HEAVEN

"Maria . . ."

"Jocko."

His arms closed around her, then one hand sank into her hair, cradling the back of her head. Slowly, he brought their lips together. The kiss went on and on; ecstasy made him dizzy, hot. Her lips parted, and through the kiss he whispered her name again.

"Don't talk," she whispered back.

The denizens of Whitechapel nurtured a myth among themselves. They drank to it in their murky taprooms on cold nights, they muttered it under their breath when the gentry drove by in their fine carriages. The myth was that beneath the fine, clean clothes and fancy airs, women and men were all the same. Only by an accident of birth was Victoria born Queen and Nelson crowned a hero. Now, that myth had been dispelled. The lady was in his arms . . . and she was not the same as the other women he had known. Not the same at all.

She was heaven—a heaven he could never hope to reach. But as he pressed a kiss to the top of her head, she raised her lips to his once again. And then he knew . . .

He had fallen in love with her.

DISCOVER DEANA JAMES!

DEANA JAMES

BELOVED ROGUE

ZEBRA BOOKS
KENSINGTON PUBLISHING CORP.

ZEBRA BOOKS are published by

Kensington Publishing Corp.
850 Third Avenue
New York, NY 10022

First Printing: September, 1994

Printed in the United States of America

*Dedicated
to
Maria Carvainis
Agent Extraordinary*

*Who has not only guided my career
but has been my very good friend.*

Love you, Tiger.

One

Melissa

"Careful, Miss Thorne. You'll fall."

Melissa started, not so much because of the husky voice directly behind and beneath her but because of the hands that gripped her calves. Her body tilted on the ladder. She dropped the leather-bound volume of Xenophon's *Anabasis* and clutched frantically for the edge of the shelf. The tips of her fingers grasped at it too late.

With a cry she fell backward onto her employer.

Lord Terence Montague warded off her flailing arms at the same time he managed to catch her about the waist. Her dress tore with a loud rip. A button popped off the waistband. He grunted as her heel banged into his shin.

She cried out again as the momentum carried them back across the floor in a tangle of limbs on the overstuffed divan. "Oh, my goodness!"

"I warned you." His voice conveyed irritation as he rubbed his injured shin.

Breathless, her first impulse was to reach for her hair. Fortunately, it was still anchored in a bun at the back of her neck. Then she bent to investigate her skirt. She could replace the button at the waist, but the skirt might not be salvageable. Fully four inches of heavy black wool serge had been wrenched from the waistband.

The sight of her white petticoat through the gaping tear embarrassed her. Cheeks reddening, she tried to poke the serge back under the band which was now loose around her waist.

Beside her Lord Terence cleared his throat. "I warned you," he repeated.

She flashed him an accusing look. "You frightened me."

"You were about to fall, my dear," he insisted. His eyes skittered downward. "Oh, you've torn your dress. Let me see." He pushed her hand aside and put his hand into the hole. "Quite badly it seems."

Lisa gasped as his fingers pressed against her waist. She tried to get to her feet, but the weight of his hand held her beside him. She shot him another startled look. Was she imagining that he was actually holding her down?

He was smiling now, a gentle smile. "You're very fortunate that I was there to catch you."

She put her hand on the arm of the divan and pushed.

"Don't try to get up, my dear," he murmured. "You've had a shock."

Hot color flooded her cheeks. She was not imagining anything. His fingers were moving, circling on the inside of her skirt. "Lord Montague—"

"If not for my quick thinking, you might have had a very bad fall." He had dropped his other arm along the back of the divan. Now he encircled her shoulders.

She pushed with her hands and heels, rocking forward, but he held her fast.

"Melissa." His voice was husky.

His entire hand had disappeared inside the hole. She could feel his heat through her petticoats. His fingers had slid upward over her corset. Unimpeded by the normally tight waistband, they found free access to her breast. "Lord Montague!"

"My dear." His breath fanned her cheek. "I would have been so sorry if you had been hurt."

She twisted around to stare into his face. Every pore in his skin, every stubbly hair on his chin, the tiny network of lines at the corners of his eyes, all were frighteningly close. His color was high. Beneath the carefully combed and waxed moustache, his overfull lower lip was wet.

She grabbed at his wrist and tried to pull his hand from beneath her dress. "Lord Montague! Let go of me!"

His response was to give her breast a painful squeeze. At the same time he craned his neck forward, his lips puckered, reaching for her own. "My dear."

"Stop! Don't! Lord Mon—!"

His mouth closed over her own. Wrapped in his arms, she tumbled backward on the divan. His weight pressed her down, so heavy she could not draw another breath. His hand continued to squeeze her breast. His open mouth sucked at hers. She clenched her teeth and clamped her lips tight together. Her heels scraped and drummed on the carpeted floor.

At last he drew back, his eyes hot. "You can't have failed to notice my admiration for you."

"No," she managed to whisper. "No. Please let me up."

"You're beautiful." He kissed her again, still pinching her breast. "You're so tender with my children. So loving."

"Stop," she moaned. "You're hurting me."

He grunted. His body twisted and pushed against her. His arm tightened around her shoulders.

"You're hurting!" Her eyes flew open. She looked into the face of a stranger.

His color had deepened. On either side of his prominent nose, the network of tiny veins had turned purple. The loose skin of his jowls sagged forward. He was breathing heavily.

"Lord M-Montague?"

"Oh, Melissa. What a darling girl you are." He squeezed her breast again. "Am I hurting you very much?"

She sucked in her breath. In her best governess's voice she demanded, "Get off me this instant."

He chuckled and buried his face in her neck. "You're perfect. Perfect. So young. So beautiful."

One of her hands was trapped between their bodies. The other was twisted at an awkward angle above her head. Despite the pain in her shoulder, she wrenched her arm down and struck at his back. Struck again and again. Instead of letting her heels kick uselessly at the floor, she pulled up her knee and drove her heel into the back of his thigh.

He raised his head. He was smiling, his discolored teeth glistening. "Little devil!"

She drew back her fist and hit him squarely in the eye.

"Ow!" He sat up, clasping his face.

She threw herself off the couch. Her skirt ripped again, but she caught it with both hands and pulled it with her as she rolled away. She came up on all fours and then used both hands to climb the stepladder. When her feet were under her, she swung round.

He was leaning back on the couch, one hand over his injured eye. But he was smiling. "Wonderful," he murmured. "Wonderful. So spirited."

She wanted to bolt for the door, but her trembling legs would scarcely support her. She braced herself against the ladder. "Lord Montague. I am your daughters' governess."

He removed his hand from his eye and touched it experimentally, then blinked rapidly. When he had assured himself that he had suffered no severe damage, his smile broadened. He reached inside his coat and adjusted his trousers. "Not really, my dear. Actually, you were merely an assistant hired to do the less desirable aspects of teaching, such as cleaning up after the little terrors."

Melissa glanced fearfully at the door. The children. What if the children should see? Or their mother? She shivered. "Your wife—"

"—has nothing to do with this." His hand shook faintly as he smoothed his thinning gray-blond hair. "Clarice is an admirable woman of excellent family. She has borne me two daughters. Which is probably just as well, because there's no chance that George's inheritance will ever be questioned."

"She is your wife."

"She is indeed, but she is a lady."

"I am a lady." Melissa's body still trembled, but her legs were gathering strength. She tested her weight on first one and then the other. Her skirts swayed. The tear gaped, exposing her petticoat. She let go of the ladder with one hand and fumbled at the edges.

He looked at her sympathetically. "I regret that your dress was torn. You'll have to go directly to your room and change. With luck, no one will see you on the stairs."

Melissa moaned in embarrassment. The servants. They would know. They would talk. Her reputation would be ruined.

As if pleased with her distress, her employer straightened his clothing again. He crossed one leg over his other. "Now, my dear, let's have a little talk."

Not bothering to answer, she sidled around the stepladder and felt behind her for the bookshelf.

He smiled pleasantly as he opened the cigar box on the table beside him. "I see you are still concerned about your dress. Don't be. If a servant should inquire—" He gazed downward, concentrating on the cigars. "—merely say you fell. It's the truth, after all. And don't worry. I'll buy you a dozen new dresses. I promise."

Melissa straightened away from the bookcase. "Lord Montague. I must leave your employ."

He rose, the cigar between his teeth, and strolled toward her. She took a backward step.

"To be sure. To be sure. You won't need to work again." He put out his hand to touch her cheek. She had not re-alized she was crying until his thumb brushed away a tear. "Beautiful. You cry beautifully, my dear. So many women turn all red-eyed and swollen."

She tried to dodge him, but he caught her by the arm. "We haven't finished our talk, Melissa."

"I—I have nothing to say to you."

He pushed her back against the bookcase. Her hip was pressed against the front of his body. "I want you, my dear. You'll be a willing pupil. You can't imagine the plea-sure your body will know when you learn to give me all the things Clarice can never give me."

Melissa almost gagged. His breath had suddenly turned rank. A bright red bruise was beginning to swell below his left eye. "Let me go!"

Smiling, he tightened his grip. "After you kiss me."

Drawing her foot back, she kicked him in the shin with all her might.

He cursed and released her. When he hopped backward, she shoved at his chest with both hands. He fell sprawling. She dashed around him and flew to the door.

He had turned the key in the lock. She fumbled wildly, glancing over her shoulder. He was cursing and rolling on the rug, both hands locked around his lower leg. She turned the key and the knob at the same time. Swinging the door open, she fled down the hall.

She did not stop to catch her breath until she had reached her own room and slammed the door behind her.

Montague climbed to his feet and hobbled around behind his desk. He dropped into his chair and pulled his trouser leg up. *Damn her.* A bruise the size of a goose egg had already popped out on his shin. The skin was actually broken in one place and, as he stared at it, a tiny bead of blood welled out. The sight made him smile grimly.

What a pleasure she was going to be!

He raised his hand to the swelling beneath his eye. Now that was going to be hard to explain. Too late for a tree branch during the morning's constitutional. He thought of other possible excuses while he opened his desk drawer and took out writing paper.

He had walked into a door. In his own house? He winced. That made him sound like a veritable clodpole.

He had forgotten to duck. What?

A book had hit him in the face. He glanced at the leather-bound volume facedown on the floor. With a slight smile he rose and fetched it. Xenophon's *Anabasis.* What a thing for a beautiful young woman to bother herself about. Probably a history lesson for the little terrors. Or perhaps she had not been reaching for it at all. No matter. It was sufficiently hefty to cause damage.

He turned the book over in his hands and ruthlessly ripped the binding off the spine. The threads snapped and the glue cracked noisily in the quiet room. He glanced at the door. Then he tossed the wreck back beside the ladder. Several leaves fluttered after it.

He nodded. A satisfied smile spread across his face. He stroked the corner of his moustache as he dipped his pen into the inkwell and began to write.

After a moment or two, he folded the paper twice and wrote the name and address across the center: Mrs. Hermione Beauforty, 27 Kingsway Mews, London.

He stared at the name. His expression softened. *Hermione.* This way would be best after all. Melissa Thorne was too beautiful for a casual seduction. He could look forward to weeks, even months of infinite pleasure from her. Their liaison at Briarfields would be over too quickly. Such things became awkward with his wife and children in residence. And they were always impossible to conceal from the other servants.

No, Hermione was the reasonable, the practical solution.

He tucked the missive into his coat pocket and went to find the porter to take it to the train station. The telegraph operator would send it straightaway.

Melissa Thorne slammed her bedroom door and flung herself against it. Fearfully, she pressed her ear to the panel. Did she hear footsteps or was that the thudding of her heart? Vainly, she sought the key. The lock was empty. She dropped to her knees and stared through the yawning keyhole. Why had she never noticed that she had no key?

Because she had never wanted to lock the door before. Her room on the third floor in the east wing was far from the rest of the house, even beyond the schoolroom and the nursery. It had always seemed so private, so pleasant. Now the location chilled her.

He could come after her and no one would hear.

She sprang to her feet and stared around at her small

room. A trundle bed, a bedside table, a lamp, a chair, a chest. A chest! She caught its corners. It was small, sufficient to her needs until this moment. She put her shoulder against it and moved it with frightening ease until it stood in front of the door. It would not stop anyone, certainly not Lord Montague, but it would rouse her. It would make noise. Someone might hear.

She leaned on the top of the chest, panting, her heart in her throat. Her eyes fell on the connecting door to the schoolroom.

"Oh, dear heaven."

A loving father paying a visit to his dear children after they were sound asleep could easily decide to pay a visit to their governess through first one and then the next connecting doors, which also had no locks.

Her heart sank. She had no more furniture to bar the way.

Distraught, she listened again at the door. Did she hear a board creak? She must not go to sleep. Her room, usually so warm and cozy, had become a place of terror. He could come to her any time he wanted. And she dared not scream. She dared not even protest. The scandal would not touch him. It would destroy her.

She rubbed her arms. They were sore. Her whole body felt sore, wrenched most likely when she fell from the ladder. When he dragged her from the ladder, she corrected herself bitterly. She longed for a warm bath and a warm bed where she could sleep forever.

She shook her head. She dared not undress. Shivering, she wrapped her shawl around her shoulders and prepared to sit up in the ladderback chair for the night.

* * *

"Clarice, my dear, I have been giving the matter much thought. The girls must have a new governess."

His wife's small white hands stilled in their incessant tatting. She stared at him over the gold rims of her spectacles. "Whatever for, Lord Montague?"

He cleared his throat. "Well, I should have thought the reason was obvious. They are getting older and require a knowledgeable head. Can't have them learning nothing but drawing and watercolors."

His wife untangled her hand and pulled the spectacles from her nose. "But Bethany is six and Juliet is only four. Melissa is teaching them their letters and to read simple papers. What else do they need to learn?"

He hesitated, nonplussed. "Perhaps—er—French. Yes, French. And Italian."

"French and Italian—at six and four!"

He nodded. "Clarice, this is 1884—the modern world. Why, I heard just the other day that a woman—a female, mind you—can take her examinations at Oxford. Doesn't seem proper, but there you have it. When our girls are of age—"

"My goodness, you sound like a suffragette. They will become excellent wives, Lord Montague. Really, we can be spared the expense of a qualified governess for several more years. And you know you are always harping about expenses."

"But—"

She hurried on. "Melissa Thorne is Mavis's daughter. You know how close she and my mother were. When Maria wrote to me of the difficulties, I was only too happy to take her."

Lord Montague's brow knitted in a frown. He had forgotten—if he had ever known—that the little governess

was a distant family connection. If she had a family somewhere— "Er—what difficulties?"

Clarice returned to her tatting. Lord Montague watched
her little fingers spread the threads and shoot the shuttle
in and out, tying each separate knot with lightning speed
and moving on to the next. The process would drive him
crazy, yet his wife did it while she spoke.

"Surely you remember. The influenza. Poor Mavis and
dear Fred within hours, leaving the poor girls quite alone.
And little Melissa only sixteen."

Terence relaxed. Both parents dead. Good.

"Well, Maria *would* go to work to earn her way in the
world. But she couldn't support herself and Melissa, so,
of course, I said—"

Good God, but she had a mind for the trivial. "Dash it
all, Clarice," he burst out. "Don't make me tell you what
the problem is."

She gaped at him. "Lord Montague?"

"This is difficult." He turned his back to her. Now that
he had her full attention, he did not want any betraying
eagerness, any expression that might cast the least shadow
of doubt. "She's a young girl with a lot of silly romantic
notions."

"Romantic notions!" Clarice's voice rose and fell.

Keeping his face carefully straight, he strode to the window and tugged aside the drapery and lace curtain. The
darkness was quite impenetrable. He could see his reflec-
tion in the pane and his wife's behind him. She had risen
and stood with her hand to her cheek. He cleared his throat
again. "I pretended not to notice until this afternoon when
she came into the library."

"The library!"

His mouth curled contemptuously. "Really, Clarice, must you parrot everything I say?"

"But, m-m'lord, are you saying she f-followed you into the library?"

"Well, give her the benefit of the doubt. Perhaps she was getting something to read to the children."

"From your father's library! Why, there's nothing in there but Latin classics and books about war!"

He shrugged off-handedly. "Perhaps—"

"Are you sure you didn't get the wrong impression?" Her voice was breathless, utterly scandalized. She had pulled a lace handkerchief from her sleeve and was fanning herself with it.

He snorted convincingly. "There may be snow on the thatch, but—" He turned and bathed her in his tenderest smile. "—I'm not dead to a pretty girl's flirtations. I'm as flattered as the next man."

His wife of seven years—the mother of his daughters—actually blushed. Of course, she was only ten years older than Melissa Thorne and almost as innocent.

"Lord Montague—"

He came swiftly across the room and took her in his arms. With more than fatherly affection, he embraced her. "Now, now. Let's not get upset about it. I'm sure she's a good little girl. Probably just—wild."

It was the proper word. Clarice arched backward in his arms. Her face had turned quite pale. Her mouth was curled as if she might be sick. "I'll dismiss her immediately. Without a character."

"No. No." He drew her back against him patting her shoulder. "No need to do that. She'll get over me in no time if you send her to one of your friends."

She stood stiff, incensed, trembling with outrage. "And

let her shift her attentions onto one of their husbands? Perhaps one who wouldn't be so fine and honest as you are? Never! Never!"

He kissed the top of her head. He realized mildly that her temper fit was exciting him. She was usually so damned placid. He kissed her forehead and held her close, then put his hand under her chin and lifted it. "My sweet wife. So thoughtful of others."

He kissed her on the cheek.

She scarcely noticed. Her body was tense, her breath coming fast. "I shall send her away tomorrow."

"And a very good idea." He kissed her ear. "But don't ruin her life for a simple indiscretion, undoubtedly brought on by grief. She's probably missing her father. Send her to one of your older friends. One of your mother's friends." He kissed the corner of her mouth.

She shivered, suddenly aware of what he was about. "Do you really think that would be all right?"

"Yes." He kissed the tip of her nose. Her little pouch of a belly pressing against his was making him hard. "Your grandmother alone must have a round dozen friends who would be pleased to have a willing young girl in their households."

She bowed her head. Her breathing changed. "Perhaps Lady Mary. She suffers so with rheumatism. But she's so unpleasant, she can hardly keep companions."

He gathered his wife tighter against him. "Then she'd be the very one." Sealing her lips with a kiss, he put *finis* to the conversation. When he drew back, her eyes were closed. "My dear, I would very much like to show you how much I cherish you."

He watched the blush flood her cheeks again. She shivered and shook her head. "I don't know—"

"Please," he said. "Go up now and wait for me."

She thought about how he hurt her, thought about the pain of childbirth, thought about the young girl who had tried to attract her husband. A tiny shard of jealousy shot through her. He was old, so old and knobby, but perhaps just tonight— Her answer was a whisper and a sigh. "Yes, Terence."

Lady Clarice did not stir until the middle of the afternoon. She sat up in her bed and stared around her groggily at the tea tray, its contents stone cold. With a groan she pressed her hand to the tender place between her legs.

Her husband had frightened her as he always did. In bed he never kissed her or held her as her mother had told her he would. Instead he flung himself upon her. When she began to cry and push at his shoulders, he gathered her wrists together in one of his big hands and jerked them above her head. Then he had begun to bite her breasts.

She shuddered at the memory. He never did the thing with her without hurting her. She closed her eyes and buried her face in her hands. What had brought this on?

Then she remembered. He wanted her to dismiss Melissa Thorne.

Lord Montague would leave for London soon. He seldom visited his country residence and his wife for more than a couple of months a year. If Mavis's daughter had only exercised a little restraint, Clarice would not have to go through the considerable bother of finding someone suitable and willing to bury herself alive at Briarfields.

Clarice groaned again. She supposed she must send the girl away, if only to protect her from her own foolishness. No young girl deserved to be initiated by Lord Montague.

The painful memory of Clarice's own wedding journey resurrected itself. She had been just a month short of eighteen when Lord Montague had flung himself upon her for the first time.

Thank God within a month Bethany had been conceived and she had been excused from the marriage bed for over a year.

She thrust her feet into her house slippers. The afternoon was moving on. She must be up and dressed and be about it. Melissa must be gone as soon as possible.

"You've been so good to me, Lady Clarice," Melissa began in a rush. "But I must leave your employ."

Clarice's mouth dropped open. She stared in shock at the earnest face. A sudden and quite awful thought burst like a comet into her brain. Her wrinkled, graying husband with his knobby hands and thinning hair and this young and quite beautiful girl.

She managed a smile and nodded. "I-I can quite understand that, Melissa. I had been thinking along those lines for—er—for some time. London is the place for a clever young woman such as yourself."

Melissa frowned. "I had not thought of London."

"I have been thinking about a position for you," Clarice raced on, her voice trembling slightly. She must get Melissa away. She must. "In fact, I have the very person in mind."

An alarm sounded in Melissa's brain. She clenched her sweaty palms in the folds of her skirt. Suddenly, she was sure that Lady Clarice had come to dismiss her and that Lord Terence had told his wife to do so.

Melissa could feel hot color rising in her cheeks. How

dare he! That evil old man! He had terrorized and insulted her and now he sought to take away her livelihood.

"—My mother's friend. Of course, she has arthritis and is not always pleasant—" Clarice tilted her head slightly until her face moved back into Melissa's vision. "—But she has a beautiful house. Your rooms will be much finer than we could provide here." Her voice scaled higher. "Melissa? Do you think you will like Lady Mary?"

Melissa relaxed her hands at her sides. "Of course I will. I thank you, Lady Clarice. I'll leave this evening."

"This evening!" Clarice all but screeched. "Oh, no, you can't leave now. Why, you'll arrive in London after dark. You can't do that. I'd never forgive myself— There's no hurry." She wrung her hands. "That is, I know you'll want to be away as fast as possible, but you can't leave this afternoon."

"I'll go to my sister's. When I arrive at the Euston Station, it won't be any trouble to get a cab to take me to Mayfair. It won't even be terribly expensive."

"Oh, of course, I'll pay you your wages for the rest of quarter. You'll have the price of a cab, but to arrive in London at night—"

Melissa's lips curved in a tight little smile. "I'll be fine. Really I will. After all, with the trains so rapid, it will hardly be full dark."

Clarice moaned. "But you'll be traveling alone. Oh, I beg you, don't go until morning."

Melissa thought of the scene in the library. Thought of her room with no keys in the doors. She smiled bravely. "This is the modern age when women may travel alone as they will. The streets of London are quite safe. Scotland Yard has policemen everywhere."

Clarice shook her head. "I'll go and pack and just say good-bye to Bethany and Juliet."

Clarice put her hand to her forehead. Then she lowered it and looked into Melissa's eyes. "I'll write you a letter of introduction." She held out her hand. "And a character that will get you a job at Buckingham Palace."

"Come with me, Melissa."

Montague's voice was low, almost a whisper. He had appeared out of the darkness, the many capes of his overcoat flowing around him. A light mist was falling and it rose faintly gray from the platform.

Melissa sprang from the single bench and brandished her umbrella. "What are you doing here? Don't come any closer."

He spread his arms displaying his empty hands. "My dear, I must compliment you on the speed with which you left. Why, I had no idea you were even planning to leave until the coachman returned. I chided my wife, I must tell you."

"I'm leaving. The train will be here in just a few minutes."

He shook his head mournfully. "As a matter of fact, the train will not be here for another hour. And think a minute. When it comes, you won't arrive in London for another three. It will be very late, my dear. Very late indeed."

"Stay away from me." She pointed the umbrella at him as he took a step.

He rocked back, slowly revealing his teeth in a superior smile. "Melissa—"

"There are always cabs about," she interrupted, praying that there were. "If not, I shall simply remain in the station waiting room until morning."

"Only think how you are putting yourself to so much trouble and discomfort. Here I stand ready to drive you to a cozy cottage not far from here. A blazing fire and a hot meal await you. And a soft bed with a warm and loving—"

Melissa slashed at him with her umbrella. "Keep your distance, milord. Do you really think I'd go anywhere with you? You were responsible for my losing my position. Lady Clarice was going to dismiss me when I told her I had to leave."

He assumed a hurt demeanor. "Now, that is simply not true. Where do you get such ideas?"

"She already had a woman in mind that I might go to."

"But Clarice has a quick mind. I'm sure the idea to send you to Lady Mary just popped into her head."

"How did you know to whom she was sending me?"

He smiled again. "She told me. Just as she told me this evening that she did not like the idea of your going to the station tonight. In fact, my being here is her idea."

"I don't believe you."

His smile vanished. "Stop this nonsense. Put that umbrella under your arm and come with me."

He stooped to grasp the handles of her bag.

"Leave my things alone!" Quicker than thought, she struck at his hand.

With a curse, he snatched his arm back, his knuckles throbbing from her blow. Anger flushed his face. He straightened and advanced. "You'll pay for that."

"Stay away from me." She retreated. Another step and she would be at the edge of the small platform. She had never been so frightened. "Please, Lord Montague. Go away and leave me alone."

"But I want to love you, Melissa." He followed her slowly, his face dark, his teeth white. "You're going to be a very fortunate young lady. I'm a generous man."

Her heel dropped off the edge. "Lord Montague, you're a married man."

"Don't think about that." He pulled the umbrella from her hand with a twist that brought her up against him. His arm wrapped around her waist and forced her against him. He fairly gloated over her helplessness. "Think about all the beautiful new clothes, the cozy little set of rooms, the leisure you'll enjoy."

"I don't want any of those things. Especially not from you." She pushed futilely against his shoulders.

"But I want you." He bent his head to kiss her. His breath was rank—whiskey, cigars, and fish.

She gagged and tried to twist her face away. "Don't. Let me go, you smelly old man."

With a growl he slobbered along her cheek, reaching for her mouth. Suddenly, she clamped her teeth down on his tongue when he tried to push it into her mouth.

He jerked back with an unintelligible oath and slapped at her. The blow missed as she ducked and twisted.

It had worked before. It would work again. With all her might, she swung the sharp toe of her high-button shoe at his shin.

He howled and clasped both hands around the injured bone, the same one she had kicked before. Hopping, he could not stop her as she grabbed her umbrella and her two bags and raced away into the darkness.

Lord Montague flopped down on the bench and nursed his shin for a couple of minutes. In the distance he could hear the shriek of the train whistle. His eyes malevolent, he limped off the platform and down the track to the signal post. Deliberately, he lowered the stop signal. Arms folded, he stepped back and watched impassively as the last train to London rumbled through.

* * *

Melissa crouched in the wet shrubbery for over an hour, listening as Lord Montague at first tried to coax, then bully, her to come out. Finally, he climbed into his carriage with a curse and settled down for what seemed to the exhausted girl an eternity.

At last he slapped the reins over his horse's back and drove away.

For another hour she waited, afraid he would come galloping back.

Finally, her teeth chattering and her clothing soaked with dew, she mounted the platform and availed herself of the relative comfort of the hard bench.

When the stationmaster arrived, he gave her a startled look. Several farmers with produce for the city also pulled up in their carts. They stood in groups on the platform, talking among themselves, while eying her bedraggled appearance and hollow eyes.

One of them offered her a pasty still warm from his wife's oven. She accepted it gratefully, choking it down, developing a raging thirst in her sore throat.

At last the train chugged into view. Melissa was the first one aboard. Only when it pulled out of the station did she allow herself to sink against the hard seatback.

As the train stopped and started, Melissa alternately dozed and woke. She was too tired to be nervous about her destination as the cars gradually filled with people. Likewise, her presence went unnoticed.

Farmers, heavy-laden with produce of all kinds, climbed aboard. Baskets of foodstuffs, fresh-caught fish from the ponds and freshly slaughtered meat from barnyards, boxes and crates of cheese and eggs all made the air of every carriage richly redolent. The freight cars gradually filled with coops of fowl and cans of milk. All were bound for London to keep the great city fed.

At last, with whistle tooting and brakes shrieking, the train pulled into Euston Station.

Numb and exhausted, Melissa stepped down onto the platform. She was immediately jostled out of the way by the big men and women hustling their bundles to meet the lorries leaving for the various markets around the city.

Dragging her bags, her umbrella tucked under arm, Melissa made her way to a tiny pushcart where she purchased a cup of tea. While she drank it, she watched the platform empty. In almost no time she was practically alone.

She wiped at tears of self-pity as she noted the time on the big clock on the station wall. Her sister Maria would undoubtedly be at work. Melissa doubted she could persuade Maria's landlady to let her into her sister's rooms.

Her odyssey of misery would not be over until she could stretch her weary body out on a bed and rest. She was tempted to buy another cup of tea but decided against it. She snapped the flap closed on her purse and pushed it into the pocket of her full skirt.

"Would you be wanting to share a cab?"

Melissa jumped and whirled around. The plump, middle-aged woman who had addressed her smiled sweetly and tilted her head to one side. The pair of turtle doves nesting in the crown of her enormous hat turned, too.

"I—I don't know."

"Two can travel as cheaply as one," the woman continued. She kicked aside the train descending from her enormous bustle and nodded in the direction of the street.

"I'm probably not going your way. I'm going to my sister's flat."

"How sweet. I have two daughters myself. They're good friends."

Melissa frowned. This woman was a stranger. Everyone knew that strangers could be dangerous. She tried to guess the woman's age. Perhaps forty or forty-five. She could be a grandmother. Beneath the black dye, the woman's hair was probably snow-white.

"You remind me of my own dear daughters," the woman continued. "I said to myself that we might do each other a good turn. You know, I'm concerned about being alone in London." She let her expressive eyes roam uneasily over the numbers of people coming and going.

Melissa nodded. "I have to admit I'm concerned myself. I'll be happy to see you home."

The woman's smile flashed. "Would you? Oh, I'd be so much obliged." She twined her arm around Melissa's. "You're such a sweet thing. Come along, my dear."

"I don't know you . . ." Melissa began. The strength of the woman's arm surprised her.

"Nor I you. But that's easily remedied." She hurried the two of them across the station. "What's your name, lovey?"

"Melissa."

"Lovely name. I'm a widow. My name is Hermione. Hermione Beauforty."

Two

Maria

"Damn!"

The unladylike word did not even begin to relieve her frustration. Maria Thorne reached gingerly into the basket of the typewriting machine to untangle three of the long metal stalks that slapped the type bars against the ribbon. In the process of getting the three unwedged, she smudged her fingers.

Her upper lip curled in distaste as she wiped away the ink and set about erasing the resultant error. With real regret she remembered the days when she had rapidly and accurately filled page after page with graceful, flowing script. Her script had been the reason she had been hired. Then Mrs. Avory Shires, her employer, had been persuaded to purchase this abomination.

"Damn!" she snarled again. She pushed her hair back out of her eyes and stared at the tiny squiggles of rubber and shreds of paper. In her frustration and distraction, she had rubbed a hole in the paper. "Damn. Damn.

"Damn!"

She looked around her, to reassure herself that the walls of books were absorbing her unhappiness.

And a bloody good thing, too, she decided.

The library had been deemed the best choice for the office where Mrs. Shires handled her voluminous correspondence in her crusade for women's suffrage. In addition to its hundreds of volumes on every subject, it was quiet, well-lighted, and private. It was a perfect place for Maria to vent her own suffering.

Maria unrolled the ruined paper from the machine and inserted a fresh sheet with a yellow backing page behind it.

Before she began typing, she flexed her fingers and allowed herself to gaze out the solitary window into the quiet square. The postman was turning the corner.

Maria stuck her eraser behind her ear and began typewriting slowly and carefully, forcing herself to concentrate on each word. She even began to pick up speed as she moved down the page. At the jingle of the front doorbell, she jumped to her feet in the middle of a word.

Today she would get a letter from her sister. When Melissa had gone to Briarfields, Maria's employer had been kind enough to allow Melissa's daily letters to arrive at Mrs. Shires's address. Now, almost a week had passed since the last letter. Maria hurried to the office door.

She could not see the mail around the butler's massive shoulders.

Friends who came to call had become accustomed to "Saint" Peter, who looked like no other butler in the whole of England. He had been hired when Mrs. Shires's strong stand on women's employment in government had brought a street gang to her door. While her former butler, a family retainer of seventy-odd, had cowered weeping, the thugs had hurled bricks through her windows and turned over her ornamental stone lions.

Now her new employee, a former boxer with a broken nose and swollen knuckles, guarded her door from dragons.

Peter riffled through the letters and papers, his lips moving as he read their addresses. His watery blue eyes were apologetic as he turned to Maria and shook his head.

She slumped back against the door. Something was definitely wrong, she thought glumly, as chills skittered over her arms. Her sister was her only living relative. She had deeply regretted their separation, but her small salary had not been enough to provide for herself and Melissa, too.

"No word, Thorne?" Mrs. Avory Shires, a woman of medium height and unprepossessing demeanor, bustled down the stairs.

Maria shook her head. Taking the mail from the butler, she turned back into the office to open and sort it.

Mrs. Shires followed her. Her bright eyes, behind amber-tinted lenses, surveyed her secretary's drooping posture. "Thorne," she announced. "I believe it's time you sent a telegram."

"A telegram?" Maria shuddered. Telegrams were death messages.

"Absolutely. We'll go together today to the office."

Maria hesitated. "I was planning to go to Briarfields on my day off."

"A waste of time and money," Mrs. Shires advised curtly. "A short drive and a couple of shillings and you'll hear from your sister in the afternoon."

Maria flashed her employer a hopeful look. "I hadn't really thought about it like that. I can't tell you how much I appreciate—"

"Thorne, you have continued to work though you're worried about your sister. I'm satisfied of that. You're a very good girl and a good worker in every way. But the last two days, I've seen the light go out of your eyes. No more spark. No more zeal. And I want zeal." She waved an imperious hand toward the butler. "Peter, send for the carriage. You will accompany us."

"Melissa has sought employment in the home of Lady Mary Hampton!" Maria's voice was barely a whisper as she read the message for the third time. "This can't be. Melissa wouldn't come to London a week ago and not contact me."

Mrs. Shires put her arm around her secretary's shoulders. "Oh, my dear. Of course she would have contacted you. Perhaps the Montagues made some mistake as to the time?"

"No. The telegram from Lady Montague states clearly that Melissa left six days ago. See for yourself." In the grip of cold terror, Maria sank down on the bench. Her hand was shaking so badly that the telegram slipped from her grasp and wafted to the floor.

Her employer stooped to pick it up. Adjusting her spectacles, she read it through, but Maria had not made a mistake. "Oh, my dear, perhaps—"

Maria clasped her hands together in her lap to still them. "Something's happened," she whispered. "Something's happened to my baby sister."

Mrs. Shires unprepossessing demeanor was a sham. A tiger clothed in the wool of a ewe lamb, she dragged her secretary to her feet. "Come, come. Let's go immediately to Lady Mary Hampton's home. Peter, the carriage again. We cannot be certain of anything until we know the facts."

The ride was an agony for Maria. Hands clenched into fists inside her muff, she scanned every face they passed.

Was Melissa wandering the streets of this huge city? Terror for her sister's fate gripped her; she tightened her jaw to keep her teeth from chattering.

Thankfully, her employer did not speak. In mute communication, she laid her hand on Maria's wrist.

Outside the Hamptons' door, the women waited in silence while Peter climbed down from the box and rang the bell. He rang it again and yet again before a caretaker answered.

Maria smothered a sob when she saw Peter turn away and come down the steps, shaking his head. Mrs. Shires lowered the glass window in the carriage door. "What did they say?"

"Lady Hampton's gone to Bath for the winter," Peter reported. "They said nobody'd come to see her this past week."

Maria could no longer hold back her tears. "Oh, Mrs. Shires."

"Call me Avory, dear Maria."

"What shall I do? Where shall I go? Something dreadful's happened."

Mrs. Shires's face was grave. "It's beginning to look that way."

A frown deepened between Peter's eyebrows. He shifted his bulky body and cleared his throat. "Er—whyn't you go to the police?"

Mrs. Shires directed a thoughtful look at her butler. "Perhaps you're right—"

Maria shook her head violently. "Oh, I couldn't. Melissa's not a criminal."

"Well, of course not, Maria. But the police—"

"What if they suspected her of a crime?" Maria all but wailed. "Think of her reputation."

"There is that," her employer agreed slowly. "But what if she has met with a criminal?"

Maria's face paled to alabaster. She covered her eyes as the world spun around her.

"I don't believe the local constabulary station will do," Mrs. Shires continued. "Scotland Yard, Peter. A very good idea you've had. We must go to Scotland Yard."

Constable Wilkie opened the door and stood back to allow them to enter. "Two ladies to see you, Inspector Revill."

Revill rose from behind his desk and came forward. He was of middle height and early middle age, his body somewhat heavier than it had been in his youth. His sandy hair receded slightly at his temples, and his mouth had long ago given up smiling.

As he eyed his visitors, his mind automatically ticked off their approximate ages and descriptions; he noted the disparity in their clothing, possibly indicating a mistress and her maid, but not quite. The younger one was frightened but not subservient.

The older of the two extended her hand. When he took it, she stepped forward and tilted her head back to peer at him through amber-tinted half-glasses. For a few seconds she took his measure, then nodded. "Inspector, is it? I would have preferred a superintendent but an inspector may be satisfactory."

Accepting her left-handed compliment, he inclined his head. "At your service." His startlingly blue eyes moved from one face to the other. "Won't you have a seat?"

"Thank you." The older woman sat immediately, planting her furled silk umbrella upright beside her like a staff of state. The young one remained standing, staring distractedly around her. When their eyes met, hers dropped immediately.

Revill put his hand under her elbow and guided her to her seat. Pulling a tiny notebook from his breast pocket, he picked up a pencil. "May I have your names?"

The older woman frowned. "My name doesn't concern you. However, I am Mrs. Avory Shires. That's Avory with an 'o,' and this is my secretary Maria Thorne." She hesitated briefly, then tightened her grip on the handle of the umbrella. "I'll come right to the point. Maria's sister Melissa has disappeared."

Immediately, Revill directed his attention to the younger woman. His pencil noted her details. *Maria Thorne. 25+. Lt blond hr. Br ys. Evn ftres. 5'5" or 6". Blk wool suit, plain blk hat, blk gloves. Mourning?* His pencil fairly flew. He raised his eyes. "How do you know she's disappeared?"

Taking a deep breath, Maria told the story. It was distressingly short.

"And you say she wrote you every day without fail?"

Oh, yes, sir."

"I can attest to that as well," Mrs. Shires inserted.

"Even if she'd been sick or unable to write, she would have contacted me the very day she came to town." Maria's voice quavered. "I know she would have."

His face grave, Revill took his seat. He aligned several papers on his desk more precisely and placed his notebook in front of him at an exact angle. The various movements gave him time to think. At last he said, "Describe her for me."

"She's just seventeen." Maria dabbed at her eyes and swallowed hard. "Yesterday, sh-she was seventeen years

old. She's a bit shorter than I am. Her hair is blond, the
same color as mine, but her eyes are blue. She has a dimple in her right cheek. She's b-beautiful. I have a photograph of the two of us, taken three years ago." She leaned
forward to lay it on the desk.

Revill noted the description in his little book, then
picked up the photograph. "And she came into Euston Station at night?"

Maria pressed a handkerchief to her nose and nodded.
"That's what the telegram said."

"I think it's unconscionable," the older woman broke in
angrily. "How could the Montagues have let her go at such
a time?"

One of Revill's sandy eyebrows rose. "Perhaps they insisted that she leave."

Both women's eyes widened. Maria muttered something
unintelligible. The older woman shifted her umbrella in
front of her knees and leaned forward on it. Her eyes narrowed accusingly. "What are you saying, sir?"

Revill shrugged. He noted the younger woman's color
rising in her cheeks even as he answered the question.
"What I'm saying is simply that she might have had to
leave because they didn't want her anymore, Mrs. Shires."
He held up his hand to forestall their cries of protest. "For
many reasons, some good, some bad. Perhaps she wanted
to leave to pursue a more lucrative career in the city."

Maria Thorne's face was bright red. Her eyes sparked
furiously. "Absolutely not."

"Governesses aren't paid much," Revill continued inexorably, "while a girl with an—let's call it *enterprising* nature
can make more in a single night than I make in a week."

Maria Thorne rose from her chair. "I can see this has
been a mistake, Mrs. Shires. Before we leave, Inspector

Revill, let me tell you that I did not come here to hear my sister's reputation maligned."

He laid down his pencil. "Yes, Miss Thorne. I realize that, but I also realize that no decent girl would travel unattended at night."

"My sister is a decent girl!"

Mrs. Shires pounded on the floor with her umbrella. "Of course she is. Inspector, I must insist—"

He held up his hand. This part of his job never seemed to get any easier. "Ladies, please think about this rationally."

"I *am* perfectly rational," Mrs. Shires stormed.

"My sister has disappeared!" Maria cried. "And instead of trying to find what happened to her, you're telling me that she disappeared because she wanted to."

He closed his notebook. "I'm offering a theory. It's what I do for a living. But I won't dismiss your sister's case on a theory. I'll investigate. I'll keep this picture and have a police artist draw a sketch from it. I'll put it out with the description to the police in the area around Euston Station." He sighed. "In the meantime we'll check the usual sources."

"And what are the usual sources?" Mrs. Shires queried.

For the first time Revill dropped his eyes. "The river, ma'am—"

Mrs. Shires's hand clenched around her umbrella. Maria's color drained away. She dropped back into the chair, her expression pleading.

Revill looked into the younger woman's eyes sympathetically. "—And the morgues. Wherever bodies come to us through misadventure."

"Misadventure." Maria said slowly as she sank back in her chair. With trembling hands she covered her face.

Mrs. Shires stamped her umbrella into the floor as she

rose to put her arm around her secretary's shoulder. "You are cruel, Inspector."

"What happened to her sister may be cruel."

Maria dropped her hands. "My sister is not dead."

Revill nodded. "If she is, we'll find her. Misadventure is a terrible thing, but it is part of living in a crowded society. Horse-drawn vehicles gallop up and down the streets at all hours of the day and night, even though we advise that they travel at a moderate pace. Unfortunately, citizens are robbed—sometimes violently. And then sometimes unfortunate girls, perhaps like your sister, depressed because she'd been dismissed, make their way to the river."

Maria held out her hands. "My sister was on her way to take another position."

"But when she arrived—if she arrived—the position wasn't there," he pointed out reasonably.

"B-but she never arrived," Maria countered. "We told you that. The caretaker had never heard of her."

Revill sighed and opened his notebook again. "What would she have been wearing?"

"Black garments," Maria replied promptly. "Just as I am. Our parents died last year. We haven't had time nor resources to put mourning aside."

He noted it and Mrs. Shires's address, then closed the book again. "I'll prepare a report."

He stood to escort them to the door.

"Is that all?" Maria cried. "Is that all you're going to do?"

"Miss Thorne—"

"This is infamous," Mrs. Shires blazed. "Absolutely infamous. I have friends in high places. They shall hear of this."

Revill sighed again. "That is certainly your right. And

if they can help you in any way that I can't, then I say more power to them. But the plain facts are these. Melissa Thorne's disappeared. If there's no body, and no one's seen or heard anything, then we have to assume that she doesn't want to be found."

"She might have been kidnapped."

He hesitated, tempted to confirm that possibility, then changed his mind. "Miss Thorne, you don't have any money. Where's the profit, if a girl's family can't pay a ransom?"

He opened the door. Mrs. Shires kept her arm around Maria, who was staring straight ahead, her face white as paper.

"I'll prepare a report," he repeated as the women stepped out into the narrow hallway. "I promise you that all the paper work will be done immediately. And I'll come round to your address the minute I know anything."

On the threshold Mrs. Shires stopped. Her steady gaze behind the amber spectacles met his. "You don't think you can find her, do you?"

He hesitated. "This might all be a misunderstanding. You never know. Just go home and wait for my message."

Revill watched them until they turned a corner, then went back into his office. When the constable entered a few minutes later, Revill passed him a slip of paper. Wilkie looked at the name on it doubtfully. "He ain't going to be easy to find, sir."

"Put out the word."

"He still might not come."

"Oh, he'll come. He knows what's good for him."

* * *

Maria could not think beyond the present, even though her mind was racing.

Her sister. Her beloved sister. Her beautiful, gentle baby sister.

A lorry thundered by. The driver's whip snapped over the backs of the horses as their steel-shod hooves clanged on the cobblestones. In her mind's eye, she saw her sister falling beneath those hooves.

With a terrified whimper she covered her face with her hands. The grim, gray waters of the Thames rolled in her mind. Her sister's drowned face, eyes closed, hair like seagrass, swirled up out of its depths.

"Maria."

She heard the voice but could not comprehend.

"Maria!"

With an effort she put her hands down into her lap. "Mrs. Shires."

The older woman leaned forward and covered Maria's hands with her own. "What you are doing does no good. You must put the dreadful thoughts aside," she urged. "After all, that man was only an inspector. What does he know? There's probably a reasonable explanation for all this."

"He said she might be dead. And worse. If she isn't dead, she might not want to be found. He as much as called her a—a prostitute." Maria gulped at the awful word.

"Well, he's wrong. It's doubtless the class of people that he's forced to associate with. Makes him immediately think of the worst."

"He said—"

"Don't think about what he said," Mrs. Shires snapped.

"He doesn't know your sister. You do. Think about what she would do and what you must do to find her."

"Me?"

"Someone must. You're her next of kin. You're the one who cares."

Maria drew a deep breath. The carriage wheels rattled along over the paving stones. Pains were starting in her temples. Surprisingly, they sharpened her senses. A plan began to take shape. "You're right. I'll go to Briarfields. They were the last people to see her. They either sent her away or allowed her to go in the middle of the night—for some unknown reason. I have to know that reason. I have to start there."

Mrs. Shires patted her clasped hands. "I agree. Good girl. The very first thing in the morning, you'll go north by train. Peter will accompany you."

"Oh, no, Mrs. Shires. I couldn't take Peter." Maria took her employer's hands in her own. "He's everything to you. And remember you have a meeting to go to tomorrow."

Avory frowned. "Peter should go with you."

"I'll be all right. You need him."

"You're right." She shook her head. "But I insist that he go with you and purchase your tickets both ways so he'll know at what time you'll be returning. That way he can meet you at the station." She smiled grimly. "No chance of misadventure for you."

"Coo, Jocko, y' owe me fer th' last beer, y' do."

"Maisie, it's watered by 'alf. I oughtn't t' pay for but every other one."

"Garn!" Maisie knocked his bowler hat askew as she sloshed the mug down on the table.

His sherry-brown eyes crinkling at the corners, Jocko Walton cocked his bowler back in its proper position, on the back of his head. Blond hair in tight curls ringed his broad forehead and temples. He blew Maisie a kiss before he blew away the foam.

The smoke in the Cock Robin was thick enough to cut with a knife, the noise made fair to deafen a man, and most of the customers had only a remote acquaintance with soap and water; but Jocko, tipped back in his chair, surveyed the scene with something akin to pleasure.

From the corner a concertina man squeezed out his music, his gravelly baritone adding to the din. His efforts would have put Gilbert and Sullivan both to the blush.

> *"Bertie and Gersity, from university,*
> *Do, dear boy, give us a call,*
> *A slasherty, dasherty, casherty, masherty*
> *Mashiest Masher of all."*

Prodded by her pimp, Mary Margret slid out from the next table and came toward him, her bustle twitching. " 'Tis a cryin' shame t' be drinkin' alone, Jocko." Her voice, a gin-soaked bass, rumbled out of her compact body. "You've a bit of coin. Why ain't ye spreadin' it around?"

Jocko grinned again. He pushed a chair out with his foot. " 'Ave a seat, Maggie," he offered amiably. "I'll buy the first one, but after that you're on your own."

Mary Margret threw a look over her shoulder at the Russian, who collected for her. His thick black brows kneaded together. She leaned across the table, displaying a plump bosom.

Jocko drank again, grinning at the display.

"Give a girl a tumble," she whispered. Her hand, clad

in a black net mitt, dived into the neckline of her dress and pulled her breast up. The nipple popped out. With her thumb and index finger, she pinched it. "Me poor ol' mither's be'ind in 'er rent."

Jocko looked across the room at the Russian, then back at the girl. "That's a 'ell of a shock, Mary Margret. I thought she was dead. Seems to me I contributed to 'er funeral last month."

The girl leaned closer still. Her nipple was only inches from the back of his hand. He could have closed his fingertips over it. She laughed huskily, exposing a gap in her upper jaw. "She's a tough 'un, she is. Why, we was lowerin' 'er sheeted corpse into th' grave when she sets right up an' ollers fer gin."

Jocko laughed.

Mary Margret leaned farther still, until her nipple actually grazed his knuckle. "I'll do whatever ye like, Jocko. Swear I will."

Maisie flounced by at that moment and slammed a tankard down, aiming it at the tip of the breast. Mary Margret screamed in outrage as foam slopped over the side onto her bosom. Maisie thrust out her lower lip defiantly. "Ye don't want no poxey whoor like 'er, Jocko," she announced to the room. "Lord knows who she's 'ad."

"Who ye callin' a poxey whoor, ye ol' bag?" Without bothering to restore her clothing, Mary Margret came out of the chair swinging. Her fist caught Maisie on the side of the jaw. The occupants of Cock Robin closest to the disturbance raised their heads. Those farther away paid no attention.

Jocko picked up both beers and agilely sidestepped the struggling women. From the relative safety of the bar, he set one pint down and polished off the other.

"That'll be tuppence," the bartender reminded him confidentially.

Jocko fished in his pocket and brought out a shilling. "Give the change to Maisie," he murmured. "She got me out of a near thing. I didn't want to 'ave to fight the Roosian."

"Got ye," the bartender agreed.

The party in question was watching stolidly as Mary Margret doubled her fists in Maisie's blond hair and pulled.

Maisie screamed and kicked, landing a pointed toe in Mary Margret's shin.

Mary Margret screamed in pain but kept her grip in Maisie's hair. They staggered back and forth until Maisie's ankle caught in a chair leg. Over they went, rolling in the sawdust.

Mary Margret tried to bash Maisie's head against the floor, but Maisie was too strong for the smaller woman. Bucking like a horse, the barmaid unseated her opponent and ended up on top. With that advantage she caught Mary Margret's wrists and squeezed.

With a cry the Irish girl let go. Maisie laughed. Her triumphant expression took in the whole room. "She's a poxey whoor," she announced. "I said it. An' it's th' truth."

Mary Margret screamed furiously. The Russian slowly, almost wearily climbed to his feet. Instead of going to rescue his woman, he sauntered toward the bar.

Jocko did not change his stance. His gaze was on a level with the Russian's beard. Though he was almost six feet tall, he would have to tilt his head back to look into the dark eyes.

Knowing he had all the time in the world, the Russian

hooked his elbow on the bar. He picked up the pint Jocko had bought for Mary Margret. "You want her?"

Jocko's grin spread. "Thanks awfully, but I wouldn't want to spoil 'er."

The Russian sneered. "You would not spoil her. She used to best."

"I'm sure she is." Jocko pushed his bowler forward on his head. Blowing the triumphant Maisie a kiss, he strolled out into the night.

The fog was so thick that the clop-clop of hooves could be heard no more than a block away. Jocko exhaled the smoke from the Cock Robin and sucked in a breath of air. It was heavy with the stench of decaying filth in the wet cobblestones beneath his feet.

He wrinkled his nose and was about to turn up his collar and stroll home when a figure materialized out of the fog.

"Jocko Walton. Just the very person."

The London bobby's uniform was enveloped by the heavy cape, but its brass lion's heads gleamed at the neck.

Jocko drew back in alarm. " 'Ey! I'm straight as a die."

"Course y'are, Jocko. We know that. Revill needs ye to do a bit of work for 'im."

Jocko backed away another step. "I *am* workin'."

"Revill'll see yer job keeps."

He retreated again, but the officer followed. "I'm on my way 'ome."

"This won't take long." The constable fastened his hand in Jocko's collar and walked him away.

Fog closed around them so thick that even their footsteps ceased abruptly.

Three

Through patches of early morning fog, Jocko Walton trotted down the deserted street, his face twisted in a ferocious scowl. The sun would not make an appearance for at least another thirty minutes, but here he was out of his bed where he should have had a couple more good hours.

He caught a whiff of baking bread; his mouth watered. Following his nose, he loped down a mews, but the aroma wafted up from a basement kitchen. No handouts there. Not even a chance to slip some baker's boy a farthing.

His stomach growled and his disposition growled back. With any luck he would have to cool his heels in front of the house on Aubrey Walk for a good couple of hours before Miss Maria Thorne came out of her front door.

At the head of Aubrey Walk, he slowed. The row of cheap rooming houses, once the servants' quarters of an estate, all looked alike. Smoke-stained gray brick, one door, nine windows, four chimney pots at each end of the roofs. He pulled the tiny piece of notebook paper from his pocket.

"Number 38." He read the number aloud, then thrust the paper back into his pocket. Six more houses and he stopped. The front of the house was dark and quiet. He thrust his hands deep into his pockets and shivered.

At that instant the door opened and a young woman

came out, dressed all in black, her face pinched and pale as chalk. Even without the sketch Revill supplied, Jocko would have guessed that she was Maria Thorne.

At the sight of him loitering and scowling, she froze. Their eyes met and clashed.

Then he looked past her to the house number. Pulling the piece of paper from his pocket, he checked again. "Number 42," he muttered, looking at the house next door and moving on down the street.

She seemed to relax. "Number 42 is four doors down," she offered in a soft voice.

"Thankee, ma'am." He did not look at her again. Instead, he nodded and hurried on down the street.

Maria paid him no further heed. She closed the door and locked it and set off in the opposite direction.

Jocko stood in the doorway of 42 Aubrey Walk and peered after her. She had seen him, had looked him right in the face. She had even spoken to him. *Blast the luck!* Now she would be far more likely to pick him out of a crowd when he followed her.

His first impulse was to abandon the pursuit and return to Revill. The inspector would have to send somebody else to keep an eye on her. Then he thought about the confession.

Revill wouldn't hesitate to use it. He'd end up in Dartmoor Prison. The gooseflesh rose on his arms and the back of his neck.

He was well and truly trapped. He had to follow her and do the best he could.

* * *

Maria snapped a glance over her shoulder. She was not mistaken. For the third time that morning, she saw him.

Maria had spent almost an hour walking toward Euston Station through an unfamiliar part of London. Suddenly, she realized she had made a mistake. Spinning around to retrace her steps, coming directly toward her, she saw the blond young man in the bowler hat, the same one who had been at her front door when she stepped out at dawn.

Instantly, he lowered his gaze. While she stood stock still, he turned down another street. When she reached the corner, she looked for him, but the street was empty. Perhaps she had been mistaken. Perhaps two young blond men in bowler hats were out for a stroll today.

The closer she got to Euston Station, the more she hurried. She could hear the noises of the big engines, feel the ground shake as they rumbled in and out. Was the one she needed to take leaving? Would she have to wait long hours to get another train?

Another thought struck her. Was the man still following her? She paused to stare into a shop window. Swiftly, she turned her head. A shiver of fear went through her. He was behind her again—his familiar bowler tipped to the back of his head. While she watched, he pulled a folded newspaper from his pocket and appeared to study it. Then he stared up at the building in front of him. Nodding to himself, he replaced the paper and disappeared into the shop.

She put out her hand to steady herself against the lamppost. Her heart was pounding so that she felt slightly dizzy. What possible reason could someone have to follow her?

She should pick up her skirts and run, but she had walked for miles and had neither eaten nor slept the night before. Now her legs quivered beneath her. She should have spent the money on a cab to the station. She was stupid not to have waited for Peter.

Too late now!

All night long, she had stared into the cold darkness, thinking about her sister. As soon as the room had lightened from black to gray, she had risen to take the train.

The search had to begin at Briarfields. She would ask questions of everyone. Someone would have seen something. Someone as beautiful as Melissa could not have disappeared off the face of the earth.

She took a deep breath and pushed herself away from the lamppost. She looked over her shoulder. The young man was nowhere in sight. She waited, taking a tighter grip on her umbrella.

A full minute passed. Perhaps she was just imagining him. Or perhaps she was mistaken in thinking she had seen the same man three times. Besides bowler hats, houndstooth Garrick overcoats were sure to be quite common in London.

With a last look at the doorway into which he had disappeared, she turned and hurried on.

Behind her, Jocko edged an eye around the corner of the shop door. He groaned. She had spotted him for sure. *Blast the nearly empty streets! And damn and blast herself for starting out so bloody early! What had she to do that she had to come out of the house before he even got his bearings?*

He pulled his bowler over his eyes and crossed the street. At least if she looked directly behind her, she might not see him. A cab clopped by, the driver drowsing in the box.

Jocko caught hold of the nag's collar and walked along beside it. In that way he kept his quarry in sight while the horse's body and forelegs shielded him.

Maria Thorne looked over her shoulder again, then turned around and scanned the entire street. Then she actually managed a relieved smile.

Jocko might have continued walking the horse indefinitely had his quarry not turned into Tottenham Court Road. It was thickly lined with market stalls and dozens of people already shopping.

The driver awakened as Jocko tried to lead the horse after her. "Hey! What d' ye think yer doin'?"

Jocko ducked the whip and darted behind a pieman's pushcart stationed on the sidewalk. In that moment he lost sight of Maria Thorne. His heart gave a leap.

"Gorblimey, bird," he muttered. "Don't fly on me now."

Still, if he went back and told Revill he had lost her in Tottenham, he would have an excuse. *Revill wouldn't use the paper over that. Even the coppers themselves lost one now and again. Hell! They lost them all the time.*

That thought nudged at him in a different way. He was better than a bloody copper. He could find her easy. He loped down the street, scanning the backs of the people ahead.

There she was! Turning into Euston Station. He thought about his light pockets, then dismissed his concern with a grin. Revill would simply have to give him more money if he had to take train rides. Still, he hoped she wasn't bound for Scotland.

He was lucky at the ticket window. He waited a minute until she moved through the gate onto the platform. No one had bought a ticket. He pulled a pound note from his pocket purse. "Same stop as the lady."

The agent eyed him coldly. "Say there, what are you about?"

"I'm her brother and I'm going to surprise her."

"You don't look much like her."

"I know." Jocko grinned pleasantly. "She's dreadful ugly, but we love 'er anyway."

The agent grunted. "Briarfield Common. That'll be two bob."

On the platform, Jocko stationed himself behind a baggage cart and spread open his paper. A quick glance over the top revealed Maria Thorne sitting primly on a bench.

Satisfied that he had found her, he raised his shield in front of his face and waited.

When the train pulled out of Euston Station, he was in a seat as far from her as possible, studying his paper as if he had a thousand pounds to invest on the Exchange.

"What do you mean she never arrived?" Clarice Montague's voice rose shrilly. "She must have arrived. She left—oh, I can't remember when—a week, six days. Oh, no. I begged her not to leave so late in the evening, but she insisted." Lady Montague tottered back onto a chair and fished for her bottle of *sal volatile*. "Oh, the poor dear."

Maria assisted the lady by opening the bottle and passing it under her nose. When Lady Montague could breathe freely, Maria continued, "Then she did leave in the evening?"

"Oh, yes. Even though I begged her not to. Oh, this is dreadful."

"What is, Clarice?"

Maria searched the face of the man who entered. He smiled pleasantly as his eyes roved over her figure.

"Oh, Lord Montague, dear, dear Melissa did not arrive

at Lady Mary's." Maria could not doubt Clarice's distress. Tears brimmed in her eyes.

Her husband patted her shoulder. "Now, now. Let's not leap to any hasty conclusions. There's probably been a mistake somewhere." He frowned at Maria. "What did Lady Hampton say?"

"I didn't speak to Lady Hampton," Maria informed him. "Her house was closed and she was in Bath for the season."

"Well, there you have it. The girl's gone to Bath."

"No, sir," Maria contradicted him.

"What? How can you be sure?" His affable manner chilled. He stopped comforting his wife to direct a heavy frown at Maria.

"She wouldn't have gone to Bath without seeing me first."

"Perhaps you weren't home."

"I would have been home at night," she reminded him bluntly.

His eyes narrowed. "Young woman, there's no call for you to take that tone with us."

His demeanor intimidated her. Her tone changed to frightened apology. "Something's happened to my sister. I'm frightened for her. Oh, please, can you tell me why she left here so late?"

Clarice began to sob. "Oh, she insisted. I didn't think it was a good idea, but—"

Lord Montague cleared his throat. "Fact is, she was asked to leave. We found her unsatisfactory."

"Terence!" his wife gasped.

Maria paled. After her conversation with Inspector Revill, she dreaded another reading of Melissa's character. "In . . .

what . . . way . . ." Each word was separate, issued between stiff lips " . . . was . . . Melissa . . . ?"

"She wasn't," Clarice interrupted. "She wasn't. Not really. She was just too . . . young."

"Oh." Maria's face crumpled. "Too young." She managed to hold back the tears. "But why did she leave in the evening?"

Lord and Lady Montague looked at each other. Lady Montague shrugged her plump shoulders. "Er—possibly she was in a hurry to see you?"

Maria thought her heart would break. "But she never came."

"Oh, my dear." Clarice pulled Maria down on the divan beside her. "I'm so sorry. Is there anything we can do?"

Maria shook her head, her eyes brimming with fresh tears. "I'll return to London immediately and go directly to Scotland Yard. When I tell them that the reason she left here was because she was too young—"

Lord Montague cleared his throat. "I shouldn't think it necessary nor appropriate to go to Scotland Yard. The girl'll undoubtedly turn up."

Maria rose. "I've already been to Scotland Yard."

"What? What's that?" He took a step toward her, his brows drawn together in a black frown.

"I said, I've already been to Scotland Yard. I spoke with Inspector Clive Revill yesterday. He promised to institute a search."

His lordship was positively glowering. "That's not a good idea at all. What about her character?"

Maria faced him, her own anger kindling. "At this point I don't care so much about her character as her whereabouts and her safety. When I find her, I'll worry about the rest."

He might have said more, but his wife hastily intervened. "Of course, my dear. You're quite right to do so. I will pray for her safe return."

When Maria left, Lord Montague was still fuming.

The young man in the bowler was stretched out under a tree, his hat pulled over his eyes, his ankles crossed. His hands were folded over his chest, which rose and fell with his rhythmical breathing. Despite the chill of the day, the sun shone full on that particular spot.

Maria's first thought was to sneak past him and hurry to the train station. She would catch the next train and leave him lost in the country. Her second thought was to find out who he was and why he was following her.

Before she could think of a third thought, she marched up to him and struck the sole of his halfboot with her umbrella. "Wake up!"

"Hey!" With frightening swiftness his body jackknifed. In an extension of the same movement, his legs whipped down, his back arched, and he sprang upright. Eyes blazing, fists clenched, he faced her.

Maria stumbled back. With a shriek, she spun and dashed back down the lane.

"Gorblimey! What'd ye do that for?" he called after her. "I think ye gave me a 'eart attack."

She halted, throwing a look over her shoulder.

He was slumped back against the tree, one hand pressed to his chest. The other fanned his face with his bowler. "Lord. Ye scared me so bad. I almost peed in m' trousers."

She flushed at his frank language, then stiffened. "I'd like to know why you're following me."

His pained expression vanished as if it had never been.

He straightened away from the tree. Dusting imaginary soil from the brim of his hat, he tilted it back on his head in its familiar position. Dusting his hands in turn, he strolled toward her. "Don't suppose you'd cop the notion that I was just takin' a day in the country, sort of a constitutional, so to speak?"

She brandished the umbrella — like a saber. "Don't come any nearer."

Raising his hands, he flashed an ingratiating grin. "Hey there. Easy. I won't. You don't have to stab m' vitals."

"You've been following me since early this morning."

"Me? Following you? Not much." He struck a pose. "I was looking for honest employment."

She looked him up and down. The smile was too affable, the circumstances too strange. She glowered in Mrs. Shires's best aristocratic manner. "You're not honest."

He leaned back, his smile a thing of calculated charm and beauty. "Now that hurts me to the quick. I'd just as lief you'd stabbed me with that umbrella as defame m' honor."

Her expression was stony. "I'm giving you one more chance. If you don't tell me what you're doing here, I'm marching right down this road until I see a constable. And then—" She blinked rapidly. "—I'll have you arrested."

He threw up his hands in terror. "Oh, don't say that. Don't say that. M' old mother'll weep and wail if she 'ears 'er darlin' boy's been taken up."

"Just see if I don't." Keeping the umbrella pointed at him, she edged around him and trotted down the road, her bustle twitching.

He followed her, his smile broad. "And what would you 'ave me arrested for?" he called. "Taking a nap on a country lane?"

"For following me and annoying me," she called over her shoulder.

He loped after her and caught up. His long legs easily kept pace with hers. "No crime in following a be-yoo-tiful lady," he crooned. "My heart fair leapt outta m' bosom—"

She stopped dead and thrust her face into his. "Will you stop? I don't want to argue about any of this. My sister is missing and, and—" She could feel the tears starting. She was going to cry again and in front of this—creature. "—I don't know how to look for her."

She spun away and fumbled at her reticule. "Please," she gasped. "Just go away."

" 'Ere now. Easy does it." He put his hand on her elbow and led her over to the grassy verge.

She leaned her shoulder against a tree while he looked away at some sheep grazing in a meadow. Finally, her tears were spent. "I have to get on to the train station," she whispered huskily. "I need to get back to London."

"Maybe I can help," he suggested.

"I don't see how. Besides," she reminded him bitterly, "you've got to go find honest employment."

He shrugged. "Oh, I'll find it someday. I'd never disappoint m' dear old mother. For right now why don't you let me come with you?"

"No."

Her handkerchief was soaked. He fished one from his own pocket, a big square of brown and white checked gingham. When he pressed it into her hand, she took it gratefully.

"At least you wouldn't 'ave to go alone." He cocked his handsome head to one side. "That's what 'appened to your sister, wasn't it? She went alone."

She froze. Slowly she lowered the handkerchief, revealing swollen, unlovely eyes. "Who are you?"

He swept off the bowler with a smile and a bow. "Jocko Walton, man about town."

The scene around her looked perfectly normal. The road was firm beneath her feet, the clouds were white in the blue sky. How then could she, the most ordinary of young women, be standing here in the middle of the road having a conversation with a stranger about her sister's disappearance? Suddenly, she wondered if she were dreaming. Unfortunately, he seemed depressingly real. "That's not what I meant. I mean, *what* are you, Jocko Walton?"

He turned her by the arm and they walked side by side toward the little station. "I'm just what I said. A man about town. London town mostly. Listen, I've got an idea. Why don't I ask the ticket agent if 'e remembers your sister? Stuff like that."

Again she wondered if she could be dreaming. Her head was hurting from the weeping. She concentrated on his idea. It had merit. "I never thought of that. Maybe I should be the one to ask."

He shrugged. "If you want. I'll just wait and see nothing 'appens." He pulled out a couple of shillings. "While you're about it, buy us both tickets. There's a good girl."

Too dazed to object, she accepted the money.

When she returned and handed him his ticket, she could barely contain her excitement. "She didn't leave until morning. My sister didn't leave until morning. The ticket agent remembered because she bought a ticket on the last train through that night, but then she was waiting on the platform in the morning."

Jocko ran his hand around the back of his neck. "Why?"

"I don't know."

He waited a minute. "A fellow might wonder where she went after she missed the train?"

Maria bridled instantly. "She wasn't doing anything immoral."

Jocko held up his hands. "Who's to say? It's 'er business if she was."

"My sister's a good girl, I'll have you know."

He nodded, his blue eyes staring down the track unfocused. "But why didn't she take the first train?"

"Do you think that's important?"

Jocko shrugged. "I ain't no bloody copper, but if a girl was on her way to London so fast she left at night, she might've been running from something."

The train whistle sounded in the distance. "How do you know so much?"

"Not me, sweetheart. I don't *know* anything. But I've been on m' own a long time." He looked at her critically. "You 'aven't. Am I right?"

She nodded. "Does it show so clearly?"

"Actually coming down 'ere was probably a good idea. Start with the last place anybody saw her."

"There you go again. You know so much."

He preened a little, rubbing his fingernails against his lapel and studying them for any imperfections. "I've been around long enough to know that things aren't what they seem on the surface. Not by a long chalk. You've got to look real deep." His eyebrows drew together as his blue eyes held hers. "And when you do, what you find may be pretty ugly."

"My sister is a good girl," Maria repeated above the screech of the iron wheels on steel rails as the train ground to a halt beside the platform.

"If you say so." Jocko rolled his eyes as he helped her into the car.

He sat beside her for the ride back to London, his hat tilted back on his head. After a few miles, he put his arm along the back of the seat. She was more of a looker than he'd thought at first. Black made her look like a crow. He was partial to blue. She'd look a bit of all right in a blue bonnet. Of course, she looked to be pretty old . . .

Maria sat next to him, very much aware of him. Years had passed since she had sat with a young man. And her former beau had not been so good looking. Jocko Walton was handsome in a raffish sort of way. His suit was a flashy plaid. And that bowler hat . . . Men who came to call on Mrs. Shires wore silk toppers or soft fedoras. Of course, he was younger than any of them. She guessed he was even younger than she was.

He caught her looking at him and grinned. Dimples flashed in both cheeks. Flushing, she snapped her face around to stare out the window.

Still smiling, Jocko shifted his weight and crossed one leg over the other. Relaxing to the rhythm of the train, her body brushed his. Later, when the sway and click of the carriage had lulled Maria Thorne to sleep, a slight pressure of his fingers tipped her head onto his shoulder.

Terence Montague looked down in disbelief at the crumpled newspaper in his fist. His eyes hardened. Maria Thorne was a "thorn" indeed, an annoying piece of debris—tiny, inconsequential, but left alone it could fester. The thing to do was pluck it out. Now.

He had planned to depart for London at the end of the week. Now he had a good reason to step up his timetable.

He tossed the paper aside and rang for the housekeeper. When she had been dispatched to pack his things, he sought his wife.

"My dear—"

Clarice jumped.

He stared at his wife, noting the way she shrank from him, seeing the trembling of her hands before she clutched the handful of tatting in her lap. She smiled bravely, but her eyes were wary.

Another time he might like to take advantage of that fear. Now he had other, more interesting, birds to pluck. He came to her side to kiss her. She dropped her face so his kiss fell on the top of her head rather than her cheek. "I must go down to London for a few days, my dear."

She did not smile. Her voice was quavery as if she had been crying. "Do inquire at Lady Hampton's about Melissa. I shall worry terribly until I know she's all right."

"I intend to go round the very first thing," he assured her. He was irritated by the request and what he construed to be reproach.

Clarice rose. Her voice followed him, stronger and very determined. "Melissa Thorne was a good girl. She was lovely with the girls. If something has happened to her, then we are responsible."

Terence froze. His hand tightened on the doorknob. "I wouldn't go so far as to say that."

"I would. Lord Montague, you must do all you can to find her."

He looked at his plump little pigeon as if he had never seen her before. "I promise that Melissa Thorne will be number one on my list."

* * *

By the time the train pulled into Euston Station, Maria had had time to think about her companion. Her thoughts had made her wary. Had Melissa been offered assistance by as pleasant a stranger as she had? Maria gripped her umbrella tighter. He would not find her easy prey.

Who was he exactly? she wondered. They had never been properly introduced. certainly they did not come from the same strata of society. He did not even speak the same language as she did. She had trouble understanding some of his words because he pronounced them so oddly. She did not even know some of the words he used.

And most important, his damned levity about the entire situation set her teeth on edge. She was certain he did not believe that Melissa was a good girl.

She wanted to scream with frustration. No one believed her. Worse, no one seemed to *want* to believe her. Melissa, her darling sister, was being erased from society. Because she had disappeared, no one wanted to find her. The horror of it was growing in her mind.

As Jocko put his hand under her arm to lead her down the platform, she flinched. "I thank you very much for your escort, Mr. Walton, but I'm quite all right now. I need to be on my way."

He tipped his head to one side; his smile slipped for an instant, then returned brighter than ever. "Sayin' good-bye, Miss Thorne?"

"Yes. Yes, I am. I need to be about the business of finding my sister and you need to be about the business of—well, whatever your business is."

"A gentleman toff always sees a lady 'ome." He reached for her arm again.

She lifted her elbow out of his grasp and started down the platform. He fell into step beside her. "That won't be necessary. I'm so tired that I'll probably take myself home in a cab."

He nodded. "Sounds like the very thing. A good idea. I'll see about gettin' one for you."

"That won't be necessary. I am quite capable of hiring my own transport."

"You don't have to be—"

"Why'n't you leave the lady go? 'Ow's about you 'n' me, Judy? This bloke ain't what you need."

A huge man half a head taller and a shoulder's width broader than Jocko stepped in front of them. His enormous hands hung almost down to his knees. Around his massive throat he wore a muffler that must have been eight feet long. "Why'n't you jus' be on yer way, Jocko? I'll take care of the lady."

Maria gasped.

Jocko put his arm around her. "Stuff it, bully boy."

"Now, that ain't nice."

Maria stared at the giant. His nose had been flattened, his jaw slanted to one side. One ear drooped. He doubled his huge hands into fists as big as coal scuttles. She threw Jocko a frightened glance.

He did not seem concerned. "Take yourself off, Tilly. This bird's mine."

The giant grinned. "So y've 'eard o' me. Then ye knows better'n t' kick up a fuss."

Jocko shrugged. "Your reputation's as ugly as your face."

Maria gasped and tugged at his sleeve. "Be quiet. Don't say anything—"

"That's all 'e's doin' is talkin'," Jocko sneered. "Tilly won't do a thing."

The giant seemed to swell. "Let go o' the lady, or y'll find out what I do."

Maria looked around frantically. Dozens of people passed them, but no one stopped to help. Everyone scurried along with heads down, rushing to catch a train or leave one. No one was going to help them. She thought of running out onto the street. "Shall I go for the police?"

The giant chuckled. "Ye can go, but ye won't find none. They know t' leave me alone."

"This is infamous." Maria took a better grip on her umbrella.

Jocko heaved a sigh. "Tilly, the lady's tired. She needs to get home and get some rest."

"Well, now, why don't I take 'er 'ome with me? I'll see t' it, she gets lots o' rest. She can lie on 'er back all night 'n' all day."

Jocko turned to Maria. "Please step back."

"What?"

"Step back."

"But—"

Before she knew what he was about, he had pushed three fingers into the center of her chest. She stumbled back.

Quick as light, his hand became a fist. He pivoted as one leg shot out, his boot heel ramming into Tilly's knee-cap. Tilly howled and dropped his hands toward the injury.

One—two! Jocko's left fist connected with Tilly's chin, then his right buried itself in the mass that was left of Tilly's nose.

The giant toppled like a tree. The platform actually vibrated under his crashing weight.

Jocko grabbed Maria's arm. "Run!"

Together, they burst out of the station door. Jocko

dragged her in front of a cab that was coming to a halt. "Aubrey Walk!" he called to the driver. "And 'urry!"

"Right-o!"

As the driver whipped up the horse, they looked through the back window. Tilly came lunging out onto the street. Blood streamed from his nose over his mouth and chin, but he punched the air with his fists. His howl of anger reached their ears.

"Oh, God," Maria whispered. "What was that all about?"

Jocko twisted back around to face front. He blew on the knuckles he had grazed against Tilly's chin. "That's probably what 'appened to your sister."

Maria turned from the window to look at him. Her face lost every trace of color. Her brown eyes were enormous, their lashes and the dark circles under them making them look twice as big. "My sister?"

"She probably met up with Tilly, or someone just like 'im."

Maria pressed her hands to her mouth. "Oh, no."

Jocko sat back against the squibs. "Young girls arriving alone in London need to remember what their mother's told 'em. Never, *never* go with a stranger."

"But I wasn't alone."

Jocko seemed to concentrate on the street in front of them. For several blocks he remained silent. "You were with me," he said at last. "And Tilly recognized me."

"Oh, dear."

The horse trotted on.

He faced her squarely. "Do you want me to get out?"

She studied the young-old face. If Jocko Walton had planned to kidnap her, he had had ample opportunity to do so. She remembered the fierceness of his attack on the giant. He was not her idea of a champion, but this was the nineteenth century. Champions were hard to come by.

"Of course not," she said primly. "It's raining."

Four

"Oh, my dear. Your trip was a disappointment." Avory's warmth brought tears to Maria's eyes.

"Yes, ma'am." She sucked in her breath and straightened her shoulders. "I'm afraid I must leave your employ."

"But why?" Avory shook her head. "Surely—"

"My sister's disappeared. Vanished." Maria's voice trembled. "No one will look for her."

"My dear—"

"At least no one will look for her the way I will."

"The police—"

Maria made a wry face. "If my sister is to be found, I'm going to have to find her. I have to be free to go from place to place and look and ask questions. I have to—"

Mrs. Shires looked alarmed. "That's very dangerous."

"Probably that is why the police don't want to do it." Maria gestured awkwardly toward the correspondence "Saint" Peter had stacked on the desk the single day she had been at Briarfields. "If I'm out and about looking for Melissa, I can't do your work. I'm so sorry, but you'll have to find someone else."

Usually reserved to the point of coldness, Mrs. Shires came awkwardly to put her arm around Maria's shoulders. "Nonsense." Her voice was gruff. "You may have all the time you need."

"But your work . . . Your letters . . . I'm so sorry—"
Maria could feel the tears overflowing. She swiped at them
with her fingers. "You'll have to find someone else. Otherwise you'll fall behind."

"Who would I find, pray tell?" Her employer shook her
head. "I must have a woman to do this work. I doubt very
seriously that a man would work for me. And what woman
would or could take over that infernal machine?" She gestured toward the typewriter under its black leather cover.

"But you know—"

"Oh, I know," Avory continued. "I know how you feel
about it. It's noisy and messy and it takes practice."

"It's not so bad." Maria's voice trailed away.

"I shall have to get someone to faircopy the most urgent
correspondence," Mrs. Shires said with a sigh. "The rest
will just have to wait." She gave Maria's shoulder a final
squeeze before stepping back. "Just promise me that you'll
come back to me the very minute you can."

Maria pulled her handkerchief from her waistband and
wiped her eyes. "I promise."

"Hey! You've been crying."

Maria stopped stock still in the middle of Mrs. Shires's
front stoop. "You're still here!"

Jocko doffed his bowler and twisted it over his arm like
a swell. "At your service."

"Why?" She hefted her umbrella. "I don't want your
service."

"Saint" Peter had started to close the door. At her words
he opened it wider and stepped outside. "You want me to
send 'im on 'is way, Miss Maria?"

With the huge man at her back, she smiled sweetly. "I

don't think that will be necessary. Do you need to be sent on your way?"

Jocko put the bowler back on his head and cocked one eye up at the butler. From the top of the Shires's stoop, Peter loomed fully five feet above the slighter man. To her amazement, Jocko chuckled. "Now, Miss—er—Maria, you wouldn't want to be the cause of this fella gettin' hurt, would you?"

Peter growled.

She tucked her umbrella under her arm and began to pull on her black kid gloves. "No one will be hurt if you'll just leave me alone."

Jocko shook his head, his expression mournful. "I'd like to, Ria, and that's the truth; but the fact is—I can't."

"My name is Mahr-eye-ah. Mahr-eye-ah Thorne. And you, Mr. Walton, *can* leave me alone."

"Mahr-eye-ah. Fine name." He nodded. "Call me Jocko and I'll call you Ria. Ria's better." His eyes twinkled. "Friendlier—er—nicer, don't you know?" His blond eyebrows rose and fell significantly.

She gasped at his presumption.

"Want me to knock him down?" Peter rumbled.

With the heel of his hand, Jocko pushed the bowler back until his tight gold curls ringed his face like a Renaissance angel's. He leaned forward, his voice lowered as if to impart a secret. "Now, Ria, you wouldn't want to get your big friend all bruised and bloody, would you? Course you wouldn't. And you remember Tilly, don't you? I heard tell last night that 'e thinks 'is kneecap's broken."

Maria could feel the color draining from her face. Her eyes fell to Jocko's hands. Even relaxed, with the thumbs tucked into the pockets of his vest, they looked powerful. She had never seen hands like that before. The backs were broad, the skin lightly tanned and sprinkled with golden hairs.

But the knuckles made her shiver. They were swollen and dotted with halfpenny-sized bruises where he had connected with Tilly's jaw.

She raised her eyes. Her voice was high and thin. "Tilly's kneecap is broken?"

Jocko made a sympathetic clucking noise. "Leastways 'e's stove up. Knee swollen the size of a melon, nose like a turnip. Pardon me, Ria, but 'e looks like 'ell. Or so I 'ear."

The thought of kind "Saint" Peter with his nose like a turnip made Maria wince. "It's all right, Peter." She smiled weakly at the butler. "I know the gentleman."

Peter looked doubtful. "You sure?"

"I'm sure."

"She's sure," Jocko said at the same instant. He offered her his arm. "Come on, Ria. Let's get on with it."

She scowled at him, but he grinned, showing dimples on either side of his mouth. He was horrible. Absolutely horrible. Where he had come from or who he was, she did not know. But she could think of nothing else to do but go with him.

Later, she would remember that she never considered fleeing back into the safety of Mrs. Shires's house. Her sister, her only family, was lost, doubtless in danger. She had to find her.

She put her hand on Jocko's arm and allowed him to lead her down the steps and then down the street.

"What say we stop for a bit of a rest and decide what we're about?"

Maria had walked so fast into High Holborn that she was breathing hard. Unfortunately, she had been able neither to lose nor discourage her companion. The wretch seemed to exert no effort at all. Just by lengthening the stride of his long legs, he kept pace beside her. She swung on him, hefting her umbrella. "Will you please leave me alone?"

He stepped back, his expression exasperated. "I can't rightly do that, but I would be mightily pleased to know where in 'ell you think you're goin'."

"A place I'm sure you don't know about. I wasn't just walking for pleasure, Mr. Walton. I have arrived at my destination." She pointed triumphantly with the tip of her umbrella.

A row of shabby buildings sagged against each other in a cul-de-sac. Half-timbered fronts canted crazily against shoulders of brick and stone. Black mildew climbed the facings around all the narrow doors. The cobblestone street provided not even a stepping stone, much less a sidewalk.

Jocko glanced into the unlovely circle. "You're going there?" His eyebrows rose and fell. "Are you sure?" He tipped his hat back from his forehead. "You think your sister's in there?"

Maria shook her head. "Oh, I wish she were, but that would be too wonderful."

"Oh, yeah, wonderful."

Giving him a threatening look, Maria began to pick her way across the slimy cobblestones.

The third house on the left was distinguished by a polished brass doorknob and a clean doorsill. Maria rang the bell and waited. And waited.

"Nobody's 'ome," Jocko said hopefully. "Might as well leave."

Maria consulted the watch pinned to her bosom. "They're probably at morning prayers."

"Oh, Lord." He rolled his eyes heavenward. "One of those."

"Please don't." She rang the bell again.

A chain rattled behind the door. It opened a crack. A pale eye stared out of a blue-white face. A dry voice whispered, "Yes?"

Maria leaned forward. "I'm here to see the Reverend Mr. Dinsmore," she whispered.

"May the Lord bless him," came the response, although the door did not open wider.

Jocko coughed noisily. The eye flitted to him.

Maria moved between them. "May we see him?"

"He's at prayers."

"Oh, well, then—" Jocko tugged at Maria's elbow. "—Wouldn't want to disturb 'is 'oliness."

Maria pushed him away. "I must see Mr. Dinsmore. It's a matter of grave urgency."

The door closed, but the lock did not engage.

"Listen 'ere—" Jocko began, but the chain rattled again. This time the door opened just enough to admit them. A thin woman stood aside.

Stepping into the entry hall, Maria could not repress a shiver. The house was colder on the inside than out and smelled strongly of cabbage. For the first time she welcomed the presence of Jocko Walton slipping in behind her. Grayness and gloom thickened perceptibly as the woman closed the door. The chain rattled again.

"A little bit o' 'eaven," Jocko whispered in her ear.

"Hush." Maria forced a wan smile. "It's good of Mr. Dinsmore to see us."

"He's very busy." An older woman spoke tartly. The one

who had opened and closed the door stood with bowed head.

"I need him desperately. I need his help."

"Who sent you?"

Maria swallowed and crossed her fingers inside her muff. "Mrs. Avory Shires."

"Wait here with Patience." The older of the two turned on the heel of her thick-soled black shoe. The hem of her black wool skirt, several inches above the floor, swished and jerked as she marched away.

Maria smiled warmly in the direction of the doorkeeper. The younger girl did not notice. She stood with her hands clasped at her narrow waist, still as a stone. Maria shifted uncomfortably, the chill rising through the soles of her boots.

"What'd you expect to find 'ere?" Jocko wanted to know, no longer bothering to whisper.

"The Reverend Mr. Dinsmore is a missionary to the poor," Maria told him. "He's particularly concerned about the degradation of poor innocent young women. He helps them back from sin. He's written many encouraging letters to Mrs. Shires."

"Beggin' for money, I'll bet," Jocko sneered.

"Well, yes. He does run this charity house."

"Who gets the charity?"

"It's for—um—girls who have gone astray but seen the light."

Jocko stepped past Maria. His blue eyes were cold as he surveyed the dark hall furnished with a hard bench and an umbrella stand. He let his breath escape from between his teeth. It made a white stream in the cold air. His heels thudded along the bare floor as he paced the hall's length and returned to stop in front of Maria. Shoulders hunched, he thrust his hands into his pockets.

She ignored him to concentrate on pale, cold Patience. The girl had neither moved nor spoken.

The door at the end of the hall opened. "He'll see you now."

Maria hurried forward. Jocko fell into step at her elbow. The older woman barred his way. "One at a time."

"Why?" Jocko wanted to know, but Maria hastened through. The door closed firmly in his face.

Maria followed the straight black skirts down more barren halls, up steps, around turns, through a small, ill-furnished room into a larger one. The meagre furnishings consisted of a chair, a small writing desk, and a potbellied stove. "Please wait here."

Maria sidled closer to the stove. She had never imagined a house could be so cold. The farther they had gone into it, the colder it became. She rubbed her gloved hands together and held them out to the grate.

"My dear sister."

She jumped as deep tones rumbled into the room. A young man stood in the doorway. At least she supposed he was a young man. On closer examination, she was not so sure of his age. The gray light sifting through the curtains revealed his hair to be midnight-black but finely streaked with gray. It was thick and combed straight back from what could only be called a noble forehead. A neatly trimmed black beard covered his cheeks and chin.

Dressed in black with a Roman collar and a simple stock, he carried a Bible. "Sister Evangeline said you came from Mrs. Avory Shires. I hope you have brought good words from that devout lady."

Maria bit her lip. She hated to lie. "Mrs. Shires sends her regards."

He moved nearer—his eyes were as dark as his hair. They stared at her unwaveringly.

Unable to face him, she ducked her head.

"You do not come from Mrs. Shires," he said suddenly.

Her head shot up. The muscles around his mouth had tightened. "I worked—work for her."

"But she did not send you," he persisted.

She felt the skin prickle on her arms. "No."

"Then what do you want?"

"I've come about my sister."

"Bit chilly in 'ere." Jocko strolled in a circle around the silent Patience.

She kept her head down determinedly.

"Course, churches are cold," he observed as if she were heeding him. "Coo. I can remember as a boy kneelin' for the communion. Thinkin' my knees would freeze to the floor."

She did not answer.

"I've heard tell of preachers like this one. Preach that heat is the devil's tool to trick people." He ducked his head to try to see into her face. Her hair was scraped back from her cheek and bound tightly in a knot at her neck. "For myself, I didn't ever get used to the cold. It was the main reason why I gave up church."

"Gave up church?" She looked up in fright. Her lips moved, but she gave no sound to the words. She flashed a quick glance at the inner door.

He grinned. "Figured they weren't doing anything but

taking my money and preaching against everything that
was joy or pleasure."

Patience clasped her hands at her breast.

He reached out and covered them with his own. Through
the black mitts, her hands were cold, the exposed fingertips
frigid. "Don't pray for me, Patience," he said gently. "I
like being a sinner."

"Oh, no."

"Oh, yes."

She backed away from him, but he would not let her
hands out of his warm grasp.

"Why don't you tell me all about the Reverend
Dinsmore?"

She shook her head, her face twisting in anguish.

Nodding, little soothing sounds coming out of his throat,
he held her hands until she stilled. Then he smiled gently.
"Are you one of 'is girls?"

"So you see, my sister is missing. But no one will help
me find her."

Dinsmore nodded sadly. "Fallen into the pit of sin from
which there is no reclamation save by the sinner herself."

Maria sucked in her breath. "But she didn't fall into the
pit of sin. She was pushed. Or dragged. Or kidnapped.
And she needs our help. I thought you—"

"She is ruined," he intoned.

"She is not ruined." Maria felt her anger rise. She had
heard this theme repeated too often. "She's somewhere in
London, in danger, being held against her will, probably
being hurt."

He seated himself at the desk, his hand on the Bible.
His dark eyes were liquid with tears. He shook his head.

"I thought you could help me find her. In the letters you wrote to Mrs. Shires, you said you went among the poor young women—"

"My dear woman, I don't actually go into a brothel."

Maria clenched her fists. Intense frustration and a sense of injustice set her whole body to shaking. "Mrs. Shires gave you money to save girls."

Dinsmore frowned. "Ah, but only girls who wished to be saved. Your sister—"

"My sister wishes desperately to be saved, I can assure you."

He opened the Bible and ran his finger down the page. "I promise you I will pray for her soul and her body."

"Thank you, but—"

He closed the book. "If I had a larger flock, perhaps I could carry His message among sinners. Unfortunately, everything is *of the world*. A place even as humble as this is costly. From time to time men and women come seeking charity. Perhaps your sister will be among them. Of course, then we will provide for her physical as well as her spiritual needs. I trust—" His black eyes looked deeply into hers. "—that she will not go away without so much as a thank you. Most try to repay in a variety of ways."

During his long speech, she had clenched her jaw so tightly that it was aching. Something was eluding her. He was saying something that she did not understand. She tried a little desperately to answer him. "Melissa would never be ungrateful."

"Of course, God doesn't need any man's thanks." He tapped with his finger on the page. The noise drew her attention. A dirty black crescent showed under his fingernail.

She sucked in her breath. His skin was soiled as well, his knuckles ingrained with grime.

"Sometimes the lost sheep are grateful," he continued. "Sometimes they ask how they may repay our kindnesses. And perhaps earn a little something to keep them from having to return."

Maria closed her eyes. "Are you saying that you might hire someone to search for my sister—someone of these 'lost sheep'?"

"It would be a way. A way to find your sister and perhaps carry a message to her—an admonition to climb out of the pit into which she has sunk—"

Her temper exploded. "Mr. Dinsmore! I'm poor. My sister and I are orphans. We both work for our living and we have almost no money saved. Surely—"

"Surely your employer . . ."

Outside in the street, Maria could feel the tears burning in her eyes. She blinked furiously. Of course, the Reverend Dinsmore had promised to help, to send word to Mrs. Shires if Melissa should appear at his door repentant and contrite. Ruined. Her sweet, sweet sister.

Not caring where she placed her feet at the entrance to the cul-de-sac, Maria stumbled and banged into the side of the building.

" 'Ave a care there." Jocko took her arm.

Blinded by tears, she allowed him to lead her down the narrow street. He could feel her body trembling against him, feel the deep shuddering breaths she drew in an effort to get herself under control.

"Crying won't 'elp a bit," he told her at last.

She halted and pulled a handkerchief from her pocket.

While he waited, she dabbed her face and eyes and blew her nose.

"Didn't your 'oly Joe want to 'elp?"

"For a price."

"Yeah."

She looked directly into his face, her reddened eyes searching. "You knew."

He shrugged. "Everybody down 'ere's got 'is ways. Nobody'd be 'ere if 'e could be anyplace else. And everybody wants to get out. Maybe the preacher thinks 'e'll get enough money to move 'is little 'ouse somewhere else. Chances are 'e isn't a preacher at all. 'E's just a man tryin' to make a bit."

Maria drew a deep breath. "Is that what you are, Jocko Walton?"

He cocked his head to one side. "I might be."

"Are you?"

"Probably."

Her stare never wavered.

"Yeah."

"Then I know where I stand with you."

"In a manner of speaking." He felt uneasy about that. Actually, he couldn't leave her if he wanted to, but she might just be his ticket out of Revill's books. "Yeah."

She caught at his arm then. Her pale face, with traces of tears on her cheeks, her lashes stuck together and spiky, close to his. She stood so close that he could feel her breath against his cheek.

He looked away from such intensity and for the first time he noticed they were being watched.

She took his hand between both her own. "Please, Mr. Walton, will you help me?"

He looked down at her, distracted.

"I'll pay you all I have. Every blessed penny and sign a note for more."

They were being watched. Time to get in out of the cold. He nodded and caught her under the arm. Grinning as if she had said something pleasant, he leaned over and kissed her on the cheek. "Right you are, love." He slid his arm around her waist. "We'll 'ave a pint right now."

"Stop!" she protested. "What do you think you're doing?"

He pulled her against him so tight that she squealed. His lips touched her ear. "Ria, m'love, this 'ere's no place for a lady to be alone. There's a couple of chaps watching us. Time for us to move."

"Who? Where?' She glanced around her. The narrow street was still gloomy, still filthy, but no longer were they the only people in it. A cab rattled along, another parked at the curbing. At the door of several houses, men of Tilly's stripe had appeared to lounge on the stoop or patrol the iron fences.

"Come on," Jocko urged loudly. In her ear he hissed, "Smile, like you're enjoying yourself."

"I'll never enjoy anything again." She took a deep breath. Her mouth curved stiffly upward at the corners.

"That's right, love. Now, put your arm around m' waist and walk with me."

"Who could be following us?" Her umbrella banged against his hip, but she complied.

"Could be any one of a number of people. Most would be following me."

"Not friends."

"No, not friends. But you're picking up your own group as we get along in this." Together they turned the corner where he pushed open the door of the Robin's Nest.

Through a dense smoky haze, Maria stared into a long, narrow room. Indeed, it was just wide enough for the bar with a space behind it for the bartender to move back and forth in front of his casks and a space in front of it for the customers to stand.

Jocko pushed her ahead of him down the line of men. Some of them turned to leer at her around white clay pipes clenched between their teeth. Her cheeks burned as one pushed his shoulder out to bar their way. In order for her to pass, she had to turn sideways, and still her breasts brushed his arm.

At last she came to a space with four tables. Two were unoccupied. Three men sat at one, drinking and smoking. At the fourth, a man held a woman on his lap. Her back was to the room, but she straddled him, her striped stockings showing beneath the edges of her petticoat.

Maria froze. "No," she whispered. "Oh, no."

"A couple o' pints o' your best," Jocko called over his shoulder. His arm like a bar across her back he propelled her to the table farthest from the couple. "Have a seat, Ria."

Her shocked eyes surveyed the room. "I—"

He pushed her down and sat beside her. The bartender brought the dark beer in chipped glass mugs.

" 'Ere you go, love." Jocko closed her hand around the handle and guided it to her lips. His eyes stayed on the door. Every muscle in his body was tense. " 'Ave a sip. You'll feel more the thing."

She swallowed, shuddering at the foul taste, staring at the woman who jounced rhythmically on the man's lap. Suddenly, he began to groan. His hands caught her hips and held her still. She put her hands on his shoulders.

Jocko reached out a hand and turned Maria's face away.

In the flickering gaslights her cheeks were red, her eyes overbright. He read the embarrassment and shock in them. He patted her cheek. "Don't you think you'd better drink your drink and let me take you back 'ome?"

She took another swallow. This time it went down without a shudder.

"No."

"No?"

Narrowing her eyes against the haze of smoke, she looked around at the couple. The man's mouth hung open. His eyes were closed, his hands clenched convulsively around the woman's hips. She had stopped moving. One hand still held onto her partner's shoulder. With the other she reached out for the beer still on the table. As unconcerned as if she sat on a chair, the woman raised the mug and drank.

Maria looked back into Jocko Walton's eyes. "I can't leave my sister here."

Jocko's mouth twisted wryly.

Maria took another sip. The bitter brew filled her mouth and unsettled her stomach. Her nostrils quivered at the heavy animal scent slipping through the smoke. "I don't have much money, but I can promise to pay you something for the rest of my life."

He started to shake his head.

She caught his hand. "I've tried everything I know. Police. Church. I've talked with good people. Nobody is willing to help. Nobody even cares very much. But here you are, Jocko Walton. I don't know why. And now I don't care why. All I know is you're the only one who'll even try. And I'll make it worth your while."

He frowned uncomfortably. "Listen, maybe I—"

She caught his other hand. Taking them both in hers,

she squeezed them hard. "Take me where you think my sister might be. We'll look for her together. I'll do whatever you say. I won't be a hindrance. I'm strong."

Her hands fit nicely into his, Jocko thought. "What if we don't find her?"

"I don't want to think about that. We'll find her. She came to London."

"Biggest city in the world," he reminded her.

"If we don't, I'll still pay you," she said coldly.

He jerked his hands away. "I don't want to 'ear that tone o' voice."

She blinked.

"Now, Miss 'Oity-Toity, you listen to me. If you want me to work for you, you've got to treat me proper." He straightened his bowler over his eyes and tucked his thumb into his vest pocket. Sitting very upright, he took a swallow of beer. "I'm not going to work for some bloody ladyship who thinks I'm not good enough to black her boots."

"I assure you—"

He held up his hand. "You'd be lyin' if you did."

She subsided.

"I'm a man," he insisted. "I might not be strictly honest, and sometime I admit I like a bit o' fun, but I'm a man. And I must be pretty good, or you wouldn't be wantin' me."

She nodded seriously. "You're more than pretty good, Mr. Walton. You're—er—bloody good with your fists."

He shook his finger at her. "None o' that bad language now, Ria. I'll call you Ria and you call me Jocko, and we'll be friendlylike and respectful."

He took another drink and she smiled slightly as he tipped his head back. "You got to treat me like a man."

"You *are* a man—"

"A *real* man. A 'toff.' A swell. Someone you wouldn't mind bein' seen with." His blue eyes bored into her own. He lifted his chin. "Even though you would."

"A swell?"

"Right."

"A toff?"

"The same."

"You want to be treated like a gentleman."

"Is it a deal?"

She smiled. "It's a deal, Jocko."

"Then shake, Ria." He grinned. "We'll find your sister, if she's around and about, and that's a promise."

Five

A sledgehammer pounded inside Melissa's temples. Needle-sharp agony lanced behind her eyes. To open them would be futile. She would be blind. She moaned helplessly and tried to swallow. Her mouth was so dry that the sides of her throat seemed to stick together.

Despite the pain, she opened one eye. Nothing but impenetrable haze. She could distinguish no shapes, nor any particular colors. Nothing.

She tried to think, to remember. Fretfully, she attempted to turn her head. Her stomach rolled.

She closed her eyes and tried to concentrate on movement. Somewhere down at the end of her arm should be a hand. If she could manage to bring it to her head, perhaps she could massage her temple and ease the awful pain.

She sent the message. For a long time nothing happened. She had no feeling in her fingers. Perhaps, she thought, she had no fingers at all.

A shard of fear sliced through her pain. Was she dead? Was death pain unrelenting? Panic restored her to sensible thought momentarily. Something had happened to her. But what?

Where was she? Her sister . . . her sister had always made things right. She tried her name. "Maria—"

The sound in no way resembled her sister's name. It did not even resemble a word. It was a dry husk of sound, a whisper deadened by lips that did not seem to work.

Why couldn't she speak? "Maria—" Better. "Maria."

The best yet. Using all her willpower, she sent a message to her fingers. Pins pricked at their tips. They lay like pegs attached to the deadweight that was her hand. She tried to picture herself moving them.

A sound. A rumbling, as of someone speaking. "She's awake."

"Wha' happen'?"

"Call Lady H."

"Better wait. She might pass out again."

She had passed out before?!

"She's moving. See?"

Melissa heard their voices. Understood them. "Wahterr," she moaned.

Someone touched her head, slid a hand under her skull. She screamed, a rasping, husky cry. Blackness rolled across her senses, but the pain flashed red fire and drove it back. Against her lips, she could feel a glass, then water flowed into her mouth.

She swallowed, choked, swallowed.

"Easy. Don't drink so fast. You'll drown yourself," a husky voice cautioned.

Melissa opened her eyes again. The haze had parted from one eye. A woman's face to match the voice hung over her. The water was taken away.

Melissa fumbled and found the woman's wrist. "Please," she whispered. "More."

"Oh, there's plenty. You can have all the water you want. Just so long as you don't drown yourself." The voice was tinged with bitterness. "Here you go. Drink it for yourself."

Melissa could feel the glass being pressed into her own palm, her fingers closed around it.

"Got it?" the woman asked.

Melissa tried to nod. Pain made her gasp. "Yes."

"Just hold your head still. That's the worst."

The support slid out from behind her neck. Somehow, Melissa managed to hold her head still and raise the glass to her lips. This time she managed the water for herself, holding a swallow in her mouth where it felt like heaven.

A doorlatch clicked.

Melissa opened her eyes, blinked once, twice. A familiar face swam out of the dimness at the foot of the bed.

"So. We're waking up," said Mrs. Hermione Beauforty.

Melissa's eyes threatened to close as a wave of dizziness made focusing difficult. She willed her eyelids to stay open. "Am I sick?"

"Oh, I do hope not," came the deep-throated reply. "Terry won't like that a bit."

"Terry?" Melissa focused on Mrs. Beauforty's face.

"Lord Terence Montague." The woman delivered the name with a trilling laugh. "Your employer."

Behind her a slender woman dressed all in black moved restively.

The woman's face was painted dead-white. Her blackened eyebrows arched high onto her forehead and were swept away into painted wings that flowed into her shining ebony hair. Her eyelashes likewise were blackened and spiky, impossibly long. Across the lower part of her face, a scarlet mouth made a wound. Melissa's eyes widened in shock.

Catching Melissa's reaction, the scarlet mouth curled

down in a sneer. The full lips expelled breath in a disgusted hiss. "Might've known she'd be a goody-goody."

Hermione smiled as she seated herself in a green velveteen Morris chair beside the bed. "Do step away, Cate. I believe you're frightening the dear girl."

Again the disgusted hiss before the woman called Cate turned on a spiked heel and stalked toward the door.

The back view of the departing figure was quite the equal of the front. For the first time, Melissa saw that the woman's dress was a wrapper of black net and lace. Beneath it, showing clearly, were black boots, black stockings, a black corset, cut almost to the waist in back, and a shocking zone of white thighs.

At the door Cate pivoted again. The black lace swirled wide. Her shapely white legs above each stocking were bisected by a black elastic strap depending from the corset.

Melissa's shocked eyes flew to Mrs. Beauforty's face.

The woman cocked her ahead on one side and smiled winsomely. "Pretty, isn't she? You shall have a costume like that eventually, my dear."

Melissa's stomach could contain itself no longer. With a terrible moan, she managed to roll onto her side to vomit.

Hermione was not quite quick enough. The rich purple skirts of her gown received the foul stuff. "Damnation!" She sprang to her feet, toppling the chair. "Hecate!"

The woman in black laughed, a nasty, dry sound.

Safely out of range, Hermione stared down at the sour mess that had ruined her dress. "You did that on purpose."

Cate shrugged her slender shoulders. "Me? I didn't puke all over the floor."

"You did it on purpose."

"I didn't give her too much."

"You—you bitch. You vicious, nasty—" Hermione advanced hissing. Her face assumed an icy calm. The quivering of the sagging flesh of her jaw betrayed her anger. Her hand swung up in a slap. The back of Cate's head thudded against the door panel.

Cate showed no sign of emotion. The vivid stain on her cheek was the only evidence that she had been struck. "Why don't you make her clean it up? I'm not the maid."

"You are if I say you are," came the angry reply. "And don't you forget it."

"I never forget who I am. Not for one minute. Nor who you are."

"That's enough." Lady H gestured viciously toward the bed. "Clean this mess up while I change."

Holding her ruined skirt aside, she started for the door, but Cate was not finished. "God Almighty spoke and you brought her here. She's not to turn a profit. And she could be trouble. You act as if he's—"

"That will do."

"Why don't you make her clean it up? Afraid she might get her precious hands rough for his bloody pimping lordship."

Hermione's hand flashed upward again, striking the other cheek as it passed.

Again the sickening thud.

Behind the two women, Melissa vomited again. The spinning room began to darken. The women's voices arguing, arguing, echoed unintelligibly and then faded as she lost consciousness.

"You're back with us again."

Melissa raised her head. Drawing a ragged breath, she

pushed herself off the cot and moved carefully to lean against the wall. "Yes. Was I poisoned?"

"I suppose so, in a way of speaking. Bert holds your mouth open and Lady H just opens up her bottle and pours it down. One time a girl didn't wake up. Sometimes, like now, they can't remember."

"Oh, mercy," Melissa whispered. She pressed her hand to her belly.

"Be sick again if you're going to be."

Melissa shuddered. A couple of tears trickled down her cheeks. Finally, she shook her head. "I don't th-think so."

"That's good." The woman in black motioned to her from the door. "I'm Cate. Come with me." She tossed her black locks. The hectic color still stained her cheeks where the other woman had slapped her.

Melissa realized she must have been unconscious for only a few minutes. "Why?"

"No reason, if you like breathing in a stench that makes you gag every time you draw breath. I've got Nessie out here to clean it up. You can watch her if you want." She swung open the door. At the snap of her fingers, a short, grossly fat person waddled in. Cate raised her black brows to Melissa. "Come if you want."

Melissa stared into the moon face of the creature bearing the bucket and mop. She could not tell whether Nessie was a male or a female. A huge apron enshrouded the body. Beneath it, gray stockings encased thick posts that swelled over scuffed brogans. Shirtsleeves gray with grime were rolled back from thick, hairless wrists. Dark eyes squinted out from beneath the folds of fleshy eyelids. The eyes slid off Melissa's face to the mess on the floor.

"Nas-s-sty."

Cate cocked an eyebrow. Her red, red mouth twisted up at one corner.

Melissa edged along the wall past the mountainous Nessie and fled through the door Cate closed behind her.

The two girls stood in a long hall. Gaslamps cast their hissing lights from brackets beside every door, casting pools of yellow light upon the thick red carpet.

Melissa looked around her dully before fixing her gaze on her companion, who tipped her head back and shook her long black hair. It was thick and heavy, curling like snakes around her shoulders. Cate met Melissa's eyes with a mocking smile.

Snapping out of her trance, Melissa reached out to take hold of Cate's arm. "Where am I?"

The smile disappeared. Cate stared pointedly at the hand. "Don't touch me."

"I'm sorry." Melissa drew back instantly. "Please. Please. Tell me where I am."

Cate crossed her arms, pushing her bosom up tight against the black lace. "The Lord's Dream."

Melissa gaped at the white skin and dusky rose nipples cresting each breast. "Not a hotel?"

Cate sneered again. "Not a hotel. Honor marks for you, dearie. You're the latest dove in Lady H's cote."

Melissa swayed where she stood. Her head still ached, her empty stomach made her feel faint. "A—a house—of—"

"Whores."

Melissa reeled back against the wall. She shook her head, trying to come to terms with her predicament. "I won't stay."

"Oh, you'll stay all right." Cate leaned her shoulders against the opposite wall. Dark and light, they faced each other, brunette and blonde, harlot and innocent. Golden light pooled around them. "Even if you left, no one, at least not a decent person, would take you in."

"My sister would take me." Melissa felt tears prick her eyes. "My sister will be worried to death. She'll be searching for me."

"But not here," Cate jeered. "No one will search here. Not your sister. Not the police. You're ruined, you see. And nobody wants you anymore. That's what *ruined* means."

"My sister wouldn't care if I were ruined," Melissa insisted with quiet certainty.

Cate slipped a white hand into a satin pocket in her robe. She drew forth a slender silver box and extracted a long, thin, black cheroot. Standing on tiptoe, she held the tip in the flame of the gaslight until the rolled leaf caught fire. With a defiant air she flourished it before drawing the smoke into her lungs. Her smile was that of a superior cat. "Especially your sister."

Melissa lifted her chin. "You don't know my sister. She'll come for me. In fact, you'd better let me go. She works for Mrs. Avory Shires. She has great influence in government."

Cate blew smoke into the air. It fled like a ghost toward the gaslight. "On any night of the week, we have all the influence in the world downstairs."

Melissa cast her eyes down the hall.

"Don't try it," Cate warned.

"You couldn't stop me."

"I wouldn't even try. But the doormen would. Not very nice gents to tangle with. One of them twisted a girl's arm up so far behind her back that he dislocated it at the shoulder." Cate moved a step and tapped the ash into a brass cuspidor. She dragged more smoke into her lungs and coughed slightly. "The poor thing screamed bloody murder when he popped it back in, but she didn't get away. Didn't even get the night off."

Melissa shuddered. "Please—"

"Save it."

"I could pay you. My quarterly wages are in my purse."

Cate laughed. "They're already in Bert's pocket."

Melissa felt a flash of anger. She had worked hard for that money. "My sister would pay you. She's a type writer for an important woman."

The door opened. Nessie came out, turning slightly sideways to edge the mountain of flesh through the door. Melissa decided that the maid was female. She seemed to have breasts lying atop the huge barrel of stomach and hips.

Cate drew back in disgust as the malodorous bucket brushed by her knees. Seizing her chance, Melissa bolted down the hall.

That is, she would have bolted down the hall, had Nessie not shot out the mop. It plowed between her feet, its ropy wet strands catching her about the ankle. She fell headlong.

Nessie giggled, a high-pitched squeal.

Cate laughed, too.

Bruised and breathless, Melissa rolled half over.

Nessie set the bucket down and lumbered forward. "Might as well take them rags."

"No."

Fingers the size of sausages, but terribly strong, dabbled at Melissa's neck, slipped inside the high collar and pulled the girl up on her knees. The porcine face hung above her, glistening with grease. With a grunt, Nessie ripped Melissa's dress open at the shoulders.

She screamed. Mortal terror and helpless despair combined to make even the huge Nessie draw back. Still screaming, Melissa stumbled to her feet and took a single step. Then Nessie's hands fastened in the back of the dress and ripped again.

This time the scream choked off in a sob. Nessie tore again, ripping the skirt away. Again. The petticoat. Again. The camisole.

Melissa could no longer scream. Only sob and sob. Her eyes were blinded by her tears

Nessie stuffed her sausage-like fingers into the single band of lawn at Melissa's waist. Rip! Her drawers came away in two pieces that slid to the floor about her slender ankles.

Clad only in stockings and shoes, Melissa collapsed against the wall. In another pool of light, she slid down it and huddled, her knees drawn up to her chest, her hands trying vainly to cover her breasts and belly.

Efficiently, Nessie bundled the rags of clothing into the bucket, picked up the mop and waddled off down the hall.

Melissa sobbed on, hopelessly.

A hand touched her shoulder.

She shrugged it away with a shrill cry.

"Come on." Cate's voice was not unkind. "You'll catch cold here in the hall. Come back to your room."

Shaking her head and struggling feebly, Melissa allowed herself to be pulled to her feet. Naked except for her stockings, she was helped back along the dimly lighted hall.

In the center of the room, she stood shivering, head bowed, eyes tightly closed, arms vainly trying to cover her body.

Cate left her and returned with a wrapper. Melissa

opened her eyes to find maroon lace hanging from her shoulders.

"Slip your arms in this."

"No. No."

Cate stepped back. "Suit yourself, but it's better than nothing."

Melissa looked at Cate's wrapper. "It's like yours."

Cate shook her head. "Mine's black. I like black. Black goes with what I do. Most blondes have to wear pink or blue. Believe me, maroon's better. Black's best."

Wanting to ask why, but not daring to, Melissa slipped her arms through the sleeves and lapped the garment across the front of her body. She wiped the backs of her hands across her cheeks.

"Here." Cate shoved a handkerchief into her hand. "Take care of that nose. Nothing looks worse than a snotty nose."

Melissa could feel embarrassed color flooding her cheeks. She hastily dried her nose and upper lip.

Cate grinned. "Got your vanity, didn't I?"

"Please let me go."

Cate strolled across the room and seated herself in the green velveteen chair. She crossed her left leg over her right, exposing herself with a graceful sweep of white limb and black lace.

Despite herself, Melissa gasped. Her color ran higher.

Cate drew on her cheroot, found it had gone out, and relighted it with a practiced swipe of matchstick against the underside of a table. Through the gray smoke, she smiled again. "The gentlemen do more than gasp."

"You're a—a—harlot."

"How biblical!" Cate's black eyebrows rose. Her smile

was bitter. "I suppose that gives a certain status to the trade. *Whore* is so low."

"You're brazen."

"Brazen! Yes, I guess I am. I've survived, so perhaps *brazen* is a good word for that. Bronzed more like."

"But you're educated," Melissa protested. "You're—"

"I'm ruined," Cate snarled.

Melissa darted across the room to take Cate's hand and try to pull the other girl to her feet. "We could escape together. My sister will take us both. She'll find good jobs for us. She'll—"

"She'll turn us over to the coppers before we get through her door." Cate snatched her hand away.

"No, she wouldn't. I know Maria. She loves me."

"Well, she don't love me," Cate's voice changed deliberately to a harsh twang. "Get that through yer bloomin' noggin. She don't love me. Nobody loves a whore." She took another drag off the cheroot and deliberately blew the smoke into Melissa's face. "And she don't love you anymore."

Melissa stepped back, her eyes watering and stinging.

Cate pointed to a bellrope. "Why don't you just stroll over there and give that a good yank?"

Melissa glanced at the thing. "Don't make me call anyone else. We could escape together."

"Pull it."

"Not until you tell me—"

"Lady H'll tell you all you need to know."

"Maroon lace. That's all wrong for this one. Cate, how could you be so stupid?" Hermione gestured impatiently at Melissa as if she were a thing with no feelings.

Cate shrugged. "Maroon sets off white skin."

"Well, of course, it does, but—"

"You'd better let me go," Melissa interrupted. "My sister will bring the police down on you."

At the mention of police, Hermione's head snapped round. "That will be all from you, my girl. You'll speak when you're spoken to." She seated herself as gracefully as a lady at a tea party. Her smile flashed. "And then only pleasantries. Threats are a waste of my time. Now listen to me closely while I explain your duties."

"I don't have any duties." Melissa's voice gathered strength. "I don't intend to stay here and work for you."

Her tormentor shook her head. "Ah, my dear. I'm afraid you have no choice in the matter. A very special man has gone to a great deal of trouble to have you brought here. You've cost him a substantial amount of time and trouble—"

"Montague!" Melissa exclaimed.

"Exactly."

"But how—?"

"In this modern age of the telegram, so much is possible." Hermione tossed the words out impatiently. She turned to Cate. "Have you told her?"

The woman in black lace shook her head. "There hasn't been time. She was sick and then the mess had to be cleaned up." She blew a stream of smoke into the air. "And then she tried to escape."

Hermione's blue eyes narrowed. "You will stop all that this instant."

"Never."

"It's quite useless. And I won't have the order of my house disturbed by it. Cate, see to the preparations."

The other girl slouched forward, sighing heavily. "I'm just a slavey around here."

"And be sure you get it right. The very idea of putting maroon on her."

"Sapphire blue would look nice with her eyes."

Hermione shook her head. Her eyes were scanning Melissa critically. "Terry will be here tomorrow night to claim his prize. Neither maroon nor sapphire will do. He likes his girls with an appearance of innocence. With those eyes and that yellow hair, I think virginal white—"

Melissa pulled the maroon lace tighter at her throat and over her loins. "I won't do what you want. I won't."

"Of course not," Hermione told her. "No one's expecting that you would. That comes later. Hopefully, much later. He's not coming here for that. Yes, white, like a bride, I think, and all that long hair washed and combed out, artistically arranged on the pillow."

"I'll never hold still for that."

"You won't have any choice."

Melissa's hair, washed and brushed until it shimmered, spread in a halo across the mattress. Her naked breasts swelled above the white satin wrapper tied in a loose knot at her waist. Below her waist the material parted to expose the nest of soft blond curls.

She strained against the straps that held her spreadeagled and virtually unmoving on the big bed. She had shed so many tears in her futile battle that she had no more to shed. Humiliation had followed humiliation as she was bathed and brushed and dressed and perfumed.

Her eyes were dry now, the dark bruised circles beneath them covered with makeup applied by Cate after two hard-handed men had tied Melissa down.

The door opened. Melissa raised her head off the pillow, then allowed it to drop back. She was exhausted.

Cate entered, carrying a tray with a decanter and glasses. She was still clad in a black lace wrapper.

Was it the same one? Or a different one? Didn't she ever get cold?

Setting it down on the table beside the green velveteen chair, Cate looked round the room with the eyes of one taking inventory. Her face serious and businesslike, she moved to the head of the bed and plumped the pillow, smoothing Melissa's hair over it.

"Let me go."

Cate's eyes skimmed down Melissa's body, looking for flaws. She bent to smooth the sheet.

"I promise you. My sister will take us both. She'll never turn us away." Melissa's voice was husky from weeping.

Cate arranged a fold of white lace and satin to better advantage. At last their eyes met. "Forget everything," Cate advised. "Forget your sister. Forget what you were. Just think about making this man happy."

"No."

Cate bent closer until her face was only inches from Melissa's. "You can't get away. But you can make a fortune, if you're smart and willing. But not too willing."

"A fortune," Melissa jeered. "Like the one you've made, I suppose."

Cate's teeth clamped together. She drew back as if Melissa had spat fire.

"If there's so much money to be made here, why haven't you made it?" Melissa raised her head.

Cate flounced away. "Who's to say I haven't?"

"I say." Melissa dropped back onto the pillow. Her eyes slid around the room. It was small, barely ten feet wide.

A bed, a chair, and a small table with a hanging mirror were its only furnishings. No other ornamentation of any kind. Heavy draperies hung on one wall, but Melissa had already checked behind them. They were a sham. The room contained no window. "No one would live here or do this to another human being—" She tugged at her straps. "—if she had any other choice, or any money to get away."

Cate tossed her head. "I advise you to forget everything. This is going to happen. Nothing you do can change it."

"But you could," Melissa insisted. "You could let me go. Give me a chance. If you want to make the money, you wait for Lord Montague."

"I've thought about it. Don't think I haven't. I'd like to see the expression on Lady H's face." Cate's eyes glittered. She bent to the mirror, lifting her breasts and studying them for flaws, turning to the side to check her figure. "I just might sometime."

"Then do it now." Melissa was half sitting up, her arms at full stretch.

Cate pressed her hands against her flat belly. "No. They'd catch you—"

"At least give me a chance."

"—and then I'd be in trouble."

Melissa's whole body shook in revulsion. "I'd never tell who set me free. I'd swear I got free by myself. Blame those two men. They didn't fasten me tightly enough."

Cate looked at her a long minute. The dark eyes flickered. Then she shook her head regretfully. "No."

Six

"Sure you don't want to try the police again?" Jocko asked.

Maria looked as if she might burst into tears. "What's the use? I can't tell them anything new."

A riverboat sounded its horn at a dock far down the Thames. The mournful sound might have been a groan.

Jocko leaned back against the bridge abutment. His hat was tipped low over his eyes, his thumbs tucked into the shallow pockets of his vest. "They might have learned something."

Her reply was bitter. "Why would they try to learn anything when they don't think we want her found?"

He grunted noncommittally. For a moment he considered telling her that Revill had sent him. She might even think he was a "peeler" himself. He grinned faintly at the thought. He did not mind lying, but he needed to think about what truths to tell and what to keep to himself.

Furthermore, she might want to ask him too many questions. His answers, based upon his own experience in the tough London underworld, would be hard for her to swallow.

"Do you think my sister's still alive?" she asked abruptly.

He hesitated. The chances were better than even that Melissa Thorne was still alive. On the other hand, by the time they found her—if they found her—she might not wish to be found. He swiftly put that idea away. No sense starting those kinds of thoughts to spinning in Maria's brain. "Probably."

She pressed her palms to her temples as if her head hurt her. "Perhaps we could go again to Lord Terence Montague. Perhaps there's something he's forgotten to—"

" 'E'd run you off."

"You don't know that."

"I know."

Maria leaned her elbows on the dark-stained granite and stared morosely across the murky waters of the Thames. Where it flowed by beneath their feet, all manner of flotsam rode its gray-green surface. For all its proximity to Trafalgar Square, the nation's tribute to its fabled hero Nelson, Waterloo Bridge also connected with roads leading into the seamiest sections of London. With a sigh she lifted her eyes to the miles and miles of rooftops stretching on forever up the rise from the Strand. "There are so many houses."

He nodded. "Couldn't visit them all if we lived to be a hundred."

"I can't give up," she whispered.

He leaned his elbow on the buttress and propped his bowler back on his head. "I might 'ave a friend who could 'elp you."

She looked at him with a flicker of hope in her eyes. "Might?"

"Do." He set the bowler straight. " 'Er name's Duchess. She's the girl who could find your sister if anybody can."

"A duchess?" Maria brightened noticeably. "Someone with influence?"

Jocko chuckled. "My friend's no duchess. She just acts

a bit uptown ever' so often. Them that knows 'er calls 'er Duchess. It suits 'er to a T."

"Does she have influence?"

"In a manner of speaking."

"And you think she would help me?"

"You'll just 'ave to see for yourself. That is, if you want to meet 'er."

She hesitated. A long, dark object floated just below the surface. It might have been a log, or a partially empty cask. It might have been a body. She tore her eyes away to collide with Jocko's. "You really think Lord Terence Montague won't help me?"

He looked at her seriously. "I think you'd be wasting your time."

"Then I'll be happy to meet your duchess."

"Where are we going?" Maria wrinkled her nose at the stench that rose from the street. The paving stones barely poked above the slime. She had to plant each foot as if she were walking on ice to keep her ankle from turning. The thought of falling flat onto that unimaginable mess sent shudders up her spine.

"You wanted to find your sister. We're going to meet someone who can 'elp." Jocko strode along unperturbed.

Maria, who had already fallen a bit behind, shot an angry look at his back. "And of course we're going to find help in the sewer."

After glancing back over his shoulder, he paused for her to catch up. "If your sister's been taken someplace by someone like Tilly, she could be worse off than this."

Along the wharf the buildings were very old and quite close together. Their walls seemed to tip inward and sag toward each other. The gray sky between was cut here and there by planks slung crazily across the narrow spaces. Chimney sweeps could cross without ever coming down from the roofs.

And why should they? Maria asked herself. Certainly, no one who did not absolutely have to walk here would do so. Probably the sun had not shone on these stones since the buildings rose around them. She straightened her shoulders. "Do you really believe my sister's in a place like this?"

Jocko hesitated before shaking his head. "No." He watched her face brighten. The exhausted, discouraged look had settled around her eyes since they met. It made her look plain—and old. He wondered what she would look like if she smiled.

Instead, she frowned. "I hope this isn't a waste of time."

He thrust out his chin belligerently. "I told you what we came 'ere for. We need 'elp. We'll find it 'ere."

"All right. All right. I didn't mean to upset you." She reached out to put her gloved hand on his sleeve.

"I ain't upset."

She stepped closer and patted his arm. "Let's go on. I'm getting chilled."

"Right."

At the end of a turning, they looked down a narrow alley that dead-ended at a wall. Huge building stones, blackened with age, dripped blacker dampness from each line of mortar. Jocko led her straight to the wall. In one corner narrow steps descended, hardly wide enough for Jocko's shoulder.

Maria looked down after him. "Where does that lead?"

He looked up at her. "Come on."

Her face had gone white. She took a step back from the edge. "Where are you taking me?"

He climbed back up to her side. "You're afraid."

She looked away. Her hands crushed her bag.

"It's just steps."

"It's not that."

He stepped back, his expression dark and brooding. "No, I can see it's not. You don't trust me."

She could have lied, made up anything. Some imaginary fear. She could not. She pressed her fist to her mouth, then took it away. "I don't want to end up like my sister."

He snorted angrily. "And you think I'm dragging you 'ere to sell you?"

Put like that, her fears seemed ridiculous. "N-no. At least I don't think so. But you wouldn't want the police to know—"

He strode away a couple of steps, his hands clapped to the backs of his narrow hips. She could hear him muttering under his breath. When he looked back at her, his eyes were blazing. "I'm a gentleman, I am." His voice was low and rough. "Before I agreed to take on this 'air-brained stunt with you, you said you'd treat me like one. Treat me like a toff, you said. That meant you'd trust me. But you lied, didn't you?"

"No." She hastened toward him, her feet slipping and sliding. "No. You are a gentleman. You are. It's just that—"

Her ankle turned inward. Her foot slipped out from under her and all her weight came down on one knee. A cry of pain burst from her as her face turned absolutely white.

But he was furious. Still standing with his hands on his hips, he watched while she caught her lip between her teeth, watched her plant her umbrella between the stones and push back to her feet. A circle of greenish muck six inches in diameter clung to her skirt, then trickled down toward the hem.

When she was on her feet, using her umbrella as a crutch, she matched him stare for stare.

"Well," he snarled.

"It's nothing personal," she said through clenched teeth. "It's just that I don't trust gentlemen, any gentlemen. I don't have any reason to. You're a gentleman. You've been kind and I know you saved me from Tilly, but you also told him I was your bird."

His stance became less belligerent. "Say, I was just warning 'im off. I didn't mean noth—anything by it."

Mentally, she noted the grammar correction. "I should hope not."

Suddenly, he grinned. The bowler hat tipped back on his forehead, exposing the tight curls. "Not that I wouldn't like you for a bird. You're a trim little thing, that's for sure."

"Mr. Walton!"

Shrugging, his grin firmly in place, he came to her side and slipped his hand under her arm. "Did you hurt yourself bad?"

She shook her head. "It's nothing that won't heal."

He bent to go down on one knee, but she caught his arms and pulled him straight. The thought of his pulling up her skirt and petticoats, not to mention pushing aside her stockings and drawers, to get at her knee made her go red in the face.

"It's all right," she insisted.

Noting the blush, he grinned broadly.

How she hated that grin!

The silence stretched between them until he asked politely, "What'll it be, Ria. Stay or go?"

She swallowed: Pain was streaking up her leg. Her knee was on fire. She wanted to hold it tightly and cry, but she could do neither. She took a deep breath and slid her arm through his. Planting the tip of her umbrella like a cane, she looked up into his face. "Go. That is, go down into the—er—go down the stairs."

By the time he got her down the stairs, she was hurting so badly that tears were slipping down her cheeks. Every time her leg took her weight, she was sure she was going to scream. Finally, at the bottom, her foot sank fully an inch in malodorous mud. She did not bother to suppress a groan of disgust.

He shrugged. His mouth twisted as the stuff squished up around his own boots. He squeezed her arm—a bit familiarly, she thought. "Now see 'ere, Ria, it's this way. You're too good for a place like this. Even if I was going to sell you, I wouldn't sell you 'ere. Who'd live 'ere, I ask you, if they 'ad any money to live anywhere else. What swell would come 'ere to spend 'is money when he can spend it up in Soho?"

"I see your point."

He stooped to the low door, hardly more than a gate, its boards sodden with greenish-black moss. Making a fist, he knocked three times, then waited, then knocked once.

"A secret sign," she whispered behind him.

He chuckled. "Right. Duchess don't like strangers.

"I don't think much of her accommodations."

"You'll see."

He waited a minute. Behind the door she could hear faint sounds, muffled words.

"Duchess," he called softly.

Again the silence.

He tugged at the string latch. "Lemme in. Me boots're gettin' all wet."

Maria listened, too, thankful for something to concentrate on besides the pain in her leg. She could not be certain, but she thought she heard his name.

He looked at her and grinned. "She'll open soon."

"If she knows it's you, why doesn't she let us in immediately?"

"Duchess can't take any chances. That's 'ow she stays free. She never takes chances."

Iron screeched across iron. Something heavy scraped across stone. The door swung inward.

Maria kept her hand in Jocko's as he stooped and led the way through the door. Another set of steps led upward toward a yellow light. "Come on," he encouraged her. "It's all right."

Limping badly, her whole leg afire, she had no choice but to follow. Suddenly the air lost its dank, rotten odor. Instead the smells of lamp oil and spices greeted them.

At the top of the steps, a tall figure lifted a lantern. "Who did you bring with you, Jocko?"

He ushered Maria into the spill of light. "This girl's lost 'er sister."

"You've come to the right place." The female voice was low and sweet, without the slightest hint of stridency. "I'll be happy to trot everybody out and let you take your pick."

"See, I told you." Jocko grinned like a boy. "Duchess, this is Ria."

"Pleased, I'm sure." The figure extended her hand. "Jocko's a careful fellow about his friends." Only the grimy fingertips could be seen. The rest was covered, as was the arm and the whole body, in men's clothing. If not for the soft voice, Maria would have taken the person for a man.

She slid her hand into the outstretched one. The grip was strong, the fingers cold. Maria took a deep breath. "I've only known Jocko for a couple of days."

Duchess flashed the man a quick look.

He shrugged. His white teeth flashed, turning on what was clearly practiced boyish charm.

Duchess stepped back from the pair. For the first time, the brim of her floppy cap no longer shaded her face. Her expression was angry. "Damn you, Jocko Walton—"

He flung up his hands in mock defense.

Maria took a step forward, supported by her umbrella. "Please," she whispered. "May I sit down somewhere? I— I've hurt my knee."

Both of them looked at her. Jocko's charming grin vanished in an instant. In a long stride he placed his arm around Maria's waist lifting her against his hip. He looked pleadingly at the duchess.

Her glare never dimmed. "Pansy, would you want to roll a keg over so the 'lady' can sit down on it?"

"No," piped a shrill child's voice from somewhere in the darkness above them.

"There you are," Duchess remarked. "No place to sit. I think you'd better take your lady bird and go."

Jocko's face darkened. "Duchess—"

"Don't say any more. You've brought someone here you don't know—"

"I said I knew 'er. I do. She's square."

"Jocko," Maria murmured. "Perhaps we'd better go. Melissa isn't here. I'm sure."

"How can you be so sure?" Duchess asked dryly.

The pain was easing a little since Jocko had helped Maria to stand. She could feel the chill of the place through the perspiration that had broken out on her body. "Because if my sister were here, she would have come to me the minute she heard my voice."

During the exchange, Jocko had located several barrels

along one wall just beyond the lanternlight. Without waiting for permission, he rolled one out behind Maria. Despite her protest, he eased her down on its end. Then he turned to Duchess.

Hat pushed back on his head, he met her toe to toe. "Now listen 'ere. This girl's sister's disappeared. My guess is some fag like Tilly's nabbed 'er. She came into town at Euston."

"That's Tilly's territory all right."

"And Bert Nance's and Flasher's—"

Duchess held up her hand. "Forget it. I know the names." She walked toward Maria. "How'd you team up with Jocko?"

Maria gave up finding the face beneath the shadow of the cap. The pain in her knee seemed to increase by the minute. She cupped her hand around it and concentrated on keeping her voice steady. "I don't really know. He just appeared one morning on the front step."

"Oh, he did." A note of amusement was just discernible. "So Jocko just turned up on your doorstep."

Jocko shifted uncomfortably and tipped his bowler over his eyes.

"That's right," Maria said. "Please don't blame him for bringing me here. I insisted."

"Here now, Ria—" Jocko began.

She hurried on. "He's been the only one to help me. He's gone with me into the country and come back. He—er—drove off that monster Tilly when he tried to abduct me."

"I heard how he did it, too," Duchess said. "Good work, Jocko."

"Thanks," he replied sourly.

"Right y'are, Jocko. Good work."

The three looked up. A dim light had appeared above them, as if someone had taken a cover off a lantern. A couple of heads were sticking over the edge of a platform. In silhouette, ragged locks of hair swayed from beneath floppy hatbrims. One neck was muffled to the ears, the other bare and distressingly thin.

"Thank you, Pansy, m'girl." He snapped up the brim of his bowler with his index finger.

"He's helped me when no one else would," Maria repeated, raising her voice for the benefit of the audience. "The only reason we came here was because he thought you might help. You see we can't possibly search through all the—er—brothels in London."

"Not in this lifetime." Duchess gave a dry chuckle.

"Not in this lifetime," came the chorus from above.

"We think my sister Melissa's been abducted into one of them. She's my only family. I love her very much. She was seventeen only a couple of days ago."

Duchess shrugged—at least the drooping clothes lifted and fell. "She's actually pretty old for Tilly."

"I'm sixteen."

"Nah, yer not," the companion with the muffler declared. "Yer nah but six. Gawd! Dumb!"

"Dumb? Me? Take 'at back!"

The heads disappeared together. The sound of thuds and slaps carried down from the platform, followed by expletives of the vilest sort. Maria looked around uncomfortably. Jocko merely grinned. Duchess made no move to quiet the disagreement.

"Give 'er another kick, Pan." A third voice entered the fray.

Maria looked up again. Where the ceiling had been in darkness, thin streaks of light suddenly appeared on both sides, beaming between the boards of another platform. And then another. And another.

Their illumination revealed a long and very narrow room, possibly the height and width of the building. Its walls were lined with platforms.

"What kind of place is this?"

"Can't you guess?" Duchess's words were tinged with bitterness. " 'Home, Sweet Home.' "

"But—"

Duchess interrupted her. "Don't worry. The peelers can't find us. And it's been forgotten by the man who owns the warehouse."

"If 'e ever knew about it," Jocko added. "Bleedin' sod."

A piercing scream came from directly above, followed by a chorus of laughter and catcalls from all sides. From time to time Maria would see the silhouette of a flying piece of cloth or a hand. Once an unidentified object sailed from one platform to another. The place must be full of children, she realized.

"Bet! Take it back 'bout me bein' dumb, er I'll bite yer ear off."

"Get off me, you li'l rat!" Bet's command was accompanied by a thunder of kicks and thumps. Evidently her efforts failed to dislodge her assailant because the next sound was Bet's scream.

"Duchess, Duchess." Another head popped over the edge of a platform directly opposite. "Pan's killin' Bet."

"I don't think she will, Alice." Duchess put her head back to the light. For the first time, Maria got a glimpse of her face. Smudged with grime, it nevertheless reflected a singular beauty.

Maria stared in awe. She knew herself to be barely passable in terms of female beauty. Her features were regular, but undistinguished. She did not even have her sister's beautiful blue eyes. She looked exactly like what she was—an English working girl of good family.

Duchess might very well have been a duchess. The brow, cheeks, and nose thrusting up from beneath the fine skin were every bit as refined as those of Mrs. Avory Shires. The jaw swept in a clean straight line from ear to chin.

Then Duchess dropped her head and caught Maria staring at her.

Above them the screaming stopped, then a ladder dropped off the end of the platform with a thud. A small figure came flying down. "She bit me. She bit me." Bet flew to Duchess, catching her around the waist, hiding her head in the layers of clothing. "She bit m' ear clean off."

Fierce little Pansy followed her halfway down the ladder. "Did not. Only bit a li'l. Di'n't no more'n break th' skin."

Duchess hugged the sobbing Bet. "Did you call her dumb?"

"Y-yeah, but she is dumb."

Pan gave an outraged cry and jumped to the floor. "Am not."

From the safety of Duchess's side, Bet snapped her face around. "Don't know 'at six and sixteen be dif'ernt numbers."

Pan halted. "They got th' same sounds."

"Betty is right, Pansy," Duchess said softly. "Six and sixteen are very different numbers. One is almost a baby and one is quite grown up."

Jocko came over to stand beside Maria. "Sixteen's still young, if you've never been off the farm."

"I come from a farm," a voice above him called.

"I be sixteen in three years," called another.

Maria looked upward into what had at first appeared to be a black vault. "What is this place?"

While Pan and Bet agreed to make up under the duchess's arbitration, Jocko bent to her ear. "Duchess found it and brought them 'ere."

"But how can they live? It's dark and cold."

Jocko smiled. "Not exactly. The platforms and ladders go all the way up to the skylights. They come and go up there. And they live better 'ere than where they were."

"Where were they?"

Jocko lifted his shoulders uncomfortably. "In sportin' 'ouses."

Maria twisted around to face him. "In brothels! But they're only children."

He stepped back, his eyes not quite meeting hers. "Some men like 'em young."

Maria twisted back around to stare at Pansy. Standing on the floor, her clothing pooled around her feet, she was less than three feet tall. Her little neck was like the stem of a flower. "She's only a baby."

Jocko had no answer. He fished in the pockets of his overcoat and withdrew a handful of sweets. "Pansy."

She dashed toward him. "You 'membered."

He poured them into her cupped hands. Then before he let her go, he caught her chin. "Now don't forget to share."

"Yes, sir."

More ladders hit the floor. More children descended. In a matter of seconds, Maria counted eight gathered around Pansy as she dispensed the treat with an air of importance. The smell of horehound drops permeated the still air.

Duchess left the children to come to her visitors. "Are you sure you want your sister back?"

Maria struggled to stand. "Oh, yes. More than anything

in the world. I want her so much that I'll keep looking as long as it takes. As long as I live, I'll keep searching. If you can help me—"

Duchess interrupted her. "You realize that if she's been in a brothel for several days, she's been used already. Many times."

Maria raised her fist to her mouth. Her face twisted with pain. "So Jocko said. So everyone else has said. They act as if she's dead, as if she's not the same person anymore."

"That's the way the world looks at it," Duchess said bitterly.

"She didn't ask to be kidnapped. She didn't make a choice. She's good. She's a sweet, good girl."

"Now she's ruined," Duchess said, her voice flat. "No gentleman will take another man's leavings."

The pain in Maria's heart was worse than the pain in her knee. "If a good man doesn't want her, then that's his hard luck. She's still my sister. I love her." She could feel the tears starting in her eyes. "She's been hurt by evil, evil men. I want to rescue her. I want her back."

"Very laudable," Duchess said coldly. "What if she's diseased?"

Maria gulped. "Then I'll nurse her and try to heal her."

"What if she's pregnant?"

"Then we'll raise the child together."

Duchess threw back her head and laughed without mirth. "It might be worth the effort to see your face in a few months."

"I assure you—"

She raised her hand. "Don't assure me of anything. You don't have the slightest idea what you're talking about." She looked at Jocko. "So you think I ought to help her?"

He nodded. "That's why I brought 'er. You know me. I'd 'ave never taken a chance if she wasn't square."

Duchess turned around. She walked the length of the room. Some eight children had gathered in a couple of tight knots, squatting on their heels or climbing onto the tops of kegs and boxes. Maria could not be certain, but she believed they were all girls. They watched her solemnly.

"Shall we do it?" Duchess asked of them.

Bet shook her head. "Don't wanta take no chances. Nah but trouble if they cotched me again."

"They've forgot all about ye," another voice jeered. "They forgot ye th' minute ye disappeared."

"They ain't forgot th' Duchess."

"Nobuddy'd forgit th' Duchess."

"Ought we gotta do it, Duchess?"

"A girl is being hurt," she replied. "Her sister wants her back."

"Roncie Jack'd kill me if he cotched me."

Maria hobbled forward. "I wouldn't want any of you to be in danger." She looked to Jocko. "Perhaps we'd better go."

He stopped her. "They go out every day to find food and fuel. They can ask questions, listen to talk. They can find your sister if anyone can."

"But they might be caught again." Maria shook her head. "I couldn't bear to think that one of them would take Melissa's place."

"That's how I found the first one. And how they've found themselves ever since," Duchess told her.

"Nevertheless—" Maria looked at Pan and Bet. "Thank you all very much."

Duchess led the way to the stairwell. "We'll thrash it about. You'll hear from me, Jocko, one way or the other."

"Much obliged, Duchess."

"Yes, thank you—er—for your hospitality. I swear I'll never reveal your hiding place." Maria clung to the wall as she descended. Her knee had stiffened in the cold. The pain was making her feel faint.

Her head was almost level with the floor when Duchess dropped down on her haunches and thrust the lantern into her visitor's face. "Do you really want her back?"

"With all my heart."

For a long moment the two stared into each other's eyes. Then Duchess took the light away and Jocko pulled the door open through the muck.

Seven

"Can we take a cab?" Maria panted. "I'll pay for it."

Jocko looked down. Despite the fading light, he could see the deep lines that creased her forehead. She was heavy on his arm. Instead of answering, he stooped to put one arm around her shoulders and another around her legs.

When his hand closed round her swollen knee, she tensed. When he swept her up against his chest, she sucked in a frightened breath. "Put me down," she protested. "Somebody will see you."

"Me," he scoffed, pretending not to understand. "Nobody cares what I do."

She hesitated. Her first impulse was to say that she cared that someone might see *her;* but then she remembered his anger when she had doubted him. She would not hurt his feelings again. He had been too good to her. Her voice was barely a breath in his ear. "I care."

His arms tightened just a fraction. The corners of his mouth lifted. He strode on as if he were still unburdened. Indeed, he increased his pace.

"Jocko, you don't need to carry me."

"Just a few more steps." He turned out of the alley. "We'll get a cab in the Strand."

"I can walk," she murmured. But her protest was half-hearted and they both knew it. Her arms settled around his shoulders. She clasped her hands beneath his ear. Her breast was pressed against his warm, hard chest. His strong arms held her effortlessly.

Her heart stepped up its beat. Suddenly, her body was warming with what she recognized as improper thoughts. A proper Victorian maiden only *thought* about being held tightly in a man's embrace. And that man must be her husband. She shivered.

"Cold?"

She gave her head a tiny shake. Finally, she said faintly, "I must be heavy."

"That you are," he agreed, with a hint of humor. "I'm fairly staggerin' under the load."

A few silent tears cut hot paths down her cold cheeks. "Oh, Jocko, you're so good."

That remark made him chuckle. "Me. No. Not likely. I'm a bad 'un. You're just tired."

A cab clip-clopped out of the gloom spreading along the Victoria Embankment. Dampness and a thick fog crept upward from the Thames.

Jocko caught his lower lip between his teeth and gave a shrill whistle. The cabbie raised his head. His horse halted. In less than a minute Maria had been bundled in and they were on their way.

They rode for some distance in silence. Somehow she had remained seated on Jocko's lap, his arms around her, her arms around him.

Finally, Maria spoke. "What do they do?"

"The children and Duchess?"

"Yes. How do they survive?"

His chest swelled as he sucked in a deep breath. "Well, now, I'm not rightly sure. I don't ask questions. It's none of my business."

"I thought—"

He shook his head.

"She's not—er—you and she are not—"

"God, no. If she were mine, do you think she'd live there? Never. My girl's going to 'ave a place. A real place."

Maria could feel the blood pounding in her ears. The throbbing in her leg had eased somewhat, but now she had a new fever. She could feel long-forgotten warmth suffuse her cheeks. She could not stop the next question. "Do you have a girl?"

"Me? No. How could I have a girl? Who'd want me?"

The cab turned into Aubrey Walk. They were nearly home. He would take her to the door and leave her with a good night and a tip of his bowler. And then . . .

As if a party to her thoughts, he asked, "What time do you want me to come tomorrow morning?"

"I don't know," she whispered. "Early. I suppose we need to plan. Right now I'm too tired."

"You need a good night's sleep."

Suddenly, Maria could not face the loss of him. How could she return to her single room alone? Alone she would think of Melissa. And think. And imagine all sorts of horrors. The fire would have to be laid. Or she would have to climb into a damp, cold bed where she would lie shivering, too uncomfortable and exhausted to sleep.

Suddenly, she began to weep in earnest.

" 'Ere now. What's going on?"

"I can't h-help it. I—I'm sorry."

He clutched her tighter. "Are you 'urting?"

"I'm ashamed to say I'm feeling sorry for myself."

"Oh, is that all?" He patted her clumsily. "No 'arm in doing that."

She shook her head, willing the tears to stop. "It doesn't solve anything. I guess I'm just tired."

"O' course you are. Who wouldn't be?"

The cabbie pulled the old horse to a stop. Jocko reached over to open the door and help her down. As if she were glass, he supported her to the door. When she had unlocked it and swung it open, he tipped his hat. "I'll be saying good night, Ria."

He started down the steps.

"Don't," she whispered. She could feel the blood rush to her face. Oh, the enormity of what she was doing. The single word had been wrung from her. She pressed her lips together too late.

He froze. "What?"

The silence held while she listened. She could not hear the polite Victorian voice within her. The voice of morality that cast blame and censure was still, frozen in the cold darkness of the entryway. In its place the hot blood pounded in her ears, of desire remembered, of ecstasy, and of loss.

"Don't say good night, Jocko."

He let his breath out in a ragged sigh. The bowler tipped backward as he thrust his head forward to search her face. His expression was serious, his brow wrinkled. He shifted his weight uneasily. When he spoke, his voice sounded a bit hoarse. "Ria, I don't think that'd be a good idea. You know I'm not a nurse, nor an old-maid companion."

"I know."

"If I stay, I'd stay as a man."

She put out her hand. It was steady, but her voice trembled in her own ears. "Stay, Jocko Walton. Please stay."

"Yes, ma'am." Pushing the bowler back straight on his

forehead, he vaulted down the steps and passed the cabbie a coin.

"Thankee, sir."

Maria turned up the lamp on the hall table. Holding it aloft, she mounted the stairs to her room. Her very daring made her dizzy. On the second-story landing, she braced herself against the wall.

Behind her she heard him closing the door, clicking the lock into place. She heard his tread in the hallway. His heels thudded on the hardwood as he came up the stairs in a rush.

A slow heat suffused her cheeks. Her throat felt dry. She steadied herself away from the wall and walked toward her door, the last room at the end. She kept her eyes carefully front as if by not looking at the doors, she could prevent the other occupants of the rooming house from opening them. A rooming house, after all, was very different from a summer house, away from everything, sheltered by vines, shaded by trees.

Before she had traveled half the length of the hall, he had caught up to her. His masculine presence crowded against her back. *Please,* she prayed silently. *Please don't let anyone hear us.* She hardly knew the other boarders— only that they all lived alone and all of them were women. They would know instantly that he should not be there.

She thrust the key blindly at the keyhole. It collided with the plate and slipped from her numb fingers. It clattered noisily in the silence.

He stooped to retrieve it. As he came up, he caught sight of her face in the flickering lamplight. "Maybe I'd better go?"

She shook her head, an abrupt gesture. "Just open the door."

Once inside, he closed it behind her. She set the lamp down and raised her arms to remove her hat. Suddenly, she could not stand its weight one minute more.

"Please," he said. "Let me."

"Oh."

His warm hands brushed hers aside and deftly withdrew the eight-inch hatpins. He tossed the hat onto the little bureau beside the door, but he did not stop there. Gently, he began to pull the hairpins out as well. Her coil rolled down her back.

She gave a frightened gasp. No man had seen her hair down since that long ago day. No man had run his fingers through her hair. She moved to step away, but his fingers were already caught in it, separating the strands.

"Your hair." His voice came close to her ear, his breath brushed it.

She shivered.

"It's so long," he whispered. "And fine." Her scalp prickled as he finished his self-appointed task. As if he were performing a ritual, he held it out from her shoulders.

"It's just hair," she whispered.

"Oh, yes," he agreed. "I've never seen the like."

"I-I've never cut it."

"That's good." He brought the strands back together and smoothed it down to the tops of her hips. Then his hands cupped her shoulders.

She tensed.

"I'll build a fire."

A fire already raged inside her. She did not recognize her own voice that murmured. "Yes. All right."

He left her to kneel on the tiny hearth.

All the time she stood transfixed, her head light, her face and body no longer cold.

As she watched, he removed his hat. His hair was a darker gold in back, but every bit as curly. Tight as a ram's fleece, it seemed to clutch at his collar. His shoulders were broad. The coat completely covered him except for the sole of one shoe. Kneeling there, his shadow before him, he fairly dwarfed the room.

Before tonight, she had thought her little bedsitter perfectly adequate for her needs. Now it was much too small. When he stood up . . .

A curl of white smoke rose from under the tinder. A tiny flame curled bright yellow-orange along one edge. Expertly, Jocko added bits of wood for kindling and threw coals on top. Then he blew air across it with the bellows. When it began to glow, he rose. "There." He rubbed his hands together briskly. "Won't be a minute till it'll take the chill off."

Her body was cold as ice and hot as fire. One minute she felt she would never be warm, the next she longed to fan herself. She had not moved from her spot by the door.

He turned. His brisk smile faded.

Slowly, she raised her hands to her cheeks. She could only imagine what more than twelve hours in the wind and misting rain had done to her. He must find her uncommonly plain. She knew she had never been more than passing pretty, but tonight she must look like the very wrath of God.

As he stared, she tried to smile. Apologetically, she pushed at the tendrils of damp hair plastered to her forehead.

"Come on." As if she were a child, he walked to her narrow bed. Still watching her, he began to turn down the covers. That done, he came to her, slowly, hesitantly, as if half-expecting her to shrink away from him. His hands reached to unbutton her coat.

"I'll do it." Her voice was raspy. She slipped the coat off and, in a practiced movement, hung it on a peg beside the bed. "May I take your coat?"

He hesitated. His eyes searched her face. For the second time he volunteered to go.

She turned around. "Oh, please, don't."

"Maria." His handsome mouth contorted. "Miss Thorne—"

"Ria," she murmured, forcing a smile. "Remember? It's more friendly-like."

"You're too tired—"

She took a quick step across the room and placed her fingers across his lips. "Jocko."

For the first time she was voluntarily close to him. His arms closed round her automatically, then drew apart. She caught one of them and brought it back around her waist. Her eyes pleaded. Her words tumbled over themselves. "Jocko. I know I'm not beautiful. Not like the duchess. I'm not even pretty. I can understand that you wouldn't— couldn't love me. I'm not a fool who reads romantic novels."

His lips moved. His breath warmed her fingers.

"Oh, please—oh, please—stay with me. I'm so lonely. I'm so afraid."

"Ria—!"

He must feel her fingers trembling, she realized. She pulled them away.

His usual grin had disappeared. No cynicism curled his lip. Instead, he tilted his head. One hand sank into her hair, cradling the back of her head. Slowly, he brought their lips together.

It was a different kiss from the few she had known. She had been expecting the roughness and heat of a man's passion. Instead, she found the tender touching of mouth to mouth. Warmth spread from all the points where their bodies touched, but especially from their lips. She breathed, commingling their breaths, and pressing her breasts more tightly against his chest.

She could feel the change in him. His body stiffened. He took a couple of steps forward, gathering her against him as he moved. Hard-muscled thighs pressed against her own. His hands were hard, too, holding her. She remembered the hard hands of the other time, remembered what they signaled.

With a sense of joy she knew that he was not going to leave her, no matter how unattractive she might be physically. He was hard and ready. He would not stop.

Then she couldn't think any more. His mouth pressed urgently against hers, demanding. Feverishly she opened her mouth and welcomed him in. His tongue thrust between her teeth. He tasted like—she had forgotten the taste of a man. It was heady. Her tongue pushed at his, slipped beneath it, drinking more.

He growled deep in his throat, pulling her impossibly closer.

Her knees trembled. She could no longer support herself on the injured one. One arm was crushed between them. With the other she encircled his shoulders and let him take most of her weight.

His kiss went on and on. Better, much better than she remembered. Ecstasy. It made her dizzy, hot. She had never felt anything so—

He wrenched his mouth away. His head tilted back as

he sucked in a deep breath. "Ria." She could hardly recognize her own name. "Damn."

"Jocko." She did not flinch at the obscenity, did not even notice it. She wriggled and twisted until she freed her other arm to wrap it round his neck. She wanted to taste him again.

"Jocko." Her lips parted, she pulled his head down to her. This time she kissed him, her mouth eagerly seeking his own.

He moaned. His hands clutched her hips as he lowered her to the bed. The tilting of their bodies broke their mouths apart.

"Ria?"

"Don't talk," she whispered. "Don't speak."

He kissed her again. His hand slid up over her waist. Through her clothing he could feel the slenderness of her ribcage and then the swell of her breast.

He touched it, closed his hand over it, pushed it up.

It was her turn to moan. A wave of pleasure swept over her. Hot blood swept into her cheeks while the same now-familiar heat and pain increased at the base of her belly.

He kissed her again, kissed her mouth, her cheeks, her eyes, her mouth again while his hand massaged her breast.

Eagerly, she edged her body against the wall and pulled him down beside her on the bed. One part of her wanted him to continue the kisses, never to stop. Another part wanted him to do more. Her other breast was aching. She arched her back, shifting her hips, trying to relieve the heat and longing between her legs.

What would it feel like this time? When she had been a virgin, the pain had been bad. She knew from the novels she had read that it was not supposed to hurt ever again. In her mind she knew, but her body could not quite believe. All those novels had ended when the couple stood in the middle of the room embracing.

With one hand he unbuttoned her shirtwaist and pushed her clothing down. From somewhere came a soft rip as stitches tore.

She gasped at the rush of cold air, then cried out, for he had covered her nipple with his mouth. She could feel his tongue circling the bit of flesh, feel his teeth. No man had ever put his mouth on her naked breast before.

She arched and twisted. "Jocko. Oh, I don't think—"

He raised his head. By the light of the fire, she could see the moisture glisten on his mouth. "Believe me, Ria. This is the way it's supposed to be."

She shuddered and managed to nod.

He ducked his head again. This time he kissed her other breast. The pleasure was so acute that she arched her back, lifting her chest to give him easier access.

He needed none. His hands were pulling her skirts and petticoats up. Then she could feel them on her thighs beneath her loose drawers.

She moaned and gasped, as his fingers touched her, parted her, probed. "Jocko. What are you doing?"

"Feels good," he murmured. "Right?"

She realized with a flush of embarrassment that she was wet. She had not been wet before. Would he pull back in disgust? No. His thumb kept up its pressure. She twisted so violently that the bed rocked.

He chuckled against her breast. His thumb followed her gyrating body. Embarrassment was making her hotter than ever. She was drowning in emotion, in feelings. Her heels dug into the mattress as she lurched up seeking—she was not sure what.

Then something struck her. Like a great wave, hot liquid

poured from her, wetting his fingers, spreading through her. She would have sworn he had stabbed her had she not felt such bliss, such ecstasy. She set her teeth, but the scream would come. She could not contain it. It ripped out of her mouth, but he was there to put his mouth over hers and catch it.

She slumped back on the bed, her hands fell away, her heels slid back along the disordered bedclothes.

He tossed aside her skirts. She could feel his hands at the slit in her drawers. Now would come the pain. That she remembered.

"Ready, Ria?" His husky voice seemed to come from a long way off.

She barely moaned assent.

He parted her, his fingers sliding over her most delicate skin. She felt his manhood at the hot, slick opening. He pushed against her. His arms slid under her knees. He lifted.

Another nudge. Then he slid inside her, gently, easily as a sword into a velvet sheath.

"God," he murmured. "Sweet Jesus, Ria." He pulled back and began to move.

Her eyes flew open. The sensations were acute, every nerve, every muscle, feeling the ecstasy. A few minutes ago she had not thought it possible to feel more than she felt. Now she thought she would die. Pleasure so acute that it was pain sang along her nerves. She pulled at his shoulders at the same time crying, "Stop! Stop!"

He hung above her, breathing hard, holding her legs. "Come on, sweetheart," he urged. "It'll be good for both of us if you'll give a bit of a move."

Good if she moved. How could she move? She was pinned to the bed. She bucked her hips upward.

"Mmm, that's it." He moaned in pleasure. "That's it." He crouched over her, holding her legs, lifting her hips, filling her with himself, the big male part of himself, that pierced her to the very heart.

She pushed her hips again, pushed them against him. The muscles of her belly and thighs tensed. He pulled backward, then thrust into her again.

"Oh, Christ," he whispered. "Ria." He stiffened, a great hard shape above her, sweat glistening on his brow in the firelight. She thought he would kill her with his weight atop her and his strength inside her. His jaw clamped shut.

Through slitted eyes, she watched him sag back on his heels, letting her legs fall from his arms. His head sank to his chest. The huge, hard shape that had almost split her in two slipped from her body on a gush of hot liquid.

"Oh, Ria," he sighed. Maneuvering himself carefully on the narrow bed, he lowered himself beside her and gathered her in his arms. "I'm sorry. Did I 'urt you?"

"No," she whispered. "Oh, no." Her own arms leaden, she fumbled for the covers and managed to pull them up around them.

He burrowed his head against her neck. "I'm glad."

"It was wonderful."

He was mumbling, half asleep. "Did you 'ave yer pleasure then? I wasn't sure. I don't usually—that is—I've never been so fast. I can go all night. It's just that you were so—"

"Please. Don't tell me what I didn't do."

He pulled his head back, trying to find her face in the dark. "Didn't do! Oh, no. You were wonderful. You were the most wonderful. So hot, so tight. I didn't know 'ow to make love to you. I've never made love to a lady. Not a lady. Not ever."

"Please. Don't say any more." He thought she was a lady. She could feel the hot shame rising in her cheeks. He must not have realized. She hated herself.

To her surprise he fumbled for and found her chin. Gently, he turned her face toward his. His mouth found hers. His tongue caressed her, his lips moved over and over hers. The kiss went on and on, comfort that began to turn to passion. Abruptly, he jerked back.

"Careful, Ria!"

She blinked and gasped. Her hands were sliding sensuously up and down his arms. "Oh."

He sucked in a quivering breath and hugged her back against him. "Listen, Ria. You're a lady. Every bit of it. You're proud—and you've got a right to be. You're so far above common . . . it was so good. I never—" He swallowed, at a loss for words to tell her without embarrassing her.

She wanted to believe his nervous speech, murmured in the dark. Their heads shared the same pillow. Their bodies touched at all points. The warmth she had longed for relaxed her body and eased her mind. At the same time another part of her cringed in shame at her weakness, her unladylike desires, her lies.

But just for this evening, just for this night, she would be warm and safe. She would lie wrapped in his hard strength and rest. Just for tonight she would not be alone with her terror.

She awakened in the middle of the night. She lay on her side facing the wall. Warmth enclosed her, weighted her at waist and thigh. Warm breath expelled by a soft snore wafted past her ear.

Lying still, she savored it all. Jocko's hard-muscled chest moved rhythmically against her back. His arm held her against him possessively. One heavy thigh pinned down her own, his knee nudging the back of her knee. It was bliss. It was pleasure. It was forbidden.

Society warned against it because of the terrible price she would be forced to pay. She had paid it twice over. First, in heartbreak. Her seducer had broken his vow and married another. Second, in disillusionment. In giving her innocence, she had tainted herself in the eyes of the man who had taken it. The irony of his betrayal had burned itself into her brain.

She turned in Jocko's arms, luxuriating in the feel of her skin against his, arching her neck to ease the prickling of her scalp as her hair slid between them. He loved her hair. He had made love to her and then reassured her that she was still a lady in his eyes.

She put her arm around his shoulders, drawing herself tight against his chest, feeling her breasts flatten against his chest, pushing her belly against his. She was a lady in his eyes. She pushed her leg between his thighs. Satin caressing satin, she waited for him to awaken so she could tell him what a gentleman he was.

She moved one leg experimentally. A muscle she had never heard from before protested faintly. She hoped she was not going to be so stiff and sore that she could not continue the search for Melissa.

The thought of her sister shattered the fragile feeling of well-being. How had her sister spent the night? She shuddered at the thought of Melissa submitting to such a thing without the attention of a gentle and polite man like Jocko Walton.

He lay on his back, his head pillowed on his arm. As she watched, his mouth dropped open. He gave a soft snort, then closed it firmly. His nose twitched.

She smiled. Never catch him with his mouth hanging open. Jocko Walton was a "proper toff."

"I say we don't!"

"There's no need to shout." Duchess placed her hand on Bet's shoulder. "We'll all listen to you. You may speak in a normal voice."

Bet subsided slightly. Her lower lip still protruded. "Naught but trouble if some of them cotch sight of us."

"They catch sight of us all the time," came a scoffing rebuttal from Alice. "They don't want us anymore. We're too smart for them. They wants green ones."

"Jocko wants us to. Jocko said—"

"They might hurt us," Bet interrupted.

"You're a cowart," Pan accused. "Stay here and hide. Duchess, I'll help—"

"We must all decide to help, Pansy, or decide not to. This concerns us all because we will all be risking our hiding place." Duchess looked around at the solemn faces.

"I ain't a cowart," Bet denied. "I'd help if it was for Jocko, but his woman . . . she's naught to us."

"I had a sister," another girl said solemnly. "She came with me from the farm, but they split us up. I don't know what they did with her. I wish I'd hunted fer her."

The quiet words reduced them all to silence. They looked around at each other. Pansy looked hard at Bet, who finally folded her arms and slumped back against the wall.

"Maybe we could hunt for them both," Alice suggested.

Duchess looked round the circle. "Is that what you all want to do?"

One after another the tousled heads nodded.

Maria edged herself out of Jocko's embrace and crawled from beneath the covers. Carefully, she tried her injured knee. It was stiff and sore but seemed serviceable enough.

Shivering in the blue morning light, she knelt to build a fire and swing a kettle over it. Then she lighted a tiny oil burner to heat water for tea. When the water was hot, she measured out the proper amount and let it steep. From the kettle she wet a cloth and washed and dressed herself. Her hair she left long, hanging down her back, the way he liked it. Then she drew the single chair next to the bed.

Jocko's arm and shoulder were bare, the skin white with a faint tracery of blue veins running over the muscles. His forearm had a golden cast of curly blond hair.

The heat of desire curled in her. She closed her eyes for a minute, summoning control. Then she laid a hand on Jocko's shoulder.

His eyes opened instantly. He rolled onto his back, throwing up one arm in an oddly defensive position.

"Good morning. I've made you some tea."

"Oh." He blinked, rubbed his eyes like a child, then grinned. "Good of you." He pushed himself up to a sitting position that left quite a lot of him bare. Somehow, he looked so much more naked in the light. Her body kindled along with a blush that rose from the base of her throat. She shifted slightly in the chair.

He took the cup and saucer from her and sipped the tea. "Ah. Just the way I like it. And a good, good morning to you, Ria Thorne. This is the life. Tea hot and sweet brought to me in bed by a proper lady."

Smiling shyly, she remembered her promise to herself. "I'm pleased to bring it to a proper gentleman."

She watched his ears turn red. The cheeky grin faltered. His bright blue eyes flickered to her face, then dropped back to his lap. Quickly, he snatched the covers up higher round his waist. "Begging your pardon, ma'am. I'll be up in a minute."

She rose quickly and turned her back. "No reason to get up after I've gone to the trouble to bring it to you. Just stay there and drink it in comfort."

Her admonition left him gaping. No one in his memory had invited him to stay in bed. Before his mother had disappeared, she had always rousted him off his pallet before light. Moreover, he had never even spent the night with any of the women he had paid for.

He rubbed his palm across the warm teacup. What would Miss Maria Thorne think if she knew that she was the first woman he had ever spent the whole night with? Not that he would ever tell her. His past was past. He wanted no questions asked about it. This precious luxury would be the first of a new set of memories.

Maria's tea had almost steeped when she heard the rustle of cloth behind her. In less than a minute he was up and dressing.

She tossed him a question over her shoulder. "What should we do to find Melissa?"

He said nothing. The chances were very good that they would not be able to find her sister. He did not tell her about the many boats that left from the Wapping Docks past the Tower. White cargo was common, although officially unrecognized, bound for the bordellos of Paris and the harems of Arabia.

Her teacup rattled in her saucer. She set both down without drinking. Her throat was so tight, she could not swallow. Yet she did. "You don't ever think we'll find my sister, do you?"

He covered the distance between them in one swift stride. His arms went around her. "If she's in London, we'll find 'er."

"And if she's not—"

He did not answer.

She heaved a sigh. "I have to believe she's still in London."

"There's a good chance. She's a little too old for the foreign trade."

When her response came, it surprised him. "Damn them all!"

He hugged her and pressed a kiss to her temple. "That's the spirit, Ria. We'll find 'er."

"You're right. We will." She lifted her teacup with a steady hand. "And I intend to go this morning to tell that Scotland Yard inspector what I think of him."

Eight

Inspector Clive Revill gaped at the couple Constable Wilkie ushered into his office. Behind Maria Thorne's shoulder, Jocko Walton wiggled his eyebrows and grinned. The inspector's mouth snapped to, his cheeks reddening as his temper rose. Walton had been ordered to follow Miss Thorne unobtrusively.

Revill rose. "Miss Thorne."

"Thank you, sir, for remembering." She did not extend her hand. Instead she stepped aside to allow her companion to enter behind her. "Inspector Revill, may I present Jocko Walton."

The inspector's eyes narrowed. His sandy brows drew together in a scowl.

Jocko Walton, Esquire, locked his hands behind him and made a great show of looking about. He studied the framed photograph of Queen Victoria on the wall, then turned his attention to Revill's service plaque.

Revill quelled the desire to order Wilkie to drag him from the room. Instead he surveyed them both with a flinty stare. Maria Thorne obviously had no notion of what Walton was about, he rapidly concluded. The inspector could foresee all kinds of problems arising from this misalliance. What if she should discover that Scotland Yard had sent a known felon to follow her about? Revill surreptitiously wiped his palm against his trouser leg. "Mr. Walton."

"Pleased to make your acquaintance." Tucking his bowler under his arm, the thief thrust out his hand.

Revill had no choice but to take it. He inclined his head stiffly.

Grinning, his eyes fairly snapping with mirth, Jocko wrung the inspector's hand with perhaps a bit more vigor than necessary.

Revill freed himself as quickly as possible and retreated behind his desk. "Where is Mrs. Shires, Miss Thorne? She seemed a most admirable woman. I would have thought that good lady would have been willing to accompany you and help you."

"Oh, she would have." Maria hurried to assure him, "but she has her work which she cannot neglect. She was good enough to give me leave, and has promised me my old job back when my sister is located." She took the chair he offered. "That's why we came today. Have you found any trace?"

Revill wished he could say something encouraging. The truth was that not a single word had been heard on the streets by any of the usual police informants. The utter silence made the situation even more grave. The possibility existed that if something had been heard, it had not been allowed to make its way to his office.

He rather expected the latter to be the truth. In which case Melissa Thorne must be in a brothel frequented and therefore protected by powerful men. His lips twitched beneath his heavy blond moustache. The very thought brought a bad taste to his mouth. Slowly, with great regret, he shook his head.

Maria Thorne sank back in her chair. Many emotions

swept across her face—pain, anger, fear, and despair. Smothering a choking sound, she pulled a handkerchief from her handbag.

"Miss Thorne." Revill inwardly cursed himself. He had nothing to offer her but wordless pity—and Jocko Walton, unrepentant thief. To his surprise, his reluctant hireling flashed him a look of disgust.

" 'Ere now, Ria. Don't give up.

She swallowed hard. The choking stopped. When she raised her head, she was composed except for some brightness in her eyes and spots of high color on her cheekbones. "I haven't given up."

"The department—" Revill stopped. The department had done all it intended to do. Melissa Thorne was missing. They had instituted their usual procedures. But she was a nobody, a young girl trying to make her own way without even a father to protest her disappearance. Revill must have let something of his emotion show in his face.

Maria stared at him, her brown eyes narrowed. The knuckles of her hand resting on the handle of her umbrella showed white. "I *will* find my sister, Inspector Revill. She's the dearest person in the world to me. I think you believe that evil men—very evil men—have kidnapped her and are hiding her somewhere in this city—" Her voice quavered. "—abusing her, terrifying her."

Revill grimaced. He rose and came around the desk with the intention of putting his hand on her shoulder, of offering some comfort.

Jocko cut him off. "I'll take care of 'er," the thief said firmly. "Let's go, Ria. We got a lot of ground to cover."

Facing off, shoulder to shoulder, Revill glared at Jocko. "Miss Thorne, I really advise against your starting out on your own in this city."

She rose. "Thank you for your time."

"Mr. Walton, surely you know how dangerous the streets are." His voice carried a note of irony as he emphasized certain words with biting clarity. "Miss Thorne would be safest at home or in the company of Mrs. Avory Shires. This is a police matter. Let us do our job."

Suddenly, Maria's temper flared. "If you would do your job, sir, neither one of us would be here."

With that she sailed out the door. Jocko threw an enigmatic look at Revill before bolting after her.

"Nice enough chap," Jocko remarked conversationally.

"He's a man and a bureaucrat," Maria snapped. She was striding down the street, skirts asail. "Mrs. Shires encounters them all the time. I've read dozens of letters from them and typed dozens of replies."

" 'E's right about one thing," Jocko continued. "It's dangerous out 'ere, you know."

Maria almost skidded to a halt. Both hands gripped her umbrella, holding it like a bar in front of her. "Do you want to quit?"

He blinked in the face of such intensity. "Me? No. Of course not, Ria. I just thought—that is—just wanted to be sure. Old Revill wasn't exactly 'opeful."

Maria stared into his eyes. The muscles in her spine and shoulders were aching from the strain of self-control.

He tilted his head to one side. His smile was gentle. "Ah, Ria. You don't 'ave to worry about me. I'm in for the run."

His words touched a chord deep within her. Emotions that she did not know she possessed welled in her. She wanted to cry, to laugh, to—love him. She wanted to love him. She wanted to throw her arms around him right here in the street, but she had to be contented with stepping close.

His eyes widened. She rose on tiptoe and laid one gloved hand on his neck. His incredulous gasp was stilled by her kiss. She held her lips against his cheek a few seconds longer than necessary. He was so still she might have believed his heart stopped beating. Then a shiver went through her, not caused by the biting wind.

She sank down on her heels. "Where shall we start?"

His face like a thundercloud, Revill stalked out of his office. "Find me Dodger double-quick," he ordered curtly. "I want an urgent message delivered to our Mr. Walton. Likewise, I want this order issued to all the patrolmen round the watch."

He slapped a sheet of paper down on his aide's desk. Constable Wilkie read it before raising his eyes inquiringly. "Trail'll be cold, sir," he suggested. "It's a shame about her, but—"

"Just do it, Constable." Revill tugged on his overcoat and strode down the hall.

Wilkie looked after him with a thoughtful frown. Then he wrote two notes. He would give the message to find Dodger to the officer on the Charing Cross beat; the second he sealed in an envelope and addressed.

He put on his hat and coat and passed through the squad room where he paused to place Revill's message on the duty roster. Then he slipped out the door to post his second note.

* * *

"That woman looks like a—um—" Maria could feel her cheeks redden, "—prostitute."

Beneath a parasol of black silk, a dusty rose velvet hat nearly as big as the parasol perched on the woman's head. The top of the brim was ringed in velvet roses. Black silk satin ribbons secured it under the chin and a black veil was draped overall. Through the lace the wearer's hair gleamed a metallic shade of blond. She tipped the amazing hat forward and smiled at Jocko with brightly rouged lips.

Maria felt a twinge of irrational anger. She tried to urge Jocko to a swifter pace as the shiny, yellow-wheeled barouche rolled toward them. "She acts like she knows you."

"Phronsie. She does know me. And you're right. She *is* a prostitute. Wait here for me."

"Jocko!" Maria protested, but he patted her hand and stepped to the curb.

The carriage halted. The two exchanged several sentences. Then Jocko stepped back to tip his hat, and the woman's carriage rolled on.

"You spoke to her!" Maria looked around her swiftly. The passersby continued about their business, apparently unconcerned.

"We're trying to find your sister," Jocko reminded her, replacing his hat and reaching for Maria's hand as they resumed what might have been mistaken for a simple stroll.

"Prostitutes are what we're trying to get Melissa away from," Maria reminded him angrily.

"Right you are. And they'd come closer to knowing where she is than any peelers or ministers." He smiled down at her. "Think that one over, Ria, my love."

His argument made perfect sense but did nothing to quell her shock and resentment. "How can she drive around the streets just as bold as brass in a beautiful carriage?"

"Because she makes a lot of money," Jocko informed her. "She can afford the horse and carriage—and she likes to show off her clothes which she buys in some of the best shops. Believe me, there are worse people riding through the streets."

"A lot of money!?" Maria's sense of outrage was growing with each revelation.

Jocko's grin spread from ear to ear. "A lot of these girls in these sporting houses make more money in a night than you make in a month, Ria. And they don't work nearly the hours."

"They wouldn't have to make very much to make more than I make," Ria sniffed. She walked on, her brow furrowed. Suddenly, she balked. Her eyes hardened with suspicion. "If Melissa's a prisoner in one of these houses, why would they tell us?"

"Still don't trust me, Ria?"

She shook her head. "I trust you, Jocko. I've trusted you with everything I have in the world. I'm just—" She hesitated. "Maybe you're mistaken? Maybe you haven't thought this through?"

"Ria. Ria." He laughed softly. "The girls, who are already established, like Phronsie, don't want any competition. A new girl's always competition. Specially if she's like your sister—young, refined, good language. The toffs don't like to talk to farm girls. Half the time a Londoner can't understand what they're saying."

Maria's eyes grew wide as Jocko continued.

"Phronsie's got her eye on the main chance, just like all the good ones do."

"*Good!* Jocko Walton, you aren't saying she's good?!"

"In a manner of speaking. She's a good girl, not much older than you are." He squeezed Maria's hand. "She's got her hopes and dreams just like every other girl."

Maria's voice was small. "What does she have to hope for?"

"She's hoping that her old regular'll get tired of trotting down here to Soho every night and set her up in a town house in St. John's Wood."

"St. John's Wood!" Maria squeaked.

Jocko nodded. "He's a widower now. His wife can't object any longer. So naturally Phronsie doesn't want him sniffing around and finding someone younger and fresher. She'd be happy to help us get your sister away."

"I see."

"But there're no new girls at Madame De Vere's."

Maria's face fell. They walked on in silence. An exquisitely dressed young woman stepped out onto the doorstep of the house in the next block. When she lifted her yellow silk walking skirt, Maria caught a glimpse of green and blue peacock eyes on the ankle of her stocking.

"Wait here."

Jocko hurried down the street to catch the gorgeous creature before she entered the carriage. The man inside it stepped out and scowled blackly at him. The young woman only smiled sweetly at them both. A minute of conversation, then she shook her head. He tipped his hat, grinning at the man who glared even harder.

He watched them drive off before returning to Maria's side. "She's not at Poodles."

Maria shot him a narrow-eyed look. "How many prostitutes do you know?"

Her words were like a knife, but he kept his eyes straight ahead as he tucked her arm in his and continued walking. The difference between their stations was painfully obvious. The delicacy of her birth and her high ideals forever separated her from him.

Take advantage of her while you can, old boy, he advised himself. *When you find the sister, she won't even speak to you on the street.*

Lord Terence Montague crushed the paper into a ball and tossed it into the fire. His jowls reddened as he drummed his fingers on the arm of his chair.

That bitch!

For the first time he experienced the tiniest tremor of disquiet. While Maria Thorne could not be said to be anything so significant as a "thorn in his side," her persistence was becoming annoying.

She must be discouraged, sent back to wherever she came from. Injury to her person did not occur to him, but the common felon who had attached himself to her was a different matter. Obviously, the woman did not have any idea that she was in danger from him. He would be doing her a favor if he eliminated this thief before she came to harm.

He consulted his watch. He just had time to have instructions delivered before his appointment with his broker.

"Spare a penny, gentleman and lady?"

Maria and Jocko looked down between the pickets of an iron fence. Duchess sat below ground level on the steps that led to the cellar. At least the patrician voice sounded like Duchess's. Greasy black hair liberally streaked with gray straggled down over a figure completely concealed under a great dirty cape.

"A penny's 'ardly worth my time to drag it out," Jocko commented with a grin.

The figure tilted its head. Dark eyes peered up between ropy matted locks. The nose and mouth were liberally smeared with grime. She might have been a crone or a witch. "You two are attracting a lot of attention."

"You sure are." Pan, resembling a small bundle of rags, squatted on the step at Duchess's feet. When she turned her little face up to them, it was like a flower out of the trash heap.

"Hush, Pansy." Duchess's hand shot forth and tapped her grimy cheek. The little one ducked obediently.

Jocko grasped the spikes on top of the pickets. Slowly, he scanned the street in both directions. "What's the word?"

"A dame and a bloke looking for a bird." Duchess tipped her head forward, so her hat concealed her face.

"Damn."

"There's more. You're both in danger now."

"Danger!" Maria's stomach clenched. She looked at Jocko for reassurance.

He shrugged. "What'd you expect? Girls like your sister are supposed to disappear quiet-like. Nobody's supposed to come looking for them. Nobody's supposed to want them after they're ruined."

"But that's monstrous," Maria protested. "It can't be. You make it sound like a horrible conspiracy on the part of society."

A dry chuckle stirred the heap of rags. "You said she was green."

"Green as grass. A real looby." Jocko winked at Maria.

"But she'll do. Anyone in particular we should watch out for?"

Maria felt heat rise in her cheeks.

"Roncie Jack's put out the word."

He looked down at the crown of Duchess's head. "That might mean her sister's at Lady H's."

"What? Where?" Maria clutched the pickets harder.

"And an even dozen other houses," Duchess reminded him. "Jack works the whole street. And Tilly's looking for you, too."

Maria could feel the trembling in every muscle. "Is Jocko in danger, or is it just me?"

"Oh, Jocko's always in trouble." Duchess's voice hinted at a smile.

"Always," agreed her small echo. She tilted her head up to look at Jocko with shining eyes. "But he's not afraid o' nothin', are you, Jocko?"

Jocko blew her a kiss, then turned and leaned his shoulders against the fence. He tipped his bowler forward at its most audacious angle. "Tilly's limping every step of the way."

Maria shook her head. "I don't want anyone to get hurt. She's my sister—"

"There's more," Duchess interrupted.

They waited silently.

"A couple of peelers are putting out the word on you. They've flashed a bit of blunt for a finger."

"What? I don't think I understand." Maria shook her head.

Jocko straightened and tipped his bowler back. "Peelers! That Revill—"

"Not Inspector Revill," Maria argued. "He wouldn't—"

"Like bloody 'ell 'e wouldn't." The color rose in Jocko's

cheeks. He slammed his fist into his palm. "Bloody peeler."

"Calm down, Jocko," Duchess counseled.

Her face white, Maria caught his arm. He scowled down at her as if she were a pesky fly. Then he glared up at the windows of the silent houses. His breathing slowed. The hot color began to fade. He lifted his chin.

"We've decided to help you," Duchess said quietly.

Maria let go of Jocko to look down into the stairwell. "Are you sure you should? It's what I prayed for, but now I'm not sure. The children—"

"We wanna do it," Pan interrupted excitedly. "Ev'rybody voted. Even me. We're gonna find 'er."

Pride rang so clearly in the piping voice that Maria thought her heart would crack. She closed her eyes, inhaling deeply, seeking control. When she opened them, the day seemed suddenly brighter.

Beside her Jocko moved restively. "We better move on. Standing around 'ere attracts the eye."

Duchess put her hand on Pansy's head. "And it's getting late. Pansy and I haven't yet earned our supper."

Maria thought about the coins in her reticule. They were few and decreasing in number every day. Likewise, since she was not working, she could not expect Mrs. Shires to pay her, even though she knew that the dear woman would not mind a small loan. Still . . .

She opened the reticule and began to count out the shillings and pence. They made a faint jingle.

"That's not necessary," Duchess began, but Pansy's sharp ears had heard it, too.

"A penny, pretty lady." In a flash she was on her feet and up the stairs, reaching a grubby little hand between the pickets. Maria pressed the coins into it. Instantly, the hand disappeared within the sleeve of her garment. Pansy scuttled back down the step to Duchess.

"What do you say?" Duchess prodded.

"Thank 'ee."

"I wish it could be more," Maria said. "I wish I had more money."

Duchess chuckled grimly. "Don't we all?" She patted Pan, sending the little girl before her down the steps where she opened a door and slipped inside. Once more Duchess raised her face to the waning light. Just before she too disappeared, she threw Jocko a meaningful look. "You be careful. Something's very wrong here."

"There's money to be gathered for the good work."

The black-clad Reverend Thomas Dinsmore rubbed his hands together over the small wood stove. The black clothing made his face look even paler as it accentuated the hollows in his cheeks and eye sockets.

Sister Evangeline, bleak as a crow, watched him. "Not from Mrs. Avory Shires," she scoffed. "She's never parted with more than a few pounds. Hardly worth the time."

"No, not from Mrs. Shires," he agreed. "Although a letter well-worded might draw more now, especially if we promise to help in the hunt for Maria Thorne's sister.

Evangeline grunted. "A waste of paper."

"Perhaps. However, I think Mrs. Hermione Beauforty might be more forthcoming. They should be willing to pay something to avoid notoriety."

His assistant smiled faintly. "How'd you come by her name?"

"The word's out," he replied. "Minions of the state and of the devil are both disturbed. The game's begun. Maria

Thorne's stirred up a hornet's nest. Or perhaps a nest of locusts, to plague and desolate the land. The unjust are stirring uneasily in their untended fields. Those fields will not bear the scrutiny of the Master."

"Hallelujah," Evangeline intoned mockingly.

He scowled. "There's money here. Money for the good work, and for ourselves. I can feel it. We only have to keep good watch and be ready to catch whatever falls our way."

The two uniformed policemen stared hard at the carriage, an expensive black berlin without any kind of identifying markings on the door. A man's voice called from the dark interior. "Gentlemen."

Casting glances to either side, they approached. A note passed to them at the beginning of their watch had instructed them to wait at the corner of Greek Street and Old Compton.

A white, well-manicured hand cuffed with linen and fine wool extended from the window. "Gentlemen, I'd like to shake your hands."

Without hesitation, they allowed banknotes to be pressed into their palms. "I hope that will be sufficient for the task," the voice went on. "You needn't let this little job lie on your consciences. The man's a thief, a pickpocket turned burglar. A sharp warning is society's gain. Do you understand?"

"Yes, sir." The pound notes disappeared into their pockets. Still, they shuffled back and forth uneasily.

The hand extended a second time with a piece of white paper. One took it and read the name. He grinned faintly and nodded. "It'll be a pleasure, sir."

"Good. He has a young woman with him."

"A woman, sir?" The second patrolman protested.

"Oh, she's no better than she should be, I assure you. She needs a like warning."

The patrolman who had taken the paper folded his arms across his chest. "I don't know about—"

"Nothing physical. She's been misled. Two fine gentlemen such as yourselves are just the ones to give her a friendly but firm admonition."

The two looked at each other. One shrugged. The other nodded.

"Come back and tell me when you've done it," the man in the carriage said smoothly. "I'd like to shake your hands again."

The evening light was waning. As the breeze died, dank air settled on them like a blanket. The cobblestones glistened. Where Maria touched her glove to a lamppost, it came away damp. Her coat grew heavier as the droplets slid into the boiled wool.

Knee aching like the very devil, she maintained most of her weight on her good leg, shifting only when the cold rising from the paving stones became too uncomfortable.

A uniformed footman came out and lighted the gas coachlamps in front of the house that fronted Kingsway Mews. While Maria watched, he took out a cloth, spat on the brass knocker, and polished it bright and shiny.

She shifted again. Where was Jocko? He had been gone much longer than on any of his other excursions. The footman reentered the house. Before the door shut, Maria heard a woman's laughter.

She was going to be angry if he were inside enjoying himself while she froze to the pavement. He had not knocked at the front door, of course. Instead, he had disappeared down the mews to the servants' entrance. Contributing to her uneasiness was the fact that he seemed to know everyone. Perhaps they had invited him inside.

Maria remained ever surprised at the style and beauty of the exteriors of the houses they had visited that day. Far from being shabby and cheap, their facades were as stately as that of Mrs. Shires's home. The couple of glimpses she had had of interiors revealed the finest furnishings. Butlers of the same imposing size as Mrs. Shires's "Saint" Peter had opened the doors on both occasions.

Duchess's unpleasant truths about society were swiftly reinforcing themselves. No woman alone could afford this house unless she had inherited a small fortune. In which case, why should she prostitute herself? Women who lived here must have very rich men who visited them and paid great sums to do so.

Maria watched a carriage drawn by a matched pair of black Hanoverians come to a halt in the street. The vehicle gleamed with shiny paint and leather wax. To cut an even more dashing appearance, the horses' necks were impossibly bowed by checkreins on their bits. Two passengers stepped down. One mounted the steps eagerly, making the brass knocker ring. The second climbed down with seeming reluctance.

"Come on. Don't stand there gawking, m' boy," the first called.

Maria frowned. The voice was familiar. She could swear she had heard it before. She cocked her head, hoping to hear the speaker's next words more clearly.

"I'd just as leave go on home, Father," replied the companion.

"Nonsense."

The door swung open. Rather than answer, the older

man motioned the driver on his way and disappeared into the house. The carriage rumbled away and turned the corner into the mews.

The son stood in the street for a moment. The butler looked at him inquiringly as the young man shrugged and entered.

"Taking his son into a brothel," Maria muttered disgustedly. How had she ever believed rich and powerful people were good? When she did return to Mrs. Avory Shires's employ, she would be skeptical of every promise made, every speech uttered.

The night was now full dark, but the street was well-lighted. Lamps graced each doorway and portico, and a streetlamp burned far down at the corner. Lights spilled through lace curtains from many of the windows.

No more pedestrians moved along the narrow walks, but well-sprung carriages drove up and down, stopping before the houses and discharging their passengers. Another halted across the street.

"This is disgusting," Maria grumbled to herself. The man who had just alighted turned his face to the lamplight. She recognized a minor baron who was a special friend to Mrs. Shires.

The butler opened the door. The Member of Parliament strode smiling into the foyer and into the arms of an elegantly gowned woman.

Maria determined to wait no longer. Teeth chattering, arms tight across her chest, she followed the carriage into the mews. Rectangles of light from the curtained windows illuminated portions of the narrow way, but the contrast left the rest in impenetrable blackness.

She was an idiot. Her sister had been kidnapped, perhaps into this very house, and she was lingering here. The man she waited for was at best a rascal, at worst something evil. Even now he might be disporting himself somewhere with one of his "friends."

She could imagine what he would be doing there. And the knowledge made her burn with anger—and jealousy.

What would she do if she did not find him at the end of this mews? They had walked so many streets today, passed so many houses that she had no clear idea how to find her way back to her own home. If she could not find him, she would have to wander alone, perhaps until dawn.

"Damn you, Jocko Walton," she whispered. "Damn. Damn. Damn."

A few more steps and she froze. The hair rose on the back of her neck. Somewhere up ahead she heard a strange sound. Faint, undefinable. A dog panting?

She took a backward step. What if the mews were guarded by ferocious animals? They would leap out and attack . . . She halted her wild imaginings. The horses and carriages had come down the mews without so much as a whimper. It could not be a dog.

"Where are you, Jocko Walton?" Her mouth framed the words without a sound.

Shuddering from head to toe, she resolved to walk to the last rectangle of light. When she reached it, she would take two steps—only two—out of it. There she would wait until her eyes accustomed themselves to the dark, then she would look around. If she saw nothing, she would return to the street and undoubtedly spend the rest of the night trying to find her way home.

The plan eased her wildly spiraling imagination. Taking in a deep, cold breath, she hurried through the last two patches of light.

One step. Two.

She stopped.

The sound came from somewhere to the right. Staring into the gloom until her eyes ached, she made out an archway and, beyond that an area of lighter darkness. The carriages must have passed on through. Nothing was in this alley except the smell of horses and the sound.

This time it was a little louder. She cupped her hand behind her ear. The sound became a moan. She took another step in that direction and her heel struck the cobblestone.

The moaning stilled.

Maria waited, shivering.

"Ria."

Her name. Jocko's voice. Jocko whispering her name.

"Jocko?"

"Ria." The sound of someone stirring. Another groan. "Ria. 'Ere."

Nine

The darkness was like peering into the depths of a well. Cautiously, Maria advanced, sweeping her arms wide and low, trying to find him. "Jocko, where are you?"

Then she stumbled over his leg. Off balance, she tilted forward. Her hands, outstretched to catch herself, slapped into his body.

His howl of pain ended in a groan. " 'Ave a care."

The words were nearly unintelligible. She froze, trying to understand what he had said.

He stirred beneath her touch, heaving himself up. Panting, breath hissing like a bellows, he attempted to roll over. Only then did she realize he lay facedown.

"Bastards," he hissed between clenched teeth. Another groan.

Stepping cautiously over his leg and moving along his body, she reached his head. Her hands found his shoulders, rocking, trembling, suspended above the ground on one arm. She put her arms around him, tugging.

"No. Oh-h-h. God."

She pulled her hands away. "I'm sorry. What can I do?"

"W-Wait."

Her eyes were beginning to distinguish shapes in the blackness. She could see his silhouette as he tilted over on his side. Then he collapsed with a groan, losing some of the ground he had gained. He was not facing her.

She knelt and leaned forward, trying to find his face. It was not even a visible blur in the darkness.

He was panting like a dog. His body gave off heat in the dank air and with it a strong odor—sweetish, cloying. Not perfume.

"Jocko! How badly are you hurt?"

He managed a chuckle. "Just about to death, Ria, m' girl."

"Oh, no." She reached down in the direction of the voice. Her fingers encountered his cheek, slid through warm, wet—blood! Her stomach heaved and she froze. Jocko Walton was bleeding. For her. Faintness rolled over her in a black wave, but she ducked her head down until her forehead touched the wet stones. The chill shocked her. She knelt up straight and whispered, "Can you stand?"

"Maybe." He took a careful breath. "In a while."

From somewhere above them a woman's laugh rang out. Maria threw a shocked glance upward at the patches of light that marked the second-story windows. Did she dare knock on the door to summon aid?

Then a pair of horses drew a carriage into the mews. *The coachman.* "I'll get help."

"No." He rolled over on his back, catching her by the coat, holding her so she couldn't scramble to her feet. "Don't. Let 'em go on."

"But—"

"They wouldn't 'elp." He slumped even though he still retained his hold on her coat.

The carriage clopped on past. The light from its lamps spilled down over them. The coachman actually glanced down, then quickly averted his face.

Maria felt a sharp spurt of anger. "I can't believe it."

"At least 'e showed me where my 'at went." She could feel Jocko strain to reach the bowler. With a relieved sigh he placed it on his head. The carriage turned the corner.

"Let me get help."

"No." He managed to lever his body until his shoulders were against a wall.

"What shall I do?"

"Gimme your 'and." He reached out for her, fumbled, found her shoulder. His weight bore down on her. He sucked in a lungful of the icy air, then pushed. His body slid up the wall.

She caught at his arm to lift it over her shoulder.

"T'other side! T'other side," he whimpered. "Rib's cracked. Arm, too."

"What?" She could not believe her ears. "Your arm's broken?"

He did not answer.

She moved to his good side. "They broke your arm?"

He was shuddering, his clothing damp with sweat. "Maybe."

He pushed at her again. Another shriek of laughter came from above. On its crest it was joined by a masculine guffaw. She shook her head. She was completely out of her element. Nothing in her life had prepared her for this. She truly had no idea what to do.

She stood there, shivering with shock. His pain was because of her. He suffered for her.

In that terrible minute she knew the agony of love and sacrifice. Her hero, her lover swayed helplessly against the frost-encrusted wall of an alley. The beautiful body she had caressed only hours before and the bright spirit were suffering. Because of her he had put himself in danger and paid the price. Only the sternest self-admonitions kept her from screaming in rage and despair.

Instead, she placed herself at his side. "What can I do?"

He pushed himself away from the wall, and she put her shoulder into his armpit. He swayed heavily against her, then righted himself and took his first step. His leg gave way, but she shoved upward with all her strength and he rallied. The next step was easier. But on the third he faltered.

"Your leg?"

"Don't think it's broken," he groaned.

"That's a blessing." She was guiding him back toward the light, but he balked.

"Not out there."

"One of the customers is sure to arrive in a cab," she argued. "When he gets out, we'll get in."

He shook his head and muttered something that sounded like, "Green as grass."

"That I may be, but surely—"

"They'd never take us up." He tried to take more of his weight off her shoulder by straightening. He failed miserably.

"Oh, Jocko."

"Let's just take it slow." Every word was an effort.

She reached to encircle his back. His arm weighed heavily on her shoulders, but no heavier than the awful fears. Her teeth began to chatter. He had said it. She *was* green as grass. If a cab would not take them up, how would she be able to save him? They were miles from her tiny apartment, miles from Mrs. Shires's home, miles from help of any kind.

Again the panic was almost overwhelming. Again she tamped it down. "Where do you want to go?"

"Back this way." He pivoted, turning her around. Together they followed the way the carriages had gone.

From the Lord's Dream behind them came more laughter. Window glass shattered and tinkled into the alley. Now the sounds carried more clearly. Someone was playing a mandolin, a popular tune. Someone was singing—not well—about blinding tears and lost pearls. A man's voice joined in, slurring the words.

Suddenly, Maria felt a frisson down her spine. Beneath these very windows someone had beaten Jocko. Not near any of the other establishments, not on the narrow streets they had traversed. Here. Duchess's warning intruded upon her whirling thoughts. They must be getting close.

She lifted her face to search the upper windows of the house. Her sister. She could almost feel her sister—

Jocko stumbled, dragging them both off center. With a muffled apology he caught himself. Stolidly, he resumed the task of placing one foot in front of the other. Sweat trickled down his face and wet her temple.

More sounds flew out into the icy night. A *mélange* of sounds of people about their noisy pleasures.

And finally—when Jocko and Maria were too far away to hear—a piercing scream.

Ria lowered Jocko to a stone bench at the Victoria Embankment. "I'm going to find a cab and take you home," she insisted.

"No." He was curled into himself, cradling his left arm. Now he raised his face. The light from the lamppost revealed the damage—swellings around both eyes, a lump standing out on his jaw, and a trickle of blood slipping darkly down from his temple.

"Oh, Jocko." She went down on her knees, reaching for him but not daring to touch.

He hated her to see him this way. He knew he looked bad. She'd be disgusted. Ladies weren't accustomed to things like this. When he tried to turn away, she brought him back with a couple of fingers under his chin. "You need a doctor."

"Oh, yes, Ria. They're thick upon the ground around here." He gave a negative shake that sent a twinge through the side of his face. "Not bloody likely. Who'd take care o' me?"

She looked up and down the embankment. "We can go to my employer. We'll get her doctor and then we'll send for the police."

"No." His voice rose.

Irritation and exhaustion burst their bonds. "You were attacked," she reminded him, her voice quivering with righteous anger.

She was going all strait-laced on him again, he realized. Ladies were like that.

"By whoremongers and only God knows what else," she went on. "This is London in the nineteenth century. Victoria is the Queen. It is our duty to inform the police."

He sucked in a careful breath. With his good hand he stroked her cheek. "The peelers beat me up."

She caught at his hand. "What did you say?"

He let his battered face sink to his chest. "The coppers, the bobbies, the bloody police. They're the ones who did it."

In the silence that followed, they could hear the Thames lapping against the granite. Somewhere through the fog came the sounds of a scuffle. Hoarse voices barked at each other. He drew in an experimental breath, deeper than any he had dared to draw. The pain was not as bad as he had feared.

Maria's voice quavered as she lifted his bruised knuckles to her cheek. "The police did that to your face? And broke your ribs and maybe your arm?"

"That's right. Sod 'em all."

"Because they caught you in a sp-sporting house?" She was trying hard to excuse what he was telling her.

"Not bloody likely," he snorted. "No. Because I was asking questions." His effort to sit straight ended in a gasp. His right side was worse then his left.

"But that's monstrous."

He could feel her shaking. He should never have let her talk him into any of this. If he were in danger, then so was she. He wanted to reach out and gather her in his arms to sooth her fears.

A foghorn groaned its deep warning from the river. She jumped and looked around. He could see her face, white as pearl, with dark circles surrounding her wide eyes.

He dropped his hand onto her shoulder. "The thing for you to do, Ria, is leave me."

"No!" Her loud exclamation startled them both, making them realize they had been speaking in the barest of whispers. "Absolutely not!"

Her answer lit a tiny glow within him. Still he insisted. "Don't you see? You can go home and be safe and sound."

"They might arrest me," she objected.

He shook his head. "For what? Stayin' out late? No, you can go 'ome and tell them you 'aven't seen me. Tell them you didn't know anythin' about me visitin' sportin' 'ouses."

"If they could beat you up for no reason, they could arrest me."

"They wouldn't arrest you anyway. They'd just warn you."

She dropped her head into her hands. "All because you're helping me look for my sister. She's just one little girl. Who would want her so much? Who would hate you so much that they'd break your arm?"

He tried to move it. The pain made him curse weakly. Any numbness had long ago worn off. He could feel the tears starting from his eyes. Instantly, he tucked his head again, but not before she saw. God! Was he going to blubber in front of her? With his good hand he squeezed gingerly. "I don't believe it's broken," he grumbled between clenched teeth. "Course, it's not from their lack of tryin'."

She huddled against him, shivering. He sucked in the frozen night air. Much longer and they would freeze to the stones. "What about Duchess?"

"What about her?"

"Can I take you there?"

He straightened, shocked at the very thought. "Lord, no. We might bring them down on her."

"Oh, no." It was her turn to sound shocked. Again the frightened glance about. "I-I didn't think of that. Are they following us?"

"Might be." He squinted through the fog. "Probably not. They've done their do for tonight."

Teeth chattering, her whole body shaking with chills, she gave him a painful shake. "Then tell me what to do. Damn. Damn. Damn you. I don't know what to do. Tell me what to do."

He looked down into her white face. Finally, he said, "I've already told you. Leave me."

"No. Oh, no. I can't."

He pushed gently at her shoulder. "You'll be all right.

You've got some friends in high places. If they take you in, just demand to see Revill. He'll see you get out in a flash. I'll just quietly disappear."

He was surprised at how much his own suggestion hurt him. He did not want to disappear from her life. As miserable as he was at this moment, as dangerous as their situation seemed, he loved the cradling arms, the real concern, the beginning of what he was sure was real respect, perhaps even friendship. It had opened a window into a world different from the one he had always known. He did not want that window to close.

"Where will you disappear to?" Her voice was husky.

He shrugged, then wished he could take the movement back. "I got some digs."

The admission galvanized her into action. She sat up straight. "I'll take you there."

"No," he replied firmly. Not for anything would he allow her to see the miserable hole in which he lived.

"Why not?" She rose and began stamping her feet to get the circulation moving.

"They aren't fit for a lady."

"Neither are the streets in front of sporting houses," she reminded him. "I won't let you go alone. How will you take care of yourself? You can't clean your face. Why, if your arm is broken—"

"I think it's all right." He lifted it to demonstrate. The pain made him nauseous.

"How would you undress yourself, fix food for yourself? If you won't let me take you to my house, I'll go to yours."

"It's too far," he groaned.

"We'll take a cab." She was a whirlwind when she got an idea into her head. She hurried along the embankment to the head of a street. "I think we can get a cab this way. I'm sure I heard a horse's hooves a few minutes ago."

He hesitated. "Doesn't make any difference. A cabbie won't go there."

Suddenly, she reeled around and caught him by the lapels. "Stop this, Jocko Walton! Stop it this instant! Where—do—you—live?"

He thrust his face close to hers, biting out the hated word. "In Whitechapel."

"Whitechapel!" She clutched his lapels more tightly. Still, she could not keep the shock from her voice as he named the poorest part of London miles from where they stood.

He nodded. "Plenty of digs for rent over there."

"I should imagine so." As innocent as she was, even she had heard of Whitechapel. "But surely you could live better than that."

He tried to shrug her off, angry and disappointed that she had taken on her old prim and proper voice. "Oh, it's a bit rough, Miss Thorne, but the peelers don't bother us none. And birds and blokes can get together friendly like."

"Don't call them *birds*," she snapped.

He gaped. *What had brought this on?*

"They're women. Girls. Like my sister. Like me—now." She was shivering, shaking him with her hands on his coat. Her voice was edged with fear and grief. She sounded as if she would burst into tears at any moment.

"Ria—"

"Don't call them *birds*." She pounded her fists against his chest and pushed herself away from him. "Call yourself a bloke if you like. Although I can't see why you'd call yourself that when you want me to treat you like a toff. Make up your mind, Mr. Walton."

She waited for his reply. When none came she turned on her heel and started off down the embankment. "I'll find us a cab."

"He'll never take us up," he called after her hurrying figure.

"He will," she vowed. "I'll lead the horse myself if I have to."

Maria did succeed in finding a cab, but not all her promising, nor the offer of every penny in her reticule could prevail upon the driver to take them past Bishopsgate Road. There he let them down and whipped his horse into a canter heading back the way he had come.

Still, the ride had rested and warmed them both. They were making good progress through the fog when Maria gave a muffled shriek.

A misshapen bundle of old rags dragged itself out of a doorway. "Ain't she kind of a step down fer ye, Jocko?"

"Shut your trap, Dickon," Maria's thief snarled wearily. "You've never seen a lady before?"

"A laidy, is her?" The beggar tilted his rag-wrapped head to one side and squinted up through the fog. "Kinda plain." He put his knuckles to the ground and hoisted himself across their path, balancing on the stumps of his thighs with careless ease. He thrust out his hand. "How's about a penny, laidy? Fer a wounded vet'ran."

Jocko winced as Maria tightened her grip on his waist and shrank back against him. "Get away from her, Dickon." He made to lead her around, but Dickon sidled crabwise to bar the way.

"A ha'penny'll do me," he whined. "A bleedin' farthin'."

Maria tried to reach into her reticule, but Jocko held her hand tightly. "Let 'im be. 'E's a faker."

The beggar set up a horrendous howl. "That's a bloody lie. I lost m' legs fightin' fer th' whoorin' queen."

Jocko pulled Maria to the left, then dodged back to the right before Dickon could execute both maneuvers.

A stream of curses followed them into the fog. Jocko could feel Maria shivering and panting against him. Beneath his coat her fingers clutched his shirt in a death grip. Her face was turned into his shoulder. At least she hadn't fainted.

Even as he was thinking those thoughts, she turned up her face. "Why didn't you let me give him a coin?"

"I told you. 'E's a faker."

"How can he be a faker? He doesn't have any legs."

"Right. 'E lost 'is when a guard knocked 'im off a coach. 'E rolled under it."

"Oh, the poor man."

" 'E was tryin' to rob it."

"Oh."

"An' don't be thinkin' 'e's seen the error o' 'is ways. 'E's got a string o' boys workin' for 'im now. Stealin'. Makes more off them than 'e ever did on the road. 'E could 'ave killed us both if 'e'd wanted to. 'E's bad clean through."

She closed her mouth and tucked her head into his shoulder. Jocko could feel her heart hammering against him. Her breathing had been labored for several minutes. She must be exhausted, but he'd be no help for her. He could barely keep himself on his feet.

Clinging together, they trudged on through the fog. Sometimes they walked on cobblestones that turned their ankles treacherously and made them stagger. Sometimes they splashed through water; as their feet slipped, unimagined substances squished beneath their soles.

Once or twice they encountered a figure, huddled in rags, seeming to pay them no attention. Around them the heavy silence was broken occasionally by a thud, a cough, a faraway cry.

Sometimes they would round a curve in the twisting streets to find light streaming out of a doorway and hear the muffled drone of voices. A glance inside would reveal a public house with a few customers drinking. Then they would turn another corner and both light and sound would vanish in the ever-present fog.

"How much farther?"

"Not much."

"How can you be sure?" she panted. "Everything looks the same. We might be anywhere."

He did not answer. Another turn, up a half-dozen slippery steps, into an alley so narrow she had to move behind him to negotiate it. And finally, they arrived at a door. He reached out to touch the latch. "I'm sorry," he whispered. "You shouldn't ought to be 'ere."

The door creaked open.

Maria held on to him so hard he could barely breathe. The only good thing about her clinging was that his cracked ribs were getting support.

"This is where you live?" Her voice was a thin thread of sound. He could hear her teeth chattering.

Three steps into the room brought him up against the table. Out of long habit he found the candle in its holder, the matches beside it. Sometimes darkness was best. He set his teeth and raked a match across the metal striker.

Maria blinked in the light. Jocko watched her face as she looked slowly around her. Embarrassment added to his pain. He would have given all he owned, which was precious little, to have hidden this from her.

A table less than a yard square, a couple of mismatched chairs, a tiny two-drawer chest, nails driven into one wall to hang clothing, and a pallet. Nothing else. Nothing.

Her eyes, carefully blank, came back to his face. All she said was, "Let's get your coat off."

Obediently, he reached for the buttons. She pushed his hands aside and accomplished the task for him. Then moving behind him, she lifted the heavy garment off his shoulders.

"Is there some way to heat water?"

He could feel his face getting hot. "No water."

"What?"

"No water," he said more loudly.

She looked around helplessly. Her eyes found a bucket in the shadow of the chest.

"Down near the roundabout there's a pump," he supplied, "but you can't go out and get some."

She lifted her chin as if to argue.

"You couldn't find it in the fog."

At his words she collapsed into the other chair. For a couple of minutes they stared at each other. She very much feared she looked as bad as he did, except for the blood. He had evidently been struck on the side of the face. Two trails of blood contrasted startlingly with the skin on his cheek. The blond hair above his ear was matted. Another bruise swelled out on the side of his jaw. But the most awful thing about his appearance was the twisted way he held his body.

"What will we do about your arm?"

He lifted it a couple of inches. His face turned white

with the effort, and sweat popped out on his forehead. "I don't think it's broken. See?"

"Please don't do that."

"What?"

"Be so brave. You're hurting, and it's my fault."

He shifted and bent over to remove his shoes. They felt as if they had grown to his feet.

Instantly, she dropped down before him and started to untie the strings.

"Get away," he ordered angrily.

She looked up at him. In the candlelight her face was thoroughly homely, strained white, eyes ringed by dark smudges, mouth pinched, lips cracked. Her hair, dark with dampness, straggled round her face. "I'll do this and then put you down on the pallet. In the morning, I'll find the pump."

"In the mornin'—" He could not go on. Dizziness overcame him. Weakness swept over him in waves. He swayed where he sat.

She reached up to catch him and guide him down to the pallet. He sprawled on the hard ticking with a sigh. She tucked the single pillow under his head and eased his shoes off. He had two blankets. She spread them over him and took his coat to wrap around her shoulders.

"Come 'ere," his whisper was so low she had to lean to hear it.

"I'll wrap myself up in your coat and sit in the chair."

"No." His head rolled on the pillow. "With me."

"You're hurt," she argued. "There's not room."

"I'll make room."

"The pallet's only big enough—"

"I'm used to it." He held out his good arm. "Please. You'll keep me warm."

She blew out the light. The room was instantly plunged into total darkness.

"Come on," he called. "Come to my voice."

"What if I stumble over you?"

He chuckled. "Then you'll know where I am."

He heard her steps edging along the floor. When her toes had found the edge of the pallet, she came down on her knees. Very carefully, trying not to jostle against him, she arranged herself on the edge of the pallet. The better part of her hip and shoulder was on the floor. She pulled the blankets up over his shoulder.

"Over against me," he murmured, his breath soft in her ear.

"I'll hurt you."

"I can stand it. What I can't do is go to sleep without your being warm and soft in my arms."

Her breath hissed between her teeth. Obediently, she hitched her hip over until it fitted into the cradle of his loins.

"Now the rest o' you."

"How badly did you say you were hurt?"

"I'm 'urt, Ria. Not dead." He pulled the pillow from beneath his head and propped his arm on it.

She snuggled down against his ribs, her head fitted into the curve of his shoulder. "If I hurt you, just nudge me," were her last words before she fell into a deep sleep.

His body a throbbing mass, he lay awake and listened to her breathing. He had really gotten himself into a pickle, but not the one Miss Maria Thorne suspected. She would have thought his major concern would be the police.

Their beating did not trouble him overmuch. He had received worse before. He was too small, too unimportant for them to come back. They bore him no malice—they were merely doing their jobs.

Likewise, Tilly and Roncie Jack and the whole race of pimps and sportin' types were quick to anger and quick to forget.

No, the pickle he had gotten himself into was one that he would never have expected, had never sought, could never escape.

He moved his head forward only an inch. His lips touched Maria Thorne's hair. Though snarled and tangled, it was fine as silk. It smelled clean and with a hint of sweet soap.

The denizens of Whitechapel nurtured a myth among themselves. They exchanged it whenever they gathered in groups beside the communal standpipes. They trotted it out and drank to it in their murky taprooms on cold nights. They soothed one another's complaints with it. They muttered it under their breath when the gentry drove by in their fine carriages or honest tradesmen drove them from their doors.

The myth was that beneath the fine, clean clothes and fancy airs, men and women were all the same. Only by an accident of birth was Victoria born Queen and Nelson crowned a hero.

"Take 'em outta their fine 'ouses an' offa their 'igh 'orses, an' y'd see."

Now that myth had been dispelled.

The lady in his arms was out of her fine house and off her high horse, and she was still a lady, still brave, still loyal. She had gone down on her knees to untie his shoes when he was not fit to kiss hers. She treated him like a toff even though she was worth ten of him, and he would be damned to hell before he would behave any way but like a toff.

Which left him with the first moral dilemma of his short life. She was heaven—a heaven he could never hope to reach. He could see a life of loneliness stretching before him.

Bad cess to Revill for ringing him in on this. He had been heart whole, easy-going, uncaring as any penny-bought thief that ever pinched a purse or fleeced a cove. Now his heart ached, he was burdened with responsibilities, and he cared.

He pressed his lips to the top of her head. She stirred and muttered something.

God! How he cared!

He had fallen in love with her.

Ten

"Lord Montague."

"Hermione, my dear. You're looking beautiful as always." He smiled with real warmth and bowed low to the lush figure.

"Thank you." Lady H's dress was magenta satin, the new modish shade, with a huge bustle at the back and a cloud of net ruching framing her plump white shoulders. Her hair was midnight-black and combed fully six inches above her face in an elaborate pompadour. With a welcoming smile she advanced with black-gloved hands outstretched.

Then, the corners of her magenta lips twisted as she watched his eyes slide past her to survey the room; beyond him, she saw the tall form of a young man. The smile disappeared as if a shadow had passed over her. Her whole body stiffened.

Lord Montague's gaze followed hers and his smile broadened. "George, don't be a laggard, boy. Step up. Here's someone I want you to meet."

Lingering in the archway, George Montague stood tall and gangly with great hands and wrists hanging out from beneath the white linen of his cuffs. Half a head taller than his father, his dark hair flopped over his forehead. Now, he tossed it back with a nervous movement that turned into a negative shake. His cold, dark eyes flicked over the woman like a whip.

"Terry," Lady H faltered. "Lord Montague. You've brought your son." In anguish she faced Montague's scion, unable to hide her lead-white face, her heavily rouged lips and cheeks, her garish dress. They proclaimed her occupation blatantly, and obviously young George did not approve.

Lord Montague chuckled as he caught his son's arm and dragged him into the main salon. "Surprised?" he asked her. "You shouldn't be. He's all grown up now." He tugged the youth forward another step. "He's just shy."

Both woman and youth glared at him in disgust.

"Tonight's the night, m' boy," the father continued. Oblivious, he clapped his son on the back with a show of heartiness. "Going to make a man out of you. And here's just the lady who can do it. Lady H, this is my son George."

In the icy silence that followed, the brothel-keeper scanned the young man's form and face. Their eyes met, his glaring ferociously. Lady H hastily looked away and attempted unsuccessfully to clear her throat. Her voice cracked as she called for champagne.

"The very thing," Terence agreed. "But not too much. Boys, you know. Mustn't dull the performance."

George's face turned a brick red. His hands balled into fists.

"Eunice." Lady H motioned to a young woman wearing a frilly white apron. She might have been simply a maid if her black dress had not been cut shockingly low. Smiling broadly, she approached the new guests with a tray of filled glasses. With an especially provocative movement, she took a deep breath as she offered George the champagne.

Instead of looking at her bosom, George looked into her

eyes. Their hard, anticipatory gleam repulsed him. His scowl blackened. He opened his mouth to speak, then closed it again. The muscles in his jaw jumped as he ground his teeth. Over Eunice's shoulder he surveyed the large salon, then gasped.

The walls alternated panels of red-flocked paper with panels of rosy nudes—both male and female—in passionate embrace. Beneath the paintings at least a dozen women posed artistically on plush divans and chairs. All of them were in stages of *déshabillé*—white bosoms, arms, and limbs exposed beneath lace and satin undergarments and robes. Draped in sheer pastel silks, one softly strummed a guitar. The blazes from no fewer than three fireplaces made the room stuffy.

As the "maid" strolled away, she revealed the backs of white legs, from the black lace edging at the bottom of her drawers to the black boots that reached halfway up her calves. The material that constituted the front of her skirt had been gathered up into an enormous black satin bustle that rustled as she swayed voluptuously.

George's eyes widened. His cheeks grew even redder.

"See anyone you particularly like, m'boy?" Terence put his arm familiarly around Hermione's shoulders.

"Terry, *please.*" Uncharacteristically, she tried to pull away, but he did not notice.

Instead, he winked lewdly and laughed. "Take your pick tonight, George. You're the one who has to be satisfied."

The young man stared accusingly at them both. Whore and lecher. He had come to realize how different he was from his father, whom he scarcely knew, in both taste and temperament.

Like most Englishmen of his class, Lord Montague had left his son's rearing to others. From his Scottish nurse, a

Presbyterian on her knees to a stern but forgiving God, George had had a strict moral upbringing. His public schooling had been Nether Stowe rather than Eton or Harrow.

The result was that he now regarded his father as something of a monster. Embarrassed and disgusted, he lowered his eyes, concentrating on the bubbles rising in the champagne.

Terence shrugged in irritation. He leaned close to Hermione's ear. "Did my—er—*protégée* arrive safely?"

She nodded. The practical side of her business reasserted itself. "Safe and sound, but very unhappy."

He took a long drink of his champagne. "That'll change." He smiled in anticipation. "I can't wait to change her mind. Just let me get this one settled." Turning his attention to his son, he slapped the youth on the shoulder. "Go on, m'boy. Get your feet wet. Learn what a woman's for."

Hermione's eyes suddenly flew wide. She freed herself from Terence's embrace. Unfortunately, she was a moment too late to intercept Cate.

"Lord Montague," the girl in black addressed him loudly. "Welcome to the Lord's Dream."

He frowned. His eyes took on an anticipatory gleam as they slid over the flawless white skin and slender figure all provocatively contrasted to midnight lace and satin. He directed his question to Hermione. "Who is this?"

The brothel-keeper pressed her fingertips to her temple and closed her eyes. "One of the girls. Don't be—"

"Actually, I'm something more than that." She tossed her head, disturbing the thick black hair that cascaded down her back. "My name is Hecate, m'lord. You know— like the witch. But I've taken the name Cate. More champagne, Eunice. Tonight is a celebration."

"Cate, please," Lady H murmured. "This is not the time."

Cate drifted closer to Lord Montague. Holding out her hand, she smiled. "We've never met, your lordship. But since this seems to be a time for introductions, I thought I'd introduce myself."

Terence's frown turned to a calculated sneer. He lifted her hand to his mouth and brushed his moustache across the pale skin. "You're impertinent, young lady. Someone needs to teach you better manners. It's really too bad, but tonight I've other plans."

"Too bad. I'd love to talk to you about manners as well as other things."

"Cate!" Lady H pleaded.

"Perhaps your son would be interested in a conversation. Why don't you introduce us? I've heard so much about you, George."

Before Hermione could intervene, Cate stepped past her to wrap her arm through the young man's. If it had been an adder, he could not have looked more repulsed. She smirked up at him. "It's an honor to meet the heir apparent. And on the evening of your initiation. How appropriate."

"Cate!" Hermione wailed. "Stop this!"

The guitarist stopped playing. The hum of conversation ceased, then began again at a higher pitch.

"I'm pleased to meet you at last, George," Cate continued.

"Who is this creature? What does she think she's doing?" Terence wanted to know.

George stared at the face so close to his. A shudder went through him. "Take your hand off my arm, madam. We have never been introduced. Nor are we ever likely to be."

She felt the tremor. Her smirk contorted into a snarl.

Pure fury blazed across her face. Shoving him rudely, she stepped back. "Rot you, y' bleedin' sod!"

She stalked away.

A silence had fallen over the salon. Men paused in their pleasures. Girls stared open-mouthed.

Hermione moaned. "You'll have to forgive her, Lord Montague."

"I think not." His hand clenched around his glass. "I don't want to see her here again. Turn her off."

"No need for that," George spoke up. "I suggest that we leave and let these—creatures continue about their business."

For an instant, his father looked tempted. But Cate was fast disappearing up the stairs and conversations were resuming. And somewhere up above, his, *protégée* awaited him. He smiled.

"Nonsense."

Melissa had tugged at the bindings until her wrists were rubbed raw. Her tears had long since dried. The mottling on her cheeks had faded. Pure misery had set in. Her whole body ached from her spreadeagle position.

Moreover, she had to listen to the sounds of people coming and going down the hall outside her door. Every time footsteps approached, her fear increased. Likewise, the noises coming through the thin walls on either side of her had appalled her.

Groans and moans, female giggles and male roars, the squeak of bedsprings, came clearly to her ears. Now she lay lax, head and body aching, reciting half-remembered prayers in which she placed no faith.

High heels came tapping down the hall. The key turned

in the lock, then the door opened. Melissa jerked her head off the pillow. Cate stood there, her face a mask of cold anger. Closing the door behind her, she leaned against it. "You're quite a sight, *protégée*."

Melissa let her head sink back. She stared at the crack in the ceiling without comment.

"Your mentor's here."

The captive shuddered. Despite her will to remain still, she strained her shoulders, tugging at the bindings.

"That won't do any good," Cate jeered. "Lady H buys only the best silk. Strong as harness leather."

She stalked across the room. "It has to be cut off. Maybe your mentor will take these—" She showed Melissa a pair of silver scissors on the bedside table. "—But only if you promise with tears streaming down those pale cheeks to fall on your knees and kiss his feet."

Melissa turned her face away. "And if I don't, will he kill me?"

"Kill you?" Cate laughed aloud. With a whirl of black lace, she stalked across the room. She poured herself a stiff tot of brandy and tossed it off. "Women don't die from this." She raised her glass toward the ceiling. "After all, God is a man. He wouldn't want to spoil their pleasure."

Melissa did not answer.

"Pleasure." On Cate's lips the word became a curse. She stalked back to Melissa's bedside. "Want to try to run for it?"

Melissa's head snapped around. "Yes."

"You'll never make it, you know."

"I might."

"They'll beat you if they catch you."

"They might not catch me."

Cate shook her head. She picked up the scissors. Only

an inch from Melissa's bindings, she stopped. *"When* they catch you, you'll tell who set you loose."

"No." Melissa craned her neck, desperate, frantic. "They'll never catch me. I'll kill myself before I let them catch me again."

Cate drew back the scissors. Slowly, she shook her head. "I'd better not."

"Yes," Melissa hissed. "Do it! Do it! Cut me free. I'll escape, or die. I swear to you."

"At least promise me—"

"I'll never tell that you were here. Never. Before God."

"Oh, that's a great oath," Cate sneered.

The tip of the blade pricked Melissa's wrist as Cate worked it under the silk. A drop of bright blood slid down the white skin. It mesmerized them both.

"Sorry," Cate muttered.

"I didn't feel it."

Cate cut the other three ties at the bedposts. In less than a minute, Melissa was free. Her mind ordered her to spring to her feet and rush from the room. In reality she managed only to sit up and bring her arms down in front of her with a great effort. Grimacing, she brought her legs together and swung them over the side of the bed.

Cate stepped back. "You're too stiff to move," she snarled. "Poor job you'll make of it. I've wasted my time."

Melissa pushed herself to her feet and listed to one side. "I'll be all right in just a minute."

"That's all you may have." Cate strode to the door and looked out. "The hall's clear."

"What about clothes?" Melissa took a few steps from the bed. Her head was spinning, black spots speckling her vision. She took a deep breath to keep from passing out.

"What about them?"

Melissa stared down at her thighs showing white through the pale blue lace. "I'm nearly naked."

"If you don't want to try, just lie back down. He'll be thrilled to find you waiting for him."

Melissa dragged a sheet from the bed and wrapped it around her. She tucked one corner into the top of her corset and tossed the end over her shoulder toga-fashion. Then she made her way carefully to the brandy.

The liquid splashed as she poured it, but she got most of it into the glass. Feeling was returning to her hands as she tossed the drink into her mouth. The neat spirits burned a path down her throat and her eyes watered, but she refused to cough or complain. "Point me toward the back way."

Cate shrugged. "There isn't any back way."

"No back way?"

"Lady H doesn't want anybody sneaking out without paying. Nor any girls trying to escape."

"What about a window?"

"All nailed shut."

"Then I'll have to go out through the salon." Melissa was shaking in every limb. Her teeth chattered. Her stomach clenched as the brandy hit it. She had to swallow as it threatened to come back up.

Cate held out her hand. "Follow me."

Unholy delight lit her face as she led Melissa down the hall. They turned a corner and came upon a brightly lighted hall at the top of a wide staircase. Cate stepped aside and bowed mockingly. "The salon's down there."

Melissa could hear the music and the murmur of voices. She shrank back.

Cate laughed nastily. "Good luck. Don't forget. You promised not to tell."

"I won't."

Cate opened the door to her own room and leaned against the jamb.

Melissa stood frozen in the hall. Blood roared in her ears. A couple of shadows rose on the wall followed by their creators. A portly man in evening dress, his cravat undone, the ends hanging down his chest like a scarf, came puffing up the stairs. He was smiling broadly at his companion, a girl in a rose negligee. She was laughing as she hurried ahead of him. At the sight of Melissa in the sheet, she froze. Her client reached out a beefy hand to pat her plump rear. She giggled and twitched away.

Melissa shrank against the wall. The sheet was a giveaway. Without it she would be dressed like the others. She could go down into the rooms below and no one would notice. Perhaps Cate had lied. There had to be more than one way out.

But she could not find it cowering here. While the black-haired girl grinned like a demon, Melissa dropped the sheet and edged her way along the railing, trying vainly to see the room below. Based upon what drifted up the stairs, it must be hot and noisy. That might be good. Perhaps no one would notice her.

If she could pass them unnoticed and leave the building, then what?

She glanced down at her garments. A blush rose in her cheeks. She pulled the lace tightly together beneath her chin. She might as well be naked. Perhaps that was good. She shouldn't have to run far before a policeman would arrest her. Therein lay her hope. If he placed her under arrest, she would be safe in jail until Maria could come for her.

Maria. She closed her eyes, drawing courage from the thought of her sister. Then she opened them. Maria would welcome her home. Her sister was the only real thing in her life.

The hand she laid on the banister was cold as ice.

Lord Montague glared at his son.

George was not behaving at all as he should. The two of them sat in high-backed chairs, the second bottle of French champagne on a table between them. One after another of Lady H's girls had paraded for George, but each had been rejected.

Montague was fast working himself into a rage.

What was the matter with the boy? These were the very best of Hermione's girls. They would have excited a nine-day corpse. *What had he sired?*

He wiped his forehead surreptitiously and looked around him. Was it his imagination or were several men staring and commenting? If the boy did not choose soon, he would gain an unfavorable reputation among the other men in the room, men who were Montague's peers.

His lordship consulted his pocketwatch. *Good Lord! How much longer?*

A little blonde in rose pink exactly the color of her nipples arranged herself demurely on a stool at George's feet. She took his hand and looked deeply into his eyes. Her luscious mouth recited a mildly ribald love poem in a sweet, husky voice.

George's eyebrows rose. He looked interested.

Lord Montague uncrossed his legs and started to rise.

His own body was more than ready after viewing all this feminine flesh. The thought of the girl awaiting him on a bed upstairs made him so stiff he wondered how he could walk across the room.

Unfortunately, when the poem ended, the girl's English degenerated into a thick Midlands accent. George blinked as the spell was broken. His eyes ran over her and he asked her where she came from. She sighed and cast her eyes downward. Her story was sad—a widowed mother, a host of little brothers and sisters. A tear trickled artfully down her cheek. She had come to seek work in the city to provide for them.

George looked at his father in horror.

"Don't believe a word of it," Lord Montague advised him. "She wants you for her protector. I think you're a little young for that, but if you're interested, something might be arranged—right here, of course."

George was not interested. Instead he asked the girl how she came to be in the Lord's Dream.

A shadow of fear fell over her face. She looked around nervously. At that moment George became aware of a large man standing in one corner, his arms folded across his chest. Though he was dressed in a footman's uniform, an eighteenth-century wig slightly askew on his head, he was bigger than any footman George had ever seen. His shoulders strained under the black broadcloth. His heavy jaw thrust out pugnaciously.

The girl looked back at George. Her expression was carefully blank under the heavy make-up. "I likes it 'ere," she said mechanically. "Where else can a girl meet such a fine gen'leman like y'rself?" She flashed an inviting smile that revealed a broken tooth. "If you'd like to come upstairs with me, I can make y' like it 'ere, too."

Deliberately, George pulled his purse from his pocket. "No, I don't think you could." He extracted a pound note. "But thank you for the poetry."

The erstwhile footman strode forward, his brows beetling fiercely. " 'Ere now. We don't 'ave none o' that. She's not supposed to ask fer money."

Suddenly, the salon grew quiet. The girl shrank back. "I di'n't, Bert. I swear I di'n't. 'E just liked me poetry."

George rose. "I'm leaving, Father. If you wish to remain here, please feel free. I'll send the carriage back for you."

"George—"

The blond girl rose, too, but her trepidation made her clumsy. She tangled her ankle round the footstool and fell backward against the footman. He caught her and stood her on her feet at the same time Lord Montague rose. The three jostled together. Montague cursed. A woman's nervous laugh rang out.

Thoroughly disgusted, George brushed past them, heading for the door of the salon. As he strode across the floor, weaving his way among the patrons about their various pursuits, he suddenly became aware that a girl in white lace had fallen into step beside him. She was not walking with him exactly, but the rest of the room might have thought she was.

They were almost through the archway when he halted. "I do not require your services."

She did not look at him, nor did she pause. Instead she bolted through the arch. He stared after her.

A few seconds later another uniformed footman, the twin of the one in the salon, dragged her back. Desperate to escape his grasp, she kicked and twisted frantically, her scanty clothing flying open, revealing her slender legs and immature body.

"Stop that. Settle down," her captor warned.

Sobbing, she bit his hand.

With a curse he let her go, then cuffed her with his injured hand. His blow knocked her off her feet, but she sprang up.

"He told me to wait in his carriage," she screamed, pointing at George.

"What?" He stared at her.

"You did. You know you did," the girl in white cried. Her eyes filled with tears. "Please. Take me with you."

Lady H joined the group. "What are you doing here?" She caught Melissa by the arm. "Take her back upstairs, Bert. This girl shouldn't even be down here."

"Right you are!" Bert twisted the girl's arm up behind her.

She screamed in pain.

"Where's Jack?" Lady H wanted to know.

"Y' sent 'im to take care of that cove in the alley. 'E ain't come back," Bert growled out of the corner of his mouth.

Lady H rolled her eyes.

"Won't somebody please help me?" Melissa sobbed.

A couple of the well-dressed men moved purposefully toward the scene.

Lady H turned and opened her arms. "Nothing to be alarmed about, gentlemen, I assure you. This poor dear has been distraught since she heard of the death of her mother. Bert will help her back upstairs, and Eunice will comfort her."

Obediently, Eunice started toward the staircase.

Bert pushed the struggling girl ahead of him, but George barred the way. "Just a minute there. Are you holding this girl against her will?"

Lady H whirled. "Of course not."

"Yes," the girl screamed. "Yes! Yes! Please help me."

"Let her go," George. warned.

The second footman closed in on the young man.

Lord Montague had recognized his *protégée*. This evening was fast turning into a disaster, he realized grimly. He hurried to his son's side, speaking in George's ear and at the same time hiding behind his back. "You really mustn't interfere here. This is a place of business."

George whirled. "This is a free country."

"Lord Montague!" Melissa screamed.

George looked from one to the other. "Does she know you?"

"Don't be ridiculous." Lady H gestured imperatively to Bert. "How could such an ignorant creature know your father? She's new and—"

"How does she know you, Father?"

Lord Montague backed away. "She doesn't. She's lying. She must have heard someone call my name."

Lady H snapped her fingers.

Bert stooped and caught Melissa around the knees, tossing her over his shoulder. Instead of falling limply over his back, she stiffened her spine.

"For pity's sake, Lord Montague," Melissa entreated, holding out her arms to him.

"My God." George's face went white. "Do you know that girl?" he asked again.

"Now, George—" Lord Montague placed a hand placatingly on his son's arm.

Melissa's struggles had knocked the footman's wig over one eye. A semicircle of avidly curious onlookers had formed. While he hesitated, the wig slipped farther down, blinding him.

"Help," Melissa cried, pummeling her captor's head. Her golden hair swirled around her shoulders. Her face contorted with effort. Tears flooded down her cheeks.

George stared at her. "My, God! I know her, too. That's my sisters' governess."

"Oh, I say," one of the onlookers remarked. "Bad form."

George started after the pair, but the second guard intervened, pushing him back. The younger man tried to elbow him aside. "How dare you! Get out of my way."

The erstwhile footman grabbed the young man's arm and twisted it behind his back just as his fellow had done to Melissa.

Several of the girls shrieked.

"Stop that," Lord Montague commanded. "That's my son."

George's face whitened with pain. The footman loosened his grasp a fraction. It was the fraction George needed. Pivoting out of the hold, he brought his fists up and punched the heavy jaw with all his power.

"Well done!" called someone from the semicircle.

"Give it to 'im," a feminine voice encouraged.

"George!" Montague shouted.

George started after Melissa, but his opponent was no quitter. He shook his heavy head, sending his white wig flying. Stepping in to bar George's way, he dropped into a boxer's stance. His knobby knuckles turned into lethal weapons. His left lanced out like lightning and caught George on the nose.

Blood spouted.

A groan went up.

" 'E's a mean one, Charly is," one girl informed her

client dolefully. "When 'e gets like this, 'e won't leave nothin' but a bloody corpse."

"Stop that!" Lord Montague stepped between them.

George wiped at the blood trickling from his nose, shook his head, then pushed his father aside and drove his right fist deep into the footman's middle.

"By Jove! Great hit!"

"A fiver on the Montague."

"That's fer you, Charly." A cheer went up among the girls.

Charly growled. His reputation was at stake, maybe even his job. He threw his best punch, a roundhouse drive delivered with all the force of his fifteen stone. George ducked, but Lord Montague took the blow to the point of his jaw.

He toppled like a tree.

"Terry!" Hermione screamed in horror, abandoning all sense of decorum. Slapping her hireling out of the way, she dropped to her knees at the fallen man's side. "Oh, Terry, dear heart."

Blood trickled from the corner of Lord Montague's mouth. His eyes were half-open but sightless. His foot twitched.

"Terry." She put her hand under his cheek. "Oh, dear, Terry."

The footman dropped his guard and stepped back. He gawked fearfully at the sight of his employer on her knees, tears running rivulets through her makeup.

George likewise bent over his father. Blood from his nose dripped onto the immaculate shirt front.

Lady H looked up at him. "How could you?"

The semicircle parted and Bert took that opportunity to

send his wig after Charly's and bolt up the stairs with Melissa.

As he lurched onto the landing, Cate burst into triumphant laughter.

Eleven

In vain did two policemen shuffle their frozen feet and huddle deep inside their thick wool capes in front of Maria Thorne's little boardinghouse. A couple of times the window curtains at the front stirred, and an old woman's face peered out. Otherwise, they saw nothing at all.

As the temperature dropped, rime formed on the sidewalk stones and the iron pickets of the fence. With every exhalation a white cloud bedewed the men's upper lips until their moustaches and chins were stiff with frost.

At first their anger built with their discomfort. Where was Maria Thorne? They damned her as a loose woman staying out so late. They discussed the threats they would make, the fear they would instill. Then their conversation slowed as their toes turned numb and their legs began to ache.

At last, they huddled together in despairing silence, waiting for the morning when they would go off watch and report to the station house.

Finally, as the leaden darkness began to lighten, they trudged stiffly away without a backward glance.

Roncie Jack's grin revealed missing teeth.

His two front uppers were long gone, splintered by a

rock flung with great strength and accuracy by a boyhood enemy. A lower canine had not survived a knock-out blow to the jaw by a constable's nightstick.

In between those catastrophes, he had been a bare-knuckle boxer. In the ring he had dealt out fearful punishment and taken all manner of blows to the head and mid-section. Unfortunately, as his career was climbing, his opponents and then his handlers came to realize that a single blow to the point of the jaw would knock him cold for an hour.

Now, he grinned in devilish anticipation at the sight of an old opponent who, by the look of him, had been knocked out of the ring into a bed of roses. Jack hunched his shoulders and clenched his fists as "Saint" Peter, dressed in his discreet black suit, collected the morning's mail from the postman.

As the butler started to re-enter the house, Jack gave a piercing whistle. "Togged out like a Nancy boy, ain't you, Petey?" he called. "I allus figgered you fer a faggot."

Peter stared at the ruffian. His brow wrinkled, then became a black scowl. "Get on outta 'ere, Jack. This street's off limits to the likes o' you."

"Oughta be off limits to the likes o' you, too. Does the lady know who she's got to work fer 'er?"

Peter squared his jaw and flexed his shoulders. He gave a superior grin. "She 'ired me 'cause o' who I was. She needs somebody strong an' honest."

"Strong!" Roncie Jack hooted with laughter. "You! Strong! Ye bloody well lied to 'er. I could beat the livin' daylights outta you the best day you ever 'ad."

Peter shook his head. A red flush spread up his thick neck. His big fist crumpled the mail.

"An' honest!" his tormentor continued gleefully, noting

Peter's reaction. " 'Ope she sleeps with 'er teeth in 'er mouth. You'll sure steal 'em if they're lyin' around."

Peter lurched down the steps. At the curb he rocked forward as if held by an invisible line. "Get on outta 'ere, you bleedin' sod. Or I'll send fer the watch."

"The watch. Lord, I'm peein' in me boots I'm so scared. I'd run, I would, but I gotta message to speak. Whyn't you crawl back up them steps and send out the ol' crow you works fer?"

"I don't need to send for the *lady* I work for. I know Mrs. Shires wouldn't 'ave no truck with the likes of you," Peter raged.

"She'd better. I gotta message 'bout that bird that works fer 'er."

"She don't know any birds."

"This 'un she does. Leastwise, she says she does. Maria Thorne."

"Miss Thorne's a lady," Peter replied haughtily.

"She's a bird that's 'bout to git 'er wings clipped."

Dressed for her morning calls, Mrs. Shires appeared at that moment in the doorway. "Who is this person, Peter?"

"Nobody, ma'am. This person's just leavin'."

Jack loped across the street. Careful to keep a prudent distance from the scowling Peter, he grinned up at Mrs. Shires. "If you know what's good fer you, lady, y'll warn yer bird off."

"Bird?"

"Miss Thorne," Peter supplied.

"What do you mean?"

Roncie Jack shuffled his feet as if trying to decide how best to deliver his warning. "Fact is, she's lookin' in a lot o' dangerous places fer 'er sister. She don't pay no 'eed to warnin's. So this's 'er last chance. Tell 'er that 'er sister don't want to be found. If she keeps on, we might jus' decide to come back 'ere and ruin the whole lot o' you."

Mrs. Shires peered at him through her amber glasses. "You can't threaten me, sir. I've met worse than you and survived."

Roncie Jack thrust out his barrel chest. "Beggin' yer pardon, mum. You ain't met worse'n me. I'm the worst there is." He spat contemptuously onto the head of the stone lion.

With a roar Peter charged.

Quick as a panther Jack sidestepped. His foot shot out and tripped the butler neatly. Peter fell sprawling. Jack jumped back out of reach of his opponent's clutch. Then when Peter pushed himself up on hands and knees, Jack kicked him under the chin. Peter's teeth clicked together.

Mrs. Shires screamed as Jack shoved his foot into the dazed man's chest. The butler toppled over, his head cracking against the step.

"Peter!" Mrs. Shires hurried down the steps and lifted her butler's head. Blood ran through her fingers and dripped onto the walk. Shocked and furious, she glared up at Jack. "Who are you? Why have you done this?"

He tipped his hat to her. "Jus' tell that bird to leave things alone."

The old woman's eyes flashed. "I assure you we'll do no such thing."

Jack laughed. "Better do like I tol' you, Grammer, er mor'n that'll be lyin' in the streets."

His threat delivered, he swaggered off.

"Not exactly what you're used to," Jocko muttered.

Maria wrung the cloth out above the pail of cold water.

"The longer I stay with you, the more things I'll discover. You have a way of broadening a woman's education."

"I wouldn't say I broadened it. There's nothing in this part of Whitechapel that a lady needs to know about."

"Ladies need to know more than they did once upon a time. The twentieth century's almost here. We'll be getting the vote soon."

Gently, she sponged the dried blood from his hair. The wound was shallow, like a scrape rather than a deep cut that would require stitches.

"How's your arm?"

" 'Urts," he admitted with eyes closed. "Like the very devil. But I'm pretty sure it's not broken."

"And the ribs?"

"I imagine they're cracked. But that's all right. They've been cracked before." He sucked in a careful breath, expanded his chest, then groaned. "Bleedin' sods." The words were out before he thought. He opened his eyes to see how she reacted to his language.

"They probably are." She grinned and winked.

He closed his eyes and relaxed as she continued to wash his face and neck. She lifted his right hand into the basin. He set his teeth as the icy water ran into the cuts on his knuckles.

"You must have given them quite a good fight."

He smiled lopsidedly. "I did my best."

She dried his right hand and then used the cloth to bathe his injured left.

His face whitened. His voice was strained when he spoke. "What do you want to vote for?"

She looked down at him in some surprise. "Because it's our right."

He shrugged. "Don't make any money out of it."

"We will indirectly. But that's not the important thing. The important thing is to be able to have a say in how things are run."

"Why? I never voted in my life. Things just keep rolling along."

"You're a man. You're lucky because other men decide what's best for them and then vote accordingly. They'll never vote to hurt themselves—most of the time they vote things that make them and you comfortable."

He looked around him meaningfully. "I'm not so comfortable."

"Then vote to change it," she replied promptly.

"Oh, sure. I make a scratch on a piece of paper and suddenly I'm a bleedin' industrialist."

She shrugged. "You could vote for the man who says he wants to run water into Whitechapel and put gaslights on the corners."

He blinked at her. His face settled into a thoughtful look. Then he dismissed it with a sneer. "Who'd do that?"

"You could find someone. Or run for Parliament and do it yourself. You're a man."

He snorted. "You're loony. You know that? I've never heard anyone talk like you."

"I type write all of Mrs. Shires's letters." She rocked back on her heels and rose to her feet. On a rude shelf above the tiny table sat an oil burner. She checked the well. Fortunately, it contained a bit of coal oil. She looked around her for matches.

"You're a man and look at all the things you need. Think about how many more things women need."

"Men are supposed to take care of the things women need," he objected.

She shot him a look that said clearly what she thought

of that idea. "Women need to vote to keep themselves
from being hurt. Men'll turn a blind eye forever to slavers
like the ones who took my sister. Can you imagine? Slavery, here in the heart of London at the end of the nineteenth century. And men in the government are protecting
it. Why? Because they're making money on it. I'm sure
there are thousands of pounds at stake."

He frowned. "How'd you figure that out?"

"It's not hard. Look at those women we talked to yesterday. The clothes they were wearing were beautiful. They
must have cost a fortune. And the houses. The outsides of
them were just as nice as Mrs. Shires's home. And the
carriages that pulled up to the—what did you say the name
of that last place was?"

"The Lord's Dream."

She rolled her eyes. "Some very rich lords must love
to dream often. Imagine how much money is paid into an
establishment like that—and I wonder who gets the money.
The girls? Probably not, unless they're fortunate like your
friend from—?"

"Phronsie from Madame De Vere's?"

"Exactly. It's the men who bring the girls in that get
the money from what they earn."

He shifted uncomfortably. Maria Thorne was a wonderful girl, but sometimes she actually embarrassed him. A
lady wasn't supposed to have such frank speech. "You're
not supposed to talk about places like that."

She was opening the containers on either side of the
burner, pleased to have found a bag of coffee beans. "That,
my dear, is the strength of the men who operate those places.
They keep women ignorant. An ignorant person is a pow-
erless person. Their mothers, their wives, their daughters

would never stand for such things if they knew. But they don't, so men can do what they want."

"It's for your own good," Jocko mumbled.

"Ridiculous." The beans clattered into the grinder. "Not for my sister's good, that's for certain."

He closed his eyes. She was right, but he didn't want to tell her so. "You shouldn't ought to know about this."

"That's true. Nobody ought to know. Nor have to know. It oughtn't to be. And I'd rather not know, but I do know and I'm appalled. If women had the right to vote, we could vote for men like you. Men who were decent. We could see that they made places like that illegal. Closed them down. And if they didn't, then when the next election came up, we'd vote them out and elect someone who would. Maybe a woman!"

Alarmed, Jocko rose up on one elbow. "Elect a woman!"

"Why not? A woman's Queen of this country. Why couldn't a woman be in Parliament? She'd see that women's rights were respected. Places like that—"

"Well, now, places like that don't actually harm anybody."

She ground the coffee beans savagely. "They most certainly do and you're lying here beaten and broken because of a place like that."

"Well, that's not—"

"It is." She dropped down and bent over him, her hand on his shoulder. "You're a person, Jocko Walton. You're a good, good person." Her voice was strong, passionate, almost fevered. Her eyes glowed. She pressed a kiss against the scrape on his temple. "And you shouldn't have been hurt."

He could feel himself blushing like a boy. "Here now, quit that. I thought you were making coffee."

She laughed and sprang up.

He could not wipe the smile off his face as he watched her busy herself. At last, he said, "I'm not all that good."

"You are. But a lot of the men you have to live among are bad. Like Tilly and the men who beat you up. They should be in jail. They're kidnappers and murderers. And the poor women. They should be free."

"To do what?"

"Why, to work."

Jocko dropped back on the pillow. "They are working."

"At decent jobs."

He grunted. "Who'd 'ire 'em?"

She sucked in a deep breath. "There are lots of employers out there. And lots of jobs for women."

He looked at her skeptically.

"They'd have to dress decently, of course." She smoothed a wrinkle in her serviceable black skirt. "More and more women are finding decent work every day. They make their own money and don't depend on anybody but themselves. Look at me."

"What do you do?" he asked curiously.

"I'm a type writer," she said proudly. Never mind that she hated everything about the machine. It proved her point admirably.

"A what?"

"A type writer. I operate a machine. Once upon a time, I copied papers and letters by hand, but now I operate a machine that prints them onto a sheet of paper. It looks almost like the page of a book."

He studied her for a moment, despair creeping along his veins. "Probably you've got to be real smart to do it."

"I taught myself."

Jocko closed his eyes. Lord help him! Not only was she a lady, but she was smart. Smarter than any woman he'd ever heard of. She could operate a machine all by herself. Not a sewing machine or a loom, but a type writer. Who had ever heard of such a thing?

Maria lighted the oil burner to heat the water. Although the tiny room was shabby and cold, she did not mind as much as she would have a couple of weeks ago. This was Jocko's home.

She felt natural being here and doing these little things for him. She was needed, she was useful. For the second time in as many days, they were waking up together. She was not alone and lonely.

She looked over at the pallet and her heart turned over. He had drifted back to sleep. Tears standing in her eyes, she tiptoed to his side. With infinite care she bent above him to tuck the thin blankets around his shoulders.

His bruised face was beautiful, so young, so dear, so like a grubby little boy. She stepped back and seated herself in the chair, prepared to wait while his healthy body restored itself. Prepared to watch over him with tender pride.

She watched him awaken. First, he groaned softly, then twitched. She could only imagine his discomfort as his injuries made themselves known.

His eyelids fluttered. He blinked. The left eye opened wider than the right. Gingerly, he raised his hand and rubbed at it. Like a child.

Then he caught sight of her. His smile held a tinge of embarrassment. "Did I doze off?"

"Yes." She relighted the oil burner to set the coffee to boiling. "You must have needed to sleep. I've always heard that sleep is healing." She lifted down two mismatched cups and stared critically into the bottoms of each. She could feel his eyes on her.

He cleared his throat. "Why didn't you ever get married?"

She did not look at him. "I didn't want to."

He waited a minute, then shook his head. "Tell me another one. I know you want to."

"Why, I never." She plastered a false smile on her mouth and pretended to be surprised. Chills of apprehension prickled up her backbone. She hated to hear the next question. He would despise her for her answer. "Whatever gave you that idea?"

He looked at her appraisingly. If he had had his bowler on his head, he would have cocked it forward. "Because you love being loved. You've got a loving heart."

His words stilled her hands. She could feel the heat rising in her ears. Her body tingled.

He stretched his legs and eased his body into a more comfortable position. The pallet rustled in the silence. "Am I wrong?"

She shook her head. "No, you're not wrong."

"So why aren't you married—a lady like you?"

She poured their coffee and carried the cups to the pallet, handed his to him, and sat on the only chair. She took a deep breath. "Drink your coffee while it's hot."

He obliged her. "It's good. You make it better than I do."

"Thank you."

"So why aren't you married?"

"Because I have to take care of my sister."

He looked at her shrewdly. "Wouldn't the man you wanted to marry take care of her?"

"I didn't ask him." She tossed her head.

"You should have. I'd take care of her and gladly—" He covered the lower half of his face with the cup. "—If I could have you."

She could feel the heat creeping into her cheeks as she stared into the dark depths of her coffee. Tears prickled at the backs of her eyes. How she had longed to hear those words. This man had made love to her, had had the use of her body, and against all the tenets of society, still wanted to marry her. She wanted to cry for shame. She had seduced a boy.

"How old are you, Jocko?"

"Old enough." He took another drink of some of the best coffee he had ever tasted. "What difference does my age make?"

"Even though you seem much older than I in terms of experience—"

"You've got the right of that."

She took a deep breath. He must not suffer for her lapse. "You're older than my sister, but not too much older. Are you nineteen? twenty?"

He shrugged. "I guess I'm about twenty."

She sank back. "I thought as much." She knew she was no beauty—and much too old for him. His confession made her ashamed of herself. She should have realized he was young and easily infatuated. Her sin was the greater for allowing—no, inviting—him to make love to her. She shuddered. For the second time she had abandoned her morals in a dark hour of loneliness and fear. And now she was a corruptor of innocents.

"In comparison to you, I'm very old. In fact I'm what people call an old maid." Her expression became tragic. "I'm twenty-five."

He chuckled. "So what?"

"Jocko, listen to me. I'm honored by your . . . that is, I would be honored to—" She did not know how to phrase what she wanted to say. She had never had what amounted to a proposal before. Her cheeks were burning. "You must find someone of a suitable age. A pure young girl who could have your children."

He swallowed hard. "You could have my children."

For an instant she pictured sweet little girls with long blond curls cascading down from bright blue bows and serious-minded little boys insisting that their curls be cut off. The picture pierced her like a knife. She opened her eyes. "I would be honored to have your children, but your children need someone who's a better person than I am."

His head snapped up. His face darkened. "Did he tell you were bad?"

She could feel the blood pounding in her throat. She had broached the very conversation she had wanted to avoid. "Not really. My sister and I were alone and poor. His parents had hopes for him. They wanted someone better, as well they should."

"But you loved him," Jocko persisted.

Maria's voice was low. She could feel old pain rupturing from wounds that were long scarred over. "I thought he loved me. He told me he did. I was foolish." She shrugged. "I . . . I let him—"

Jocko cut across her stumbling explanation. " 'E acted like a bloody hound."

"No. I just don't think he loved me enough." She drained her coffee. It was bitter at the end. "My mother was dead. My father was—very old and sick. He died. And then there were just me and my sister. She was only seven years old. He was just starting out in life. I couldn't ask him to take care of her, too."

Jocko made a rude sound. "Sure you could, Ria. You were just too proud, too much of a lady."

"Jocko, please stop saying that. I'm not a lady. I've—I have loose morals."

"Not because you let me love you," he denied vehemently. "We both of us wanted that. It made us feel good."

"It was wrong," she insisted. "I was the older. I should have been strong for both of us."

He laughed out loud.

"It's true. I'm a fallen woman. Gentlemen don't marry women of easy virtue. They say they can't trust them—"

"I've heard that one before," he scoffed. "It's a lie. The one not to be trusted is the liar and the thief who wants the girl for the night and promises he'll marry her tomorrow. He's a bleedin' beggar. Love 'em and leave 'em. I'd never be that kind."

She went down on her knees beside the pallet. "No, you never would, Jocko. You're a good, good man. And when you get a little older—"

"My father was that kind. Left us, he did. Mam didn't have the heart to turn tricks. When she met Mr. Mac-Naghten, we were starving to death."

"Mr. MacNaghten?"

"Best picker in London, maybe in England." Jocko grinned and waved his fingers at her. "Taught me everything I know, 'e did. And Mam was glad of it. Took me and Mam to raise. 'E said she was the best thing that ever 'appened to him. She was sweet like you. And had a loving 'eart. 'E never left 'er side when she was ailin' at the end." His eyes met hers, then flickered and dropped as if he realized he had said too much.

In the silence that fell between them, Maria stared at him. Jocko Walton had been taught everything he knew by a picker, a thief. She, Maria Thorne, cared for him deeply, trusted him, and yet, he must be a thief, too. He was the only one who would help her. She corrected herself. He was the only one good enough to help her.

As a law-abiding citizen, she should be scorning him because he was bad. Yet he loved his mother and the picker who had taught him and cared for his mother.

She felt the tears pricking at her eyes. The thief on the cross was forgiven as was the Magdalene. She reached out to close her hand over Jocko's. "Your mother was very fortunate."

His head whipped up, his smile radiant in his bruised face. He drank the rest of his coffee and set the cup aside. Never taking his eyes off her, he tossed back the covers. "Come here."

She shivered. "You're hurt."

"Yeah, but I'm not dead." His mouth quirked in his cheekiest grin. "You'll be good for what ails me."

She shook her head. "I don't think this is a good idea."

"Come on. You wouldn't deny a sick man his medicine?"

She slid in beside him, mindful of his damaged arm and cracked ribs.

He shifted on his side and leaned above her. His heat instantly enveloped her. His lips came down on her own, touching, teasing, imploring her to open for him. She had no will to refuse but took his tongue into her mouth.

Where the top of his thigh pressed against hers, she felt him growing, hardening. The feel of him, the scent of him, aroused her, too. She knew a momentary twinge of guilt. He really was too young. She really was too old. But his kiss drove those thoughts away.

He broke their kiss by lifting his head. His smile was

heavy-lidded. "You'll 'ave to 'andle the details, Ria, my love."

Speechless with desire, she lifted her hips. Thinking she was indecent as well as wanton, she pulled her skirts up and pushed her drawers down. "What about—?" She could not bring herself to ask the question, did not know the words. She tried again. "Shall I—?"

He grinned. "Not just yet." He slid down her body, kissing her clothed breast in passing, and ended with his mouth on her belly.

She gasped. "Jocko."

"Ssh."

His breath heated her skin, yet her flesh prickled as if she were chilled. Painful desire curled in her loins. Her belly muscles clenched.

His tongue traced a delicate path from her navel down the fine line of nearly invisible hairs to pale blond curls at the top of her thighs.

"Jocko," she quavered, "Please. I—" Her teeth clenched over her bottom lip.

"Ssh, Ria. I've got to 'old myself up on my right arm. My left's all but useless. Somethin's got to touch you. Right?"

"But—"

He pressed his mouth against her curls and blew his hot breath down into them.

She moaned. Her hands caressed his head, the thick golden fleece, twining the curls in her fingers, sliding her fingertips over his cheeks. She felt his tongue gliding down into her, parting her. He touched her, caressed her, circled the mass of nerves until she thought she would go mad.

"Jocko-o-oh."

"Ria. Tell me you're ready for me."

She knew what he meant. She was steaming hot, her loins liquid, swollen, ready for him. "Yes."

"Say it."

"I'm ready. I want you. Oh, Jocko."

"Help me, sweetheart."

She spread her legs, used her hands to free him from his clothing, touched him in a way she had not thought ever to touch a man. She should have been desperately embarrassed, but he was hard and so strong. He fitted her hand and moaned as she wrapped her fingers around him. A single drop of hot liquid slipped over her thumb.

He must want me very much, she thought.

"I want you, Jocko," she repeated. Her voice sounded strange to her ears. She had her eyes closed, her head thrown back. She could feel him move between her thighs.

"Then please yourself, Ria. Take me and do what you want with me."

She brought him down to the opening in her body, felt the essence of him mingle with the essence of her. She guided him, then released him. At the same time she lifted her legs around his hips. "Now, please."

He thrust into her, her own legs pulling him to her, holding him, letting his power lift her and drive her down onto the pallet. She cried out almost immediately. Her body shuddered and seemed to fly apart. She would have sworn her very heart and breath were stopped.

Then he gasped. His own body stiffened. He collapsed over her, then gasped again as his bad arm took some of his weight.

Quickly he snapped straight, sitting back on his heels, eyes closed, body slumped. She hung from him like a limpet, her ankles locked, her mouth open, her arms fallen at her sides.

Gradually his breathing slowed and hers resumed. She opened her eyes and unlocked her ankles. "Did I do it right?"

He grinned as he tipped over onto his right side and stretched out. "I think you were just about perfect."

She put her arms around him and guided his head to her shoulder. It was morning. They should be going, but for now, the world would have to wait. She would revel in her depravity and hold him while he rested his arm. He was a magnificent lover.

She had never felt so much a woman.

A pounding on the door awoke them both. Fear brought Maria upright, clutching the blankets. Jocko sat up more slowly, cradling his aching arm.

The pounding came again.

"Whaddya want?" he yelled.

"Jocko," the voice growled. "The man wants to see ye."

"Bloody 'ell 'e does."

"Step lively."

"I'm sick."

"Ye'd better get well quick if ye know what's good fer ye." Footsteps moved away.

Jocko sank back with a moan and threw his good arm over his eyes.

"Who's 'the man'?"

He took the arm away and looked at her. "You don't know, do you?"

She stared at him in some confusion. "Should I know?"

He shrugged. "I guess it won't make any difference." He looked longingly in the direction of the small oil burner. "I could use another cuppa."

"I'll fix it." She crawled out from under the covers and began to don her clothing.

Silently, he followed her example, then sat at the table. The bruises in his face were beginning to turn purple. While the water boiled, she brushed as much of the soil as possible from his coat. As she draped it around his shoulders, she noticed the bloodstains on his shirt.

"Do you have another?"

"In the chest."

She fetched it and helped him into it. When she set the cup of coffee in front of him, he said without preamble. "I'm a thief."

"Are you really?" So her guess had been correct. And he was an honest one, admitting everything. She smiled. "You're going to be doomed to disappointment if you try to rob me."

"Don't laugh. I'm a bad 'un through and through. A year ago I was in the Assizes on my way to Newgate."

"I won't believe you're a 'bad 'un.' "

"Revill likes to think the same thing. 'E thinks 'e's re-formin' me."

Score one for Revill. She must change her impression of the inspector. Indeed, she did not think she could ever look in the same way at a single person in the whole of London. "He's succeeding admirably. You've helped me more than any man should."

He ducked his head and swirled the coffee round in the cup. Then he took a long swallow and set the cup down half-empty. "The fact is, Ria, I had to."

"I don't understand."

"Inspector Revill sent me."

She waited. A hard lump formed in her throat.

" 'E's got my confession. 'E made me write it out and

sign it, and 'e's got it in 'is box in 'is desk. Now whenever there's a job that needs doin' that he can't put one of 'is bloody peelers on, I'm 'is man."

She relaxed. "So you're a policeman of sorts."

"No, ma'am. I'm a thief." He stood and began to pace, holding his sore arm, working it gingerly, clenching the fist, straightening it. His breath caught, but he kept on walking. "I'm only tellin' you because I can't leave you 'ere alone. There's too many that know where I live. You'll 'ave to go with me to see 'im. But from now the truth's what'll be between us."

"I wondered why you sought me out."

"Now you know." He stopped, his eyes searching her face for scorn, for condemnation. "Why aren't you angry?"

"Why should I be? At least now everything is in perspective." She picked a piece of straw from her skirt.

"Don't say it like that," he growled.

"Like what?" She pretended not to understand.

"Like a bloody martyr." He made a slashing motion with his good hand. "Like I've betrayed you. This doesn't make a bloody bit of difference with anythin' 'cept that you know why I was there on your doorstep that mornin'. From there on in what's 'appened between us 'as been square."

She wanted to believe him. She dropped her eyes so he would not see the naked hope.

"Do you believe me?"

"I don't know what to believe. First, you're a thief. Then you're working for Scotland Yard."

He put his hand under her chin and raised her face. "Believe that I'm a thief," he whispered. "And not near good enough for you. Believe that I've told you the truth this mornin'—about everythin'."

She did not answer. She could not think of an answer. Her heart was full.

He straightened away. "Say, listen. You're better off knowin' that I'm not a bloody Good Samaritan nor one of Bobby Peel's constables. When I started out, I 'ad to protect you or go to jail."

"And now?"

"I think Revill's callin' me in to tell me to leave you alone."

She sprang to her feet in alarm. "He can't do that! You're the only one who can help me. You've worked so hard. We've worked so hard. And we're close—I know we're close. Why would he pull you off?" Her eyes narrowed with newfound cynicism. "Because we're getting *too* close."

Jocko considered that idea. "Could be, but I doubt it. I wasn't supposed to be seen by you. But you saw me the very first mornin'."

"You were waiting on my doorstep."

"How'd I know you'd be comin' out at dawn?" he grumbled.

She chuckled. "I was trying to get away from 'Saint' Peter."

"Wouldn't you just know?"

"Do you think Revill sent the two to beat you?"

"I don't think so." He shook his head. "Why go to that trouble if you're goin' to call me in the next day and tell me to get away? 'E knows 'e could get in a lot of trouble if you were to tell people 'e'd set a thief to watch you."

"So are you going to get away from me?" She laid the question on the table before them like a test. "Considering the condition you're in and the danger, you'd be wise to do what he says."

"Not me." He put his good arm around her and gathered her close. "From now on, you're my responsibility, Ria. I'll 'elp you, no matter what."

She rose to kiss his mouth and caress his cheeks. "I'll be grateful to you always. And when it's all over, I promise—"

He interrupted her vow with a swift, stirring kiss. "Let me get you out o' the woods before you promise anythin'."

Twelve

"Mrs. Shires!"

At the sight of her employer coming from Inspector Revill's office, Maria rose from the bench in the station house hall.

The sound of someone calling her name roused Avory from her distraction. Even so, she had to search for the person who had spoken. When she found her, her face crumpled. She reached out for her. "My dear Maria. Oh, my poor dear child. It's so terrible."

Maria was taken aback. The militant suffragette had always been such a tower of strength. Now her mouth trembled and her bright blue eyes were red-rimmed behind the amber spectacles.

When Maria held out her hands, her employer clutched them as if they were a lifeline. "Mrs. Shires, what are you doing here? What's happened?"

Jocko rose, too, but more slowly. His arm, despite his proud boasts, was giving him the very devil. When Maria had proposed a sling, he had refused saying that the arm was fit even though it gave him a twinge now and again. The real reason for his refusal had been that he had not wanted to be seen to be handicapped. Since the peelers had softened him up, too many of his enemies would leap at the chance to finish him off.

He put his hand in his trouser pocket and slouched up to the two women.

"Peter's been hurt." Avory's voice quavered. "Attacked by quite the foulest man I have ever seen."

"Oh, no."

"Oh, yes, indeed. In front of my own house, in the heart of London in the nineteenth century." Her voice gathered the strength of righteous wrath. "I sat on the sidewalk for at least ten minutes, holding the poor dear fellow's head off the cold, wet stone. Blood was everywhere." At the memory, her face turned pasty white. She swayed where she stood.

Jocko put his good arm around her shoulders and gently guided her to the bench.

"Thank you so much, young man." She smiled at him wanly, then grasped Maria's hand and pulled her down. When their faces were close, she whispered, "Have you found your sister?"

Maria shook her head.

Jocko dropped down beside them, a fine dew of perspiration on his forehead. "Who knocked out your man?"

"He was able to identify his assailant." Revill's deep voice answered for her.

The three looked up, startled to find that the inspector had come out of the office to join them. Jocko cocked his head to one side. His mouth quirked up at the corner as he noted Revill's quick eye sliding over the bruised jaw and the cut disappearing into the hair above his ear.

Avory peered haughtily at him. "I believe we have finished our interview, Inspector."

He inclined his head deferentially. "Mrs. Shires, you're welcome to wait in my office. I've sent for your son to take you home."

"You've sent for Dudley?"

"Yes, ma'am. You need someone."

"But he and I—" She slipped her arm through Maria's. "That is, my son and I do not share the same opinions."

Revill did not react to that statement. Instead, he frowned at Jocko. "Where were you last night?"

"He was with me." Extricating herself from her employer, Maria rose to face the inspector. "You needn't scowl at Mr. Walton like that. I know that you sent him, and I'm here to tell you I am most grateful."

Revill's annoyance seemed to deepen. "He wasn't supposed to tell you that. He wasn't even supposed to let you see him. He was sent to observe and report to me."

Maria's expression was stern. "How fortunate for me that he disobeyed your orders. If he hadn't made himself known to me, I would have been carried off, too. Perhaps that's what you were counting on."

The inspector flushed. "Now, listen here, young lady—"

Mrs. Shires rose unsteadily. "Inspector Revill, I must add my voice to hers. Obviously, we are dealing here with desperate men. They are a menace to all law-abiding citizens, to the very fabric of England itself." Her voice strengthened as her speech became oratorical. "My good servant was attacked this very morning. I held his head on my front step while blood ran over my hands."

Revill looked around him uncomfortably. Everyone in the hall was looking. Some of his colleagues had stepped out of their offices to listen.

Maria put her arms around Avory. "I'm so sorry."

"That terrible man told me that I was to carry a message," she continued in ringing tones.

All three of them looked at her in amazement.

"Are you sure about that?" Revill protested. "Maybe an

old enemy came round to settle a grudge? Your butler wasn't—er—of the best character."

Maria gasped in outrage. Jocko's mouth quirked even more.

Mrs. Shires clenched her hands over the top of her handbag. "Peter has an excellent character." She looked into Maria's eyes. "The man came for you. In insulting tones he called you a *bird*. And he said that you were to stop hunting for your sister, that she didn't want to be found."

"We must be getting close," Jocko growled.

"He said if you didn't stop hunting her, you would be hurt, dear Maria." Mrs. Shires fixed her steely gaze on Revill. "And he threatened me—the widow of a peer—on my very doorstep."

The inspector looked around him nervously. "Perhaps we'd better go back to my office."

"I don't see why I should," Mrs. Shires replied. "You couldn't wait to get me out of there before."

"To talk this through," Revill pleaded.

"Of course we must," Maria agreed excitedly. "You must help us. You must. Jocko was beaten up last night. Hurt badly. And now someone's hurt 'Saint' Peter. And, most important, threatened Mrs. Shires. Oh, Inspector, how can you doubt that what we're doing is right?"

"Yes, well, come along."

He opened the office door and stepped aside to allow Mrs. Shires and Maria to enter. Before Jocko could follow them, Revill pushed his hand into the young man's chest. "Let's you and me have a little chat."

Jocko's breath hissed out between his teeth. Had his shoulder not been only a couple of inches from the door facing, he would have staggered. As it was, he sagged back. His face whitened.

Revill tightened his jaw. "Sorry."

Jocko's smile was mocking "Not to worry, guv."

Maria had helped Mrs. Shires to a chair. She lifted her eyes to the two men facing each other in the narrow doorway. "Jocko," she called. "Please help me."

Her plea snapped the tension between them.

"Right away." Jocko straightened his body away from the door.

With a final warning look, Revill strode behind his desk and motioned toward the chairs arranged in front of it. Jocko followed him and eased himself down with a sigh.

Maria felt a stab of pity to her vitals. His whole body seemed huddled around the arm. Beneath the bowler his forehead was sheened with sweat.

"Now." Revill opened his notebook and extracted his pencil. "Perhaps you'd better tell me the entire story."

"We went hunting for my sister," Maria said. "We hunted all day long, asking questions wherever we went. At the last house of the day, Mr. Walton went round back to the alley where he was severely beaten."

Instead of sympathizing, Revill glared at Jocko.

Maria intercepted the look. "Don't you dare give him a look like that. It's your fault. And mine."

"I beg your pardon." Revill's pencil popped from between his fingers and rolled across the desk.

"You wouldn't help me. Or at least you wouldn't give me any serious help."

"I told you—"

"You wouldn't, Inspector," Mrs. Shires chimed in. She nodded to the two sitting beside her. "You told us to go away."

Revill hunched his shoulders. "Citizens shouldn't get in the way of police business."

"It was police business to find my sister," Maria argued. "You told me to forget her."

"Now listen—"

"So when Mr. Walton came along and was so successful in routing—what was that fellow's name?"

"Big Tilly." Jocko managed a real grin.

"Exactly. Then I knew I had a good man to help me find Melissa."

Revill's jaw set. "Do you know who this man is?"

"Yes, I do."

Revill was taken aback. "You do?"

"He's a thief. He told me so. But he works for you. You're reforming him." She smiled. "That's so clever of you, Inspector. He's a good man. A very good man."

Jocko's mouth spread in a wide grin. With his good hand he tipped his bowler.

Revill looked from one to the other. His stare wavered and dropped to his notes. He turned back through the pages of his notebook, read his almost illegible scribble, then cleared his throat. "So where were you when you were attacked, Jocko?"

"We were investigating the Lord's Dream," Maria answered.

Revill turned back to the current pages and made the notation. "And that was the last place you'd gone to?"

"Yes," Maria said.

Revill scowled at her before directing the next question to Jocko. "But the alley was dark, so you can't be sure your attackers were from the Lord's Dream?"

"I'm pretty sure they weren't."

"Ah. They could have followed you from anywhere you'd been during the day?"

"Well—"

"What are you trying to do?" Maria demanded. "He went down the carriage drive to the back of the house. I was standing out front—"

"You were out front!?"

Even Avory Shires looked aghast.

"You were standing in front of the Lord's Dream?" The inspector's voice rose.

Instantly, she saw her mistake, but refused to back away. "I was waiting for Mr. Walton."

"Oh, Maria," Avory moaned. "What have you done?"

"You took her to the Lord's Dream?" Revill thundered. Jocko sprang from his chair and backed away. "I—I—"

Maria rose, too, waving her hands violently. "Stop!" she cried. "Stop it!"

"Miss Thorne—"

"Just stop it, Inspector Revill. Of course I went with him. He went with me to Reverend Dinsmore's and to—"

"Going to a mission is not the same thing as going to a brothel!"

"Oh, Maria. How could you take such a chance with your reputation? My dear—" Avory rose to her feet.

Jocko had backed all the way to the door.

Maria hurried to put her arm around his waist. She could feel him trembling. The look that he flashed her was white with pain and panic. "You will both stop this," she all but shouted. "This man has done nothing but what I asked him to do. He did not want to take me with him, but I insisted. *I*. Do you hear me? Moreover, he is the only person in the whole of London who has really tried to find my sister. And for his pains, he's been attacked and beaten."

"Ria," he muttered. "It's all right."

"It's not all right." She lowered her voice, but the defiance was still evident. "They both act as if you've done something wrong." She shot Revill a look of pure malice. "If anyone's done anything wrong, it's I. I'll take the blame."

"Maria, no one is suggesting that you have done anything wrong. It's merely how your presence will be construed." Avory's voice quivered.

Revill heaved a great sigh as he let his hands fall limply to his sides. Shaking his head, he went back to his desk. "Sit down," he said quietly. "Sit down, all of you."

He noted grimly how Maria helped Jocko back to his chair, how the young man eased himself back down on it. A muscle ticked in the side of his jaw. Revill cleared his throat. "So they beat you up at the Lord's Dream."

"Roncie Jack works there," Jocko reminded him.

"That's the man who hurt Peter," Avory said excitedly.

"Yes, ma'am." Revill nodded. "But Jack works all over Soho. Was he the one who beat you?"

Jocko shrugged. "I doubt it. To tell the truth, it was that dark in the alley and they came at me in a rush."

"You said there were police," Maria reminded him.

Jocko shot her a warning look.

"What?" Revill was instantly alert. "What about police?"

"Nothing."

"That's not true," Maria insisted. "You told me two 'peelers' beat you up."

Revill winced at the slang. He looked for confirmation to Jocko, who shrugged and nodded.

"Did they call the police on you?" Revill's voice contained a note of triumph.

"That's not how it was," Maria protested.

"Oh, I think we know how it was," Revill declared. "Don't we, Jocko?"

"If you say so."

"What are you implying, Inspector?"

"What I mean, Mrs. Shires—"

A knock at the door interrupted the inspector. The door opened and the Honorable Dudley Cedric Shires burst into the room. His portly figure radiated irritation. "What's going on here?"

Avory actually winced. She sat down in her chair with an air of one greatly put upon. "I'm sorry that you were summoned, Dudley."

He loomed over her. "Mother, what are you doing in the police station again? You promised me."

"Dudley, this has nothing to do with my political activities, I assure you."

"Inspector—"

"That's true enough." Revill rose. "We are actually investigating an attack on her butler."

"On her butler!" Dudley sputtered. His face reddened. "That—that pugilist. I told her she should never have hired him. A man with a bad reputation."

"Dudley, please—"

"Mother. This is enough and more than enough. This is the last straw. I have had messages from some very important people regarding your activities. You will cease them immediately."

"My activities? Some very important people?" Avory looked pleased.

"Sir Leland DeCamp. Clarence Rippington. Lord Terence Montague. To name a few."

"Montague and Rippington, too." Revill noted the names in his book.

At the name of Lord Montague, Maria stiffened. A horrible feeling spread over her. She opened her mouth to speak. Jocko's hand closed round her wrist. She sank back in her chair, pressing her lips together hard.

"Inspector Revel—" Dudley began.

"Revill." He rose from his chair and offered his hand. Dudley looked at it as if it might contaminate him but he shook it. For the first time, he seemed to take his irritation under control. "Is there any reason for my mother to remain here?"

"She is certainly not charged with any crime. I have her statement as to the events that transpired in front on her house."

"Then—"

"But, Dudley—"

"Come, Mother." He took her firmly by the arm.

She shrugged it off. "I'm not a child."

"Of course not." His eyes spoke volumes to Revill, who nodded. When she stubbornly refused to rise, he exerted more pressure.

Maria felt her own temper rising. *How dare they treat her so!* "Mrs. Shires—"

Dudley looked at her coldly. "Who are you?"

"She's Miss Thorne, my type writer."

"Your services are no longer necessary."

"Dudley!"

"My mother is coming with me into the country. Her house will be closed for a time."

"It will not," Avory stoutly declared.

Her son transferred his grip until both hands were under his mother's shoulders. Willy-nilly, she was set on her feet and propelled toward the door. Jocko and Maria both rose, deeply concerned, but Dudley reached around his mother and opened the door. "Thank you for contacting me, Inspector Revel. The family will handle this from now on."

"Dudley, please behave yourself. You can't just—"

The door closed behind them.

Maria drew herself up to her full height. "Thanks to men like you, Inspector Revill, the malefactors in this town have free rein."

A red stain flooded the inspector's cheeks. His mouth thinned. "Miss Thorne—"

Her skirts whirled around her as she turned. "Let's go, Mr. Walton."

Jocko caught up with her to open the door.

"Mr. Walton—" the inspector began, pronouncing the name with thin-lipped anger, "—must remain here. There are some questions we need to ask him."

She paused in the doorway. "Is he being charged with a crime?"

"He may be." Revill started round the desk.

Jocko sidled out the door into the hall.

Maria stood her ground. "But at this minute he is not."

"Not at this minute, no. But we need to take his statement."

"I need him to help me find my sister." She closed the door before he could reply.

"Come on." Jocko caught her arm. Rather than object, she ducked her head and let him pull her along past the startled Constable Wilkie. Together they burst out the doors of the station house.

"This way," Jocko called as he leaped down the last three steps. She cried out with shock when her narrow boots hit the pavement. Pain stabbed to her knees, but she managed to keep her balance. Jocko broke into a run, dragging her with him. She looked over her shoulder to see Revill on the sidewalk behind them.

. He waved angrily. "Hey, there! Stop!" From the door Wilkie blew a shrill blast on his whistle. "Stop!"

But Jocko did not stop. His long legs carried them out into the middle of the street, dodging under the noses of a team, matching pace beside it, then ducking behind a heavy brewery wagon as it rumbled by. Again, they ran along beside it for a few yards, then ducked into the alley.

Maria's heart was pounding. Her breath came fast. She could hear the shriek of more whistles, but she could not imagine stopping. Instead, a guilty thrill went through her. They were escaping, running free. The cold air snapped at her cheeks and burned into her lungs.

They sped down the alley. A brick wall with a spiked iron gate blocked their way.

He let go of her hand and sprinted forward. A leap. His hands caught the top, his strong arms pulled him atop it. He clambered up and stretched out.

"Jocko." She gaped at him. "Your arm."

"Plenty o' time for that later," he gasped. He reached down with his good hand. He was grinning thinly around the pain. "'Ere, love."

"But I'll hurt you. And besides—" She looked at the hand almost a foot above her head. "I can't—"

"Can't never did nothin'."

She shook her head in wonderment. Hooking her umbrella over her wrist, she reached up to clasp his hand in both of hers. Like magic, her feet left the ground.

"Oooh."

Their faces were inches apart when he began to slide off on the other side. "Throw your leg up, Ria, m'girl."

She did not have time to think, nor object. He pulled

her forward onto her chest. She swung her leg up and scrambled over onto her stomach.

"Good girl." Again the grin. He held up his arm. "Come to me, love."

For the first time she shook her head. Twisting around, she slid off on the other side.

He caught her hand. His color was gone and sweat trickled down his cheeks, but he fairly radiated pride. "Done like a reg'lar dodger."

"That's nice to know. If I'm going to lead a life of crime, I want to be good at it."

He dropped a kiss on her upturned face. "Oh, you're good, Ria. You're really good."

"So are you, Jocko."

The whistles shrieked in the distance as they hurried away.

"A man and woman actually ran out of the station house and escaped?" Captain Lawrence tugged at his moustache. "How was this possible? I've never heard of such a thing."

"No, sir." Revill wished now that he had let them go. He could always pick Walton up later. And as for the Maria Thorne . . . He sighed.

"Can you explain it to me, Inspector?"

"Yes, sir. At the same time I was thinking that the best course of action would be to send out a call for these two. They can't have gone very far, sir. They're actually not criminals. At least the lady's not."

The captain grunted disapprovingly. "Doesn't sound like much of a lady to me. Shocking thing—to run from the police. Sets a bad example. I want her brought in and severely reprimanded. A charge should be brought against her. Resisting arrest."

"She wasn't actually resisting arrest," Revill replied. "She wasn't guilty of anything. We had no cause to arrest her."

The captain's scowl deepened. "Inspector, is there more to this than you're telling me?"

Revill hesitated. To tell of his total involvement in the affair, to reveal his connections with Jocko and his surreptitious investigations of the brothels would be to cause problems for himself. The case was nowhere near ready to file. He straightened. "No, sir."

The captain leaned back. His mouth worked as if he had tasted something bad. "You're very sure?"

"Yes, sir."

"I refuse to allow people to run out of the station house. Very bad for discipline." He rose and planted his knuckles on his desk. "I want your report of this incident and your progress on the case that precipitated it on my desk as soon as you can get it written. I want them both picked up and brought in. Even if no charges are filed, I want them made very respectful of police authority. Do I make myself clear?"

"Yes, sir."

"What happens now?" Maria leaned her elbows on the table in the darkest corner of the pub.

"Now?" Jocko leaned back and drained the mug of strong dark ale. With a sigh of pleasure and well-being, he set it down and eased his hurt arm into a more comfortable position. "We order another round and wait until we 'ear what Revill's goin' to do."

"And how are we going to 'ear what goes on at Scotland Yard?" she teased.

"Sure we'll 'hear,' love." He shaped his mouth around the 'h' and expelled his breath to make the sound. "Nothin' goes on at Scotland Yard that we all don't 'hear.' "

She shook her head. Her gaze went round the smoke-swathed room where the customers drank and gambled. "It's all so amazing."

His own gaze followed hers. "We've got a life, too, don't you know? We even 'ave a good time, when nobody's lookin'."

"I believe you." She drank from her mug with never a quiver. The beer tasted good. It cheered her, put heart into her, satisfied her burning thirst. "How many miles do you think we ran?"

He shrugged. "Not so many if you could cut straight through."

Another couple came in. The girl was laughing, her hair a bird's nest of brighter-than-natural red curls. The man's big hand cupped her shoulder and held her tightly against his side. He called for gin for them both.

Maria smiled. "I never realized that there were such places. I thought they would be full of people who were depraved and cruel. I don't know how I pictured them, but I didn't picture them like this." She looked down at her ruined clothes. "And I don't look any different."

Her hair had escaped from its knot and trailed down from under her hat. A couple of buttons were gone from the front of her coat, torn off when she had scrambled over the wall. Her skirt was spattered with mud and filth all around the hem. She picked a clod from it and dropped it off into the sawdust.

Quickly, she took another sip of beer.

He pushed his bowler back on his head. "You don't 'ave to stay 'ere if you don't want to. You can go on back to Mrs. Shires."

"Never."

Jocko held up two fingers to the barmaid. Then he studied the brew in front of him as if he had never seen it before. In a low voice he suggested, "They might be right, you know?"

Maria raised her hand to push at her hair but stopped when she saw the palm of her glove. Her lip curled in disgust as she stripped off one and then the other. "You mean about my sister not wanting to be found? They're not." She slapped the gloves on the table. Particles of dirt sprayed in all directions. "They just say that because it's easy. I know Melissa."

"But what if they were?"

"Then I'll hear it from her own lips."

He nodded as he pulled another coin from his purse and laid it on the tray.

Maria slapped the gloves again, this time against the table leg. "What's our next move?"

He heaved a sigh. "I'm about done for today."

Instantly, she was solicitous. "Of course, you need to rest. Shall we go back to my room?"

He looked appalled. "Scotland Yard'll 'ave it guarded."

"Your place will be, too," she guessed.

He nodded.

She pressed her hands to her temples. "I can't believe this is happening. We haven't done anything. We're only trying to find my sister and right a terrible wrong."

He reached across the table to catch her wrist and bring her hand down. His eyes were blue as sapphires and glistened with emotion. "We ran from the police, Ria. They yelled at us to stop and we didn't. That's against the law. You didn't know that, but I did. Don't you see? I'm a bad 'un. Revill's still got my confession. 'E can use it if 'e wants. I don't think 'e will, but 'e might. Now 'e'll want you, too."

Her lower lip quivered. "Then I'm a fugitive."

He shrugged, then grinned. "And a bad 'un. Duchess likes bad 'uns. She'll give us a place to rest."

"Won't we bring our troubles down on her? I thought you said—"

He looked very serious. "We very well could, but I think Revill is after the same thing we are. 'E won't follow us too tight because 'e knows we're close. I think your sister's in the Lord's Dream." He heaved a tired sigh. "What we need is a place to rest today and make a plan. Duchess makes great plans. Smart as a whip, she is."

Maria felt a stab of jealousy. The beautiful, aristocratic Duchess was also smart as a whip. *Damn. Damn. Damn.* Outwardly, she smiled sweetly. "You make it sound so simple."

He shifted, trying to find a more comfortable position for his injured ribs. "No use complicatin' it. When your sister's free and clear, we'll go in and give ourselves up. Revill'll yell at you. 'E might lock me up for a bit, but you'll walk away."

His words sent a shard of ice through her. She must never for a moment lose sight of the fact that this man had risked his life for her and was putting his freedom in jeopardy. She clasped his comforting hand in both her own. "He'll never lock you up if I have anything to say about it at all. And if he won't believe me, I'll go to the newspapers and tell them all about how wonderful you are."

"Ria." Jocko shook his head and grinned. "You're really somethin'."

"I mean it."

The bartender brought the drinks. Jocko flipped another coin onto the tray. When he was gone, Jocko hoisted the mug. "Good luck to you."

She clinked hers against it. "And bad luck to those we're looking for. As for you, Jocko Walton, you're all the luck I need."

Thirteen

"I think we should start back at the Lord's Dream."

"I don't think *we* should start anywhere," Jocko objected from his pallet on the floor.

Maria looked down at him from her seat on a keg. "Please, don't tell me that. We're in this together. I more so than you. This is my problem."

"The Lord's Dream would be very dangerous now," Duchess cautioned.

"It's where my sister is. I know it."

Sunlight and cool, fresh air filtered down through the windows in the roof of the warehouse. One of the older girls had propped them open on her way out. Maria and Duchess sat at the table. Jocko lay on his side on a pallet the children had made up for him. He stirred and tried to ease himself into a more comfortable position. The movement made him grimace.

"You mustn't be stubborn, Maria," Duchess continued. "You can't be sure that your sister is there. Surely Jocko told you Roncie Jack works around. He does jobs for a half-dozen houses and operates for himself on the side. He thinks of himself as a businessman with a string of profitable enterprises."

"Namely girls." Jocko tried to bite off a piece of hard bread with his teeth. He gave it up with a sigh when the pain in his bruised jaw grew too severe. He looked at the dark crust morosely.

"But Roncie Jack didn't beat Jocko. Policemen beat him. Severely. Why? And in that alley? Because we were getting too close. My sister must have been in that house."

"They could have been following you from somewhere else. Somebody back along your trail might have complained. Or maybe they just didn't like Jocko's looks. The peelers might have done it for a very different reason," Duchess explained softly.

But Maria would not be dissuaded. She rose from the overturned keg and began to pace. "I know my sister's in there. If I could just get in for a few minutes and catch sight of her—"

"No one gets in or out of the Lord's Dream except by the front door," Duchess told her bluntly.

"No one?"

"Absolutely no one."

"How is that possible?"

"They've got all the back and side doors nailed shut and hidden by draperies and such."

Maria completed another circuit back and forth. "What about deliveries to the kitchen? Food? Drinks?"

"All passed to the servants through holes in what used to be the doors."

"But why?"

Duchess looked at Maria pityingly. "Think about it. I'm sure several reasons will occur to you."

A silence followed while Maria's face mirrored her dawning understanding and despair.

Then Pansy came down the ladder and skipped up to the table. "I betcha I could get in. I'm small. I could get in through th' littlest 'ole 'n' be out slick as a whistle."

"Hah! Y'd be cotched afore y' took two steps." Bet swung her legs over the edge of the sleeping platform and kicked her feet back and forth.

"Would not."

"Would. Y're nah but a babe. With a big mouth."

When Pansy whirled to attack, Duchess caught her by a piece of her outsized garments. "Pansy, listen to me."

"I could get in," Pansy insisted stubbornly.

"Yes, dear, I know you could." Duchess took the dirty little face between her hands and looked deeply into her eyes. "I know you could, sweetheart, but once you got in what would you do?"

"I'd find 'er sister."

"But you don't know what she looks like."

The little eyes widened. "Oh."

"You are small and you could slip in," Duchess said. "But you wouldn't be able to do any good. Do you see?"

Pansy pondered the question. At last she nodded. "Yes."

Pansy skipped back to the ladder. At its foot she stuck her tongue out at Bet.

"Yer still nah but six."

"But a very brave six." Maria spoke for the first time. "Thank you, Pansy, for offering."

"Yer welcome," came the reply.

Despite her concern, Maria exchanged a smile with Duchess. "We have to do something. My sister resembles me, but she's much prettier. She has blue eyes and her hair is blond and long." She rose and began to pace. "Revill has the last photograph that was taken of her. He was supposed to give it back, but there hasn't been time to get it. And now I—can't—get—it."

Her voice quavered. Suddenly, her knees gave way and she sank to the floor, covering her face with her hands.

"Ria!" Jocko hiked himself up on the pallet.

She waved at him weakly. The other hand covered her face as she rocked over, her head bowed.

"It's all right." Duchess also waved him back. "It's been too much, hasn't it?"

Maria nodded

"Are you crying?"

This time her head wobbled from side to side.

Dimly, from the depth of her misery, she was aware of the silence around her. Even Bet and Pansy were quiet. Moreover, she was ashamed of her lapse. Such lack of control hurt her cause and her sister's chances.

She must be strong. She must straighten up and sit properly upright on the keg, hands folded in her lap. She must review the situation and make plans. She willed herself to do so, but for the present, her body defeated her will.

"Shall I fetch you a drink?" Duchess's cool voice came from a long way off.

Again Maria managed to shake her head. With a supreme effort, she straightened and sat back on her heels. Her voice still shook when she said, "I'll be all right in a minute."

"I suggest we forget about this for the rest of evening," Duchess advised. "You're both exhausted. You need sleep. Jocko, you look as if you've gone twenty rounds with John L. Sullivan."

He had already sunk back on the pallet. "Maybe thirty."

Maria pulled herself to her feet and dropped down on the keg. "I can't sleep," she whispered. "Over and over I imagine Melissa in the hands of people like the ones who did that to Jocko. It's made me sick."

Duchess poured them each an ounce of gin. She passed

one cup to Jocko, who took it with a slight nod. The other she shoved across the table to Maria. "Drink it slowly."

Maria looked as if she might refuse, but Duchess took her hand and wrapped her fingers around the cup. "Drink it and then we'll all take a nice nap."

"The only strangers who get into the Lord's Dream are new girls and eager men with money."

Duchess passed around hunks of fresh warm bread, stolen off a bakery rack minutes before.

"Maybe I could pretend to be one of those girls?" Maria suggested. "I could get in and meet all the others."

Both Jocko and Duchess looked at her pityingly.

"It's an idea," she faltered.

"Not a very bright one," Duchess observed.

"At least—"

Jocko reached up from his pallet to take her hand. "Sayin' you could get in, Ria—which wouldn't be likely because you're too old—'ow would you get out?"

Maria flushed at Jocko's plain speaking but pressed on with her plan. "I wouldn't have to get out. In fact, I'd wait there and protect Melissa until you could bring the police in for me."

"We'd never get them to come," Duchess pointed out reasonably. "If they did, Lady H would tell them you went in of your own accord. They'd go away and then you'd never get out."

The silence fell again.

At last Maria suggested, "I could dress up like a man and go in."

Jocko shook his head. "Too short. Voice is too high. And too many curves in the wrong places."

Maria flushed again.

"Don't act out of desperation," Duchess advised.

"But if my sister's in there, we must get her out."

"And what if she's not in there?"

Maria hesitated. "I could look at all the girls. If I didn't see her, then I'd tell them I didn't see a girl I liked and leave."

Duchess shook her head. "Tell her, Jocko."

Jocko groaned wearily. "They'd knock you in the head and take your money. You'd 'ave to see somethin' you liked."

"Melissa—"

"She might be with another customer. She might not be there. Even if she was there the other night, they might've sent her someplace else by now."

Maria could feel the tears starting. "I shall go in there," she declared. "I don't care what you say. My sister—"

The door creaked open. One of the older children came thumping up the stairs. She was tall, her hair cut short and straight across her forehead like a boy's. Her clothes were the same castoff masculine garments the others hid beneath.

"What have you heard, Alice?"

"There's a man callin' 'isself Saint Peter 'untin' fer Jocko."

"Saint Peter!" Maria's head snapped up. "Mrs. Shires must want to see us." She rose from the keg excitedly. "Let's go."

"Not now." Duchess caught her arm.

"Why not?"

Duchess rose and guided Maria away from the table. In the deep shadows, she caught her by the shoulders. "Listen to me and listen well. You're going to have to start thinking about all the things that can happen to you."

"My sister—"

"What about your friend?"

At first Maria did not understand. She frowned.

"What about Jocko?" Duchess's voice was low and intense. "He's hurting."

For the first time Maria looked critically at the figure on the pallet. He was lying perfectly still, his body curled around his arm, his good arm pillowing his head.

"He's not in any shape to take on Roncie Jack and the rest of the crew at the Lord's Dream. But he would if you dragged him to it."

"I wouldn't expect him—"

"No, you wouldn't expect him to do anything more, but he'd do it. He's protected you, taken you everywhere, even gone back and faced Revill with you. At least let him rest today."

"I didn't think." Maria could feel the tears brimming again.

Duchess released her shoulders. "You could use some rest yourself. Why don't you stretch out there beside Jocko? I'll take Pansy and Betty out so they won't disturb you. We'll see what we can find out. We might even talk to this Saint Peter. Why do you call him that?" When Maria would have answered, she waved her aside. "Never mind. I'll ask him myself."

The following day at two, "Saint" Peter opened Mrs. Shires's door to them. Maria led the way. Duchess, her street rags covered by Maria's long cloak, followed with cool aplomb. A nervous Jocko brought up the rear.

"My dears, I'm so glad you're finally here." Avory immediately ordered tea. "You can't know how worried I was. I sent Peter out as soon as we had ascertained that he was only superficially wounded. My goodness, what stamina the man has."

"Thank you, ma'am." The butler beamed.

"I convinced Dudley that he would be wrong to take me into the country. It wasn't hard to do," she explained with a sunny smile. "He hates the country."

"Would he approve of our being here?" Maria asked.

Avory sniffed. "He hasn't approved of anything I've done since he was ten years old. Why should one more thing matter?"

"We hate to impose," Maria argued.

"You're not imposing." The old woman fairly radiated indignation. "I don't mind telling you that I was furious after Dudley dragged me out of Inspector Revill's office. His attitude was intolerable, and so I told him. I can't think when I've been so incensed."

"I'm so sorry," Maria apologized humbly. "I feel responsible."

"How ridiculous." Avory waved the idea away with a wave of her lace handkerchief. "It did me good. It's very exciting to be fighting on the front lines again. I had slowed down in my old age."

"If it hadn't been for me, you wouldn't have been in that police station."

"I've confronted the police before," Avory reminded her. "I've marched and carried placards, don't forget. No. Dudley has never had any spirit. Just like his father. Conservative businessman. I was a trial to Cedric and now my son has inherited me and my rebellious ways." She laughed.

Jocko sat at strict attention on the maroon brocade chair. His eyes shifted uneasily from side to side, taking in the Kashmiri shawl draping the piano, the Staffordshire ornaments, and the dozen or more photographs in their silver frames on the side table. Compared to his room or even to Maria's little apartment, this place was very fancy.

Moreover, all the things about him made him uneasy. What if some of them turned up missing after he'd gone? He'd end his days in Dartmoor for sure.

Duchess gave the room no more than a passing glance, her beautiful face skeptical. Mrs. Shires might be serious in her desire to help. More probably, she was like the great majority of do-gooders of her class—contented to hold a meeting and then tell their friends they had affected a change.

Maria's face commingled hope and guilt. She was certain they were very close to rescuing Melissa. Still, she could not forget the pitiful trembling of Mrs. Shires's mouth when she called to her in the police station. Nor the grasp of her employer's hands, cold through their gloves. When "Saint" Peter reappeared bearing a heavily laden silver tray, the white bandage was clearly evident on his head.

As Avory lifted her teapot, she gave her guests a conspiratorial wink. "Come, come. Tell me what you're going to do and how I can be of help."

Duchess and Jocko glanced at each other. Duchess's perfectly arched black brow lifted. The thief shrugged faintly and cleared his throat.

"We agreed that one of us needs to get inside the Lord's Dream and find Ria's sister. I'm the logical one, but—" He spread his arms, displaying his clothing. His garments had clearly seen better days. Cheaply made to begin with, they suffered from the hard usage to which they had been subjected over the last forty-eight hours.

"I don't fit the bill this way," he continued, "but dressed up I'd be a bit more the thing. Maria said you wouldn't mind the loan of a coat and a hat." He smiled engagingly, using the bright expression that had cut many a rich man's purse in his younger days.

Maria broke in. "I thought perhaps we could borrow a coat of Peter's and a vest—"

Mrs. Shires adjusted her spectacles and ran a practiced eye over Jocko's lithe form. "Peter's much bigger than you are, young man. I don't believe his clothes would do you any good." She tilted her head to one side and smiled. "You really are a rogue, aren't you?"

A blush rose in his cheeks. His smile wavered, his blue eyes dropped. "Oh, I don't mean that in a critical way. I've known a couple of rogues in my time." She heaved a sigh. "Unfortunately, I didn't marry either one of them."

Jocko sent Maria an uneasy look. She shook her head. Duchess merely smiled.

"I'll be happy to help you." Mrs. Shires motioned to the table. "Drink your tea, my dears. We have many errands to run before your appearance at the Lord's Dream tonight."

"Father, I want an explanation." The Honorable George Montague stood over his father, his mouth tight with indignation.

Lord Montague kept his face directed toward the fire. Anger, guilt, and resentment were all at war within him. For the present, guilt was winning. He had remained in his bed as long as he dared, pretending his injury sustained at the Lord's Dream was more serious than had been first believed. His valet had kept his son out and brought his meals on a tray.

"Father."

Terence heaved a martyred sigh. "Stop hanging over me," he demanded peevishly. "I still have a bruise on my jaw. Two of my teeth are definitely loose. You are a great trial to me, George."

"Father, what was my sisters' governess doing in that house?"

Lord Montague crossed his leg and pulled his body deeper into the chair. "I suppose she was doing what she had always wanted to do. My wife, your stepmother, had to dismiss her."

"What for?"

"For impropriety," Lord Montague barked. "And obviously with just cause. Just look where she ended up. I only hope that your dear sisters were not contaminated by her immoral—"

"Father, she didn't want to be there," George reminded him angrily.

Lord Montague shook his head.

"She begged you for help. She tried to escape."

"Well, doubtless she had decided that the work wasn't what she thought it would be." Lord Montague smiled weakly. "Now, George, Lady H runs a fine establishment."

"She runs a brothel," his son contradicted flatly. "She fills it with horrid, ghoulish women, ugly, ignorant, and no doubt ridden with disease."

"George! We'll have no more talk like that."

"So you have no intention of doing anything about the poor girl's situation?"

Lord **Montague** huddled deeper into the chair. "It's not my place. She's nothing to me. Nor to you."

"Father, I'm returning to the Lord's Dream to see what can be done for that poor girl."

Alarmed at the thought of George discovering his secrets, Terence sprang to his feet. "You can't! I absolutely forbid it."

"What was her name?" George demanded.

"I don't remember. You can't go back there and ask for a girl."

George smiled. "Oh, I'm sure I can. After all, that's what men do at the Lord's Dream, isn't it?"

With that he turned and stalked to the door.

"George! I expressly forbid you to set foot out of this house."

But the door had already slammed behind the Montague son and heir.

"A donation, Mrs. Beauforty, and in exchange a word of prayer for your soul and a word of warning."

"Dinsmore, you're no more a preacher than I am. Why should I give you a penny for your little operation?"

His expression remained unctuous. "Because I have my sources, my dear."

"A message from above," she scoffed.

"Amen," he intoned. "However, in this case, a little bird, a very little bird, told me that a certain recent acquisition of yours has a sister that has been twice to the police."

"She won't get very far there."

"Fools rush in where angels fear to tread."

"Get to the point."

The minister held out his pale hand.

Lady H opened her desk drawer and withdrew a box. Positioning it carefully, so he could not see its contents, she withdrew a pound note and laid it over his palm.

He did not move.

"Gouger." She added four more.

"The name of Lord Terence Montague has been mentioned more than once in Revill's reports. The inspector is no fool. A word of warning might serve you well, Lady H. One that you would do well to pass on to the estimable baron."

"This won't work." Jocko protested faintly.

"Of course it will, my dear boy," Avory replied, patting his shoulder.

"My God, I can't—"

"I believe this jacket will fit him perfectly." The salesman in the haberdashery at Harrod's brought forth a fine black wool frock coat.

Jocko backed away in alarm, coming up short against the full-length mirror.

"It's perfect." Avory nodded her assurance.

"Indeed, madam, it is the very latest style patterned after the finest custom. Note the shawl collar, a distinctive feature."

"It costs a bloody fortune," Jocko protested again.

"Nonsense," Avory proclaimed. "If you are to be seen, young man, you must be seen in the proper clothing."

He lifted a hand to the scab on his temple. His head was throbbing—not from the half-healed wound, but from his own nerves. He didn't belong here in the best department store in London. He'd never be able to pay for all this.

"If you'll just slip your arms into this," the salesman said as he guided him back around and held the coat.

"I've 'urt me arm," Jocko said.

"Which one?"

"Er—left."

"Then we'll slip it on first."

Nothing would stop them. The haberdasher determinedly outfitted him in the latest style from black wool frock coat to fine leather pumps.

When he carefully set the black silk topper on Jocko's curly blond head, the young man groaned. "No."

But Avory Shires clapped her hands. "Perfect. Box up his other things and have them sent round."

"Yes, ma'am."

She offered Jocko her arm. "Now," she said, "you look quite the gentleman of fashion. You would be welcome anywhere—the best homes, Parliament, even in the presence of the Queen—and, sadly, the Lord's Dream."

"I look like a bloody fool," her charge muttered.

Maria placed her teacup in the saucer with a careless disregard. "I hate this waiting."

Duchess, her street rags covered by Maria's full-length cloak, smiled her cool smile. "There are worse things."

Maria just managed to conceal her frustration and annoyance. The blood hummed through her veins and her stomach trembled and twisted. Mrs. Shires was busy with Jocko in Harrod's while she sat in the window of a shop sipping tea and looking out at traffic on Bromptom Road.

And while she sat, time seemed to race faster than the people in the streets hurrying about their pursuits, faster than the horses trotting by, drawing the rumbling carriages and wagons. Melissa sank deeper and deeper into a terrible pit which would leave its mark on her forever. Her baby sister.

She met Duchess's eyes. "I don't know of anything much worse than waiting."

"Being there," Duchess replied with heavy irony. "Having it done to you."

Maria's face twisted. She touched her napkin to her lips, then stared at her hands as she lowered the cloth to her lap. She could feel the nerves tingling beneath the skin. She wanted to scream, to run to the Lord's Dream, to batter down its doors.

"Your sister might not be at the Lord's Dream," Duchess repeated softly. The words ran like ice through Maria's mind.

Suddenly, Duchess smiled, her entire face taking on a different expression. Again Maria was struck by her beauty. "I'm not a mindreader, but I know how you feel."

"Do you have a sister?"

"Many." Duchess took a sip of tea, grimaced, and set the cup down. Her mouth pursed at the taste. "Sometimes I feel as if I have thousands. I know I must have hundreds."

"Like Pansy."

"And like your sister. I can't do much to help them, not really. I'm only one. And I know that if I do too much, Roncie Jack or someone like him will come after me." She was no longer looking at Maria. Her clear eyes stared unseeing at the teeming traffic.

The skin was like satin stretched over the sculptured cheekbones. Maria felt coarse and clumsy beside Duchess. Even Melissa, young and fresh as spring, could not compare with this inborn elegance. Her curiosity grew to bursting, but good manners forbade asking questions. Instead she said, "So you take care of a few. That's so good of you."

"Perhaps so. Perhaps not."

Puzzled by her cryptic answer, Maria thought about how to phrase her next question. "Have you known Jocko long?"

"A bit."

Again Duchess was reticent. Maria smoothed her napkin. "He's a good man."

Duchess cocked her head to one side. "No, he's not a good man. Not in the way you mean. Don't call him good. He's one of the best thieves. But good? No. Not Jocko Walton."

Color stained Maria's cheeks. She lifted her teacup, hoping its rim would hide her embarrassment. "You say he's a thief. He says he's a thief, but I can't believe that. Surely you're both exaggerating."

"Oh, no." Duchess's smile was catlike, humorless. "He's been one since he was a child. It's the profession his stepfather taught him. He and his mother were starving to death."

"He told me about Mr. McNaghten," Maria offered. She watched Duchess's smile stiffen. "Oh, he's been very honest with me. I say he doesn't have to stay with that profession." Maria sat straighter in her chair. "I was a fair copier and now I'm a type writer. He's young. He can change."

"He's older than you by a lifetime," Duchess sneered. "Compared to him, you're nothing but a girl."

"I still say, he could change. He could be anything."

"Could he really?" Duchess's tone was bitter, her face cold. "And why should he want to?"

Maria spluttered. "Because—it's what everyone wants. It's—it's—"

Duchess leaned forward. "Stop. Don't say things about which you know nothing. Jocko Walton taught himself to speak well so he could move among people who had valuable things to steal."

"But why not get an honest job?"

Suddenly, Duchess lost all patience. She leaned across the table, her fist clenched. "Honest jobs are for men who have the right background or for those who don't have sense enough to do anything except break their backs."

Maria's eyes widened. "That's not so. All kinds of jobs are—"

"Listen to me," her tormentor hissed. "Jocko's stepfather taught him to steal because he couldn't teach him anything better. McNaghten was one of the best in the business. He saw Jocko's potential. When he was a little blue-eyed, curly-headed tyke, he was the best pickpocket on the street. The swells would give him a tip for watching their horses. Then he'd cut their purses while he was helping them into their carriages. He was making a good living and McNaghten was collecting a percentage of the profits. Then he got so big that the gentlemen wouldn't let him near them anymore, so he burgled houses until Revill caught him."

"That's appalling." Maria did not say that what was really appalling was the fact that McNaghten had used Jocko. Revill had used Jocko. And now she was using Jocko. The realization made her sick to her stomach.

Duchess shrugged. "To you, perhaps. To him it was survival. He and McNaghten took care of his mother until the day she died."

Maria sighed. "Jocko speaks so fondly of him, when he was being so used. But his mother didn't have to stay with that evil man. There are alternatives. I read about them all the time in the letters I type for Mrs. Shires. There are aid societies. What about her church?"

Duchess made a rude noise. "Streetwalkers in Soho aren't allowed in churches. Missions maybe. But they'll starve there, too, or freeze to death while some sanctimonious preacher rings a peal over them morning, noon, and night. At least if they're walking the streets, they can sleep in a warm bed and have a hot meal and a mug of beer."

"I don't know what to say."

"Don't say anything. Just listen. And don't ever look down on any of us again. Don't pity us. Don't think you're better than we are." Duchess's eyes flashed, clear and bright as cold steel. She lifted her chin and dared Maria to contradict her.

"I would never look down on Jocko Walton or you, either," Maria said humbly.

"Just see that you don't. We do the very best we can. Jocko has no formal education. He can barely read. He can't write. So he can't be a type writer or a teller in a bank. Do you know what he could do?"

Maria shook her head dumbly.

"He could break his back as a stevedore on the dock or muck out stables or carry out slops in a great house. That's always supposing he could get a job any of those places without references."

The two women stared at each other. Duchess was breathing hard. Suddenly, she dropped her eyes and the color left her cheekbones as her anger drained away.

Maria searched her mind for something to say.

Duchess swallowed. Her next words were totally unexpected. "You may be the worst thing that's ever happened to Jocko Walton."

"Because of Roncie Jack?"

"No."

"Then I don't understand."

"You're going to take the spirit and the steel out of him. You'll make him ashamed of what he is. He'll try to change to please you, and it'll break his heart."

"I want him to change," Maria admitted. "He needs to be free of guilt, free to do what he wants instead of what other people force him to do. But he doesn't have to change."

Duchess laughed unpleasantly. "It takes a brave do-gooder to let a thief steal. I can't wait to see what you do when you get your sister back. The chances are she's been raped and violated ten or a dozen times every night. She'll scream and carry on. A couple of months from now, you might find out she's pregnant."

The future looked incredibly bleak. Maria loved Jocko's spirit, his courage, his strong body, his bright smile. But could she love his profession? What if Melissa had lost her mind? What if she were ill? What if—?

Her thoughts must have been mirrored in her face, for Duchess sat back, her lips curved in a sneer. "You see."

"I see, but I won't give up on either one of them."

Duchess pushed the cup and saucer away from her. "I really don't care for tea. It's too weak for my tastes. Coffee is my drink. Strong and black. No sugar."

Maria signaled to the waiter.

"What do you think, my dears?" Mrs. Avory Shires tugged a stiff, slightly red-faced young gentleman to their table.

Both young women stared. Duchess found her voice

first. "Why, Jocko Walton, don't you look perfectly splendid. A real 'toff.' "

"Lay off, Duchess," he muttered.

"Doesn't he look wonderful?" Avory continued to Maria. "Still a rogue with a twinkle in his eye, but quite, quite marvelous."

They all smiled at him. Gone was the checked suit, the Garrick caped coat. In its place was a fine dark gray, three-piece suit with jacket, waistcoat, and trousers. Over it was a black frock coat and in his hand he carried a black silk top hat.

Waiters came hurrying to pull out Avory's chair and seat her with proper ceremony. Before they would allow Jocko to sit, they took his coat and hat, all the time murmuring ingratiatingly.

Jocko, definitely out of his element, scowled the entire time. "I feel like a proper fool," he grumbled as the waiter pushed the chair against the back of his legs and spread the napkin across his thigh.

"But you look so handsome," Maria declared.

"He does," Avory agreed. "I can't think when I've seen a better figure in a suit. Those broad shoulders, young man. That height."

Even Jocko's ears were flaming. He ran a finger inside the high, stiff collar of his new shirt. "I'll probably choke to death."

"You'll be so handsome they won't bury you for a week," Duchess teased. "They'll just keep you laid out in the parlor for all the girls to come and weep over."

"Cut it out, Duchess."

Even with a lump on his jaw and his hair combed carefully over the bruise on his temple, Jocko was easily the handsomest man in the shop. In Maria's eyes he was the handsomest man she had ever seen. His wonderful blond hair was parted on the side above his high forehead and tamed with a sparing application of macassar oil. He was freshly shaved and smelling of bay rum.

Maria felt her heart step up its rhythm. "You look very handsome, Jocko."

He glanced at her. For a second his face was open and vulnerable.

The look was like a blow. *He loves me,* she thought. *Heaven help us both. He loves me.*

Fourteen

While they drank their coffee and ate scones with clotted cream, Maria kept looking at Jocko. He was utterly splendid. Not only did his new clothes fit him beautifully, but his freshly barbered face and hair changed his appearance completely.

When she saw him wince as he lifted his left arm to manipulate his cutlery, she remembered the savage beating. She could not bear to think of him being hurt again. "What if someone at the Lord's Dream recognizes him?"

"Oh, I hardly think that's likely, dear Maria. No one inside that dreadful place has ever seen him," Avory insisted. "At least not dressed like this." She smiled at Jocko like a proud parent. "Isn't that right, young man?"

"Right," he growled. He was still feeling like a fool. The stunned expression on Maria's face told him all he needed to know: He looked like a dressed-up monkey. She was laughing at him. He knew it. Any sane person would. Jocko Walton, thief, dressed up like the bloodiest "toff" in London. How had he ever gotten into this?

"Even if someone thinks he looks familiar," Duchess supplied, "they won't be able to place him. They'll never believe Jocko Walton could look like that."

"If they did, they'll think I've lost me mind."

Avory ignored his self-deprecation. Instead, she clapped her hands in delight. "Then the disguise is perfect."

Maria was struck by another thought. "I'm afraid you've spent such a lot of money."

Avory patted her arm. "Nonsense, my dear. All in a good cause. We must save your sister. At the same time perhaps we can be instrumental in exposing some of this vicious practice."

All three young people looked at her.

"What do you mean—exposing?" Jocko asked warily.

"Simply that I've contacted an acquaintance of mine," Avory told them. Her eyes sparkled with excitement. "A journalist."

Duchess and Jocko exchanged glances. "Revill's not goin' to like this above 'alf," Jocko whispered. " 'E'll 'ave me in Dartmoor before I can spit."

"A newspaperman?" Duchess asked.

"That's right. William Stead is his name. He works for the *Pall Mall Gazette.* Of course, it's just a scandal sheet."

"Scandal sheet," Maria murmured weakly.

"That's right. Not at all like the *Times,* but, nevertheless, it is much read and discussed." Avory smiled like a child at a birthday party. "He's been very supportive of our cause. He truly wants to help women. I sent a message to him."

"Oh, Lord," Jocko whispered, sinking lower in his chair.

Duchess put a comforting hand on his arm. "What kind of a message?"

"Oh, just that if he wants a great story, he should come to the Lord's Dream tonight. In disguise, of course. He'll see and hear everything that happens."

Avory smiled cheerfully despite the gloomy silence her announcement had cast upon the table.

"Including the girls' names." Maria sighed. Every day brought some new problem in her quest to free her sister. If a newspaperman wrote Melissa's name into a story, her ruin would be certain. Any chance to spirit her away and pretend it never happened would be lost.

"Oh, I doubt he'll use the names of the girls. I told you—they've been exploited, too. In fact, he probably won't report many names at all—just the names of the criminals and such."

"Lord a' mercy," Jocko whispered.

"Don't worry." Duchess tried to reassure them. "When this Stead turns in his story, his publisher will probably cancel it."

Maria looked at her hopefully.

"Oh, no," Avory assured her. "His editor is a crusader."

"Dartmoor," Jocko predicted darkly.

The door opened, throwing a rectangle of light onto Melissa's huddled form. She threw up her hand to protect her eyes from the sudden onslaught. Between her fingers she could distinguish silhouettes. She recognized Hermione's voice.

"Get her out of there and get her bathed and dressed. If she puts up a fight send for Charly and Bert."

"She won't give me no trouble."

Melissa had been without water or food for more than forty-eight hours. When she struggled to make a sound, her voice came out in a rasp. "You'd better let me go. They know where I am now."

Lady H laughed unpleasantly. "They've always known where you are, you fool."

"Let me go," Melissa insisted, her voice gaining strength.

"I won't be what you want me to be. I'll fight. I promise, I'll fight. You'll be very sorry if you don't let me go."

"So you'll fight, will you? Good. I'm sure Terry will enjoy that. As for me, save your breath. I've heard it all before." Lady H stood aside for Nessie to edge through. "She's to be dressed *à la Turk* when he calls for her. That will teach you, girl."

Maria closed her eyes as she leaned against Jocko's broad chest. Her arms encircled him, holding him close without pressing against his tender ribs.

"Ria." His lips shaped the syllables against her hair. She could feel his warm breath.

Eyes closed, she breathed in the scent of him. Of clean, new fabrics—cotton and wool—of soap and bay rum, and—most important—of Jocko Walton himself. "You mustn't go," she murmured.

He tensed. "Why not?"

"You've been hurt. They might hurt you again."

"What about your sister?"

She made a swift negative movement with her head, just a hint of a shake.

"What about 'er?" he pressed.

"I don't know. Yes, I do. I love her. I love her with all my heart. I want to find her, but I don't want you hurt."

"Why is that?"

"Because—" She turned her head, pressing the other cheek against his chest, refusing to let him see her face.

"Why?" he insisted.

She could feel his heart step up its rhythm. His chest swelled with each breath. He was so vital, so alive. And he made her feel alive. Her own body responded powerfully to his. She could feel her breasts swell as a melting ache curled in her loins.

"Because—you are very precious to me." She wanted to say more, wished she could give him the answer he wanted. She remembered Duchess's warning. Above all, Jocko Walton must not be hurt. She tipped her head back. "You're free of any obligation you had to me. I'll tell Revill that I wouldn't allow you to put yourself in danger. He won't blame you. Just don't go."

He looked down at her with eyes blue as the skies on a rain-washed day. How could a face look so young and so old at the same time? He tightened his arms fractionally and dropped his mouth on hers, kissing her, his lips moving over hers, drinking her sweetness.

She was dizzy when she broke the kiss and stepped away from him.

He adjusted the silk topper at a proper angle. "I'll always remember you said that."

The Honorable George Montague had never felt so uncomfortable in his life as when he descended from his father's carriage in front of the Lord's Dream. On the ride over he had questioned his own sanity in returning to a house of prostitution. They were evil places. His nurse, his stepmother, his tutor, the teachers at his school, had all warned of the dangers of such a place, the lewd, immoral behavior, the diseases.

Perhaps his father was correct. Perhaps his sisters' governess had behaved improperly. Good girls could not know of such places, much less find themselves inside them. Could they?

A footman whom he instantly recognized as Charly stood

at attention at the door. The man's eyes flickered at the sight of George. He flexed his powerful shoulders inside the forest-green livery. His thin lips peeled back, revealing his chipped front teeth.

George swallowed. He almost climbed back into the carriage. Then he remembered the beseeching eyes—tear-filled, desperate, a breathtaking shade of blue.

Giving his father's gold-headed cane what he thought was an intimidating twirl, he mounted the steps. His stare collided with the footman's. Then to George's infinite relief, the brute dropped his eyes and bowed. On a spurt of confidence, George entered.

Tuesday evenings were quiet at the Lord's Dream. The business and excitement of the weekends were over. For several years Hermione Beauforty had been accustomed to leaving the premises and retiring to a quiet house in Bayswater. There she kept all her account books, concentrated her energies on the Stock Exchange, and pretended to her neighbors that she was a respectable middle-class widow.

Cate's heavily rouged lips pulled back from her sharp white teeth when George entered. "Why, it's Mr. Montague," she purred, laying her talons on his sleeve. "And how is Lord Montague, your esteemed father?"

George regarded her as he might an adder coiled about his arm.

Cate lifted her chin defiantly. "Did the old bugger lose a couple of teeth the other night?"

"No."

"Too bad." She led him through to the main salon where a few girls were lounging. Eunice came to take his hat and cane.

"I'll just keep this," he told her, clutching the stick tightly.

Cate drew back. "Planning on giving someone a hiding, are you?"

"Only if someone gets in my way."

She laughed. "Champagne for Mr. Montague."

"No!"

She stared at him inquisitively. One black eyebrow rose like a vulture's wing in her dead-white face.

"That is, I don't care for any." He managed what he hoped was a knowing smile. "It mars the performance."

At this she did laugh, tilting back her head and exposing her long, white throat.

He looked around nervously, trying to scrutinize the faces of the girls without appearing to do so.

The laughter stopped. "What did you really come for?"

He did not trust her. "A woman."

She swept her arm wide. "Choose."

"Someone special."

The hand dropped to her hip. She stepped away from him and posed, her bosom thrust out beneath the starched white blouse. Feet apart, she flicked back the edge of the black serge skirt. The movement exposed her leg halfway up the thigh. "I'm special."

He could not keep his lip from curling in disgust.

"Liar."

"I don't know what you're talking about, my good woman."

"Oh, spare me." She dropped the skirt back into place. "Does your father know you're here?"

"What difference does that make?"

"It might make all the difference." From an alcove on the other side of the room another liveried footman appeared. George recognized him, too. The girls had abandoned their provocative positions; they huddled together in two groups, whispering and staring.

George could feel himself losing control of the situation. "I want the girl who—er—the girl my father intended for me."

Cate shrugged. "Which girl was that?"

"I didn't find out her name. There was a misunderstanding."

"You might say that," Cate jeered.

Suddenly, George took her arm and pulled her to the side. "Listen to me. I can't give you much money, but I can give you some. And I can promise you a great deal more. Just let me talk to that girl."

"Talk? I think you plan to do a lot more than talk."

Every word this woman spoke seemed to have a double meaning. More than that, he was a little frightened of her. George hesitated. "We'll begin by talking."

"St. George," Cate jeered. "Come to rescue the maiden from the dragon, have you?" She leaned close to him. "We were all maidens once. Even me. I was a maiden once."

Something dark flickered in her eyes beneath the blackened lashes and brows. He could not read it. His grip tightened in frustration.

Cate slapped at his hand. "Have a care there. You're hurting me."

He had never hurt a woman before, but he could hear the silence in the room, feel the menacing footmen. He squeezed even tighter. "Take me to her."

Cate's eyes went dull. "Let me go."

Slowly, he opened his fingers.

She let her arm drop and turned on her heel. "Follow me."

* * *

"Shall we pick him up, Inspector?" Constable Wilkie watched the elegant figure descend from the carriage.

"Not yet." Revill shook his head in wonder. Under ordinary circumstances he would never have recognized Jocko Walton. The tall, well-dressed figure walking up the steps of the Lord's Dream might have been any one of a number of young lordlings who roamed the night streets in this particular section of London.

A peculiar mixture of pity and pride ticked somewhere near the edge of Revill's conscience. His thief looked nothing like the shabby felon Revill had apprehended last year. The type writer and her suffragette employer had taken him in hand and introduced him to a life he would not want to leave. With Jocko Walton's gift for language and his inherently good nature, perhaps he would never have to.

The footman bowed obsequiously at the door as Jocko handed him the silk topper. His carefully arranged curls shone like guinea gold in the lamplight as he disappeared from sight.

Wilkie started forward. "Let me go in and get 'im, sir. That blighter can't walk around bold as brass."

"No."

"But, sir—"

"Wilkie, there's no reason to stop any man from walking into a brothel. In the first place, no such place exists officially. And in the second, he hasn't done anything."

"He ran." The constable's fists were clenched, his moustache fairly bristling in his eagerness to pursue the thief.

Revill looked at him appraisingly. "Perhaps he had good reason to do so, Wilkie. My understanding is that he was beaten very severely the other night right outside this place."

He watched the constable carefully. Did the man cast him a wary sidelong glance?

"This is a rough neighborhood, sir."

"I know, but in this case he swears the police were the ones who beat him."

"Liar, sir. They're all liars."

Revill waited so long to answer that Wilkie was finally forced to meet his gaze. The inspector gave the constable a long, searching look. "That may be true," he said, choosing his words carefully. "Or it may be that something strange is going on in the department. Perhaps orders are being misunderstood."

Again he waited. He could imagine Wilkie's heart pounding. Then he sighed. "I believe we'll let Mr. Walton do whatever it was he set out to do. Perhaps he will find Miss Thorne."

The constable looked away, muttering under his breath. Suddenly the carriage that had brought Jocko rumbled into the alley, then paused. Revill heard the door open, then close before the vehicle continued on.

While he watched, two female forms slipped out of the darkness and hurried across the street to hide in the shadows. Revill would have bet a monkey that one was Maria Thorne. But who was the other? Surely the elderly Mrs. Shires had not let herself be led into this dangerous adventure.

"Inspector?"

"Patience, Constable Wilkie. We may get more here than we bargained for."

"Yes, sir," the constable muttered.

As they watched, a cab pulled up in front of the Lord's

Dream and two men climbed out. Business was brisk for a Tuesday evening.

"Quite a place," the younger man remarked. His eyes scanned the salon eagerly, taking in the scantily clad girls.

"About as usual, actually," his companion remarked. "Put your eyes back in your head, Markham, and look sharp. I didn't bring you with me to spend the evening indulging yourself."

"Oh, I say, Will, a bit of a tickle wouldn't hurt."

"I'm afraid it would, Markham. We're here for business."

Smiling invitingly, Eunice approached, balancing a silver tray with a couple of wine glasses. "May I introduce you to any particular girl, gentlemen?"

William Stead took in the maid's costume. "Are you the proprietress of this establishment?"

Eunice's smile faded. "No, sir. She's engaged at the moment."

"Perhaps we'd better wait for her." Stead helped himself to the glasses, handing one to his assistant. "Thank you," he told Eunice politely. "May we just move around and meet everyone?"

Eunice's smile returned. "Of course, sir. Just let us know how we can serve you." With a quick curtsey she turned away.

"Oh, I say," Markham gulped at the sight of her legs beneath the black bustle.

"Eyes back in your head, if you don't mind," Stead suggested drily. "Really, Markham, we're here to investigate and report. Nothing more."

Markham almost choked on his wine. "I'll be happy to investigate her."

Stead elbowed him in the ribs. "Look sharp. Who's that?"

Lord Terence Montague strode into the Lord's Dream, his anger obvious to all. As Charly trailed him in an attempt to take his cloak, Montague cursed the footman.

"Milord," Eunice gasped at the sight of the baron's face. She dropped into a deep curtsey.

"Yes, yes," he acknowledged her impatiently. "Where is Lady H?"

"Er—she's not here tonight, sir." Eunice peeked out from under her lashes at him and grimaced. Fortunately, he did not notice.

Lord Montague's nose was hideously swollen and purple. The bruising had spread into the pouches under his eyes and down the sagging jowls. He thrust his face into hers. "Not here? I never heard of such a thing. This is her house. You're lying, girl."

"No, sir," Eunice squeaked. "Indeed, I'm not." She motioned to Bert who was grinning in his alcove. He ambled over. "Find Cate! Hurry!"

He nodded. His speed did not increase as he mounted the curved staircase. Eunice cursed silently.

Lord Montague tossed his cloak and hat to the hovering Charly and strode toward the stairs.

"Oh, please, sir, have some champagne." Eunice chased after him, stepping in front of him and taking his arm. Another girl had grasped the situation and hurried forward with Eunice's tray.

"I didn't come for champagne," he snapped. "I need to see my son. Has he come here? Where in hell is Hermione?"

"This champagne is from the new French shipment." Eunice took the stem from the tray and pressed it into Lord Montague's hand.

He looked at it distractedly, then drank it. "Has my son been here?"

"I'm—er—not sure," Eunice replied vaguely. "What does he look like, sir?"

"Look like? He looks like a young man—tall, well-built, blond."

"Oh, him." Eunice appeared to think. "Actually, sir, we have three young men here, all tall and—"

"Lord Montague." Cate came down the stairs, her eyes glittering.

He recognized her and stiffened. "Send for Lady H immediately."

"She's not here," Eunice repeated, stepping back

Cate paused on the first riser. One hand on her hip, she faced Montague, eye to eye. "I'm in charge today."

He came closer. "You'll never be in charge."

Her eyes flashed with hatred. "Of course I will. Of everything."

His fury increased the rate of his breathing to the point that his words came out in gasps. "I'm surprised that Hermione has not sent you away before now. But pack your bags, girl. When I speak to her, you'll be gone."

At the explicit threat Cate merely smiled. "Waste your breath if you like."

"Bitch! I'll—"

Even as Terence Montague raised his fist, he saw the footman come down the stair. Somewhere behind him was another. Then he became aware of the silence in the room. For the second time in less than a week, he was the center of attention in this salon. He glanced around him. Only three other men were there, two together and one in an alcove. All were staring at him.

Lowering his arm, he stepped ever closer to Cate, seeking to intimidate her with face and voice. "Send for my son, or I'll make you sorry for the day you were born."

Cate's eyelids drooped, her mouth shaping itself into a *moue* that mocked its promise. Then she pivoted on her heel. As she mounted the staircase, her laugh floated back down.

George poked his head out and checked the hall. It was empty and every door was closed. His pulse began to pound. Sweat trickled down his spine. He passionately regretted ever embarking on this errand. What could he have been thinking of? He was no knight errant and nineteenth century damsels in distress were most probably prostitutes.

Still, he had come this far. He might as well attempt to do the thing. He would set himself a limit. If he opened all the doors and did not find her, then he would consider that he had done his best. If he found the girl, he would question her and abide by her wishes.

With that resolved, he tried to tamp down his fears. If the bruisers attacked him, they would get as good as they gave. And he knew they would not really hurt him—his father was too important. He crossed the hall and flung the first door open.

He opened and closed five doors without finding anything except unmade beds. They were such small rooms and so sparsely furnished, that they offered no concealment. A glance was sufficient to assure himself that they were empty. He was beginning to feel damned foolish when he came to one that was locked.

He twisted at the white china knob, but it resisted. He smiled slowly. The door he had tried previously had had a key in the lock. Most locks were the same. In a moment he had the room open.

The girl who had recited poetry for him leaned up in bed.

She was naked. George gaped as her heavy breasts swung forward. Then he saw her face. Both her eyes were black and her mouth was swollen.

He sprang across the room. "My God, what happened to you?"

She pulled the sheet up across her chest and turned her face away. "Fell down stairs," she mumbled.

"What?"

"Stairs. I took a tumble."

He started to sit down on the bed beside her but froze. Her back was bare from hip to shoulder except for the long fall of hair that failed entirely to cover the purple bruises. "You've been whipped."

She shuddered.

George came around the bed, trying to get a look at her face, but she drew her hair over it. "Please, miss, won't you let me help you?"

She shook her head. "Leave, why don't you? I'm all right."

"But who did this?"

Her voice rose. "For pity's sake, get outta 'ere. You'll get me in trouble."

He stood. "If that's what you want." He was almost to the door when he stopped. "Can you tell me where the other girl is?"

She lay back down, turning her face into the pillow and hunching her shoulder up. He could see nothing but the wealth of curly blond hair. "What girl?"

"The one that caused such a disturbance the other night."

The figure on the bed did not answer at first.

He was half-way out the door when she whispered, "Next to th' last door on your left."

Poised at the top of the staircase, Cate watched George use the skeleton key and enter the room in which Hermione had confined Melissa Thorne. Her lips peeled back thinly in a parody of a grin. So the son had come back to sample the father's private stock.

That for you, you old bastard!

She started back down. When Lord Montague would have mounted the stairs, a flick of her hand brought both Eunice and Bert forward.

"Best wait, sir," the footman advised. "Sometimes the girls aren't exactly ready to receive guests."

"Milord," the little maid said most respectfully, "please have some champagne."

Lord Montague ground his teeth as he accepted the glass. His eyes met Cate's over the rim. Unbridled hatred crackled in the air between them.

The dressing stool caught George on the shoulder. Fortunately, it splintered like kindling. The blow sent him staggering across the room.

Eyes slitted with determination, Melissa Thorne came after him brandishing the leg of the stool. Her second blow landed on his forearm, but he was ready for her. His hand whipped around and fastened on the broken end.

With a twist of his wrist he wrenched it from her grasp.

George was almost a foot taller than Melissa. He looked at the stick and then at her. She shrank from him.

George recognized her. He vented his anger on the piece of wood by flinging it into the corner.

With a cry Melissa darted for the door, the harem bells around her wrists and ankles chiming wildly. The diaphanous trousers and sleeves ballooned around her.

George easily caught her shoulder. "Wait."

"Let me go." She tried to twist out of his grasp. "Let me go!"

"Wait," he repeated. "I'm here to help you." He threw his arm around her waist and pulled her firmly against him. "Listen to me."

Beyond understanding, she continued to struggle. "For mercy's sake, let me go."

He managed to turn her around in his arms. His hands touched bare female flesh. The little bolero had been wrenched open. Her breasts were naked. In fact, most of her whole front except for a narrow strip of green velvet below her navel was naked. His mouth was suddenly dry. "Stop struggling."

She must have understood the change in his tone, for she looked up at him. What she saw there redoubled her efforts. "Let me go! *Let me go!*"

"Tell me your name."

"No."

"Listen to me. I think I know you." He shook her hard. He must have hurt her, for she cried out.

She tucked her head so he could not see her face. "You don't know me."

"Yes, I do," he insisted. "You were my sisters' governess."

"Bethany and Juliet?"

"That's right."

"Your name is Montague?"

He smiled. "That's right."

She stopped struggling then. Her head went back. "Monster! I hate you."

He dropped his hands. "Why?"

"Because Lord Terence Montague put me here."

Fifteen

"Just let me make you a little more comfortable, sir."

Jocko stared, hypnotized by the long blond curls swinging against the leg of his trousers. They framed a deep shadowy cleavage between white breasts that seemed to swell and billow as their owner lifted his foot onto a brocaded stool. Her pink negligee spread around her in a circle of net, lace, and marabou.

"No." He jerked his leg involuntarily as her hand slipped up above the top of his boot and wrapped around his bare calf. "That's not necessary," he protested. "It's—er—quite comfortable like it is."

If he had been nervous and uncertain before he entered the Lord's Dream, his state of mind was now chaotic. He could feel himself blushing, an embarrassing consequence of his light complexion. The cigar smoke stung the back of his throat. With great difficulty he lifted the excellent Havana high and tried to control his breathing.

She looked up at him and smiled. Her big blue eyes were outlined in black. Her face was powdered dead white with heavy rouge spots on the cheekbones. In the middle her nose was a little button turned up at a saucy angle—an Irish nose.

For Jocko the nose spoiled the entire thing. Ria's nose—and therefore Melissa's—was straight and narrow, a bit patrician. Reasonably safe to say, the girl so earnestly rearranging his body bore not the slightest resemblance to Melissa Thorne.

Still he could not take his eyes off the kneeling woman. Through the lace and net he could see a pink corset that barely covered her nipples and came down just below the tops of her thighs. From it, pink suspenders latched to the tops of sheer pink stockings that started just above her knees. Her shoulders and a large portion of her thighs were bare.

The only whores of Jocko's acquaintance were rough and ready girls like those in the Russian's string. They wore layers of skirts and shirtwaists, as well as heavy coats and mufflers to protect them from the cold of the streets. Even their legs were covered with several pairs of stockings held up by crudely tied elastic garters. A man had to find his target through the slit in their drawers.

Here he could see everything and it was all within reach. He ran a finger around the inside of his stiff collar and kept a firm grip on the cigar. The salon was warm, too warm. He could see how it would need to be with all these girls sitting around with half their bodies bare. He tore his eyes away and looked around.

A maid in a black uniform strolled by him to serve two other gentlemen. Her bustle swished back and forth tantalizingly above the backs of her plump white thighs.

His eyes followed her across the floor. Without thinking, he puffed on the cigar, drawing the burning smoke into his lungs. It made him light-headed—at least, he blamed the feeling on the smoke. His manhood was growing heavier and harder by the minute.

With a supreme effort of will, he concentrated on the task he had set for himself. Look at each of the girls' faces—

Remember, Jocko, faces!

Find the one who resembles Maria.

Think about Ria, Jocko. She wouldn't approve of any of this.

There was one with Maria's color of hair. Damned if he could see the color of her eyes.

Eunice whispered something to the footman standing beside the irate customer at the foot of the stairs. Then with a smile, she came toward Jocko. "Have you seen anything to fulfill your dream, sir?"

"My dream?" he croaked.

"This is a house of dreams," she prompted, leaning down to offer him more champagne. In the process she displayed the deep cleft of her bosom. The heat wafted her scent to him. It was female, heavy with her own perfume and promise.

He cleared his throat. "I—I like—er—blond 'air—er—hair, but—er—I don't think this will do."

Eunice straightened, a frown dropping the corners of her heavily rouged mouth.

"That is—er—she reminds me of my sister."

The girl in pink stopped massaging his calf and rose. Still smiling, she patted his hand. "Just you keep me in mind, sir. You don't make me think of my brother at all."

Eunice signaled to the girl in the deep red negligee and black hose. "Maribelle is blond."

The woman mincing toward him on high-heeled black shoes laced halfway up her calf was at least a couple of inches taller and probably older than Maria. She posed in front of him, her hands on her hips, her head tipped to one side. She licked her lower lip and smiled at him.

He gulped the champagne but managed to shake his head. "I don't think so. She's a bit old for me, don't you think?"

Maribelle's look should have shriveled him where he sat. She flounced back to her *chaise longue.*

Another blonde who owed her color to a bottle swayed forward, but her eyes were brown and her nose flat. She in no way resembled Maria. In fact, Jocko found her singularly unattractive. "I don't like her at all," he complained to Eunice, "Are these all you've got? Some dream!"

"Some of the girls are upstairs today," she informed him coldly. "If you'd care to wait—and have another glass of champagne—perhaps I can prevail upon a couple to come down."

"Why don't I just come up and see for myself?" he suggested blandly. "It'll save us both a bit of time."

"My father!" George turned white. "You must be mistaken."

Melissa shook her head violently. She backed away from him and stripped the green satin sheet from the bed. The harem bells tinkled as she wrapped it around her. When she was decently covered except for one shoulder, she faced him defiantly. "I was kidnapped in the Euston Street Station by that horrible woman downstairs—"

"The one they call Lady H?"

She nodded. "—And brought here for your father to—to use."

"You're lying."

"Why would I lie?"

"He said you were improper. My stepmother dismissed you. You came here of your own free will."

She pointed to the wall behind him. "Why would any girl in her right mind come here of her own free will?"

Fearfully, he turned. His face grew impossibly whiter.

From a row of ordinary clothes pegs dangled an array of whips and leather cuffs and straps. "My God."

While his back was to her, she tried to slip past him toward the door.

"Wait." He caught her arm.

"Don't. Don't touch me. Let me go."

"I can help you. I will help you." Unsmiling, he placed his hand over his heart. "I promise on my honor."

She hesitated, trying to read his face, afraid to believe him.

"I swear on my family name."

"Don't swear on the name of Montague," she sneered.

He dropped his hand. "On my mother then. She's dead, but she was a Richmond. An old and honorable family. I swear on her name. And on my own honor."

"You'll help me escape?"

He smiled. "It's what I came here for. Don't think of me as a Montague. Call me George."

"George."

"That's right." He held out his hand. "And I'll call you Melissa, if I may?"

She hesitated, afraid to trust him, doubting, hoping. Their gazes locked. Finally, she took his hand. "You really did come back for me?"

"Yes."

"George."

"Yes."

Her face crumpled. All her courage, all her defiance dissolved into tears. "I thought I was lost. I thought my sister couldn't find me. I had come to believe no one would ever help me."

She would have sunk to her knees if he had not caught her. Clumsily, he wrapped his arms around her and pulled her against his chest. She stiffened, fearing his touch. So many people had hurt her in the past three weeks. Had it really been only three weeks?

"I'll help you, Melissa," he repeated, awkwardly patting her shoulder.

Valiantly, she tried to force back the tears. Then she admonished herself to remember that she was not free yet. This might be a trick. He seemed strange. He was so tall. He smelled of bay rum and macassar oil. His chest was flat and hard-muscled beneath his clothing.

She shuddered violently. He could hurt her if he wanted. But he did not seem to want to. He would not allow himself to be bullied by the likes of Nessie and Lady H, but Bert and Charly were very strong.

She lifted her head. "What will you do?"

He looked affronted. "I'll take you out of here."

"They'll never let you. There are big men—"

"I'm the son of the man whom you say brought you here," he reminded her bitterly. "If you're correct, then my father must be a man of some importance to these people." He let his arms drop and stepped back. His jaw clenched. "They wouldn't deny me what I desire."

"They did before," she reminded him.

"I'm more determined this time." He grinned boyishly.

For the first time she wondered about his age. He could not be much older than she. He didn't understand. She tried to explain. "You don't know them. Huge, strong men work here. Ex-prizefighters, so the other girls say. They can kill a man with their bare hands. They're very dangerous."

"I met one of them. Remember?"

"And you weren't able to stop them from carrying me back up here."

He thought for a minute. "Then we'll go down the back stairs."

"There aren't any."

"No back stairs?" He sounded incredulous.

"No one slips out without paying at Lady H's."

He strode to the window and pushed aside the curtains and drapes. It was not a window at all. A blank wall stared him in the face. "What the hell—!"

"You see?" She twisted her hands together. "Oh, it's impossible. You must leave here and go to the police."

He came back to her. "If the police are involved, your reputation will be ruined."

"I don't care about my reputation. I don't care about anything but getting out of here. Nothing is worse than what they have planned for me." She could see the possibility for escape slipping away. "Please. Go get the police. They'll listen to you."

But he would not leave her. "What about the room across the hall? There have to be rooms with windows somewhere." He took her hand. "Stay close to me."

"Where are you going with him?" Lord Montague snarled as Eunice led Jocko past him up the stairs.

"Now where would she be going with him?" Cate sneered. "The gentleman's here to have himself a bit of fun. Not hunting for his bloody son."

"When Hermione hears about this, you'll be walking the streets in Whitechapel," he prophesied. "I'll see to it personally."

"Oh, is that where you hang out? Dip in up here, dip in down there. Lady H likes her regular customers not to bring in pox."

His eyes fairly sparked as his rage mounted to apoplectic proportions. "I'll not tolerate this insolence any longer!"

Before either Bert or Charly could stop him, he sprang at Cate. Catching her hand where it rested on the banister rail, he whipped her by him. She screamed piercingly as she was flung down. Fortunately, Bert stood at the foot of the stairs—he thrust out his arms and Cate fell into them.

"I say," called the younger of the two gentlemen. "Bad form, sir, to fling a woman around like that."

Montague's eyes were wild. "Go to the devil!"

Cate levered herself out of Bert's arms. Massaging her shoulder, she came back up the stairs. "Charly! Bring him back down."

The guard sprang up the steps. He reached Montague on the wide staircase and caught his arm.

Montague sent him a steely look. "Take your hands off me."

Charly released him but did not move. "Let's go back down, guv, quietlike."

Montague came down a couple of steps until he literally hung above Cate. "I promise you that you'll be deported to Australia."

From the bottom of the steps, Cate flung back her head. "This is the Lord's Dream. Not bloody Eton. You can't go up those stairs to find your son." She snapped her fingers. "Charly, escort the gentleman to a seat by the fire. Eunice, get Lord Montague more champagne."

Charly reached for Montague without touching him. At the same time he stood aside so that the lord could descend with a modicum of dignity. Eunice met him at the bottom with champagne.

He ignored her and marched straight to the chair beside the fire where he seated himself, glaring.

Cate returned his glare. Then, with her back straight and her chin high, she marched up the stairs.

The room directly across the hall from Melissa's had no window, but the room at the end of the hall had one. George tore down the draperies and unlocked it. When he tried to raise it, he discovered it was nailed shut. "Good Lord. What happens if there's a fire?"

Melissa shuddered. "I suppose we all burn."

He cursed. "Lock that door." He raised his foot and set it against the sash bars. "Now, scream!"

She blinked, startled.

"Scream!"

She clenched her fists and closed her eyes. The noise ripped out of her throat.

The sash bars caved outward and carried four panes with them.

"Again."

She screamed again and the rest fell away.

"Good job." He leaned out. "We're in luck." He drew his head back in and held out a hand to her. "Come on."

"What was that?" Champagne spilled down the front of Markham's vest as he started to his feet.

"Get yourself under control," Stead cautioned.

"But I heard a woman scream." Glass tinkled faintly somewhere in the distance.

"Quite. Unfortunately, this seems to be that kind of house."

"My God."

The woman screamed again. Sweat started on Mark-

ham's forehead. He looked into the face of the young prostitute who sat beside him. Her smile had frozen around
her mouth, giving it a pinched look. She blinked rapidly.

"What's going on here?" Markham demanded.

She shrugged. "Oh, just one of the girls having a bit
of a lark."

"Doesn't sound like a lark to me," Stead remarked.

"Oh, yes, it is," she tried to explain. "Sometimes the
gentleman's so special—" The lie froze on her lips.

Cate appeared at the head of the stairs. "Charly! Bert!"
Both of them vaulted up.

Montague flung his cigar into Maribelle's lap and started
after them.

Markham rose. "There's a story up there, sir."

Stead nodded. "I think you're right, Mr. Markham."

George helped Melissa out onto a ledge behind a knee-
high balustrade built to mask the windows of the top story.
Her toes curled as she put her bare foot onto the slippery
stone. Then her foot slipped into the concave lead guttering
that ran along beneath the ledge. She squealed as her toes
sank in watery muck. Hastily she pulled back and set her
foot on the narrow ledge. The harem bells on her costume
jingled as she struggled for balance.

The wet wind blew through the satin bedsheet as if she
were wearing nothing. A look over the edge made her head
swim. She fell back against the casing. "What are we doing? We'll never make it."

"Of course we, will," George said heartily. "Don't look
down. We'll walk along here—"

"But we're going nowhere," she wailed. The wind
whipped her hair. Her teeth began to chatter.

"Come on: At the end we'll go over the roof and onto the next house. It'll be like a Dickens novel."

She was shivering so hard she could not speak. He looked back at her.

"Damn. I should have put my coat around you." As he started to shrug out of his garment, his body tilted out over the balustrade.

"No!" she cried. "For heaven's sake, don't fall. I'm all right. K-k-keep going."

He righted himself and led her cautiously toward the next window.

"Stop right there, damn ye!"

Both teetered against the railing. Melissa threw a terrified glance three floors straight down into the kitchen basement.

George caught his balance and then pulled Melissa against him. "Go on ahead," he ordered.

"Where'n 'ell do ye think yer goin'?" cried Charly.

"But—"

"Go on." Pressing back against the sloped roof, he passed her by him.

Behind them Charly thrust half of his burly body through the broken window. He wrapped his hands around the outer sashes and held on for dear life. "Bring that girl back in 'ere, ye bloody fool."

George assumed an air of disdain. "I advise you to go back in, my good man. We'll be on our way."

Charly looked down and cursed. The wind whipped his scraggly hair. His next threat was made with less conviction. "Y'ain't goin' nowhere."

"Leave us alone or you'll be sorry." George clenched his fists. "I whipped you once."

The challenge stabbed at Charly's pride. He grinned, revealing his broken teeth. "Not this time, bucko."

"George!"

"Go on, Melissa."

She reached the end of the balustrade and set her bare foot on the roof slates. Instantly, it slipped back down. "I can't climb it!"

"You must."

"Stop right there, if ye know what's good fer ye!" Charly yelled. He braced one hand against the sloped roof. With his body at that angle, his first step was his last. His foot slipped off the ledge, through the slimy muck in the lead gutter, and between the pillars of the balustrade.

"Gorblimey!" Bert yelled, making a grab for Charly's shoulder.

"Watch it, man!" George called.

Charly cursed and grabbed for the railing. "Come back in 'ere. Ye'll get us all killed."

"You go back, or you'll kill yourself."

Melissa threw herself onto the roof, clutching for handholds and toeholds, anything that might give her purchase. Spread-eagled on her stomach, hair streaming across her face, she found one, and then another. Groaning with effort, she managed to pull herself to the peak of the roof. "George!"

"Go on. I'm coming." He backed toward her carefully, keeping his eyes on Charly.

"Oh, be careful!"

Just as she yelled, both feet slipped off the ledge. He windmilled his arms violently and caught the third gable.

Behind him, Charly cursed. "Ye bloody fool."

George's face was white, his stomach trembling, but he

righted himself and took another step. The lead gutter actually was easier going.

Melissa threw her leg over the ridgeline. The next house was only a few feet lower, with a flat rooftop. She could lower herself with no trouble. "Come on," she called to George. "We can do it."

"Stop! Damn ye both to bloody 'ell!" Charly yelled. He made a half-hearted effort to free himself, pushing with all his shoulder strength from the top of the balustrade. Unfortunately, his thigh was trapped between two pillars. Panic seized him. The ex-fighter grabbed his leg with both hands and tried to heave it upward.

George edged past the last window. Looking back over her shoulder, Melissa smiled encouragement to him. "Be careful. The roof tiles are slippery."

He nodded. Their eyes met. He reached his hand toward her. Suddenly, he looked down at his feet. He cried out and twisted, making a swipe in her direction. The sheer terror in his eyes locked with her own as his body tipped slowly away from her.

"George! No-o-o!"

With a flailing of arms and a great cry, he toppled over the balustrade.

"Miss Thorne, I believe."

Maria jumped six inches.

At her elbow Inspector Revill had materialized out of the darkness. "What is the particular fascination that this establishment has for you?"

Maria regained her balance, but her heart was still pounding wildly. Though she despised the gesture, she realized she was pressing her hand to her chest. "Inspector, you frightened me half to death."

"But not—I'm afraid—enough to get you to leave the vicinity," he observed. "And who, please tell me, is your companion?"

Maria threw a nervous glance over her shoulder. "Oh, a friend. Just a friend. And now we've got to be on our way.

Duchess had already begun to edge down the sidewalk, but Constable Wilkie appeared out of the darkness at her back.

"Don't let me drive you away," Revill said. He tipped his hat. "You are the estimable Duchess, I believe."

She would have bolted had the constable not laid hold of her arm. "Answer the inspector."

Maria hurried to step between them. "I've told you she's a friend, Inspector. She's just keeping me company."

"Why?"

"I know my sister's in there. I'm waiting for her to come out."

"Since the first is highly unlikely, the second is virtually impossible." He assumed a stern pose. "And even if she were there, how would keeping company with street riffraff like this bring her out?"

Maria drew herself upright. Eyes glittering under the streetlight, she advanced. "This woman is my friend. When you insult her, you insult me."

"She's a thief," he declared bluntly.

"Thanks to you I have made the acquaintance of several thieves," she countered.

He looked away, embarrassed.

She plunged ahead. "And let me tell you that they have been unfailingly kind, considerate, and helpful. In fact, they have been much kinder, more considerate, and more helpful than Scotland Yard. My advice would be to dismiss some of the policemen and hire thieves who—"

He opened his mouth to interrupt her tirade.

A cry of terror followed by a piercing scream cut him off.

"Good Lord!"

"Melissa! That's my sister's voice." Maria picked up her skirts and bolted into the alley.

Revill followed at her heels. Wilkie and Duchess pounded after him. Another piercing scream led them on, and another.

At the back of the house, in the mews, light from the kitchen basement did little to dispel the blackness toward the roof.

The screams were constant now. Revill scanned each window trying to locate their source.

Then the leaden clouds parted and a three-quarter moon illuminated the scene. On top of the house, straddling the ridgeline and wrapped in a sheet that was trailing across the tiles, a girl lay screaming.

Maria recognized her instantly. "Melissa! It's my sister!"

Her voice did not carry, or perhaps Melissa Thorne was too hysterical to hear her. Maria caught at Revill's arm and pointed. "She's there. There! She's trying to escape! Melissa!"

Some distance back along the balustrade a man hung on for dear life, one leg dangling between the columns.

"And he must be trying to stop her."

Before Revill could speak, a servant threw open the door to the kitchen. Light flooded out into the basement.

"Good Lord," Revill whispered.

George Montague's lifeless body hung like a ragdoll over the iron fence that ran across the back of the house.

No fewer than three corkscrew spikes thrust up through his back.

Duchess cried out and hid her face.

Constable Wilkie gave a grunt of horror. Shaking his head, he stooped to lift the boy's wrist and search for the pulse. "No good, sir," he murmured. "He's dead."

Maria kept her eyes fixed steadfastly on the roof peak. Cupping her hands around her mouth, she summoned all her strength. "Melissa! Melissa! Listen to me! It's Maria! Melissa! Hold on, dearest! We'll get you down. Melissa!"

The hysterical screaming continued to pierce the night.

Sixteen

"George," Terence Montague whispered. "George."

Revill had needed the help of both Charly and Bert to lift the boy's body off the corkscrew spikes. They had carried him into the salon of the Lord's Dream, while Constable Wilkie had been dispatched to summon help.

They had laid him down on a divan of deep red satin. Revill closed the sightless eyes with his own hands and covered the body with his overcoat. Then he drew his omnipresent notebook from his breast pocket. "Who knows this man?"

Montague was on the point of collapse. He swayed, his hands pressed to his temples. "He's my son. My son, George Montague."

"And you are?"

"Terence Montague."

"Lord Terence Montague." Revill repeated the name between his teeth as he wrote it down in his notebook.

Very little blood drained onto the satin. The terrible wounds from the force of the fall had emptied George's body in minutes. The boy's face had not struck the pavement; it remained unmarked. The golden blond hair, tousled from the wind and damp from the fog, lay on his forehead. He might have been asleep.

"George." His father fell to his knees, clutching the lifeless hand, weeping. "George, open your eyes, son. Please."

"He's dead, I'm afraid. Terrible way to go." Revill tried to think of something comforting. "But swift."

"He can't be. He's just lost consciousness." Montague brushed at the boy's hair. "Here. He's cold. Bring more blankets."

When no one moved, Lord Montague seemed to go mad. "Bring more blankets, damn you!" he screamed. He lunged to his feet and threatened them all with clenched fists and blazing eyes. "And coals from the fire to warm his feet! By God, I'll have the lot of you on the next boat for Australia if you don't take care of my boy."

Cate silently signaled to Maribelle, who seemed the most self-possessed of the salon girls. Glad to be away from the sight, the girl in red hurried up the stairs. Charly was just on his way down.

The footman's wig was gone, his face white as parchment. He wiped the moisture from his eyes. " 'E seemed like 'e was all right, Miss Cate. An' then 'e just flipped. Right over the edge, 'e did."

"Were you struggling with him?"

Charly did not hesitate. "No, ma'am."

Her eyes seemed to bore into him. "Just be sure you're telling the truth."

When he reached the foot of the stairs, he ducked his head and tried to slip into the first curtained alcove.

Revill fixed him with steely eyes. "Is the lady brought in from the roof?"

Charly shook his head. "Not by me. I couldn't take the first step. It was that slippery.

"You mean the girl is still out there?" Revill started for the stairs.

Charly shrugged. "There's a couple of people tryin' to get 'er in."

Revill gave only one quick instruction to Charly. "Don't try to leave, man. You have some questions to answer."

The footman nodded unhappily.

At the top of the stairs, Revill met Cate. She pointed the way down the hall. When he would have rushed past her, she caught his arm. "May I assign Charly to the door, Inspector? He'll be of greater benefit at his post turning any customers away."

"Yes. Yes." Revill hurried down the hall.

Serene, her face expressionless, she glided down the stairs. "Go to your post, Charly. You, too, Bert."

"Maybe somebody'd better send for Lady H," Eunice suggested.

"She's already been sent for," came the curt reply.

"You can't go out there." Jocko caught hold of Maria's arm as she hiked up her skirts and tried to climb out onto the ledge.

"I have to get Melissa."

The thief pushed his lady back and held her by the shoulders. "You won't do Melissa any good if you're killed. I'll go."

"She won't come to you. She won't recognize you."

Melissa's screams had subsided into wails and then into weeping.

Jocko thrust his head and shoulders out through the gaping hole. "I'll get 'er."

Before Maria could protest further, he climbed nimbly onto the ledge between the roof and the balustrade. "Melissa," he called. "Melissa Thorne."

The sobbing continued.

"Melissa, I'm Jocko. I'm Maria's friend." He began the treacherous journey along the roof, one foot on the ledge, one in the slippery lead flashing.

"George," came the pathetic whimper.

"I'm Jocko. Stay right where you are. I'm coming to get you." Attempting to place his foot, he looked down. A dizzying black void gaped just on the other side of the low balustrade. He tilted his body sideways and hugged the roof tiles. Then he slid along, leaning against them. A feeling of real regret flashed through his mind. His beautiful new suit would be ruined.

He passed three windows until he could pick up the corner of the trailing sheet. "Come on and slide down to me, Melissa."

"No. Stay away." She tried to edge herself forward on the ridgeline. The bells jingled, the sheet shielding her legs from the cold tiles slipped. "Stay away!"

"Come on." He kept his grip on the sheet, though he doubted it was sufficiently anchored to her clothing to allow him to pull her back with it. Beyond the roof was another roof, but if she went over the side, she would probably slide to her death. "You're all right. Maria and I've come to take you away."

"Keep away!"

"Just come to me. I'll take you inside where it's safe and warm."

"I'll never go back in there," she vowed. The terror on her face was apparent even in the half-darkness. She must be freezing to death, he thought. Every surface was slick with fog and dew. He could hear her teeth chattering, yet she still had the courage to fight.

Jocko grinned. "You're Ria's sister, all right."

"Ria? Maria." Her voice quavered. "My sister."

"Melissa," a voice called behind him. "Go to Jocko."

A glance over his shoulder almost gave him a heart attack. Maria Thorne balanced awkwardly on the ledge not six feet behind him. One gloved hand was braced against the roof, the other reached for the next grip. "Bloody 'ell, Ria," he cursed. "You're causin' a bloomin' traffic jam up 'ere."

She ignored him as he had known she would. "Melissa," she called again. "Please go to Jocko. We'll all come down together and get in where it's warm."

Melissa shook her head. "George said we were going over onto the next roof. I can see the way from here. You don't know, Maria. I can't go back in there."

"Nothin's goin' to 'appen to you," Jocko told her patiently. "I won't let it."

"He really won't, Melissa," Maria assured her. "He's very brave."

"George was brave." Melissa wrapped her arms round her body. "He fell." She closed her eyes. Her chin dropped to her chest. "He's dead, isn't he?"

Jocko looked for confirmation to Maria, who nodded. "Yes, ma'am."

"Come in, Melissa," Maria begged. "I promise you'll be all right. We won't let anything happen to you. The police are here."

"Bloody 'ell," Jocko cursed again. "You didn't tell me that."

"The police?" Melissa raised her head sharply.

"That's right, Melissa. You'll be safe inside. The police will protect you."

"That's right, Melissa. I'm Inspector Revill of Scotland Yard. It's safe for you to come back in." He was leaning half out the window, holding his hat with one hand. "Is she coming?" he asked Maria.

"Inspector—"

"Come to me," Jocko coaxed. "Just slide down the sheet. It'll be like landin' in your sweet papa's arms."

"George fell." A gust of wet wind lifted the long, damp locks of hair off her naked shoulders. She shuddered weakly. "You're sure you can catch me?"

"You don't weigh much more than a sack of feathers." Jocko grinned as he stretched up a hand, anchoring the other around a shutter.

With some difficulty she swung her leg back over the roof edge. Then she held out her arms and tilted herself forward. She slid only a couple of yards before she was in his grasp.

"I love you, Jocko," Maria called as he helped her sister slip between him and the rooftop and make her way into Maria's arms. "I'll never be able to thank you enough."

When they were all safe inside, Revill clapped Jocko on the shoulder. "Good work, man. Best job I've ever seen."

"Thank you, sir." *But is it good enough to keep me out of Dartmoor?*

"I want everyone in the house gathered in the salon," Revill ordered Cate.

"Does that include the kitchen staff?" Standing straight in her severe black skirt and blouse, her hands locked in front of her, her face stern, she conveyed an intimidating aura of haughtiness and self-possession.

"Are they in the house?"

"Yes, but they can't get into the upstairs rooms."

"Why's that?"

"The kitchen and laundry can only be reached from outside back."

Revill pulled his notebook from his pocket and noted that information on a new page. "Let them stay where they are for now, but we'll want to take their statements. I'm assuming that the boy's body fell in front of the kitchen. They might have seen or heard something."

A rather unprepossessing gentleman approached him. "May I introduce myself?"

Revill eyed him closely.

"I'm William Stead of the *Pall Mall Gazette.*" The stranger extended his hand.

Revill sighed as he shook it. "A reporter. It wanted only that."

Stead smiled blandly. "We'll be happy to help you get to the bottom of this tragic business. This is my associate, Mr. Markham."

"Two reporters."

Markham nodded with great solemnity. "Terrible tragedy here tonight. Any ideas as to why it occurred?"

Ignoring the question, Revill noted their names in his book. "I don't suppose the two of you frequent this establishment."

"Not at all," Stead replied. "A very public-spirited lady directed us here tonight."

Revill sighed again. "I think I may know her. Mrs. Avory Shires."

Stead smiled. "You're here for the same reason."

"Not exactly." The people in the salon stirred, drawing his attention. The inspector left Stead and moved to the foot of the staircase.

Maria Thorne was bringing her sister down. Her eyes

swept the room, spying Duchess in the shadow of the entrance alcove and Revill at the foot of the steps. She threw him a glare that shouted I-told-you-so.

Cate also followed Maria's glance around the room. At the sight of Duchess, she stiffened.

Jocko carried Melissa Thorne, wrapped in Maria's cloak. The garment fell away from her bare feet and ankles. The harem costume with its noisy bells had been removed. Long blond hair, damp and curly, the exact shade of Maria's, streamed over Jocko's arm.

As they came into the salon, Revill studied the girl's pale face. Her lips were quite colorless. Her eyes skipped everywhere, recognizing the faces, registering violent emotions.

"Inspector Revill." Maria's voice was overloud. "This is my sister, Melissa Thorne. She has been held prisoner in this house."

Bert and Charly exchanged anxious glances. Cate's mouth curved in a cynical smile.

"Oh, I say!" Markham exclaimed excitedly, looking at Stead for confirmation. " 'A Prisoner in a West End Brothel.' " He pulled out his notebook and began to write.

Revill hunched a tired shoulder. This was going to be a long night.

The most startling reaction came from Terence Montague. He swung round from his kneeling position beside his son's body. "She's responsible! She killed him."

Clive Revill and William Stead both stared at the peer of the realm. Markham flipped a page and kept on scribbling.

"She's the cause of this!" Montague repeated. He swayed as he climbed heavily to his feet, his hand still clasping his son's. He pointed an accusing finger at Melissa, who made no sign that she understood his accusation. "My son is dead because of her. She seduced him and he fell to his death. Arrest her, Inspector. Immediately."

" ' . . . Seduced him, fell to his death . . .' " Markham muttered as he wrote.

A banging at the front door drew everyone's attention. Bert hurried to answer it, admitting Hermione Beauforty.

The sight of Duchess in the alcove made Lady H's eyes widen. She opened her mouth to speak, then closed it. Lifting her chin at an arrogant angle, she swept into the room, her heavy wool cloak flaring out around her. "What *is* going on here?"

Cate hurried to her side. "A man's been killed."

"What? In my house? That's not possible." Lady H's carefully manicured nails clutched at the thick fabric even as she was removing the garment. Still her demeanor remained queenly. "Perhaps some unfortunate gentleman has been overcome with—" She hesitated fractionally. "—emotion."

"The man didn't die in—er—the pursuit of pleasure," Revill contradicted dryly.

"And who, sir, are you?"

"Inspector Clive Revill of Scotland Yard. And you are the proprietress of this establishment?"

"Hermione—" a voice croaked.

"Terry?"

He staggered toward her. Tears suddenly flooded down his cheeks. "Hermione. George has been killed."

The woman seemed to crumple. Her hands clenched, then fell open. Her shoulders slumped, her head drooped. "George?"

Terence reached for her, his whole body shaking. "Hermione, he's gone."

Her legs would have given way had he not reached her and supported her.

"George," she whispered.

"Yes."

She shook her head vigorously. The high pompadour bobbed. "You must be wrong."

"Oh, if only I could be."

Oblivious to the onlookers staring in utter fascination, Terence led her to the divan. She took one look and screamed. Tearing herself from Montague's arms, she flung herself across the body. With infinite gentleness she took the boy's white face between her hands. "George!" she crooned. "George, open your eyes."

Terence put his hands on her shoulders. "He's dead, Hermione."

"No. No. No. He's not. Open your eyes, sweetheart. Look at your mother."

A concerted gasp went up from the onlookers. Cate sucked in her breath sharply and looked away.

"You're going to wake up, sweetheart." Hermione looked to Terence for reassurance. "He will wake up soon. My son."

"And mine," he nodded, his own frame shaking with grief. "Hermione, he's gone."

She bowed her head on the dead boy's chest and gave herself up to wracking sobs. Tears streamed down her face, dissolving her mascara, making black runnels through the heavy white powder and French rouge.

The inspector cleared his throat. "Perhaps someone had better help her up to bed," he suggested. "Obviously, she can't contribute to this investigation since she only just arrived."

Brushing past Lord Montague, Cate put her hands on

Lady H's shoulders. "Come on," she murmured gently.
"Let's go upstairs."

"No. I want to stay with my son."

Cate looked to the inspector for direction. He shrugged.
The sobs increased to a desperate wail, a sound so deep
and mournful that it threatened to tear her apart.

"Good Lord," Revill whispered.

Maria put her arms around Melissa who was still in
Jocko's arms. The three huddled together, the younger sister's head between the two of them.

Cate bent over Hermione. "Lady H," she said sternly.
"Lady H. Please let me take you upstairs."

"No. No."

"Then you have to be quiet," Cate admonished. "The
inspector is trying to conduct an investigation. He's trying
to find out how it all happened."

The words penetrated Hermione's curtain. "He's investigating?"

"Yes."

The tears continued to flow unabated, but the noise
stopped. Hermione clutched George with all her strength,
as if her grasp could somehow force life into him.

"Now." Revill faced the room. "I'd like to begin with
the man on the roof." He motioned Charly forward.

The footman had recovered some of his nerve. "How'd
ye know I was on the roof?"

"I saw you. We heard the young lady's screams and ran
around to the back of the house in time to see you, my
good man, or someone who looked very much like you
trying to free himself from the railing. Did you fight with
young Montague on the ledge? Did you send him toppling
over the railing to his death?"

" 'Fore God, no." Charly cringed. "I wasn't nowhere

near the bloke. Me bloomin' leg was stuck. I was in a fix."

"Then how did he fall?"

"Must've been an accident, guv. Th' gutter's lined with lead. Slippery as glass up there, an' that's a fact."

Inspector Revill looked unconvinced.

"I couldn't believe it when George fell." Melissa Thorne spoke for the first time. Jocko had set her down near the fire, adding coal and wood until it blazed high. She sat huddled in her chair, her bare feet drawn up under her, her eyes closed as Maria chafed her icy hands.

"Perhaps you'd tell us what you mean by that," Revill asked gently.

Her speech was slow, reflecting exhaustion and shock. "He was reaching up to me, starting to climb. He looked up at me and smiled as he was reaching for me. And then—he looked down and started to fall."

She clutched her sister's hand tighter. "Maria, I'm so frightened."

"You don't have to be afraid anymore. I promise I'll protect you. We'll all protect you."

Revill was still unsatisfied. "Was anyone else near him?"

"I don't think so, sir. He was coming around the corner of the window, smiling. Then he looked down at his feet and toppled over backward."

"She pushed him." Terence Montague thrust his way into the conversation.

Melissa slowly shook her head, her words slurred with exhaustion. "Why should I have pushed him? He was trying to help me escape."

"So you say. But you're a whore. A whore!" Montague spat the words, his face purple with hatred and grief. He staggered toward the huddled figure. "You refused him. You led him on—"

"I didn't! I didn't!" Melissa began to cry.

Revill caught Montague by the shoulders and pushed him back. "That will be enough."

"Inspector." Maria rose with fire in her eyes. "My sister has suffered a great shock. She was almost killed tonight. Please let me take her home where she can rest."

"As soon as she gives a statement, she may go," he agreed. Sending a prayer to heaven to bring Wilkie and a squad on the double, he led Montague back to the other side of the room where he motioned to Eunice. "I think Lord Montague would like something to drink."

"Ch-champagne, sir?"

"Coffee. Black."

"Yes, sir."

"Now then, Melissa Thorne." He came back to the fireplace and pulled a small stool in front of her chair. "Please tell us in your own words what happened."

"George—Mr. Montague was trying to help me escape."

"Why?"

"Because he felt he should. He wanted to repay me."

"That's ridiculous," Lord Terence snarled from across the room. "Why would he waste time on a common little whore."

"I'm not a . . . what he said. I was his sisters' governess," Melissa said softly. "Lord Montague had me kidnapped and brought here."

"Lies," Montague snarled. "Lies. She's a whore."

" 'Lordly Procuration for the West End,' " Stead remarked to Markham. "Write it down."

"Yes, sir."

Revill could feel his job falling into jeopardy. The whole

stinking cesspool was about to be opened up. Yet he could not ask Stead and Markham to leave. They had been in the house, too. Eventually, he would have to question them as witnesses. He wrote the information in his own note-book. "How do you know this?"

A bit of color rose in Melissa's cheeks. "Because Lady H told me so when I was brought here and she made me wear the harem dress."

Murmurs rose around the room. Hermione pulled a handkerchief from her reticule and wiped at her eyes.

"What did she say? What kind of dress?" Markham asked eagerly.

Revill fixed him with an icy stare. "Mr. Stead, your associate is interfering with a Scotland Yard investigation. If he interrupts again, I'll place him under arrest. Go on, Miss Thorne."

"A few nights ago, Lord Montague and George came here. I tried to escape. I managed to slip down the stairs. I was almost to the front door when Bert caught me."

"And what happened?"

"I recognized him. Lord Montague." She pointed at her former employer.

"Lies," he hissed. "Liar."

"I begged him to help me."

"And this took place in this room?"

"Yes, sir."

"In front of witnesses?"

"Yes, sir." She looked around. Several young women, including Eunice, avoided her eyes.

"And what did Lord Montague do?"

"He pretended he didn't know me. But George recognized me."

"Who witnessed this?" Revill asked.

Hermione rose to her feet. Her expression warned her employees. "No one. The girl is a liar."

But Cate laughed. "I saw it."

Revill turned a page in his notebook. The severely dressed girl with the thick white make-up appeared different from the others. "And your name is?"

"Cate. With a 'C.' Short for Hecate. She's a witch, you know."

"I'll want to question you later." He turned back to his original notes. "Continue, Miss Thorne. Tell us what happened tonight."

She began to tremble. "George came into my room alone."

"She's nothing but a whore," Montague insisted.

"And how did you behave?" Revill went on inexorably. He looked around the room at the other girls, gathered in groups, listening to the story in fascination. "Were you dressed in your undergarments?"

"I was wearing the harem costume, sir. With sheer sleeves and trousers. And b-bells. I didn't have anything else, sir. They took my clothing. Even my shoes." Through the heavy wool of Maria's cloak, she clasped her hand over her bare toes.

"So you were wearing—"

"A green bolero and a pair of harem trousers." Melissa's voice was so low Revill could barely hear it. Color rose in her cheeks.

"And how did you greet Mr. Montague?"

"I broke a stool over his head."

"And he still tried to help you escape?" Revill asked incredulously.

"Yes, sir."

"Whose idea was it to go out onto the roof in the first place?"

"George's. He knew we couldn't get through downstairs. They'd tried to beat him up last week."

"Is this true?" Revill looked straight at Montague. "Was there a fight in here last week?"

The baron quickly raised his hand to cover his face and hide his broken nose. Guilty silence spread like a pool around him.

"I suppose the woman Cate is the only witness to that also," Revill remarked sarcastically as he made a notation. "So, Melissa, you opened the window and climbed out on the roof?"

"George kicked out a window."

"Why didn't he just open it?"

"Because it was nailed shut. All the windows are nailed shut—I suppose because they don't want the girls trying to kill themselves," Melissa said bitterly.

" 'Death Before Dishonor,' " Stead intoned.

" 'Conditions in a West End Brothel,' " Markham added excitedly. "Great stuff!"

Hermione Beauforty threw him a look of sheer hatred. "This is obviously a pack of lies. This girl killed my son and now she's trying to lie her way out it. We all heard her admit that she hit him over the head. Obviously, when he chased her to punish her as she deserved, she pushed him off the roof."

"Are the windows nailed shut?"

"Some might be." Hermione shrugged indifferently. "To prevent thievery and runaways."

"The girl was running. No doubt about that," Revill agreed. "But I doubt that she could have pushed him off the roof. She was on the peak when we saw her."

"She could have climbed up there to escape."

"It was my sister's screams that brought us to her," Maria interrupted. "What about the man who was on the roof with her?"

"I didn't do nothin'," Charly grunted as he lumbered into the room. "The cove fell from the roof all by 'isself. It was slick as glass up there. First step out after 'em an' I like to gone over m'self. Foot slipped through th' railin' an' I was stuck. If it 'adn't gone through, I'd of ended up on a skewer like 'e was."

"Who else was above stairs?"

Cate stepped forward. "Eunice brought that gentleman up." She pointed directly at Jocko, who froze. He had known that eventually the questioning would turn in his direction.

"Say, that's right," Eunice chimed in. "What'd he want to go upstairs so much for? He said he was looking for a certain blonde."

"I was looking for Melissa Thorne," Jocko said reasonably. "Her sister had sent me in to find her."

"Maybe he found her," Cate suggested triumphantly. "Maybe he saw her being chased down the hall. Maybe he stopped George Montague by pushing him off the roof."

"No," Maria cried. "That's not possible."

"Who is he?" Suddenly, Terence Montague added more fire to the flames. "What's he doing here?"

Revill looked only slightly less uncomfortable that Jocko.

Maria glared at the police inspector. "He's a friend. He's been helping me find my sister. When you wouldn't," she reminded Montague. "Of course, you wouldn't. You had put her here in the first place."

"Perhaps you are the one who killed my son," Montague accused loudly.

Maria stared at him incredulously. "I? I was standing out in front of the house with Inspector Revill."

"But you ordered him to do it."

"No. Why would I do that? I didn't even know your son."

Montague's eyes were wild. He lurched to his feet. "Inspector, I demand that you arrest all three of them. They plotted together to kill my son. I'll personally see that you receive a commendation for this night's work."

" 'Murder in the West End,' " Markham exclaimed gleefully.

"I warn you, Mr. Markham." Inspector Revill rose from the stool and came to the peer. "Lord Montague, get control of yourself, man. This is unseemly."

"Unseemly!" Hermione Beauforty screeched. *"Unseemly* is my son lying there dead and those persons standing here lying as bold as brass."

"He demanded that we take him upstairs." Cate's voice purred with malice.

"Who is he?" Montague demanded again.

Revill's face was turning red. The situation had gotten completely out of control. Where were the reinforcements the constable had gone to fetch? He needed help in the worst way.

Jocko sidled closer to Maria's back. "I've got to scarper off," he muttered.

She stiffened. "No. You mustn't."

"They'll 'ave me swingin' in another mo."

"The young man wasn't even on the roof," Revill protested. "I saw the scene less than a minute after your son fell. There were only two people up there." He motioned to Charly. "Where was Miss Thorne when Mr. Montague fell?"

"Up on the top," he replied promptly.

"And yourself?"

"I never got no farther than ye saw me."

"And where was Mr. Montague?"

Charly's brow wrinkled in deep thought. " 'E was just about past the last window."

"Was there anyone at that window?"

"Do ye mean inside it?" Charly thought again. "I can't say, sir."

Revill turned to Markham. "Would you make yourself useful, Mr. Markham?"

"Glad to, Inspector."

"Please follow this fellow up the stairs and find that window. See if it's open or will open."

A tense silence followed.

Suddenly a wild-eyed Montague lunged at Jocko, grabbing him by his lapels. "Who are you?" he screamed. "Why'd you kill my boy?"

Revill caught the crazed man and dragged him back. "Here, stop that."

Montague struggled to free himself. Revill dropped his notebook, breaking his pencil underfoot. Bert moved away from the door to get a better view of the fight.

"Now, Jocko," Duchess called from the archway.

"Right-o." The thief leaped across the room, his hand under her arm.

"Stop them!" Hermione Beauforty cried to her footmen.

But before anyone could move, they dashed out the front door.

Seventeen

" 'Old yer 'orses. 'Old yer 'orses."

Clad in a shabby robe that had probably seen use in a boxing arena, a bleary-eyed "Saint Peter" opened the door to Maria's persistent ringing and knocking.

"Miss Thorne." His irritation quickly changed to sympathy.

A young woman who could only be Maria's sister had sunk to her knees on the stoop.

"I'm sorry to wake you, Peter." Maria's voice broke. "I had to bring her here. I don't know where else to take her."

With a gentle smile he opened the door wide.

Maria bent over Melissa. "Come, dearest. Just a few more steps."

Melissa's head rolled wearily.

"Let me, Miss Thorne," Peter rumbled. With no effort at all, he scooped Melissa up in his arms and carried her into the warm hallway. The girl's head lolled with exhaustion.

Once inside, with the door closed and locked behind her, Maria put her hand to her head. They were safe. Her little sister was safe. Whatever had happened to her inside that awful place could be healed and forgotten with love and time.

She dropped her hand and looked around her, desperately conscious of the terrible imposition on Avory Shires. Still she felt she had no choice. Melissa's tragic experience had brought home to Maria how helpless girls were when they were left alone.

"Want me to put her in one of the guest rooms?" Peter suggested.

"Oh, yes. Would you? I couldn't think for a minute. That would be so wonderful. I don't know how I'll ever repay Mrs. Shires."

"You shouldn't think about that, Maria. I'm so glad you brought her here." They looked up to see the old lady coming down the hall toward them belting her robe. Her enormous white mobcap bobbed with every step. "Where else would you have taken the poor dear, I'd like to know?"

"Thank you so very much." Maria could feel the tears starting. In a different way, her ordeal had been no less than Melissa's. And like her sister's her own life was forever changed.

"Bring her this way, Peter," Avory ordered. Gathering up her robe, she led the way up the stairs.

When the two sisters were alone, Melissa fumbled for the catch on Maria's cloak. When it fell away, she pulled off the remains of the green velvet bolero with the shredded gauze sleeves. With a sob she flung the thing from her as if it were poison.

"Melissa," Maria said softly. "It's all right."

But Melissa did not heed. Shivering, her jaw set, she crossed her arms over her naked breasts. "Please get me something decent to wear," she moaned. "I want to take every bit of this off. Please."

Maria helped peel off the harem trousers and put her cloak back around her sister's shaking shoulders. Then she led her to the bed. "The wool may be coarse, but you can't sleep naked. You'll never get warm."

As if on cue, Peter's knock sounded at the door. "Miss Thorne," he called, "I've brought a warming pan for your sister's bed."

"Climb into bed," she bade Melissa. Opening the door, she smiled her gratitude at the butler. "You're the dearest man. I can't ever thank you enough."

He grinned a little. "We're all glad she's back with you. Is she all right?"

"Just exhausted. She needs to rest."

"Yes, ma'am. Mrs. Shires told me to tell you that you're to ring when she wants food. Otherwise, she's to stay in bed as long as she wants."

Returning to the bed, Maria slid the pan in between the covers. "They're so good to us."

Melissa, who had drawn herself up into a tight ball, thrust her feet against its smooth side and sighed. "Yes, they are good." She stared at Maria with haunted eyes. "Am I really safe, Maria?"

Maria tucked the covers around her sister's shoulders. "You're safe, sister. Did you hear what Peter said?"

"Yes." She hesitated over the word. Her body lay tense beneath the covers, fighting sleep.

Maria could see her eyelids flicker. She caressed her sister's cheek with the back of her fingers. "You can relax and go to sleep, Melissa. Listen to me. You're safe here. Everything will be all right. Avory will take care of you."

"Avory?"

"Avory and Peter. I have to go."

Melissa's eyelids had begun to close. Now they opened wide. "Go?"

"Yes, I have to."

"But it's night."

Maria looked toward the windows. Not even the faintest trace of light could be seen behind the lace curtains. "It's almost morning."

"Where are you going?" Melissa reached out a hand.

Maria took it and tucked it back beneath the covers. She noted the warmth stealing up from the pan. "I have to find Jocko Walton."

"Who?"

"The man who carried you downstairs. Without him you wouldn't have been rescued, dearest. I couldn't have found you by myself. And now he needs help."

"He escaped." The word was slightly slurred.

"That's right. He escaped. But he mustn't run away and hide from the law. He's innocent. And he needs my help."

Melissa's eyelids were closing inexorably. "Help?"

"That's right. He needs help. I have to go." Maria bent and kissed Melissa's forehead.

This time the response was the merest upturn of the corner of her mouth. Her sister slipped into a deep sleep.

Hermione Beauforty had aged twenty years in one night. Only rage and grief kept her from complete collapse. She would not allow George Montague's body to be carried from the salon. Instead, she ordered Inspector Revill and his squad as well as the two reporters to leave. Then she set Charly and Bert to bathing and dressing her son's body while she stood at his head, color burning in her cheeks.

Lord Terence Montague sat by the fire, drinking steadily. His tormented eyes scanned George's body throughout the entire process, searching for a flicker of an eyelid or a sudden intake of breath that would mean that his son was not dead.

The girls of the Lord's Dream scurried up the stairs to their rooms to huddle together and relive the evening's excitement and the revelations that came from it.

To think that Lady H had a son and he was a lord. Or he had been a lord. Now he was dead. A good-looking swell, too, and such a gentleman. Wasn't that always the way?

In the salon, Bert turned gray-green around the mouth as George's clothing was cut away to reveal the three wounds. He had fallen almost face down on the fence. One spear-point spike had gone through his upper chest in the vicinity of the heart, one through his belly, one through the groin.

"Steady there." Charly tapped his companion on the shoulder.

Too late. Bert's eyes rolled. He fell almost straight backward, crashing like a tree.

Hermione did not move. "Give him whiskey, Charly. Get him back on his feet."

"Good idea, Lady H." Charly knelt beside the semiconscious man. "Come on now, Bertie. Just play like it's a picture."

"When you've finished here," she continued, "I have more work for you to do."

Cate rose from the divan. "Lady H," she said softly. "Why don't you come upstairs and lie down?"

The older woman shook her head. "I'll get to be with my precious son only a few more hours. I only just saw him and now I have to lose him again." She smoothed the silky blond hair back from George's forehead. His face was unmarked, as was the rest of his body save for the terrible wounds. "My precious baby."

"You're going to make yourself sick."

"Sick," Hermione scoffed. "I'm dead. My son is dead."

Cate shuddered. "Please don't say things like that."

"I want that creature out of my sight." Terence flung his tumbler into the fireplace and tried to push himself to his feet. He pointed a shaking finger at Cate as she backed away, cursing unintelligibly. "Throw her out in the street, Hermione. Throw her out, I tell you."

His drunken fury seemed to crack the ice in which Hermione had frozen herself. "Terry, calm yourself."

"It's her fault."

"You're loony." Cate faced him defiantly. "And blind drunk besides."

"Not drunk," he sneered. "Not drunk at all. She did it. She's the cause of George's death."

"Terry." Lady H tried to step between them, but he brushed her aside with a sweep of his arm. "Please stop this."

Cate laughed. "Me?" As he staggered close, she stabbed all four fingers into his chest. He reeled backward. "I didn't bring him here." She pursued him, plowing her fingers into his chest again. "I didn't put him in the way of his sisters' governess."

"You . . . you—" Apoplectic, Terence staggered and reeled to the side.

"Cate!" Hermione cried.

Cate laughed. "A peer of the realm. Look at him."

"Terry." Hermione took his arm to steady him.

Montague threw one arm over her shoulder. His foul breath made her grimace. "She—" Spittle struck Hermione's cheek. "—wouldn't let me upstairs." He swallowed hard as the whiskey nauseated him. "She kept me waiting down at the bottom, just as if—" He lost his train of thought. Eyes glazed, mouth agape, he shook his head. The movement destroyed his balance. Had Hermione not steadied him, he would have fallen. She guided him back into the chair.

With a lacy handkerchief, she wiped at her cheek. "Don't drink any more, Terry," she counseled. "It doesn't make it any better."

He looked up at her, his face contorted. "Lemme drink, Hermione. Drink until the pain goes away."

In the act of denying him, she caught sight of her handkerchief. It was soiled with her powder, mascara, and rouge. She could only imagine what she looked like.

"Lemme drink, Hermione." He pawed at her.

Wearily, she nodded. Then with a steady hand she filled another tumbler. Behind her, Cate withdrew to the far side of the salon while Bert and Charly began to wrestle George's body into a new suit of clothes.

"Ria will want to see you," Pansy objected.

"I can't see her. I've got to get out of London completely." Jocko sat with his hands clasped together between his knees. "Being 'ere could get the rest of you in trouble."

"Pansy's right, Jocko." Duchess put her hand on his shoulder. They were both unutterably weary. Jocko had seen his life tossed and torn asunder. Duchess wondered what complications might arise from Revill and from Cate seeing her. She gave Pansy a gentle shove. "Climb up on one of the platforms and get some sleep."

"You can sleep with me," Pansy offered solemnly. "I'll keep you good an' warm an' I don't snore."

"You're my sweetheart, Pan. I couldn't ask for a better

bed partner." Jocko patted her hand where it rested on his knee. "But it's my snoring that would keep you awake."

"Naw, it wou'n't. Bet snores ever so loud, but I sleep right through it."

"I don't snore. If ye sleep so sound, how come ye think I snore?" Bet sneered. "Gawd, yer dumb, Pan."

For once, Pansy ignored Bet's insult. She leaned her head against Jocko's shoulder. "Yer sad, Jocko. Whenever I'm sad, I cuddle up with Bet an' I'm not sad no more."

He put his arm around her and hugged her close. "You're my best girl, Pan. I'd cut off my right arm before I'd let anythin' 'appen to you. That's why I've got to be goin'. They'll be lookin' for me in a couple of hours, just as soon as the watch changes. I don't want them to find me 'ere."

"This is all her fault," Duchess cried angrily.

"No."

"I tell you it is," she insisted. "While we were waiting outside for you, Revill walked up just as bold as brass. He knew we were there. She must have tipped him."

Jocko shrugged. "Doesn't make a mill of difference, Duchess. I never expected this to last. I'm a thief. She's a lady. She's got 'er sister back. Why'd she want to know the likes of me?"

"Oh, Jocko—" She put her arms around him.

They held each other tightly for several seconds. Pansy put her arms around their waists and hid her head against Duchess's side.

"Where will you go?" Duchess asked when he stepped back.

"Wherever my feet will take me." He lifted Pansy and hugged her, then set her carefully down.

Duchess caught his hand. "Tell me."

"I think I might 'ave a talk with the Russian before I leave." He grinned half-heartedly.

"The Russian!"

" 'E knows more than most. 'E's been in and out of all the flash 'ouses. The Russian might 'elp me put two and two together. And if I get four—" He laughed. "I might try to get a last word to Revill before I disappear. Maybe it'd be enough to get 'im to tear up that paper."

Duchess crossed her arms in front of her chest. "Don't ask too much of the Russian," she cautioned. "Soho's secrets are dangerous to know."

Jocko looked down at her. He put his hand to his curly head. Too late he remembered. The new silk topper rested in the cloak room of the Lord's Dream. His bowler was gone into a ragbag at Harrod's. He settled for touching Duchess's chin with his index finger. "Dangerous secrets for sure, Duchess. Like where'd you get those clear blue eyes and skin like milk? And where'd you learn to talk like—"

She brushed his hand away. "Leave it, Jocko."

"Right." With a grin he was gone.

George was dressed in a fine morning suit. A messenger was sent for the Reverend Thomas Dinsmore. Eunice was told to have all the girls in their best dresses and assembled in the salon.

Hermione herself, dressed in unrelieved black with her face half-hidden behind a black veil, had ordered all the curtains drawn. The fire had been extinguished on the hearth, but banks of candles burned at George's head and feet.

She pressed a thick roll of bills into her doorman's hand. "Charly, find Roncie Jack. You and Bert get him to help you bring those two back." He closed his fist around the roll, testing its thickness. His eyebrows drew together in a tight frown. "Who?"

"Melissa Thorne and Jocko Walton."

"Cripes!" Charly exclaimed. His hold on the bills loosened fractionally. "Ain't we got enough trouble, Lady H?"

"Not nearly so much as *they* will have," she replied.

"The peelers'll be lookin' fer 'em, too," he reminded her. "We might find 'em and then the peelers could get us all. We don't want no truck with them."

Her mouth was a thin, pale scar in her white face. "Then you be sure you find them first."

" 'Is bleedin' lordship ain't gonna like it if the peelers come back."

Charly jerked his head in the direction of Lord Terence, who had finally passed out in the chair. His mouth hung open. His drunken snoring broke the peace of the room.

She threw a look of pity in his direction. "He will agree with me. Just find those two and bring them back."

Cate walked across the room. Her dress was also black, but unlike the older woman, high color blazed in her cheeks. Her eyes found the wad of money in Bert's hand. "What's going on? What's that for? What are you doing?"

"None of your concern," Hermione snapped.

"What are you giving him money for?"

Hermione motioned to Charly. "Get on about your business."

"Right-o, Lady H." He shrugged and strode out.

"What's his business?" Cate would not let the matter rest.

The older woman shuddered. "He's going to bring that girl back."

Cate shook her head violently. "No! What for? We don't

want anything more to do with her. And especially not with her sister. The girl used to talk about her sister. She said Maria Thorne—that was her sister's name—would never rest 'til she found her. And she didn't. She was here last night. She brought Revill. For God's sake, Lady H, let them go."

"If Maria Thorne tries to interfere, Charly will take care of her."

"That knot of muscle doesn't even know where to look for her."

"Roncie Jack will."

Cate's hands knotted into fists. "You'll wreck everything and land us all in the courts."

"Lord Montague will protect us."

Cate swept her arm toward him. "Sure he will. That drunken sot, that cock-hound—"

Lady H slapped her.

Cate did not make a move to touch her cheek. Her dark eyes blazed.

Lady H shuddered and clasped her hand as if it had been the injured rather than the injurer. "You'll not speak of him that way. Nor will you use words like that in my presence."

Cate's voice was like dry leaves scraping over an icy pavement. "I'm sure he's been called worse by worse women than me. He's that and more. He's the one you should blame. This is all his fault. Don't forget he took your son."

"He had to have one."

"Then he should have taken the mother along with the son."

"He's a lord. I'm—" She could not go on. Her shoulders rose and fell helplessly.

Cate made a dismissive gesture with her hand. "This is 1884. That old bag in Buckingham Palace is the only one would say a word. Even her own sons don't mind her."

"Things were different in 1866."

Cate shook her head. "You're an absolute and utter fool."

Hermione sank onto a chair for the first time since she had entered the Lord's Dream almost ten hours before. "Cate," she whispered wearily. "I love him."

"Here's a face I never expected to see again." Duchess stood at the top of the stairs, one hand on her hip.

Maria wearily toiled up the steps. "I kept getting lost."

"Of course, I should have remembered. Inspector Revill doesn't know about this place." She paused significantly. "Until now."

Maria snapped a look upward. "Inspector Revill?"

"Your friend. You seem to travel everywhere with him."

Maria shook her head. Exhaustion and nervousness had taken their toll on her body, but she had thought her mind was still functioning clearly. What was Duchess talking about? "I don't understand."

"You understand, all right." Duchess did not step back from the top of the stairs. Instead, she stretched her arm like a bar across the narrow entry. "Amazing how conveniently that peeler appeared last night. Just stepped right out of the dark and spoke to you."

"I was as shocked as you were. I didn't think he ever stepped out of his office."

"Don't tell another one like that," Duchess sneered. "I may be sick."

A band of steel tightened across Maria's brow. Her temples began to pound. She closed her eyes, struggling to understand this woman whom she had counted if not as a friend, at least as a sympathetic acquaintance.

One thought drove the confusion from her mind. She had left her sister's bedside, dragged herself through the streets, for one reason only. "Where's Jocko?"

Duchess's eyes flashed fire. "Fat lot you care. He's gone. Running from the peelers and the pimps both. I warned you not to hurt him. Stop! Don't you come in here."

Angered in her turn, Maria ducked her head and pushed the smaller woman aside. "Where is he?"

"See if I'd tell you."

Maria caught her by the shoulders. "Where is Jocko Walton?"

"Is Revill waiting outside?"

"No. You don't think I'd lead him here to you and Pansy and Bet. Don't be stupid."

"Stupid, is it? Is Jocko supposed to go somewhere with you where they're waiting? Or maybe you'll just take him back to Revill over at Scotland Yard. Save Revill the trouble of finding him."

"I haven't seen Revill since last night." She looked over Duchess's shoulder into the darkness.

"You've set the runners on Jocko."

"Never. As God is my witness."

"Your type calls upon God often. Down here we're too far away for Him to pay any attention."

Maria's head began to throb in earnest. She tightened her hands on Duchess's shoulders. "Tell me where he is."

Duchess wrenched herself free. "He's gone. He's leaving London. You've run him off completely. No need to worry about him telling that your precious sister spent three weeks in a flash house. Unless, of course, she turns up big-bellied."

Duchess had put a name to Maria's greatest fear. Hands clenched into fists, she struck at Duchess's shoulders and face like a madwoman. "You tell me where he is! Tell me!"

Duchess dodged and ducked, scrambling away, lunging behind the table.

In the lofts above, the girls awoke, sitting up, looking over, calling out. Pan and Bet squealed in fear and excitement.

Maria caught the other side of the rickety table and dodged to the left. Duchess instantly dodged to the right. Maria dodged back. Eyes locked, they circled, keeping the scarred piece of furniture between them.

"You've ruined Jocko," Duchess accused. "Made him into a toff. Gave him a taste of the good life. Made him fall in love with you. Then when you got what you wanted, you tossed him aside."

"Is that why you're acting this way? Are you jealous?"

"Me? No." Duchess's eyes flickered. Then she rallied. "Jocko's a friend. Nothing more."

"He's my friend, too. I came to help him. And I'll never toss him aside."

"Your kind tosses people away every day."

"You believe that because you want to believe it," Maria countered. "Otherwise, you wouldn't keep these children locked up here like animals in a zoo. You'd take them to churches and orphanages where they could live and learn in the fresh air."

"Your kind never helps the poor. We're just dirt to you. You just used Jocko."

"I'm here, aren't I? I didn't use Jocko Walton. I've come to rescue him and take him back with me. Now tell me where he is."

"Never."

Abruptly, Maria halted the game. She straightened her hat and took a deep breath. "This I swear to you. If you don't tell me where he is, I will go back to Revill. I'll not only tell about this place, I'll bring him here."

Duchess shivered. Her eyes shifted around the dark, high room. "He wouldn't care."

"Oh, I think he might."

"I haven't done anything wrong."

But Maria understood the way of things better than she had three weeks before. She smiled silkily. "Revill's superiors would care. Some of them undoubtedly frequent the places where Pan and Bet came from."

"You wouldn't do that."

"Where's Jocko?"

Duchess gave her a look of intense hatred, but she knew she had lost. "He said something about paying a visit to the Russian."

"Who's the Russian and where do I find him?"

Duchess smiled nastily. "He's a pimp. He'd like you just fine. He runs an older string."

Maria flushed. "Where?"

"He sometimes has a drink at the Cock Robin."

"How do I get there?"

"It's in Whitechapel. Revill knows where it is."

Maria struck the table with her fist. "Damn you! Listen to me. I didn't tell Revill to meet me outside the Lord's Dream last night. He probably decided to do it on his own. We told him Jocko was beaten behind it. Perhaps he put two and two together. He's not stupid, you know."

Duchess took a deep breath. For the first time a flicker of doubt appeared in her beautiful face. "No, he's not stupid."

Maria leaned forward. "If you want to help Jocko as much as I do, you'll tell me where the Cock Robin is. You might even show me the way there. And if you really care for Jocko, you'll introduce me to the Russian."

Duchess looked around her at the solemn faces of the two little girls. "What do you think?"

Bet shrugged. "She ain't one of us."

But Pan nodded solemnly. "She must love Jocko terrible t' want t' go after 'im to the Cock Robin."

Duchess smiled at that. Her grin took on a malicious cast as she regarded Maria. "All right, milady, I'll take you. But you can't wear what you've got on. The Cock Robin doesn't cater to ladies."

Eighteen

"What happened to you?" The Russian let his black eyes wander over the remains of Jocko's sartorial splendor. A derisive smile might have been hidden beneath the heavy black moustache, but he did not try to hide his amusement.

Jocko shrugged. "Business."

"Good business, *dah.*" The Russian raised two fingers in the direction of the bartender. "Sit."

Jocko dropped gratefully into the chair. With the Russian a man never knew how he would be greeted. For the first time in twenty-four hours, he seemed to be in luck.

The Cock Robin was relatively quiet at this early time of evening. Stale tobacco smoke hung in the stuffy air—no one wanted to open the doors and let out any of the heat. None of the girls and very few of the regulars were in evidence. The concertina man dozed in the corner, his instrument beside him.

The Russian motioned to the plate of stew before him. "You want some?"

Jocko's mouth began to water. Had he really eaten his last meal at the teashop across the street from Harrod's department store? Half his life ago? Half a century ago? He nodded.

Again, the big hand gestured.

The bartender set the dark beer before them and went for more food.

"So." The Russian ladled another spoonful between his luxurious beard and his moustache. "Speak."

" 'Ere's to you." Jocko took a long drink of the bitter beer. It slid down his throat like nectar. He wiped the foam from his upper lip with the back of his hand.

"Nice suit," the other man observed. He reached out and pinched the sleeve of Jocko's coat between his thumb and third finger. "Very nice."

"It was," came the mournful reply.

"Climbing rooftops is very hard on wool."

"You 'eard."

"Dah. Always I wait. Before long I hear."

Jocko lifted his elbows from the table so the bartender could set the stew in front of him. He stared at the food for a minute, trying to remember why he had come. At last he looked into the Russian's obsidian eyes. "A man fell off the roof and died."

"Some say was pushed."

"Do they? Who?"

The Russian made a dismissing gesture.

Jocko sighed irritably and picked up his spoon. "I don't know anythin' about that. Lord, I didn't even know anythin' was up till I 'eard the girl screamin'."

"Some say it was you pushed him."

Ignoring that comment, Jocko bent his head to take a bite. The stew was so hot it burned the roof of his mouth. He had to suck in air to cool it. But it was hearty with plenty of fish and onions, even a few potatoes. He took another bite and shrugged his shoulders morosely.

The Russian continued thoughtfully. "Revill not say it. He not say one way or other. But he want you."

" 'E can keep right on wantin'."

"Maybe you did it after all?"

"I didn't do it," Jocko insisted, laying down his spoon. " 'Ell! I didn't even know the bloke. Just my usual run of luck. Wrong place at the wrong time. I was upstairs 'untin' for the girl, Maria Thorne's sister. Turns out she's the bird tryin' to fly the cage. I come down stairs. Revill's there. 'E gives me a dirty look. Someone yells, 'E's a thief!' So I must be a murderer, too."

"They say the one that fell was a lord's son."

"They say right."

"But they also say that he was Lady H's son."

"That's what she claimed. And that's why I'm 'ere." Jocko studied the Russian's dark face and expressionless eyes.

"You want to know about Lady H."

Jocko took another bite and washed it down with the beer. He tore off a piece of bread. "She might want to 'urt someone special to me. I'd like to give my lady a little insurance."

The Russian nodded ponderously. "When I knew Lady H, she was young and very beautiful. You can see for yourself. Beautiful like princess. Like queen."

Jocko sopped the piece of bread into the stew and nodded.

"She is very smart. Not fool like most. She all for business."

"She's done well for 'erself," Jocko agreed.

"Dah. Very well." He tipped back his mug and sent the beer pouring down his throat. While Jocko watched, he drank the entire contents before he set the mug down. After a reflective belch he opened his eyes. "She had very valuable thing. More valuable than beautiful body. When the time came, she sell."

"A son," Jocko breathed.

"Dah." The Russian's black eyes were infinitely sad. "She sell her son."

"I know that much," Jocko said. "But there's more to the story. Otherwise, George Montague fell off that roof by accident and everybody's in a tear over nothin'."

The Russian pounded a fist into his barrel chest and brought forth another belch. "Maybe he did fall."

"Somehow I can't believe that."

"I know nothing about what happen last night, but this I will tell. Montague is wolf. Not care who he hurt. His wife and his woman were both with child. They give birth two days apart. But one is dead, the other live. He beat his wife, threaten her. He give house to his woman. Give money for live child. Next year same thing."

Jocko finished his beer. A few more people entered the Cock Robin. Maisie, the barmaid, donned her apron and tucked her skirt up into her waistband exposing a length of red and white striped stocking.

"Wife knows about woman. She does not like, but she not have choice. They make pact, the three of them." The Russian clasped his big hands together in front of his face. "Wolf makes them swear. Then woman have son, wife have daughter. They exchange. Montague happy. He have son. Wife happy. Montague no beat her. Woman happy. Her son becomes lord."

Jocko stared in silence, his amazement growing at the cold-bloodedness of the tale. His own mother had loved him in her own way and been good to him. He had always known that. What kind of mother would give up her children? He took another bite of stew. "What about the daughter? What happened to her?"

The Russian laughed hugely. "Who cares? She just woman, right?"

"But—"

"Look." The Russian pointed. "See what comes."

Maria tried to drape the shawl more decently across her naked bosom.

Duchess caught the gesture and pulled the material back down. Roughly, she caught the ends and knotted them behind Maria's back at the waist. "Let's see the flesh, dearie," Duchess jeered. "You're supposed to be a girl who's out to make her living. You won't sell anything if your customers can't see what you've got."

Maria glared at her tormentor. "Enjoying this, are you?"

"You wanted to find Jocko."

A confusion of noises, liberally threaded with curses, reached their ears. "Are you sure Jocko's in there?"

Duchess shrugged elaborately. "If he's not there, he's someplace else. We'll look until we find him. Cheer up. It's tit for tat. He changed his clothes for you."

Before Maria could argue the difference between a suit of fine clothes from Harrod's and a whore's rig from the rag bag, Duchess opened the door of the Cock Robin.

"Happy hunting, lady," Duchess whispered as she pushed Maria into the dismal interior.

A few men's heads swung in her direction. Maria found she was blushing hotly. If she touched her hand to her bosom, she was sure her palm would blister. She stood frozen just inside the room, acutely conscious of the picture she must present, praying silently. *Please, Jocko, be here.*

Instead of a high-necked blouse, Duchess had given her

what amounted to a chemise, pulled up by a drawstring around the bare neck. At first that had not seemed so bad until Duchess had laced Maria into a wide corset that pushed her breasts up and made them spill over in a manner that could only be described as lewd.

Maria glanced swiftly at her chest, then closed her eyes as her face turned scarlet. Her breasts were like small melons. She had never even known she had breasts of such shocking size.

From her waist a whole assortment of petticoats and skirts billowed about her. Unfortunately, they were indecently short. Clad in scarlet striped stockings, her limbs were visible from ankle to just below the knee.

"Too bad about the shoes," Duchess had remarked, "but we can't take the time to find your size."

Maria swallowed her embarrassment and looked around her. The smoke was thick, the conversation noisy. The concertina player was squeezing out a popular air. Many men were leaning on their elbows at the bar—she could see the faces of only about half of them. She would have to walk up and down the room to see if he was there. If only Duchess had not tied the ends of the shawl, she could throw it over herself.

While she was wondering if she could get it undone without spilling out of her top, a gallant stepped forward. " 'Ow's about a pint, m'darlin'?"

"Er—no—"

He swept off his hat. His bald head fairly glowed with greasy perspiration. He leered, exposing stained, chipped teeth. "Yer new around 'ere, ain'tcha? Me name's Samuel Lytton. At yer service."

"I'm hunting—"

"Right-o, darlin'. Don't 'ave to 'unt no more. Y've found me." He tried to take her arm.

Someone else laughed.

At a back corner table, a huge black-bearded man rose and beckoned.

She was trying to avoid Samuel Lytton's clutch when the other occupant of the table turned around, a mug in his hand.

Jocko almost choked on his beer; his face turned red.

Samuel Lytton had managed to catch her elbow, but Maria shrugged him off. "Thank you very much for the offer, Mr. Lytton, but I see my husband over there in the corner."

"Yer 'usband?"

Jocko hurtled across the room. "Ria! Where'd you come from?"

She fairly flung herself into his arms.

Samuel Lytton shrugged. "Whyn't ye say so? I don't 'ave no truck with a married woman."

Jocko put his arm around her protectively and led her back to the Russian's table.

The black-bearded man surveyed her with a critical eye. "You start your own string, Jocko?"

A shock went through Maria, but she had agreed to play a part. " 'E may." She flashed what she hoped was a seductive smile. "Jocko's managin' me as a sort of trial." She turned to Jocko. "Do I look all right, luv?"

A slow grin spread over his stubbled cheeks. He looked with particular interest at her breasts. "You look fine to me, Ria. Where'd you get the togs?"

"Duchess fixed me up right an' proper."

"I might 'ave known. I'll 'ave to let Duchess know 'ow I appreciate 'er 'elp."

The Russian reached out one of the largest hands Maria

had ever seen and lifted a lock of her hair that Duchess had pulled down about her shoulders. "Is real," he muttered. "Real gold."

His touch made Maria's skin crawl, but she smiled as saucily as she could. "From me mum. 'Er's was so long she could sit on it."

"We need to get out of here." Jocko pushed his chair back and felt in his pocket for a coin. "Thanks for the food and the information."

Maria rose also, so swiftly that she pulled her hair out of the Russian's fingers. "Ready when you are, luv."

The Russian sat back, his teeth gleaming out of the dark tangle of beard. "You're welcome, Jocko. Come again. Bring your lady."

They both stared at him.

"I ain't no lady," Maria protested.

"No?" The Russian shrugged. "Maybe not. Maybe so. Good luck. Say to Hermione, I have sorrow for her son."

"What are you doin' here?" Jocko's voice was low and anxious as he hustled Maria out of the Cock Robin. "And dressed like that?"

"I came to find you. Be careful," she protested. Her foot slid sideways on the slippery street. If he had not held her, she would have fallen.

"I *am* bein' careful." The way he dragged her into the darkness of the alley belied his words. Once inside, he spun her toward him and caught her by the shoulders. "You're the one who's not bein' careful. What do you think you're doin'? You could get your throat slit."

Maria's hair bounced as he shook her. "Jocko—"

"When I saw you walk in lookin' like—" He pulled her

against him. Somewhere in the dark, his mouth came down on hers with punishing force.

When she gasped, his tongue drove into her mouth. His arms whipped round her and lashed her to him.

He lifted his head. She could feel his chest heave. "Ria." He kissed her again, more gently this time, but with a terrible intensity.

She wrapped her arms around him and caressed his tongue with her own. Passion heated her blood and curled in her belly. Somehow, one stockinged thigh slid up over his hip.

With a groan he closed his hand round it and pulled it impossibly tighter. "Ria."

He was going to take her in the alley behind the Cock Robin. A shudder ran through her as she acknowledged that she wanted him to.

Suddenly, he tore his mouth from hers. Tipping his head back, he sucked in a great lungful of fog-laden air. As he let it out, he squeezed her thigh and pushed it down. His other hand trailed across her back to grasp her shoulder and hold her away from him. He stepped back. For a moment they both stood swaying.

"Where'd you get that outfit?" he demanded.

"From me." Duchess's aristocratic tones came from behind them at the entrance to the alley.

Jocko did not turn. "I might have known," he growled. "What in hell are you up to?"

"She said she wanted to find you. She couldn't go into the Cock Robin looking like a suffragette." Duchess's voice was bitter. "And Revill's boys were probably following her. I fixed her up so they'd lose her."

Jocko's grip tightened fractionally, then fell away. He stepped back. "Did Revill follow you?"

In the dark she could not judge his reaction, but his voice had lost its emotion. "No. That is, I don't think so. I've been with Duchess since before dawn."

"She showed up in the middle of the night," Duchess corroborated grudgingly. "I kept her out of sight all day. No sign of the inspector or any other peelers when we started."

"That's good." Jocko moved to join Duchess at the end of the alley.

Maria could not believe her ears. He had manhandled her for dressing like a prostitute, when Duchess had all but forced her into the clothing. Now instead of berating Duchess, he was all but thanking her. With an outraged gasp Maria hastened after him and caught his arm. "Jocko Walton, do you actually think that I'd bring Revill here to find you?"

He hesitated. "Maybe not on purpose."

"My God!" As she stamped her foot, her heel rang on the cobblestones. "You think I'd try to have you arrested after you saved my sister? I don't understand you!" Her voice broke as angry tears started down her cheeks.

"Now don't get all upset. There's no harm done. Duchess just knows more about how the peelers operate. She's—"

"Oh, yes. Duchess is perfectly wonderful," Maria sneered. "Except if she cares so much about you, why was I the one who followed you across London and put myself in danger to find you?"

"I don't know," came the soft reply. "Why did you?"

Her anger melted. She swiped at her cheeks with her fingers. "Because I want you to be safe, you fool. I came to help you."

"Help me do what?"

She threw up her hands and tried to push between them. "Nothing. Nothing. Let me pass."

He would not budge. Instead, he caught her wrists. "Hold on. Tell me why you came?"

"I came because I wanted to help you, to do whatever you need me to do," she explained with exaggerated patience.

"I've already found your sister," he muttered.

Maria squealed in frustration and tried to twist free. "Duchess said the same thing. How can you think I would put you in jeopardy? If nothing else, I owe you a debt. Hasn't anyone ever paid a debt to you?"

A silence grew in the alley.

"You don't pay our kind," Duchess said at last.

"Damn, damn," Maria muttered as she tried to move past their united front. When they would not move, she began to struggle with the knotted ends of the scarf.

Jocko hunched his shoulders. "You don't owe me anything."

"I won't continue this conversation," Maria stormed as she jerked the scarf around in front of her. "I came to help you. And I will."

Decently covered, she dug her fists into her hips and faced Jocko Walton. "Now listen to me. Knowing what I know about Scotland Yard, they don't do their jobs. We had to find Melissa or she would never have been found. By the same measure, we have to find out what really happened to George Montague, or you'll be blamed for a murder you didn't commit. Am I right?"

Jocko was surprised she had even thought about it. But she had come to the same conclusion as he. "I can do it on my own."

"How gracious of you!" Her words dripped sarcasm.

" 'Thank you very much, Maria. Go back home again and leave the important work to us.' No!" she raged. "Oh, for heaven's sake! I'll pay my debt and then I'll go away and never bother either one of you again."

He caught her by the shoulders again, but she raised her arms and knocked him aside. Furious because she was crying again, she burst through them and out into the street. "Don't! Don't touch me. I was longing for your touch. I wanted you so badly. I wanted to run into your arms and feel warm again. I knew we could straighten this out together. And now you treat me like this."

Jocko groaned as he followed her, "Ria, I didn't mean—"

"Maria!" Duchess said sternly. "You're hysterical."

"Yes, I am, and with good reason. I'm also exhausted and half crazy. I thought when my sister was safe, I'd feel better. But saving her put you two in danger. And—" She tottered away from them to lean against a wall and stare out into the dark street. A faint drift of music from the concertina blended with the voices from the Cock Robin. "—I only feel worse."

"Ria." Jocko came up behind her and put his hands on her shoulders. "Ria. I'm sorry I doubted you. It's just— Duchess told the right of it. Nobody ever repaid a debt to us."

She remained stiff and silent.

He slid one arm across the front of her and gently drew her back against him. His lips caressed her temple. "Ria. Did you mean it?"

"What?" she asked abruptly.

"Did you really want me to be safe?"

"Not now."

He kissed her cheek. She relaxed, tilting her head so he could continue. "But you meant it then?"

"Maybe."

He slipped his other arm around her waist and hugged her close. "You'll have to be patient with me. I can't get used to this. You're a lady and I'm a thief. When you came to me, I thought you were just going to use me."

"Oh, Jocko . . ." His words sliced into her conscience and into her heart. He knew. He had known he was being used and had given her the right to do so. Just as he had accepted Revill's and probably his stepfather's as well. Jocko Walton needed her desperately. And in that moment she loved him with all her heart.

He kissed her again. "And then when you'd got what you wanted, I expected that you'd go back to your safe world."

She put her hands over his. "And that was all? You were just going to disappear into the night?"

"That's what a good thief does."

Her voice shook. "You would have done that to me? You would have left me alone? If I hadn't persuaded Duchess to bring me here, I'd never have seen you again?"

"Ria." He leaned his cheek against her own. His words were liquid gold. "I'd never do anything to hurt you."

She twisted in her arms and took his face between her palms. "Oh, you good, good man. Don't you see? You would have hurt me much, much more if you'd never come back. Oh, Jocko—"

"I think I'll just slip away quietly." Duchess brought them back to the present with her sarcastic tone.

They broke apart. Maria fanned herself with a corner of her shawl as Jocko adjusted his clothing.

"Did you learn anything from the Russian?" Duchess asked as they struggled with their feelings.

"Quite a lot, actually. Accordin' to 'im, Lady H really

was George's mother. She sold 'im—hold on." His voice dropped to a whisper. They flattened themselves against the wall.

Out of the fog three huge men came stalking by and pushed open the door of the Cock Robin.

"Who is it?" Maria whispered.

"I swear one of 'em's Roncie Jack," Jocko breathed.

"And Charly and Bert," Duchess added. "They must have followed us."

"But we were so careful."

"Maybe," Jocko said. "Maybe not."

The concertina and the din of voices blared as the trio opened the door to the Cock Robin.

Duchess moved quickly to the entrance of the alley and peered around the corner. "Let's go. They're all three in there. We can get away."

"Wonder what they came for," Jocko mused.

"You, undoubtedly. Hurry!"

"Listen . . ." he said.

The music had ceased. Likewise, the hum of voices had died. Suddenly, they heard a great roar.

"It's the Russian."

The noise blared with shocking force as the door was flung open. Three women catapulted out and ran away down the street. Then a couple of men slipped out the door with full mugs of beer in their hands. Rather than flee, however, they stood together guzzling and watching through the foggy window.

One chuckled and elbowed the other as things began to crash and bang. Furniture splintered. Someone howled in pain.

Jocko started for the door.

"Come back!" Duchess called. "You can't go in there."

He grinned back over his shoulder. "Can't miss a good fight."

"The Russian can take care of himself," she reminded him.

"Three against one when one is Roncie Jack might be a little stiff even for 'im." Jocko side-stepped another exiting patron and ducked into the bar, which was fortunate because a slab of wood came flying through the door.

"We have to help him," Maria said, starting for the door.

"Don't be ridiculous." Duchess caught her skirt. "You'll get hurt. A barfight's no place for a woman."

"There's at least one barmaid in there."

"She's probably cowering under a table."

Maria twitched her skirt away. "I'm going in."

Her first impression was that the Cock Robin seemed remarkably well organized for a fight. Around the wall and behind the bar, men and a few women were standing two and three deep. Money passed freely from hand to hand— Fingers fluttered as they placed bets on the outcome.

In the center of the place, the Russian whirled like a great black bear, kicking and punching, a steady stream of curses in several languages rumbling from his throat. Just out of his reach, Charly and Bert circled, splintered tablelegs in their hands, trying to find an opening.

Clutching his mid-section and howling, Roncie Jack writhed on the floor beneath the Russian's feet.

Maria almost had a heart attack when a hand fastened in her waistband dragged her backward.

Jocko put his arm around her shoulders and hugged her hard. His face was split in a big grin. "Come to see the mill?"

She took her cue from his attitude. "Oh, yes, luv. I wouldn't miss this for the world."

"Not what you're used to, I'll bet."

"Type writing's going to be dull from now on," she agreed.

As they watched, Charly succeeded in edging his way around the circle until he was almost opposite Bert. Some bettors groaned, others grinned in anticipation. The Russian was caught between them with no place to go. Roncie Jack let go his belly and pushed his way up on all fours.

"Things look like they're going to get unfair," she observed.

Jocko shook his head. "The Russian'll be unfair to them. Watch."

Quick as a bear's paw, the Russian's foot slashed out. The toe of his heavy boot drove into Jack's stomach again, rolling the pimp over onto the floor like a turtle on his back.

Charly's club came whistling toward the Russian's undefended back, but the big man had never stopped moving. He dodged to the side and the blow never fell. Instead, Charly's momentum carried him forward as the Russian caught his wrist and tripped him. Charly's howl of pain choked off as he fell facedown in the sawdust.

Bert took a better grip on his club. At the same time, he fumbled beneath his coat.

"Excuse me," Jocko murmured to Maria as he hurled himself through the air. His body crashed into Bert's. As he twisted the man's arm, Bert howled; an ugly-looking knife clattered to the floor.

The Russian spun around. His grin widened as he nodded his thanks.

"My pleasure." Jocko gave the struggling Bert a shove. The ex-fighter stumbled toward the Russian, who was waiting for him with a series of uppercuts to the belly, to the jaw, to the side of the head.

Maria expected to see Bert collapse alongside the other two, but he took them all on stolidly. He let the table leg slide from his hand and raised his fists—his right poised in the air nine inches in front of his nose. Swift and deadly accurate, he punched the Russian twice with his left. One blow fell on the cheekbone, one on the eyebrow.

The noise increased as the crowd recognized the professional fighter. More bets went round. The Russian stepped back, shaking his head. The two circled each other cautiously.

Jocko returned to Maria's side. He was still grinning. "Great fight."

"If you say so."

Roncie Jack had rolled out of the way. Now he came to his feet and pointed a bloody hand at Jocko. " 'Ey, Jocko, why don'tcha be a sport an' come along?"

Jocko set his lady to one side. "Who wants me?"

Roncie Jack shook his head. "Who do ye think? Bloody Queen Vick, o' course."

"She's too old for me."

The fighter growled. "You can't get away. Why dontcha c'mon with us peaceable?"

"We'd best be goin'," Jocko said to Maria. " 'Ey, Russian," he called, "you goin' to be all right?"

The Russian gave a great bellowing laugh. As if he had been toying with Bert, he waded in and flattened the man's nose until blood spattered. Bert went over backward. Charly had crawled beneath a table where he nursed his arm.

"Is over," the Russian yelled, throwing his arms wide and wading toward the last opponent standing. "Roncie Jack, you want broken nose or wrist?"

Roncie Jack stopped in his tracks. The Cock Robin fell suddenly silent as the spectators waited eagerly, straining to hear his answer. With a wordless snarl he bolted out into the night.

A cheer went up. Men and women crowded forward to congratulate their champion and collect their bets. The bartender began to draw mugs of beer and pass them down the bar.

The first went to the Russian, who drained it in one swallow. He thumped his chest, gave forth an enormous belch, and then laughed uproariously.

The second went to Jocko, who passed it to Maria and took the next one. Together they clicked their mugs and drank.

As she drank it down beside her man, elbow on the bar, one ankle crossed over the other beneath her shameless short skirts, Maria Thorne had never felt so alive in her life.

Type writing was a very, very long way away.

Nineteen

As they stepped out, the streets were gray with morning light sifting through the fog. Jocko put his arm around Maria's waist and they matched steps.

She leaned her head against his shoulder. "Where are we going?"

"Where do you want to go?"

"With you."

He hugged her harder. "I'll take you 'ome."

"That'll be nice. I can't remember when I went to bed."

They walked until a dray caught up with them. They clambered onto the back of it and settled down, swinging their feet like children. Farther on, they passed the street-sellers hawking fresh milk and hot bread, and Jocko treated his lady to a sumptuous breakfast.

As the bells began to toll at St. Luke's, they made another change of transportation.

"I feel as if we ought to go in and give thanks," Maria murmured. "We've come through the worst."

Jocko made no answer. His eyes were suddenly bleak.

She watched him closely. "You don't think that's right, do you?"

"No."

She put her arms through his. "Still, we'll get a good day's sleep. Everything will look better then."

She opened her front door and led him in without the faintest twinge of embarrassment.

He hesitated. "Someone might see."

She pulled his head down and kissed him full on the lips. "The way I feel about you, Jocko Walton, I wouldn't care if the Queen herself were sitting here in the hallway. Poor old girl. She doesn't have anyone to love."

Her kiss drove the weariness right out of his bones. He hugged her.

Inside the room, she bent down to build a fire, but he pulled her back up. "No need for that."

"I'll just make the room warm," she insisted. "Nobody's been here in so long, the sheets are probably damp."

He untied the shawl from around her neck and tossed it away. "We'll warm them up."

Before she knew what he was about, he had buried his face in her breasts. "Jocko!"

He did not raise his head, his lips moved over the sensitive flesh pushed upward by the corset. At the same time, his hands pulled the drawstring loose in the chemise. It slid down her shoulders, baring her. He sucked his breath gustily. "I've been wanting to do that for hours. If it hadn't been for the Russian, I swear I'd have kissed you in the Cock Robin. When you walked in there—with your hair hanging down—"

"Duchess helped me—"

"—And your breasts—"

"—Look as indecent as—"

"—I thought I'd explode."

She never finished her sentence. He was suckling her nipples, kissing her breasts, squeezing them between his hands. She had no will to stop him, only a yearning to experience again the power of his passion.

She moaned and plunged her hands into his thick golden hair. It curled around her fingers. She lifted her breasts to him and held on tight. Her heels, then her toes left the floor. She locked her ankles around his waist.

"Ria."

"Oh, yes, Jocko."

He lifted his head and found her mouth waiting for him, open, thirsting. At the same time, she pushed her body against his. He was hard through his clothes. Only the thinnest of lawn drawers separated them. Desperately, she pushed against him. "Jocko," she moaned. "Jocko!"

He must be aware of her need, she thought, must know the feelings boiling inside her. "It's all right, love."

"But, I can't—"

"Yes, love. Yes, you can."

She felt it coming, felt the waves of ecstasy, the pain, the pleasure erupting from the center of her being, the spot that sought to close over him, frustrated by their garments.

She pushed harder.

He rotated his hips.

It was enough to send her over the edge, screaming, rising against him, arms on his shoulders, pushing upward, pulling her nipple from between his teeth.

He took two steps and sprawled onto the bed. Pressing himself against her along his entire torso. His mouth found hers, but she wrenched her head away. "You with me," she rasped. "Now."

He fumbled for his buttons, found them, pushed them through the buttonholes. He burst out before he was half undone. The undergarment was still between them, but her hands dove between their bodies and found the slit. Grimacing, she ripped it apart.

"Now," she said again. "Now."

He drove into her, sliding up to his full length. She felt herself close round him, pull him in, caress him, encompass him.

"Ria!"

"Yes, Jocko. Yes, sweetheart."

He drove her mad with delight, he carried her farther and farther up with him, until she was laughing and sobbing, and clawing at his shoulders.

"Ria!" he called.

"Yes-s-s."

A wild wind roared in their ears. The bed beneath them heaved and tossed like a ship in a Channel gale. They exploded together in a burst of lights.

Neither made any attempt to restore order. He slid to the side, she cuddled against him and they slept.

Clarice, Lady Montague, choked over her morning tea. The cup rattled into the saucer and then tipped over as she swept the newspaper up for a closer look.

A stain spread across the linen cloth. Her daughters Bethany and Juliet gasped then looked guiltily at their mother. She had not noticed the accident. Instead, her face looked strange.

She read the story a second time. Tears formed in her eyes and trickled down her cheeks.

"Mother," Bethany said uncertainly.

She looked up, her eyes wide with shock. "Yes?"

"Are you all right?"

She took a deep breath. "I think there has been some mistake, but I must send a telegram. If you will excuse me. Go right on with your breakfast. I must send a telegram."

Juliet frowned. "You just said that, Mother."

"What?" Lady Clarice rose from the table. "Finish your breakfast, dears."

The maid came in with the chafing dish of kippers and coddled eggs, but Lady Clarice did not even realize she had not yet eaten. She walked unsteadily to the door, the paper under her nose, reading it again.

"Madam," the maid said softly. "May I help you?"

Clarice glanced up. She was trying to find the knob on the panel next to the door.

The footman bowed and left to carry the telegram to the depot. She sank onto the divan beside the window. Bright golden sun streamed in. The garden was beginning to bloom, with tender sprouts shooting up through the black soil even in the most exposed places. Clarice stared at the damning black type.

"Heir Falls to His Death"
By William T. Stead

From a maelstrom of vice where virgins are violated for the pleasure of peers of the realm, Lord George Montague, a beautiful youth, the only son of Lord Terence Montague, Knight of the Garter and Member of Parliament, fell to his tragic death.

This reporter was on the scene within minutes after the unfortunate young man plummeted from the roof of the infamous brothel called euphemistically The Lord's Dream. There he lay, his silver skin pierced in no less than three places by spikes from the iron fence surrounding the establishment. Oh, that the spikes had been sufficient to keep him out of this den of iniquity rather than to catch him as he fell.

There was more, but Clarice could not bear to read it again. George. Kind, good George. Her stepson, but more than her stepson, her friend. Her precious daughters' big brother. She pressed her handkerchief to her eyes and wept. She could not bring herself to tell Bethany and Juliet. Her grief was too raw. She would wait until their father returned.

"Terence," she whispered. "Oh, poor Terence."

She looked around her, not seeing the beauty of the day. Resolutely, she made a decision. She must go to her husband. A wife's place was with her husband in this time of grief.

Tucking her handkerchief into her sleeve, she rang for the housekeeper to order her packing.

"I never knew it could be like that."

Maria ran her hand over Jocko's shoulder. The muscles rippled as he sighed with pleasure. Her fingers trailed down the underside of his arm where the skin was like the very sheerest silk. Her fingers found the golden hair of his armpit, just as soft and curly as the hair on his head. Devoid of shyness, she laid her cheek against his shoulder and tickled him.

He growled and flexed his shoulder, playing at throwing her off.

She set her teeth lightly against the skin. "I'm going to bite you."

He laughed and rolled over suddenly, catching her in

his arms, wrestling her on top of him, hugging her. "Bite away."

"Well, perhaps I won't bite you." She moved her hips into a more comfortable position.

"Careful," he warned.

"I won't be careful," she murmured. "I love you and you'll never hurt me."

He kissed her long and deeply. "I never knew it could be like that either."

"We'll do it again and again."

He kissed her again and rolled over until she was lying on her back and he was lying beside her. From there he sat up. "I think we need to get dressed. I'll take you to your sister."

Maria sat up, too. "Lord, I had forgotten about Melissa. I can't believe it. My precious sister, and all I could think about was you."

"Lord Montague is away from home, madam."

Clarice bit her lip in vexation. Other than a black wreath on the door knocker and a black armband on the butler, the Brooks Mews residence showed no evidence of mourning.

"When will he be returning, Patterson?"

The butler fixed his cold stare six inches to the right of her face. "I really couldn't say, madam."

"Perhaps I should speak to his valet."

The muscles around the butler's mouth tightened as if he wished to say something but could not quite bring himself to do so. Finally, "The valet too is away from home."

Clarice's palms itched to grab the man by the lapels and shake him. She drew herself up to her full height. "Are they staying at Lord Montague's club?"

Patterson lifted his eyes to heaven. His sympathies were all with the lady of the household, but the lord paid his wages. He sighed mentally. "That might be where they are."

A high color stained her cheeks. "If I were to call for the carriage and ask the coachman to take me to Lord Montague, do you think he could do so?"

Patterson broke decorum insofar as to shift nervously. "I really can't say, madam. Perhaps."

"Then I shall have my lunch and lie down for a brief rest. If Lord Montague has not returned, I shall be needing the services of that coachman. See that you tell him so, Patterson."

"Yes, madam."

"Evelyn? You're not Evelyn."

Hermione Beauforty bit her lip. "No, Terry. I'm not Evelyn."

Montague stared at her, his brow wrinkling. Then his eyes glazed and wandered. "Good." He fumbled for and found the tumbler of brandy. "Never liked her anyway."

He finished off the liquor and leaned forward to reach the decanter. It was almost empty. He spilled a bit before he managed to slosh it into his glass.

He took another drink, coughed, and lifted the glass, staring at the brown liquid as if it had betrayed him. "Evelyn never loved George," he mourned. "Not like she should've. Damn her. She was damned lucky I didn't divorce her. Should've been happy when I fixed it. Fixed everything. She had everything she wanted. But she should've loved George."

Hermione removed the decanter of brandy. She dropped

a hand onto his shoulder. "Terry, you need to get bathed and dressed. The reverend will be here for the service."

He looked up at her. His face twisted, helpless tears trickling down his cheeks. "George," he murmured. "George. My son, Hermione. My only son."

His words lanced through her, but the pain was already so intense it made no difference. She had cried until she had no tears left. She motioned to the maid. "Eunice, bring the valet down. He'll have to help Lord Montague up the stairs."

"I'll take care of him, Eunice."

Lady H looked uncertainly at Cate, who smiled sweetly back. She put her arm around the old man's back. "Let me help you, Lord Terence."

He looked up at her. A flicker of puzzled recognition, then it faded. "Don't need help," he sneered. "No help. No help."

Rather than leave him alone, the girl in black exerted surprising strength and lifted him from the chair. "Come along with me," she insisted. "I'll make you feel better."

"We'll be a family, Jocko," Maria said. "You and me. We'll have Melissa for a time, but then she'll marry and—"

He wouldn't allow himself to listen to such a dream. He contented himself with watching her as she mended his suit.

"This will never show," she promised as she carefully placed the edges of the torn cloth together and interwove the darning thread. "It brushed down nicely, don't you think?"

He nodded, guided by the inflection in her voice. Whatever she had said must be right. Ria was usually right. He took a sip of tea. It was strong and hot. It made him feel good. He looked around the quiet little room. The furniture was shabby, but she had made it into a home. A shawl draped over the lamp table, pictures of her parents and grandparents in silver frames, prints on the wall, a vase of dried flowers.

She spoke of being a family, but how would they live? He had never had an apprenticeship. While he could read and write and do sums after a fashion, that sort of education fitted one to be a clerk. And to get a clerk's job, a man needed a reference.

Who would write him a reference?

He thought of the confession in Revill's possession. He wanted to curse, to punch his fist into something hard, preferably Big Tilly or Roncie Jack. He was better than they were. He knew it. But that confession would haunt him the rest of his life.

"Here you are, love. I think this will do nicely." She held it for him to slip into.

It was the sort of service a wife would perform for her husband every morning. Then she smoothed it over his shoulders, touching him with love and affection. He turned around and she adjusted his cravat and stepped back. "You look wonderful. Just as good as new."

He looked down at himself and grinned. "Wish I 'adn't lost the topper."

"We'll replace it," she promised. "For now, let's go to Mrs. Shires. I know Melissa must be worried half to death." She turned to straighten her hair in front of the mirror.

He came up behind her and put his arms around her. "Ria, I'll take you to Melissa, and then I 'ave to go."

"Go? Where?"

He kissed her cheek. "I 'ave to leave London. Roncie

Jack won't stop until 'e finds me, especially not since the mill last night. 'E wants my blood."

She stared at him in the mirror, not knowing what to say. She pressed her cheek against his. "Does this mean that you're trying to desert Melissa and me?"

"No!" The word sounded more explosive than he had intended. "Of course not."

"But you're not making plans to take us with you."

"I can't take you with me. I don't know where I'm goin'."

She clasped his wrists and pulled them across her chest. "You could send for us as soon as you're settled."

"I might never be settled." He kissed her again and tried to extricate himself. "I can't take you with me and I can't send for you."

"Jocko."

He stepped back. "No! Don't you see? I'm a thief with no prospects. I'll 'ave to take work where I find it. I may not find it immediately. I'll probably 'ave to go back to stealin'. I'll probably end up in Dartmoor."

She went after him and caught his hands. "If you took us with you, I could work until you found something."

"No! My wife—" He tried to bite the revealing word back.

Her smile bathed him in golden sunshine. "Go on," she urged. "Your wife—"

"I won't be supported by a woman."

"Why not? It's done all the time."

"Not by nice people. Not by your sort."

"My sort are your sort of people. And besides, I like working. I'm a good type writer."

"I can't listen to this." He threw up his hands. "You can't go on workin' after we're married—" He broke off with a cry and shook his fists at the ceiling.

"I'll be happy to marry you, Jocko Walton," she said demurely. "How long I've waited for you to ask me."

"No," he howled. "I've done it again. We are not goin' to be married."

"You just said we were," she accused.

"I didn't."

"You've thought of it. You've tried to figure out how to do it. You've wracked your brain about how you could earn a living for us."

"No."

"But you didn't think about my working. Or Melissa working. Just until you could get on your feet."

"Oh, my God!" he all but shouted. "Put your 'at on."

"We could do it, you know. We could do just as you said. We could go somewhere else. To Brighton or Bath. Mrs. Shires has lots of friends in both places. She would write me a reference in a minute. I know Lady Montague would write Melissa a reference." She clapped her hands. "It will work, Jocko. I know it will."

"No!"

But she caught him by the shoulders and kissed him hard on the lips. "I love you."

"Christ!"

Lady H looked at her battered minions in disgust. "I send three of you to fetch one little girl and one murdering thief, and you come back alone and looking like this."

Bert hung his head but tipped it back swiftly when his broken nose began to throb.

Charly growled under his breath. "'E 'ad 'elp."

"And the three of you could not help each other?"

Roncie Jack flexed his heavy shoulders belligerently. "That damned Roosian conked me when I wasn't lookin'."

"The Russian?" Lady H's expression hardened. "He wouldn't have had to sneak up on the likes of you."

Jack shot her a burning look, then hastily dropped his eyes. " 'E conked me from behind, so 'elp me Gawd."

"If you tangled with him, you're lucky to be alive."

"We just asked where the bloke was. And 'e conked us," Bert finished lamely.

Lady H looked as if she would like to conk them all. "God help me if I have to depend on you to handle more than the occasional drunk."

They shuffled their feet and nursed their hurts, shooting accusing sidewise looks at each other.

She consulted the small watch on her lapel. "Can you be trusted to find the girl?"

Roncie Jack was eager to redeem himself. "Sure thing, Lady H. Like as not, she's at that old woman's place where Petey works. 'Er sister was in th' Cock Robin last night 'angin' onto Jocko like a second skin."

"Do you think you can bring her back here, or should I give you money to hire some more boys?"

Jack writhed at the sarcasm in her voice. "It's done," he boasted. "She'll be back 'ere 'fore ye can turn around."

"Don't bring her in during the service." Lady H cautioned. "Take her around to the kitchen and hold her until it's over."

"Ye got 'er." Jack started for the door.

"Take Bert with you." Lady H made a dismissing motion. "A broken nose shouldn't create a problem with using one's fists."

Bert looked longingly after the unfortunate Charly, who trailed out, bound for a bed in the stables.

* * *

"No, ma'am." The coachman shook his head. "I can't recall where I took Lord Montague."

Clarice looked him up and down. He did not flinch but kept his face carefully impassive. She sighed. Her husband's servants were loyal to him to a fault. Their refusal to locate him aroused her curiosity at the same time that it made her so frustrated that she wanted to scream.

"Where is George's funeral to take place?"

"I couldn't say, ma'am."

"What is going on here, Patterson?" She turned to the butler. "Inform this man that I am the mistress of this house, George was my stepson. I wish to satisfy myself that arrangements for the funeral are complete."

"I'm sure that everything is as it should be, madam," Patterson stated lamely.

"That's just it. You never know anything. Or at any rate you refuse to tell me." She lifted her coat from the rack beside the door.

Patterson hastened to help her into it.

"Thank you. Coachman, I hope the horses are ready."

"Yes, ma'am. Where will you be wanting me to take you?"

"To the *Pall Mall Gazette*. I'm sure Mr. Stead can help me. He has all the facts pertinent to this story."

"I want Jocko Walton in this office by noon today," Revill snarled. "He was there on the scene. He may have seen something he doesn't even realize he saw."

"He was out on the roof himself. Maybe he did it. They

was both chasing after the girl," Constable Wilkie suggested.

Revill shook his head. "He didn't come out until much later. Of course, he might have raised a window and tripped the victim. But that's not Jocko's style. He's a thief."

"Maybe he got caught stealing," Wilkie hazarded.

"He wouldn't kill someone. He's been caught before."

"Maybe he's branching out?"

"He's not a murderer. Why kill someone you don't even know who's chasing a girl out onto a rooftop? Especially when the whole house is full of girls eager to serve you. No, Jocko didn't do it. But he may know who did, and not even know that he knows."

"He may be hard to find, sir."

Revill allowed himself a small smile. "Find Miss Maria Thorne and Mr. Jocko Walton will not be far behind."

"If you say so, sir."

"I do, Wilkie." He fixed the man with a deadly serious look. "And, Wilkie, see to it that he's not beaten up by any of our boys."

Wilkie's face went very still. A slow red color crept upward into his cheeks. "Sir, I can't—that is, you can't—"

"See to it."

Twenty

Bert's nose was a deformed purple mass in the middle of his face. Mousy yellow hair drooped around his bristly cheeks. He breathed noisily through cracked and broken teeth.

At the sight of him lumbering down the hall, Melissa let out a piercing scream.

He blundered to a halt and dashed the sweat from his brow. "C'mon now, girl. Don't make it 'ard."

At that moment, she recognized him. He was one of the bully boys who worked for Lady H. He had come for her. But she would not go back. Sucking in a deep breath and letting it out in another scream, she tried to rush past him.

He sidestepped into her path, arms outspread to herd her back down the short hall and trap her in a corner.

Once she would have cringed in terror, pleading for mercy. Now she drew in a deep breath and screamed again, coolly, deliberately, making the sound come from the very bottom of her lungs. At the same time, she doubled her fists and waited.

"Now, ye don't want t' do—"

His hands were inches from her shoulders when she drove her left fist into Bert's swollen nose.

The walls fairly reverberated with his howl of mortal agony.

She ducked and fled past him down the hall. A heavy weight thudded behind her, followed by a great crash. She did not spare a glance but sprinted for the top of the stairs.

The scene below froze her in her tracks. Mrs. Shires lay crumpled half in, half out of the front door. "Saint Peter" was locked in violent combat with a man she had seen once or twice at the Lord's Dream.

She threw a glance over her shoulder. Bert was climbing, hand over hand up the wall. Halfway up, his knees buckled and dropped him back. He shook his head dizzily. Blood dripped from his nose. His eyes were closed. Clearly, he was not paying attention to her.

Good.

Below her, Peter broke free and threw a roundhouse punch at Roncie Jack. If it had landed, it would have torn the pimp's head off, but Jack ducked and danced out of reach.

"Yer still a pushover, Petey," Jack crowed, ducking and weaving. "Bad eyes."

"I'll show you bad eyes." Peter raised his guard and followed Jack down the hall.

Melissa raced down the stairs. At the door she knelt beside Mrs. Shires. The old lady had propped herself up on one elbow. Muttering to herself, she was having trouble replacing her amber-tinted spectacles on her nose. One temple bar was twisted and a lens was cracked.

Melissa caught her under the shoulders. "Come on! We have to run."

"Oh, no," Mrs. Shires protested. "You go on."

"Not without you." Melissa tugged at her.

"Hey, girlie," Jack yelled.

"Run," Mrs. Shires urged. "They don't want me."

Jack threw a punch at Peter. The butler caught it on his

shoulder and countered with a right cross that connected on Jack's cheekbone and rocked him back.

"Bad eyes, huh?" Peter snorted. "Watch yerself, Jack."

"Come on." Melissa tried once more to lift the old lady, but Mrs. Shires shook her head.

"Go on. I insist."

Bert came stumbling down the stairs, still holding his nose. Peter would soon be outnumbered.

Melissa rose. "I'll be back." She took a deep breath and let out another piercing shriek. Catching up her skirts, she dashed down the steps. "Murder! Help! Police!"

A cab came rolling down the street. She ran toward it. "Help!"

The cabdriver pulled his horse to a halt. "What's that ye say?"

She dashed to his side. "Help! Some men—"

"Melissa!" Maria swung the cab door open. "Dearest! Get in."

"No. We have to get help."

"What's wrong?" Jocko Walton leaped from the cab.

Melissa threw herself into his arms. "Thank heavens, you're here. Bert's there, at Mrs. Shires's. And another man. They're fighting. Oh, hurry."

Jocko sprinted away.

Maria climbed down and embraced Melissa. "Are you all right?"

Melissa managed a smile. "I'm fine, but Mrs. Shires—"

"Mrs. Shires is hurt?!"

Melissa nodded. "They knocked her down."

"Oh, Lord. Stay here with the cab." Maria followed Jocko.

She found Avory sitting on the doorstep, her spectacles in place, lopsided and cracked. The former militant suffragette waved cheerfully to Maria. "They're fighting."

The smack of fist against flesh followed by the sound of wood splintering confirmed her statement.

Maria knelt in front of her and took her hands. "Are you all right?"

The old lady grinned. "Never better. This is just like the old days."

From inside the house came the sounds of more fists connecting. Roncie Jack cursed. Maria craned her neck to see in the front door.

Melissa hurried toward them. "I've sent the cabdriver for the police."

"Good idea, my dear." Avory readjusted her glasses.

A thundering crash made them all wince.

"There goes the refectory table," said the mistress of the house. "Help me up, Maria. I'm missing the mill. And it sounds like a good one."

"Mrs. Shires!"

"Don't look so shocked, my dear. You remind me of Dudley."

Jocko looked back over his shoulder, a broad smile on his face.

Bert stood beside him, shielding his injured face with his hand. His breathing rasped, and blood still dripped down the front of his shirt. Avory drew a handkerchief from her sleeve and offered it to him. He accepted it gratefully.

Beyond them, squared off in the parlor, were Peter and Roncie Jack. Toe to toe they stood, fists wheeling, jabbing in and out at each other, feinting, ducking and diving, pounding each other with bare knuckles. Clearly, both had lost the sense of the original purpose for the fight.

"Great show," Jocko remarked. "Wish I could make book on it."

"A fiver on Peter." Avory chuckled at the disapproving

expression on Maria's face and nudged her companion. "You're a rogue after my own heart."

"We've sent for the police," she said.

Bert started up from the doorway. "Finish 'im, Jack," he called hoarsely. "The peelers is on the way."

Roncie Jack could do no more than nod. His teeth were set. Blood dripped from a cut in his eyebrow. He feinted right, then jabbed left.

Peter parried the blow with his forearm and followed it back in. Roncie Jack grunted as the right cross caught him on the ear.

"C'mon, Jack." Bert urged. He turned his head to one side, listening. "I can 'ear the bloody whistles, Jack. Yer pardon, ma'am." He nodded to Avory and was gone.

"Nice young man," she remarked. "Perhaps I can use a second bodyguard."

Maria rolled her eyes.

"Where can the police be?" Melissa cried.

"Never one around when you want 'im," Jocko observed darkly.

Peter grunted as Jack pummeled his ribs with straight rights and lefts.

"Get him, Peter. His guard's down," Avory cried.

Melissa gasped and covered her eyes. Maria turned her face away, but she and her sister were obviously the only ones not enjoying the spectacle. If she lived another fifty years, she would never understand her employer, who took Bert's place and grinned as she nudged Jocko in the ribs.

The shrill blast of a policeman's whistle sounded from the street.

Peter and Roncie Jack both froze. Their blazing eyes met across their bloodied fists. As if by common consent,

they stepped back. Peter jerked his head in the direction
of the window. "Run for it, Jack."

"Right ye are, Petey."

"He's letting him get away," Maria protested.

Jocko grinned at her. "Sure. They're friends."

Later, after the policemen had departed to make their
reports to Inspector Revill, the five occupants of the house
gathered around the table in the kitchen. Melissa offered
to make tea. Avory cleaned the cuts and abrasions on Peter's hands.

He looked at her with adoring eyes, Maria thought. Except that she had seen him in anger and in action, she
would have continued to believe that Peter really was their
dear "saint." Of course, saints could be militant as well.

Jocko congratulated Peter again. Mrs. Shires praised his
right hook. He basked in their compliments.

Maria watched them all. She was thoroughly irritated with
both the butler and Jocko for letting Roncie Jack and Bert
escape. These men had hurt her sister, kept her against her
will, and would cheerfully have taken her back to slavery
and prostitution. They should be jailed and deported or even
hanged.

And they should all be discussing how to bring an end
to the vice of the Lord's Dream. But instead they were
discussing the details of the fight.

She shook her head in wonder. Nothing. Absolutely
nothing was as it had been only a month before. All the
boundaries of her life, all the rules by which she had lived
and which she had tried to instill in Melissa had changed.

The sedate widow of a peer of the realm was anything
but sedate. The butler was a boxer who was a friend of

the pimp who had beaten him to the pavement. And the thief looked and talked like a gentleman with a moral code that was proving to be quite as straitlaced as a bishop's.

And the upshot of all these goings-on was that Peter and Jack were friends. And Bert had Avory's handkerchief. And Melissa had been kidnapped by a Member of Parliament. And she and Jocko were wanted by the police.

Her emotions stirred as she looked at the curly blond head bent to share a laugh with Peter and Avory.

And Maria Thorne was in love with a thief.

"Does that feel better?" Avory asked.

"Yes, ma'am." Peter nodded. "Feels just fine."

"You were beating him," his employer continued loyally.

"Roncie Jack. I don't know about that." Peter flexed his hands. " 'E was givin' as good as 'e got. We 'ad a long way t' go."

Melissa served the tea in china cups. Peter drank it gratefully. Jocko grimaced at the weak taste but drank it anyway.

Maria looked around her. "What are we going to do?"

"Oh, they won't bother us again," Avory said as she laid her hand on her butler's shoulder. "They'll get short shrift here with Peter to meet them."

Maria shook her head. "That's beside the point. We don't want them to come back. We've got to do something. Otherwise, Melissa will never be safe."

Jocko nodded solemnly. "She's right. They came after me last night and Melissa today. This must be the old man's doin'."

"Lord Montague!" Melissa shuddered.

" 'E wants someone to pay for 'is son's death."

"It was probably an accident. I'll never forget it." Melissa rubbed her arms. "The roof was wet and slippery. The wind was blowing. The gutter was round, so my ankles kept turning, and I was barefooted. I can't imagine how he could have made it with leather-soled shoes."

"What about the man who followed you? Could he have pushed him over?"

"Charly? I doubt it. He slipped the first step he tried to take. He was hanging on for dear life back at the window. George was reaching up to take my hand."

Jocko set his teacup down without finishing his drink. With an air of one who has reached a decision, he rose. "I'm goin' to Revill."

Maria started. "You can't. He'll arrest you."

"That's not likely. If 'e'd wanted me real bad, 'e could have paid Dodger to rat."

"But you were leaving London to get away from him."

He looked directly into her eyes. "I'm still leavin' London, Ria."

Silence fell.

"Oh, my dear boy," Avory sighed.

The scent of lilies and beeswax hung heavy in the air. Soft music from the little pump organ faded away.

The Reverend Thomas Dinsmore sent his most beatific smile over the assemblage. The strangeness of it appeared to have no effect on him. The fact that he and Evangeline were preaching and playing in the main salon of the Lord's Dream did not give him pause. He gloried in this opportunity to go among the sinners, preaching to those who might be reclaimed to God. If they could not be reclaimed, they could assuredly be prevailed upon to make a generous donation to His holy work.

Dinsmore's eye rested with unctuous brightness on the

woman dressed in black, so thickly veiled that her face was barely visible. Sitting front and center and close to the coffin, she could have reached out and laid her hand upon it. She was the grieving mother. Likewise, she was the proprietress of this unfortunate establishment and the one who had paid him to come. He hoped her generosity would be unbounded when he finished the service.

Her veils wafted as she lifted her head. He smiled encouragingly.

A man sat beside her, his expression dazed. He stared unblinking at the corpse's pallid profile just visible above the black-draped coffin. He wore a tailor-made suit and close behind him hovered a man who must have been his valet.

The Reverend Dinsmore counted his blessings. Perhaps more than one generous donation was to be gained here.

Behind the two sat a bank of young women, each dressed in black, but in a variety of styles. Some wore gowns suitable for the opera with feathers and sequins and extreme decolletage. These they had sought to cover with scarves. Some wore walking suits probably purchased for very modest prices. A few wore shabby garments that drooped off their shoulders and sagged at the hemlines.

Despite clothing which seemed to vary according to their different stations in life, all the solemn faces were scrubbed bare of makeup. No one looking at them would have guessed their occupation.

George Montague's coffin was draped in black velvet. A spray of creamy white lilies lay on his breast. At his head and feet were more vases of white lilies and braces of lighted candles.

Dinsmore clasped his prayer book more firmly. The lady

in black had gone to a great deal of trouble to make the occasion all that it should be.

"Let's get the damn thing over with!"

The Reverend Dinsmore jumped. The one who should have behaved with the most sensibility had shattered the solemn moment.

"Please, Terry," the veiled lady murmured.

The gentleman clenched his fist. "Get it over with!" he snarled. "Over and done."

Dinsmore frowned and cleared his throat. "Let us begin with a word of prayer. Dear Heavenly Father . . ."

Revill rolled his eyes heavenward in a prayer for divine strength and guidance.

Then he rose to come round the desk to greet and escort Mrs. Shires to her seat, noting without comment the cracked lens of her spectacles. Maria Thorne, her expression mutinous, took a chair beside her. Then in silence Revill faced the man who had come in with them. A peculiar thrill went through him as he looked at his creation.

Jocko Walton in a new silk topper and fine black suit was a sight to behold. A good sponging and pressing had restored the suit to most of its pristine glory. Avory Shires had sent to Harrod's for a replacement for the hat that had been left in the cloak room of the Lord's Dream.

But more than the clothing, Revill realized that the way Jocko Walton carried himself was different, too. The former thief stood straight and tall without a sign of either fear or bravado. He had assumed a quiet air of purpose. Revill had seen a number of the queen's own advisers—he had even met and shaken hands with a few. Jocko Walton would pass among them unremarked.

Silently, Revill extended his hand and Jocko shook it.

"We were attacked in our own home yesterday," Avory Shires announced.

Revill reseated himself behind his desk and opened the report. "Yes, ma'am. I've read all about it. Unfortunately, both the attackers were able to escape. However, from the descriptions you were able to give the officers, we should be able to pick these men up."

"Descriptions be damned," Maria said bluntly. "I and my sister were able to give names and addresses."

Revill stirred uncomfortably. "We're looking into it."

"And what have you discovered so far?"

"One of the men whom you claim was at your home was in his bed at the time. He had been attacked himself and beaten severely. His employer vouches for him."

"Of course she would," Maria agreed. "And what about the other man?"

"She never heard of him."

Avory Shires shook her head. "I've never heard of anything so outrageous. We are law-abiding citizens—"

"So is Lord Terence Montague," Revill countered.

"No," Maria contradicted flatly. "He is not."

Revill spread his hands in a helpless gesture. "But you have no proof, my dear lady."

"You saw him yourself in the Lord's Dream."

He leaned forward as if explaining an oft-repeated lesson to a very young child. "That does not prove that he was guilty of kidnapping your sister."

"One of the girls—"

"The word of a prostitute against a peer of the realm?"

Jocko put his hand on Maria's shoulder. She bit her lip, then repeated her accusation. "He sent men to kidnap my sister from Mrs. Shires's house."

"We can, of course, arrest the one."

"Inspector Revill. My innocent sixteen-year-old sister is in hiding with a guard at her door. She is afraid to show her face on the streets of London, much less seek employment. I would be afraid for her to attend church or be seen in society where she might meet some young man who would recognize her for the brave, good girl that she is and want to marry her." Maria pulled a handkerchief from her purse and dabbed at her eyes.

"When Mrs. Shires identifies the man who came into her home and attacked her, he will be brought to justice."

"But that doesn't really take care of the problem," Jocko said, speaking for the first time. "The ladies are in danger, Inspector. Lord Montague is determined to find someone to blame for the death of his son." One corner of his mouth curled up in a mocking grin. "In a way, 'e's sort of like us, wouldn't you say?"

"I don't understand."

" 'E doesn't 'ave any faith in Scotland Yard either. 'E knows what you're worth."

Revill flushed to the roots of his hair.

Three pairs of eyes stared at him accusingly.

He cleared his throat. "We have no reason to think that George Montague didn't meet death by mischance."

"And it's easy to report it like that," Jocko said silkily. "No investigation, no blighter to catch. Everybody happy and the peeler takes another stroll around the block."

"Lord Montague was stunned with grief," Revill argued. "When he has had time to regain his control, I'm sure he'll see the right of it."

"But so far he hasn't seen the 'right of it,' " Maria argued. "And what will happen if he captures Jocko and

Melissa? They'll tell him they didn't have anything to do
with his son's death. And then what happens?"

"Well, I—"

"Will he have Bert and Charly and maybe Roncie Jack
beat Jocko, except this time, unlike the members of your
department—"

"Miss Thorne, I can assure you—"

"—They won't stop when he's unconscious? They'll
beat him to death."

"My dear young lady—"

"And my sister? Will he rape and torture her?"

"Miss Thorne!"

Heedless of his protests, she raised her voice. "What do
you think he will do, Inspector Revill?"

He lifted the report on his desk. "If people would only
let us do our jobs—"

Jocko laughed. "Come on, Inspector. You don't 'ave a
job. 'Alf the time, just sit around makin' reports and filin'
papers. And the other 'alf, like as not, you don't get to do
it. And you're glad of it. The poor 'andle their own troubles. The middle-class don't cause much trouble. The rich
pay their way out of trouble—they don't want you snoopin'
around in their lives. Am I right?"

"You most assuredly are *not.*" Revill's clenched hands
wrinkled his papers.

"If I'm so wrong, then why am I workin' for you?"

"I—you're—er—"

"It's 'cause you can't be seen to be workin' on anythin'
that 'as to do with Lord Terence Montague or anybody
else who's got a 'lord' or a 'sir' in front of his name."

"That'll be enough!" Revill thundered.

"What this young man says is the truth," Avory insisted.
"You know it is and we know it is and there's nothing any

of us can do about it." She waved her hand in the air as if to dismiss that problem and go on to another. "So what can we do about these young people? They cannot be harassed for the rest of their lives."

"Madam—" He looked from one to the other. Then he slumped back in his chair. "What would you want me to do?"

Maria regarded him sternly. "We think you should at least arrest Bert and Charly and Roncie Jack. They have attacked private citizens all over town."

Oddly enough, Jocko came to Revill's defense.

"Wouldn't do a bit of good, Ria. They'd be replaced before the law gets them into the dock. And maybe by fellows who aren't such nice blokes." He looked at Revill. "I've been givin' this some thought. I think I ought to let them capture me."

"Oh, no, Jocko—"

"My dear boy. You're putting yourself in danger."

Revill regarded him narrowly.

"I'm not a bloody 'ero. Lord knows I never wanted to be. And I'm deciding that being a toff isn't much of a crack either, but you set me up to do a job. And I 'ate to leave anythin' unfinished."

"No, Jocko, you can't do this," Maria repeated.

But Revill's expression was thoughtful. "What's your plan?"

"Let 'em take me up at the Cock Robin, just like they tried to do the other night. I'll slip the Russian the word. 'E can be out of the place and Dodger can let Roncie Jack know I'm there. Sort of rattin' on me, don't you see?"

"This is absolutely awful," Maria objected.

"Then they take me in. And I find out what really 'appened."

"They'll kill you."

"Naw. Not until they go over it and over it. And in the process, someone's goin' to peep—"

"It's taking a chance," Revill observed.

"Too big a chance," Maria agreed.

"I think it'll work," said Jocko.

"What's to keep them from just killing you the minute they get you?" Revill asked.

"I'll let 'em know I've got Melissa and Maria. They won't kill me until they find out where they are."

"You're crazy. But it might work."

"What happens then? Do we just leave him in there?" Maria was almost in tears.

"No." Revill stood up. "He has two hours. Exactly two. Then I come in with a squad and get him out."

"They could hurt the dear boy very badly in two hours," Avory murmured.

"Not me," Jocko boasted. "I'll set them to doubtin' each other."

Maria put her arms around Jocko and kissed him hard on the mouth. At first he stood stiff, resisting out of embarrassment, but her lips were insistent. His arms went around her tentatively, and then he was kissing her back with a desperate passion.

Revill pretended to study the papers on his desk. Mrs. Shires removed her battered spectacles and wiped at her eyes.

When they broke apart, Jocko was red-faced. He backed away from her. "Ria," he whispered. "What was that for?"

"You're a hero, Jocko. A real hero. You're a gentleman through and through."

* * *

"You're discharged." Lady H snarled at Bert.

"I'm leaving." His words were almost unintelligible, so badly swollen was his face.

She dismissed him with a wave of her hand and he slunk away. Then she scowled at Roncie Jack. "You look as if you ran into a buzzsaw."

"Met an ol' pal," Jack declared cheekily.

"But you didn't bring back Jocko and that Thorne girl."

"No, ma'am, y' see—"

"I do see. You cannot be trusted to do the job. Men!" She shuddered meaningfully.

He hung his head.

Her hand lashed out and slapped his face, hard, leaving a bright red print to stain through the stubble and grime on his cheek.

He snarled as his head snapped up, but she thrust her face close to his. "They're not getting away with killing my George," she told him, fairly spitting each word into his face. "If you haven't enough strength to bring them in, perhaps I can set you a task you can do, and they'll come in by themselves."

Twenty-one

The door splintered and burst open beneath Roncie Jack's foot. The hired tough behind him lunged up the dark stairs.

Duchess slammed a two-by-four against the side of his head and toppled him back against a third man. They fell together, stopping Jack and a fourth man in a tangle of bodies.

"Lights out!" Duchess screamed.

Within seconds the invaders were trying to climb up into total darkness, a terrible disadvantage when they themselves were backlighted by the spill through the broken doorway.

Duchess waited in silence, though any noise she might have made would have been concealed by the cursing and scuffling in the narrow space at the foot of the stairs. The agonizing seconds ticked by and then they came again in a rush.

The first to put his foot on the warehouse floor got her club in his midsection. He pitched backward, but his companions caught him and bore him up.

Duchess shot a look over her head. The skylights opened. Figures scrambled into the night sky. Unfortunately, the extra light destroyed her cloak of darkness. Still, she connected with another head as it popped over the steps.

"Hurrah!" Bet jumped up and down in the darkness be-

hind her. She brandished her little fists like a prize fighter.
" 'It 'em again."

"Yes, hurrah!" Pan agreed, taking her cue from the older girl.

"Get out!" Duchess yelled. "Run! Hurry!"

Bet caught Pan's hand. "C'mon!"

"No!" The little one dug in her heels. "We can't desert Duchess."

Their voices were like bells in the darkness. Duchess whirled. "Go on! For God's sake! Get out!"

Her command ended in a cry of alarm. Roncie Jack crawled over the top of the stairs and caught her by the ankle. Staggering, she twisted and kicked at his head, but his grip was like a manacle. Instead of trying to move toward her, he ducked and dragged her toward him.

She sprawled backwards, the two-by-four jolted out of her hand when her elbow hit the hard-packed floor. Still game, she kicked at his hand and at his face, calling him every vile name in her extensive street vocabulary. He merely grunted when her boot struck his cheek.

"Duchess!" Pan broke away from Bet and dashed forward. Like a small fury, she kicked at Roncie Jack's head. One good boot caught him in the ear, but the second went wild.

"Pansy!" Duchess screamed. "Get away! Run!"

"No, 'e 'urt ye! I'll kick 'im in th'—"

Roncie Jack's eyes were becoming accustomed to the light. Ignoring the impotent kicks, he moved to the attack. He lumbered on up the stairs, raising Duchess's ankle as he came, keeping her pinned and at a disadvantage. "C'mon," he growled to his men. "I've got 'er. Bloody cowards."

Pan kicked on his shin just above the heavy shoe. "Got ye!"

"Pan!" Bet shrieked. "Leave 'im be. Run! Gawd!"

Jack's big arm swept down and wrapped around his small assailant.

Pan screamed in terror.

"Ye let 'er go!" Bet charged forward and drove her head into his belly.

He barely flinched. Dropping Duchess's ankle, he grabbed Bet by the arm and lifted her half off her feet.

"Ow! Lemme go! Lemme go!" Bet kicked at his legs and pummeled him with her fists, but he paid her no mind.

Duchess sprang up, swinging her weapon, but Jack's toughs had found their courage. They swarmed up the stairs and surrounded her. When she swung at the ones in front, another dashed in and pinned her arms behind her.

"Ye want us to get the rest?" The others looked up doubtfully into the pitch blackness of the warehouse.

"Naw." Jack hoisted the two squirming children. "We got enough."

"Duchess! Duchess," Pan sobbed.

"Let her go! She's just a baby." Duchess struggled frantically, but her captor hauled her in front of Roncie Jack.

He squeezed both children until they squealed. "Just like little pigs."

"For pity's sake—"

"Lemme go! Lemme go! I ain't no pig!"

"Quiet!" he roared. His big arms squeezed until his two squirming burdens hung limp. " 'At's better." His men hustled Duchess forward. "Now you're gonna listen to me real good. Ye can 'ave 'em both back when ye give us what we want."

Duchess went still. "Which is?"

"Jocko Walton." Roncie Jack growled.

"Never heard of him."

Bet began to sob noisily.

The pimp shook his head. "Ye know 'im all right—'im and 'is bird."

"Even if I did know him, I don't know where he is," Duchess said. "I heard he left town."

"Find 'im," Jack insisted. "Or I know where I can get a fair price for these two."

"You harm them, even a little, and I'll use your guts for garters," Duchess promised. Her dark eyes glittered in the half light.

He laughed nastily. "Oooh, I'm shiverin' in m' boots. Bring 'im to the Lord's Dream an' ye can 'ave 'em back." He shook the two little girls again. Pansy's head snapped on her neck, and she wailed piteously. "Meantime, I'll teach 'em some manners."

He lumbered down the stairs, his crew following at his heels. Duchess sank to her knees and wrapped her arms around herself in the cold darkness.

"I'm Clarice Adelaide, Lady Montague. I wish to speak to Mr. William Stead."

The copy boy gaped at the pale, lovely woman who paused just inside the door of the *Pall Mall Gazette*. Her dark suit in fine tweed with black velvet lapel and collar was obviously hand-tailored. Her hat was also black with heavy veiling, but it followed fashion rather than practicality. In short, he had never seen her sort inside the newspaper office.

Markham sprang up, abandoning his paperwork. "Lady Montague, please come in." He hurried forward, extending his hand before he realized it was badly ink-stained. He whipped it behind him and looked around desperately. "Er—please, won't you have a chair?" He glanced at the copy boy, murmuring "Get the lady a chair."

Clarice smiled at him. "Are you Mr. Stead?"

"No, ma'am." Markham looked around anxiously— where had Stead disappeared to? "I'm his assistant, Charles Markham."

She waited politely.

"I'll—er—I'll go fetch him." He backed away, calling, "Gus!" The copy boy remained frozen, his mouth hanging open. "Bring Lady Montague a chair."

Stead was in heated argument with the typesetter when Markham found him. He came on the run, wiping his hands on a rag, tossing it aside, buttoning his coat, adjusting his plain neckcloth. "My dear lady."

She held out the paper to him. "Did you write this?"

He glanced at the article and braced himself for a tirade. "Every word."

"And you declare it to be the truth."

Puzzled, he inclined his head. He had expected her to begin chastising him. "Again I say, 'Every word.' "

She hesitated, then seemed to make up her mind. "Then you know where this establishment, the Lord's Dream, is located?"

"To my shame and sorrow, I do."

She looked over her shoulder. Besides Markham and the copy boy, the typesetter and an assistant editor had gathered to listen. "May I speak to you in private?"

He started. This was a lady, and a young one. He would bet by her slight drawl and clear-eyed look that she was country-bred. "I'm not certain that's a good idea."

"Please." She came a little closer, but only a little. "I

have a desperate request and I believe you are the only one who can help me."

"Come this way." He led her into the only private office.

Stodgy John Morley rose in dismay. He cleared his throat, his eyebrows beetling as he tried to assess this unusual situation.

"Mr. Morley will be glad to give us a few minutes' privacy." Stead looked directly at his publisher.

"Thank you." Clarice flashed him a shy smile of gratitude.

"Of course. Of course. Take as long as you need." Morley managed a confused smile before he bowed himself out.

Stead offered Clarice a chair, but she shook her head. "I must be brief. Lord Montague is not at home."

The journalist drew back.

She waved a gloved hand. "Oh, please, don't go all stiff on me. According to my servants, my husband has not returned home since our son—was—killed." Her voice quavered, but she managed to continue. "Lord Montague's had a terrible shock. George was his only son, his heir. He fairly worshiped the boy."

"Lady Montague—"

"Wait. Hear me out. None of my staff will cooperate. They seem to think that if they tell me where he is they will betray a confidence. I had to come to you. If he is at this terrible place where George died, I must go to him."

"You don't know he's there," Stead pointed out.

"I believe he is," she insisted. "Where else could he be? I've sent messages to his clubs and to his friends, what few I know."

"I see."

"And more than that. I know him. He's not a young man, though he would not have anyone know it. And, please, Mr. Stead, I know he's overcome with grief. Who knows what might be happening to him in that place when he's surely not thinking as clearly as he should be?" Her voice quivered, but her eyes were not afraid.

He shook his head. Obviously, she was sincere, but she couldn't have any idea what she would be getting herself into. "I don't need to tell you, Lady Clarice, that ladies don't go there."

"I must go to my husband."

He thought rapidly. He stood to be censured for taking a lady into a brothel. Most women of good family pretended not to know that the places existed. On the other hand, people's tastes in newspapers were changing. There was good chance to get another article from this visit.

"They may not admit you."

She lifted her chin. "I shall not leave until I see him."

He decided quickly. He would not make mention of Lady Clarice in the article. If she actually succeeded in gaining entrance to the Lord's Dream, the further doings of Lady H and Lord Montague would provide juicy reading. As a gentlemen he should refuse; as a journalist he cleared his throat. "Then I will take you there, Lady Clarice."

"Lock them in the closet in my room."

Lady H was dressed in unrelieved black. On her bosom was a jet mourning brooch. Around her ring finger she wore a lock of George's gold hair braided into a band. Her eyes were shadow-ringed, sunken in her head. Her mouth looked as if she had never smiled.

Bet took one frightened look at the dead-white face with the staring, bloodshot eyes. She ducked her head and slid her arm around Pan's shoulders as much to still her own trembling as to comfort her little friend.

Pan thrust her lower lip out and hiccupped as she swallowed her tears. "Ye'd better let us go," she warned. "Ye'll be so sorry if ye don't."

Lady H barely glanced at the grimy, tear-streaked faces. She had seen them all before, had been one of them. Whether they lived or died made no difference to her. "Take them out of my sight, Eunice. Just be sure you take all the clothes out of the closet before you put them in. They're filthy as rats."

"Ye'll be sorry," Pan warned again. "Jocko Walton'll get ye fer sure."

Lady H looked at the child for the first and only time. "That's what I'm counting on."

Cate met the sorry procession on the stairs. "Where did these come from, Eunice?"

The maid looked weary and uncomfortable. "Lady H had them brought. I'm to take them upstairs."

"What for?"

"Who knows? Get on with you," she snarled as Pan pulled back against Bet's hand. "I don't even want to touch them. They're so filthy I'll probably get lice."

Cate laughed. "A new trick for the Lord's Dream. Urchins in bed with MPs."

"Ye better let us go," Pan threatened.

Eunice drew back her hand to smack the child, but Cate forestalled her. "Would you like to come with me?"

"No!" said Pan.

"Are ye gonna lock us in th' clawset?" Bet asked tearfully.

"Not unless you're bad."

"I'm not bad. Pan's bad, sometimes, but she's nah but six."

"Then you'll have to keep her good. Follow me."

"Lady H wants 'em in the closet in her bedroom," Eunice called half-heartedly.

"Maybe later," Cate said. "If they're bad."

Jocko was not in his room.

Duchess sent all the remaining children out to scour the town for him, then she went to see Mrs. Avory Shires. Repeated knocking and ringing brought no stir. All the curtains were drawn. Duchess went round to the kitchen. No one answered her knocks and calls. No one moved behind the door. And most important, she could not smell food cooking.

She sank down on the back step, her forehead pressed against the heels of her hands. If the children did not find him, she was stymied. She did not know the address of Maria Thorne's rooms.

"Oh, Jocko," she whispered. "Please. Please don't be gone."

She closed her eyes and opened them immediately as horrid pictures flitted through her mind. Bet and Pan being stripped and bathed by ugly, hurtful hands. Their immature bodies dressed in little petticoats and drawers and white stockings, then turned over to relentless brothel keepers. If they were lucky they would be fondled and raped. If they were unlucky they would be whipped until they bled. All for the pleasure of evil old men whose excesses had worn out their bodies.

Duchess put her head between her knees and breathed slowly and deeply until the nausea passed. A sudden chill spread over her. The sun had dropped behind the buildings on the other side of the park. Night was coming.

"Pansy," she whispered. "Betty."

She walked quickly back down the carriage drive. She would go to the Russian at the Cock Robin. If he didn't know where Jocko was, then she would have to assume the thief had already left town.

And if he had gone . . . she shuddered. She could not leave Pan and Bet to their terrible fate. She would have to put on her old clothing and go back into the Lord's Dream herself.

"You make dangerous plan, my friend." The Russian poured Jocko a drink. "How come you do dis?"

The concertina man strolled from table to table.

> *I'm a dooced big toff of a fellow,*
> *My makeup I reckon's immense,*
> *I live in a manner peculiar,*
> *But I'm somewhat devoid of sense."*

Jocko scowled at the word *toff,* then grinned to himself at the last line. The song might have been written about him.

"Why you do?" The Russian urged.

"Revill. Don't you remember? 'E's got me paper."

"Nyet." The big man's teeth flashed white beneath his thick black moustache. "Revill? 'E not make you do dis. Dat girl. She make you." He pushed the glass across the table.

Jocko reached for it. "You're wrong, Roosian. The girl doesn't 'ave anythin' to do with this. It's Revill."

The Russian watched him toss the liquor down, belying Jocko's reputation for never drinking in a hurry.

Maisie moved among the tables with a heavy tray. The men pulled foaming mugs from it and slipped money down the front of her blouse. As the concertina man followed her, he sang,

> *"O-o-o-oh, you ought to see my Maisie . . .*

The men howled with laughter. One squeezed the bar-maid's breast. She slapped his hand away and grinned.

> *She's a spiffin bit o' stuff,*
> *She's gonna drive me crazy.*
> *She's nature in th' rough."*

The pair came to the Russian's table. " 'Elp yerself, Jocko," Maisie sang in rhythm with the concertina.

"Much obliged, old girl." He raised his head and grinned a little blearily. "Roosian's takin' care of me."

"Takin' me business," the barmaid accused in mock outrage.

"Is same till," the Russian replied. He topped off Jocko's glass from the bottle. "What was you sayin'?"

"Revill!" Jocko said louder than he had meant to. His next remark dropped to a near-whisper. The Russian leaned forward. " 'E's about to turn me into a bloomin' peeler."

Jocko drank again. The draught tasted warm and a little bitter. "I'm thinkin' when this case is over, I might get 'im to write me a recommendation. What do you think? Just picture me in a blue suit with a badge on me chest." He set the glass down and blinked at the fire in his stomach.

"You turn rat," the Russian scowled. He tipped the bottle over Jocko's empty glass. Liquor sloshed into it. As a drop spilled onto the tabletop, the Russian swiped it up with a blunt finger.

"Not on your life." Jocko pulled the glass toward him, a little liquor sloshing over his hand. "That ain't the way it works. Not at all. What I'd do, I'd be special investigator for the swells only. None o' the small stuff. Like Revill. That way I wouldn't 'ave to do a thing but walk around and sweep trash under the bloody rug." He drank again.

The Russian looked very sad. "You good boy. You be a good peeler."

Jocko stared at him. A film seemed to slide across his eyes. He blinked rapidly. It would not clear. "Damn you!"

"I work for lady, too," the Russian said by way of apology.

The concertina man was back, his words coming and going in Jocko's ears.

> *"I met a little charmer,"*

The crowd sang the next line.

> *"So did I,"*
> *"And I said I wouldn't harm her,"*
> *"So did I."*
> *"I took 'er int' Short's,*
> *And I stood 'er wine by quarts,"*

The chorus broke like thunder.

> *"So did I, old chum,*
> *So did I."*

Jocko slumped forward.

The Russian lifted him by the shoulders and guided him to the back of the bar.

Duchess opened the door. "I've got a cab waiting."

The Russian's black eyebrows rose at the sight of her. "You go someplace?"

She wore a maroon wool spencer trimmed and frogged in black that buttoned tightly down to her tiny waist. Her skirt was an apron of the same wool swept back over knife-edge pleats of black. She carried a neat black purse. Her face was veiled beneath a tiny hat.

She reached out and stroked Jocko's cheek with her black-gloved hand. "I'm going with him. I wouldn't take him into that place and leave him."

The Russian's laugh rumbled out of his big chest as he heaved the unconscious Jocko into the cab. "You no look like bag o' rags. You look like lady. I t'ink I go with you."

In the alley next to the Cock Robin, Revill's Scotland Yard police waited for perhaps another half an hour. At last they strolled in with an air of nonchalance. At the sight of the Russian's empty table, they froze. Jocko Walton was nowhere to be seen.

"Revill'll have our badges," said one.

They galloped away at a pace that would have done a Bow Street Runner proud.

"How could you lose him?" Revill flung open the door of the coach and stepped out to confront his minions. "Was he expecting you to follow him?"

"I don't know," said one miserably. "He said he was just going in to get a line on the pimps. We waited. We waited for an hour."

"An hour!" Maria cried. "You waited an hour!"

Inwardly, Revill cursed the fact that she and Mrs. Shires had flatly refused to go home and leave the detective work to the men. So far the impression both were getting was highly unfavorable to the department.

"You mean your men can't even keep up with someone who wants to be followed?" Avory demanded incredulously of the constable in charge.

"That wasn't exactly the way of it, ma'am." The man looked at her miserably. "We kept thinking any minute he was going to walk out. We hated to go in and queer the whole bit."

Maria's heart pounded against her ribs. She clasped Avory's hand tightly. "He's already been in their captivity an hour. We promised him we'd bring him out of the Lord's Dream in two."

"Oh, my dear."

"Climb on, both of you." Revill struck the top of the coach with his doubled fist and sprang inside. "The Lord's Dream! And don't spare the horses!"

Try as she would, Duchess could not contain her feelings as the cab rattled over the dark cobblestones. Prickles of dread raised the hair on her arms.

She was returning. She, who had vowed never to set foot inside that infamous door again, was returning.

Breathing heavily, Jocko Walton lay with his head in her lap. The cab jolted as it turned a corner. He stirred and mumbled. She stroked his curly hair. In her other hand she held the new silk topper.

He had no business in the Lord's Dream either.

A small sob slipped from between her lips.

The Russian heard it. His great bulk fairly filled the seat opposite them. Even in the dark his eyes glittered. "You cry, Duchess?"

"No. Never." She hesitated. "Yes."

"Maybe tonight things come to light."

She shook her head. "I don't want things to come to light."

"You hide in dark too long. Time for beauty like you—"

"Don't! Don't say any more."

Jocko stirred again. His hand batted weakly at his face as he tried to wake himself up.

"Everyt'ing be all right," the Russian promised.

"You don't know that," she said through clenched teeth. "I don't know that. It's a horrible place. A dangerous place. And I'm responsible for drugging one of the truest friends I have in the world and taking him into danger."

"I drug 'im," the Russian contradicted amicably.

The cab turned again. Duchess pulled aside the curtain. "We're almost there."

"If you are doubtful, my dear lady Clarice, or feel even the least bit of trepidation—" Stead left the sentence unfinished.

Clarice shivered beneath her heavy coat. Living in the country since Bethany's birth, she had not stayed up much past nine o'clock. Now somewhere a clock tolled the half hour. Half past eleven.

Stead considered her carefully. "Lady Clarice?"

"Of course I'm afraid!" she burst out. "Terribly afraid, Mr. Stead, but I'm also determined. My husband needs me. I'm deeply concerned about him."

"Still—"

"I believe that he would do the same for me." She turned her head to stare out the window. Not that there was anything for her to see. Another vehicle of some sort lumbered past them at great speed, the driver liberally applying the whip. The fog was too thick for her to discern what it might be.

Stead leaned back against the squabs to contemplate Lady Clarice. He should never have brought her. Mentally, he began to compose a story.

This dear and gentle lady, this symbol of motherhood and purity on which the very foundation of the British Empire rests, set out to offer her unquestioning love and support to her noble husband. With every fiber of her being, she feared for him, wept for him at the loss of their son, longed to be at his side to comfort him. She cared not what dreadful shocks, what sordid sights might await her. Like Gloriana herself, Clarice, Lady Montague, would rescue her husband.

Stead swallowed a bitter taste in his mouth. He had met Lord Montague and had been privy to his behavior on the night of his son's death. Likewise, he knew why Montague had brought George there in the first place and deplored the practice.

He sighed. He very much doubted whether Lord Montague would have come home from his club or in this case, his favorite brothel, if Lady Montague were suffering.

The cab slowed and came to a halt. Stead thrust his head out the window. "Are we there?"

"Nigh to," the driver called. "There's just a couple of coaches in front of us letting off passengers."

Twenty-two

At the cold, wet kiss of the night air, Jocko managed to pull his eyes open. "Where am I?"

The Russian dragged him from the cab and stood him on his feet against a pillar outside the Lord's Dream. He lifted Jocko's chin. "Wake up!"

Jocko shook his head, then put his hand on it to stop its spinning. "Why'd you drug me, Roosian? I thought you an' me were friends."

"He did it because I asked him to."

Jocko looked around him blearily. "Duchess?"

"Yes." She took his arm. "I'm so sorry. And now we have to go into the Lord's together."

He hung back. "We're going into the Lord's Dream? You're taking me in there?"

"Yes. Don't argue."

He twisted his arm from her grasp. "Bloody 'ell! Why didn't you tell me? You didn't 'ave to drug me. I'd 'ave gone with you like a lamb. I was goin' there anyway."

Duchess sucked in her breath sharply. "How was I to know?"

"Tell 'er." Jocko tugged at the Russian's sleeve.

White teeth flashed in the light of the carriage lamps. "Is right."

Outraged, Duchess turned on him. "You knew this! And you didn't tell me?"

The Russian cocked a dark eyebrow. "I work for pay."

Jocko struck the big man a harmless blow to the shoulder. "The least ye could've done was let me make my own offer. I'd 'ave paid you more than she did to leave me alone."

The Russian chuckled. He caught the arm that had struck him and locked it with his own. "C'mon, Jocko. We make entrance."

All she could see of the four men were the tops of their caps. From the third-story window, Melissa watched as they came together on the walk in front of the house. One disappeared from view and the knocker banged against the door. Its falling echoed in the empty halls and up the stairwell. It banged again. And again. Then silence.

Two of the remaining three in the street broke off and disappeared from her view. Presumably they entered the carriage drive at the corner. The one remaining in the street tilted his head back. Instantly, Melissa stepped back from the lace curtain, so even her shadow would not show.

A minute later, knocking sounded at the servants' door. It gave way to pounding as if the unwanted guest had lost patience.

Melissa shuddered. Minutes later, she watched them converge again on the walk. The four of them stared upward. She could almost feel their eyes scanning every window for some sign of movement.

At last the leader raised his arm. As a fashionable coach came down the street, the four climbed in and set off.

Melissa was still standing at the window when the butler brought in a silver tray. "Tea, Miss Melissa."

She nodded. "Thank you, Peter."

While he poured, she continued to stare out into the street. The afternoon was wearing on. Jocko would be putting himself in danger for her sake. He was just like the heroes in books by Mr. Dickens.

George Montague's words flashed through her mind. *Just like a novel by Dickens.* George had been brave to try to rescue her.

Her own dear sister would be following Jocko Walton. What a heroine Maria was! What a fighter! Melissa would never have thought a prim, quiet lady could be so brave.

Even old Mrs. Shires had refused to leave her house. She had gone back in to see the fight. If it had gone against Peter, she would have been in some danger, but she refused to desert her man. She was brave, too.

And her butler was brave for fighting Lady H's brutal guards.

In fact, everyone seemed to be brave except Melissa Thorne, the cause of all the problems.

The heavy draperies should be drawn over the lace curtains, for the evening chill was seeping in through the panes. Melissa moved to the fire while Peter performed that service. She stared into its depths, while shivers coursed down her spine and raised gooseflesh on her arms. Over and over, the same sentences marched through her mind while she tried to find the courage to say them.

Gritting her teeth, she set the tea down untouched. "The way I see this, Peter, is that you have two choices."

The butler eyed her suspiciously. "Me, miss?"

"You can stay here hidden in Mrs. Shires's house with all the doors and windows locked, or," Melissa continued, "you can accompany me to the Lord's Dream and stay by my side while I'm there."

"The Lord's Dream." He shook his head. "You can't go there, miss. Mrs. Shires said I was to keep you here until this business is settled." He offered the explanation as if she were a very young child who might not understand big words.

"But they're all going to the Lord's Dream to help me. I should be there."

"You'd be likely to get in the way, miss."

"But you could protect me." Her voice gained strength as she argued. She smiled at him, letting her dimple show. "And, of course, if that big fellow you fought came at me, you'd get another chance at him."

The light of battle shone in Peter's watery eyes. He touched his fingers to the lump on his jaw where Roncie Jack had clipped him. Then he rolled his shoulders and stretched his neck in the stiff, upstanding collar. A dull red flush rose in his cheeks. When he looked at her, he tried to keep his expression forbidding. "You're supposed to stay safe, miss."

She rose purposefully. "The only way I'll ever be safe is to make everyone see clearly once and for always what happened that night. I was there on the roof when George fell. Perhaps there was something I didn't say, or something I could say that would make it clearer. I've thought and thought about it. Peter, I must go."

"It's too dangerous."

She put her hand on his forearm. "Not if you come with me. You'll never let anyone take me prisoner again. I know I'd be safe with you."

He swallowed, trying to resist the beautiful young face upturned to his. "Please, Miss Thorne, don't—"

"Come with me, Peter. Be my champion. Help me make it all right." She took his big hand between both of hers. Her smile was incandescent.

Still shaking his head, "Saint" Peter allowed himself to be led from the room.

The Russian kept Jocko's arm twisted up into the middle of his back until the three of them had been ushered into the main salon.

Only when Bert and Charly, bandaged and plastered, were flanking them did the black-bearded man let go.

Jocko pulled his arm gingerly around in front of him, scowling angrily and rubbing his wrist. *The Russian enjoyed his work too much.*

Duchess waited calmly enough, though her stomach churned. All around her the sights and smells of the place set bells clanging in her mind. She felt as if she were being smothered in the unfamiliar fashionable clothing. She tried to think of Pansy and Betty.

Looking around the room, Jocko recognized Lord Montague snoring in the wing chair by the fire. A glass and a nearly-empty decanter stood on the small table beside him.

The mantel clock chimed a single note as a log crackled and broke in the fireplace.

Lord Montague stirred, breaking off his snore. He rolled his head on his shoulders, then allowed it to drop down to his chest again. His snoring resumed almost immediately.

The Russian sucked in his breath. The faint sound drew both Jocko and Duchess to his gaze—then they followed his stare.

Hermione Beauforty, otherwise known as Lady H, was coming down the stairs. Her hair must have been dyed as a sign of her deep mourning. It was so black that light disappeared into it. Dead-white makeup with no rouge or mascara covered her face. With pale lips and no eyelashes or eyebrows, she might have been a corpse herself.

Duchess rallied first. "Lady H, I've come for my children."

"Are they yours?" the brothel keeper inquired nastily. "I had thought you too much of a prude to accept a man, much less burden yourself with a litter of brats."

Duchess appeared not to hear the insult. "They're orphans. I've been taking care of them, as well you know."

Lady H looked at Jocko and then pretended to scan the room. "And where is the little slut?"

"I couldn't find her."

"Then you must not want these children very badly. Not that I blame you. Filthy little beggars."

Duchess clenched her fists, ready to do battle, but the Russian stepped forward. His dark eyes reflected the light as he made a courtly bow to Lady H.

"Yaroslav," she murmured. What might have been a smile flitted across her lips. She extended her hand. "Yaroslav."

"Hermione." He took it, his lips brushing the back of it before he turned it and kissed the palm.

She shivered. "I hadn't thought of you in a long time, Yaroslav."

"Long time," he agreed.

"How do you do?"

He spread his big arms wide. His greatcoat fell open, exposing a black silk blouse with huge sleeves, belted at the waist in the Ukrainian style. "Well," he boomed, "little older, little fatter."

She smiled, a slight upward twitch of her pale lips. "I see only a great bear of a man."

"And I see a beautiful woman."

She shrugged. "I'll never be beautiful again." Her bleak eyes went round the room. "It's all dust and ashes. My son is dead." She looked at Jocko with sheer hatred. "Murdered."

He held up his hands. "Not by me."

"You're a thief. You came into my house under false pretenses."

"I'm not a murderer."

"You'll be sorry you were ever born. And then I'll destroy the inspector, the man who sent you here. I have powerful friends."

"I think you'd better reconsider, Lady H." Cate came down the stairs, dressed severely in black. Unlike her employer, she wore no makeup at all except a little powder.

"I will do what I must. My son's death must be avenged."

"He fell, Lady H." Cate spoke with the air of one who has repeated the same statement until it has no meaning.

"The inspector who was here that night—of course, he would say it was an accident. He sent the thief—the murderer—into the house." Her speech had grown almost reasonable with repetition.

"The gutter and the ledge were slippery. Charly almost fell," Cate parried.

"That little slut didn't. Perhaps she's the one who did it. She was trying to escape."

"It was an accident." Cate spaced every word.

Lady H waved her hand imperiously toward Duchess. "I don't want to discuss any of this until this creature brings the little slut to me as well."

"I have no idea where she is," Duchess protested.

"Then send the rest of your rats out. Let them scuttle around the streets until they find her."

"They're just children."

With a cry of mortal agony, Lady H flew at her, her nails curved like talons. Only the quick intervention of the Russian kept her from lacerating Duchess's cheeks. Sobbing, she struggled bitterly against his strength.

He wrapped his big arms around her and turned her face into his shoulder. She would not be pacified. Like a wildcat she clawed at his satin shirt, cursing and weeping. "I don't care what they are!" she screamed. "I don't have any children. And I loved my son. I did. I did."

The noise awakened Lord Montague, who sat up, holding his head. He looked around him slowly, his bloodshot eyes lighting on nothing he seemed to recognize. "Wha's matter?"

Lady H slumped against Yaroslav's chest. She shuddered. "You can let me go now."

"I like holding you," the Russian murmured.

"Damn you, Yaroslav." She pushed against him with her fists.

He shrugged and let her go.

Her girls had begun to wander downstairs, their faces blank with bored resignation. Not one showed any sympathy. They wore various combinations of *déshabillé,* even though Lady H seemed to have no intention of opening for business.

One of them wandered over to Lord Montague. "What's your pleasure, sir?"

"Kiss," he mumbled. "Kiss me."

"Get away from him," Lady H screeched.

Her words came too late. Montague caught the girl round the waist and pulled her down on his lap. "Kiss," he mumbled again. "Kiss."

Lady H darted across the room. She struck the girl's

shoulder and toppled her out of Montague's lap. "He's in mourning," she cried. "Don't you have any respect for the dead?"

Lord Montague stared at her mourning costume. Then his eyes wandered again, seeking some explanation. They returned to Lady H, who stood over him panting. "Too old," he muttered. "Too damn old."

The woman looked as if she might explode.

"Visitors, Lady H." Bert's words were almost unintelligible coming out from behind his damaged nose.

"Jocko!" Maria Thorne ducked around the footman and flung herself into Jocko's arm. "Are you all right?"

He put his arms around her and held her tight. "Right as rain."

She raised her hand to his cheek. "They haven't hurt you?"

"They'd not had the time." He grinned. "You're early."

Revill shrugged. "I told her you were all right, but she wouldn't believe me." He allowed himself a small smile as he surveyed the couple. "It appears as if the lady may have it bad for you, my lad."

Jocko's grin spread into a smile of pure joy. He tried to speak, but the words stuck in his throat.

Avory stood in the doorway, open-mouthed. "So this is the way of it," she remarked to no one in particular. "Oh, my. My, my, my. I never thought I'd live to see the inside of one of these places."

She looked up at Bert. His much-abused nose had swollen until it was a monstrous purple turnip in the middle of his bruised face. "You're lookin' pretty good, my boy. But you should be resting and putting cold packs on your face."

"Yes, ma'am."

She patted his arm tenderly. "You come to work for me. I'll take care of you."

Lady H had recovered herself sufficiently at the sight of Revill. "Inspector, I demand that you arrest this man. He pushed my son from the roof of my own house. You saw it happen."

"No, ma'am. I did not see it happen," the inspector denied. "What I did was arrive on the scene almost immediately after the fact. George Montague was already dead."

"That thief killed him." She pointed at Jocko with an imperious finger. "Arrest him!"

"Visitors, Lady H," Bert announced again.

Avory Shires's eyebrows rose when she recognized one of the newcomers. "Mr. William Stead, I believe?"

He bowed quite gallantly. "Yes, ma'am. You have the advantage of me."

"I'm Mrs. Avory Shires, the mother of Lord Dudley Shires. Now that I see you are really here in the flesh, I'm moved to believe the stories in the *Pall Mall Gazette.*" She offered him her hand as if they were meeting at a tea at Marlborough House.

He took it, his expression bland. "Ah, yes. You were the one who sent me here in the first place. And, of course, I have heard of your work for women's suffrage." He looked round him. "I'm surprised to find you here, but now that I think about it, there are women here who need the vote."

She smiled. "I'm so glad you recognize that fact."

He stepped aside. "May I present a friend?"

His companion had moved past him across the room. Lady Clarice stared open-mouthed at the whore in peach lace and net and knee-high riding boots.

The prostitute glanced up. At the sight of the lady staring at her, she squealed in embarrassment. Hiking her garment up, she struggled to her feet. The effort made her nipples pop out above her corset. She covered herself with her hands and backed away.

"T-Terence?" his wife whispered.

The old man did not hear her.

"Terence," she repeated.

"Who are you?" Lady H bristled. Her white makeup was cracked and her India-ink hair had escaped from the pompadour on one side.

Clarice flinched at the sight of the brothel keeper, but maintained her good manners. "I do not know you," she replied haughtily. "We have not been introduced."

"This is my house." Lady H stabbed her thumb toward her bosom. "I think you'd better tell me who you are and state your business—or leave."

Clarice lifted her chin. "I am Clarice Adelaide, Lady Montague. I have come for my husband. He needs his loved ones beside him in his hour of grief."

Her voice trailed away at the end of her sentence as Montague reached for the glass and decanter. He giggled softly as he poured himself a stiff drink and tossed it down.

Lady H brayed with laughter. "So you're the new wife."

"I beg your pardon. I have been his wife for seven years."

"He was mine first," the brothel keeper bragged coarsely.

"Then you must not have meant very much to him," Lady Clarice said proudly. She marched across the room and put her hand on Montague's shoulder. "Terence."

His head swung toward her, but his eyes were sightless. He brushed her hand aside as if it had been a pesky fly.

Lady Clarice's nose wrinkled at the smell of his body. "You've gotten him drunk," she accused Lady H.

"I sell liquor. He wanted liquor," came the angry reply.

Cate put her hand on Lady H's arm. "Let her take him away. A sodden, old fool like him is bad for business."

"Hush! He's mine. Terry." She pawed at Cate's hand.

Meanwhile, Lady Clarice bent low to whisper in the intoxicated man's ear. "Terence."

He stared blearily into her face. "Who're you?"

She drew back grimacing at the whiskey fumes and stale cigar smoke. "I'm Clarice, your wife."

"Wife's name's Evelyn." He slumped back, reaching for the glass.

"Don't drink any more." She tried to take it away.

"Leave go, dammit." He slapped awkwardly at her hand.

Clarice became aware that they were performing for a fascinated audience. A large, ragged circle, but a circle nevertheless, had formed around them. Avid eyes watched their every move. Two of the women near the center of the salon were standing on the divan to get a better view.

Clarice took a deep breath and bent toward him. "Please Terence. Let me take you home."

"Take me where?"

"Home. You're ill, Terence. You need to rest."

"Don't feel sick. Don't feel—anything. Feel—just fine." He looked up at her without recognition. Suddenly, his face twisted. Tears trickled from his eyes. "George is dead."

"Oh, Terence." She smoothed the strands of hair back from his forehead. It was so thin on top. For herself and others to see him in this condition was a disgrace. She did not love this man, but he had her deepest sympathy. He needed to be home. "Mr. Stead."

The journalist came to her side. "Ma'am?"

"Will you help me get him out of here?"

"I'm sure we can arrange something."

"Terence, can you stand up?"

He looked up at her again. "Do I know you?"

"I'm your wife. Clarice." She tried to urge him out of the chair, but he refused to budge.

"My wife's name is Evelyn."

"He doesn't remember you," Lady H insisted. "I told you. He belongs here with me where I can take care of him."

Clarice rounded on her. "One look at him shows how well you've cared for him. He belongs at home with his daughters. He does not belong in a brothel." She pushed harder. "Get up, Terence. Get up."

Stead came around and lifted Montague from the other side. Together they managed to get him on his feet. With a sudden movement, he tossed them off and sat back down. "No. Lemme go. Don't want to go anywhere. Pour m'self 'nother drink."

He reached for the decanter.

"Mrs. Beauforty—" Inspector Revill pulled a pad from his pocket and noted the date.

"If you've come to arrest that monster, then do your job." She pointed at Jocko. "Otherwise, get the hell out of here."

"Visitors," Bert interrupted again.

"Melissa!" Maria cried.

"Peter, what is the meaning of this?" Avory wanted to know.

"I had to come," Melissa explained simply. "We have to get this cleared up once and for all."

"You little slut," Lady H stormed. "I didn't think you'd have the nerve to show yourself back here."

"I didn't either, Lady H." Melissa faced her bravely. "But you have to agree to leave me alone. I didn't kill George Montague. I'm as sorry as anyone about his death."

"That I doubt."

"It's true. I would never have harmed him. He was helping me to escape. I never wanted to be here in the first place."

Suddenly, Lady H was uncomfortably aware of the law and the press listening to a very incriminating conversation. "What an ungrateful slut you are," she sneered. "After I took you off the street and kept you from starving."

"You're lying," Melissa denied. "You offered to share a ride with me in Euston Street Station. How was I to know that Lord Montague had paid you to kidnap me?"

Lady H would have attacked her had the Russian not caught her in his big grasp. "Shut your mouth, I tell you! No one will believe a lying little slut like you."

Stead had abandoned Lord Montague to his drink and pulled out his notebook. "You say he paid to have you kidnapped?"

"That's not so!" Lady H cried.

"He wanted me to leave my job as his children's nursery maid and become his—" She choked.

Clarice, too, abandoned her husband. She came to the girl's side. "Oh, Melissa."

"I'm sorry, Lady Montague. I didn't want you to find out. I tried to leave quietly."

"When were you brought here, Miss Thorne?" Stead asked, pencil poised.

She considered. "It must be almost four weeks now."

"And you were kept for this man's particular pleasure, or were you to service other customers?"

"Here, now," Revill interceded. "Watch your language."

"Merely a turn of the phrase, Inspector."

"This girl is lying through her teeth," Hermione objected. "Why, I never heard of such a thing. She came to me starving. I took her in out of a sense of Christian charity."

"I would suggest you be careful what you say, madam," Revill said sternly. "Your words are being taken down." He displayed his notebook. "They may be used against you in a court of law. I may not be able to arrest you for brothel keeping, but if you are a kidnapper, I can assuredly arrest you for that."

Lady H turned on him like a fiend incarnate. "I think not, Inspector. Not without ruining everybody's reputation."

"I will write the truth, madam," Stead intervened. "No innocent reputations will suffer here tonight."

Beset on all sides by enemies, she nevertheless faced Revill with a look of pure malice. "If you don't arrest Walton, I'll see that important people know that you sent a thief into my house, Inspector. If you value your job, you'll arrest this thief and this slut for killing my George. She tried to get away from him. She was always a troublemaker. When he followed her out onto the balcony, as any noble youth would have done, she pushed him over the edge. She's a cold-blooded murderess. She should hang and her confederate along with her."

Her face was red beneath her ruined makeup. Revill looked at her with something like real sympathy. Then he looked around him, ticking off faces on his fingers. "I think we should all go upstairs," he said at last. "To the scene of the crime if crime there be. There we'll recreate the events of the night and see what happened."

Twenty-three

"All of you who were in the salon at the time of Montague's death, please remain where you are," Revill instructed.

Eunice, Maribelle, and several of the other girls exchanged disappointed looks. The moment Duchess and the Russian had brought Jocko Walton in, word had spread like wildfire through the Lord's Dream. More and more girls in *déshabillé* had drifted down the stairs to cluster in little knots around the salon. While they appeared to gossip among themselves, their eyes focused avidly on the main participants.

"The rest of us will move upstairs and return to the rooms we occupied that night."

A real moan followed his announcement. He looked around him in some surprise. "Surely you women realize that we are conducting an investigation here."

"Sure thing, love," called Maribelle. "And it's as good as Drury Lane."

He fixed her with a stern eye. "This is a very serious business. I must have everyone's cooperation. Remember, it's to your advantage to have been here in the salon. You could not possibly have been involved if we should prove foul play."

"And you will," Lady H snapped. "Inspector, I insist on going up with you."

Revill had been addressing the room at large, his back to Hermione. His face went absolutely blank, then his mouth curved upward in a pleasant smile. He turned. "I was going to invite you to accompany us, madam. This reenactment is for your benefit."

William Stead said nothing, but he flipped another page over in his notebook and continued taking notes.

Watching him, Maria wondered if he were writing about two stories at once—the events of the night and the solving of the crime.

Revill inclined his head to Maria. "Will you assist me?"

She blinked. "Me? Of course."

He passed her his notebook and pencil. "It's my understanding that you are a secretary."

She nodded. "I'm a type writer, but I take notes very fast."

"She's excellent," Avory added with a proud smile.

"Very good." He turned again to the assemblage. "First, the women who were—er—occupied upstairs will go up and take their places in their rooms. Please close the doors, unless they were standing open."

In an uncomfortable silence, a half-dozen young women trooped obediently up the stairs.

"Shall I take their names?" Maria asked Revill.

"We can get them later," was the reply. "And I'm hoping that even that will not be necessary. Now, who else was upstairs?"

"I was." Jocko volunteered immediately.

"I was," Melissa stammered. "Can Peter come with me?"

"Was he in the building?"

"No, but he makes me feel safer."

Peter had been standing with arms folded, a silent sentinel. At her plea he strode forward, his shoulders squared. His voice rumbled out of his chest. "I 'ave to stay with 'er, sir."

Revill did not blink. "Of course you do. Go on." He waved his hand. "Now, who else?"

"I, Inspector," Stead called. "My assistant Markham was with me that night. We went up right behind Lord Montague."

Both he and Revill glanced in the direction of the drunken man.

Fascinated by the proceedings, Lady Clarice had abandoned her efforts to rouse her husband. She had merely removed the decanter and glass from his reach.

Revill shrugged. "We'll let you stand for the three of you, Mr. Stead."

"Yes, sir."

Clarice raised her hand timidly. "I think I should stand for my husband. Then I can tell him all about it."

Revill hesitated. She looked very determined. "As you will."

"And I'll be happy to stand for Mr. Markham," Avory offered eagerly.

Revill rolled his eyes. "I appreciate your willingness to serve, Mrs. Shires, but that will not be necessary." He thought he heard her say "Damn" as he turned his attention to Charly and Bert. "Now, boys."

They looked at each other, shifting uneasily. Both were bruised and scabbed as a result of Lady H's quest for vengeance. Charly shrugged his heavy shoulders. "We was up there, all right. But we didn't lay a finger on the poor blighter. Swear to God."

"I didn't even see 'im go over." Bert supplied.

Revill motioned them up the stairs. "I believe you, boys. But you can tell your story on the spot. Now, who else?"

"Me." Cate's sneer was back in place. "I'll be glad to show you where I was if you want to waste your time." She flounced up the stairs, hips twitching.

"And that's the lot?" Revill looked around the room. Maribelle and Eunice nodded.

Duchess put a hand on his sleeve. "Inspector, two little girls are in one of the rooms upstairs. I need to get them out of here."

His eyebrows drew together. "Little girls?"

"Yes, sir."

He shifted a narrow gaze at Lady H, who opened her mouth to object. He raised his hand. "No doubt they are starving beggars who begged Mrs. Beauforty to take them in." He inclined his head to Duchess. "Despite the good woman's Christian spirit, little girls don't need to go upstairs in this type of establishment. Go ahead, miss."

"Thank you." Duchess preceded him up the staircase.

He nodded to Maria. "Let's be about this, Miss Thorne. Hopefully this night will see this unfortunate incident laid to rest and—"

"My sister and me out of your life forever," she finished.

"It will be simpler," he agreed.

At the head of the stairs, Cate was waiting along with Charly and Bert.

Revill looked to the right and left down narrow, thickly carpeted halls. "Explain the plan of this floor."

Cate looked as if she wanted to refuse. She heaved an exaggerated sigh as she described the construction with her hands. "It's got three halls. We're standing in one here at the top of the stairs. Two lead off to separate the rooms."

"And which hall were you on, Miss Melissa Thorne?" Inspector Revill asked.

She was quite pale, her hands clenched, her jaw set. "This one." She walked to the right then turned the corner. They all moved to follow her. In front of a door midway down on the left, she stopped, Peter trailing her like a shadow. "I was in this room."

"Where is the third hall?"

"It's here," Cate walked away to the left. Revill followed forty feet along a thick carpet that muffled footfalls to a hall turning off to the right, again with doors on both sides.

"And is this identical to the first one?"

Maria followed him, sketching as she walked.

"Identical." Cate raised one eyebrow. "Except some of these rooms have different sorts of equipment."

"I'm sure," Revill replied and went down the right hall to Melissa's room. "Now, Miss Thorne, will you please tell us what happened?"

The perfect butler, Peter opened the door. Steeling herself, Melissa stepped inside. She had been expecting a terrible rush of feelings, but from the doorway the room looked like an ordinary bedroom. Peter crowded in behind her and made a tour of it. She looked back at Revill. "It has no windows."

The Inspector entered. He looked pointedly at the draperies and swags beside the bed.

"Would you open the curtains, Peter?"

The butler-cum-bodyguard swept them aside. The same red-flocked wallpaper covered the area.

"Please note, Miss Thorne, that this room has no window," Revill dictated. He rotated slowly, then froze. His eyes fastened on the array of whips, cuffs, and leather straps hanging from the wallpegs beside the door. He walked directly to them, touching the pony lash with the tip of his index finger. "Make a list of these."

Maria Thorne had covered her mouth with her hand. Eyes wide, she took down the data with lightning speed.

Revill smiled encouragingly at Melissa. "So Mr. Montague wanted to rescue you?"

"Yes." She looked around her. "I didn't have any clothes. And no shoes." She glared meaningfully at Lady H. "They had all been torn off and burned."

The brothel keeper stirred uneasily. "They weren't fit." She excused herself. "Dirty and lice-infested."

"That's not so." Maria said defensively. "My sister—"

"Not only were my clothes good, serviceable, decent garments," Melissa interrupted, "but you took my quarter salary that my employer had paid me the day before."

"You will certainly be repaid," Lady Clarice whispered, wrapping her arms around her own body. She shivered remembering her sexual experiences with her husband; silently, she vowed he would never touch her again.

"I think we've seen and heard enough here." Revill led the way back into the hall. "Make a note of the salary, Miss Thorne."

"Yes, sir." She wrote it and underscored it, the light of vengeance in her eyes.

In the hall Revill fixed his eyes on Lady H. "Tell us where you went, Miss Thorne, you and Mr. Montague, when you saw you could not climb out a window in your room."

"I wrapped a sheet around me and we ran out the door.

I knew we couldn't go down the stairs because of Charly and Bert."

"Ah, yes. They wouldn't let you leave."

"No, sir. Nobody could get by them." She threw Charly an accusing look. "So we ran into the room across the hall, but it didn't have any windows either." Melissa opened the door to illustrate. It was empty as it had been that night. "We ran to the door at the end of the hall." She led the procession to it and turned the knob. It was locked. "It wasn't locked that night."

"The key," Revill requested peremptorily.

Cate stepped forward and opened it.

Cold air blasted in their faces. The room was pitilessly dark. The draperies still lay tangled and crushed beneath the hole gaping into the night sky.

Revill strode to the center of the room and looked around him. Then he motioned to Maria. Cate followed. A match rasped across a striker and in a few seconds, light drove the shadows back. Unfortunately, the rectangle where the window had been looked blacker than ever.

Apart from the ruin of the window and drapery, the room looked very much like a bedroom one might find in any house. Its very ordinariness was somehow an affront to what had happened. In silence, the others trailed in behind them— Jocko, Stead, Lady Clarice, Hermione Beauforty, Charly and Bert, and Melissa, followed by the omnipresent Peter. The weight of their emotions seemed to fill the room.

Duchess waited in the doorway. When Cate turned from setting the lamp chimney in place, Duchess caught her arm. "Where are the children?"

"They're safe."

"Tell me!" Her hand tightened around Cate's arm.

Cate shook her head. "As soon as this charade is over

with. Stay and see for yourself. It's as good as a night at the opera. And besides," she added momentously, "aren't you curious? You should be."

"The window was nailed shut." Melissa forced herself to walk to the center of the room. "George told me to scream."

"Scream?" Maria could not help but interrupt.

"He was going to kick out the window. The noise I made covered the breaking glass."

"And would not be remarked on in such a house of misery and de-gra-dation." Stead pronounced the words softly, spaced apart, as he wrote them into his notebook.

Lady H looked as if she wanted to kill him.

"Just tell us in your own words," Revill said, ignoring the others. Maria noted her sister's words.

"He said we'd go out and over the roof to escape. He said it'd be just like a novel by Dickens." Melissa's voice broke, then steadied. "He climbed out first and then helped me out."

"And then the slut pushed him to his death."

"No!"

Lady H made a start toward Melissa, but Peter cut her off with a fancy piece of footwork.

"Continue, Miss Thorne. What happened next?"

Melissa steeled herself to move to the window and lean out. The wind caught her hair and blew her bonnet back on her shoulders. "The ledge was so narrow. You can see." She showed Revill.

"Bring that lamp," he called.

Her face a cold mask, Cate shoved it out between them.

"Make a note, Miss Thorne," Revill called. "I make it barely three inches wide."

"The gutter beneath it." Melissa shuddered at the memory. "I stepped off in it. It was slippery and full of muddy water."

"Quite," was all Revill said.

"I was afraid. But George said we could make it. He was leading me along it."

Revill looked to the left. "How far had you gotten?"

"Just to the next window."

Revill pulled his head in. "Mr. Walton."

"Yes, sir."

"Will you go in the next room and open that window? Will you accompany him, miss?" he asked, looking at Cate.

Maria took the lamp. Cate left with Jocko to unlock the next room.

"Why didn't you go in the other direction?" Stead asked suddenly.

They all looked at him. "Because the mews is on that side," Revill supplied. "Please don't interrupt, Mr. Stead."

A minute later, after a crash and a rending of wood, Jocko's foot came through the next window. Another crash and he stuck his head through. Revill leaned his own head out. "Mr. Walton, was that necessary?"

"You said to open the window. Just following orders."

"So you found the window nailed shut?"

"Tight as a drum."

"Miss Thorne—"

"Excuse me, Inspector," Stead interposed.

Revill heaved a sigh. "What is it, Mr. Stead?"

"When we heard her scream, we all came up," the reporter volunteered. "That young woman—" he pointed to Cate, who had returned to wait in the doorway, "—came to the head of the stairs. She motioned to those two—"

Charly and Bert shuffled their feet. Charly growled a vile word under his breath.

"They ran up the stairs. Lord Montague waited until they were out of sight and then he followed them. And Markham and I followed him." Stead had paused in his writing as if he were trying to remember exactly the order of things. "I can't really say if anyone else followed us."

Revill fixed his stare on the two ex-fighters. Charly assumed a belligerent pose, Bert merely hung his head. He was sweating even in the frigid room. Revill held the lamp high, illuminating Charly's angry face. "Let's have your statement, man. Speak slowly now, so Miss Thorne can write it all down."

Charly looked at Lady H and at Cate. Neither gave him any direction for his speech. With a sigh, he let his massive shoulders slump. His fists relaxed and dangled at his side. "I swear to Gawd, I didn't do nothin'."

"Don't lie," Revill cautioned him. "Three people in this room were on the scene in less than a minute. We saw you."

"Ye saw me hangin' on fer dear life about to piss in me pants." Charly's belligerence flashed, then disappeared in a blink.

"Just tell us what happened."

"It was Cate 'at sent us in 'ere." He looked to her for confirmation. She nodded, her face expressionless. "An' Bert was right be'ind me. I went over to the winda and looked out. 'E was leadin' 'er along the roof."

"Along the ledge?"

Charly shrugged. His hands began to shake. "I dunno. I guess so."

"Go on."

"So I yells at 'im."

"What?"

"I dunno. 'Ell. 'Get back in 'ere.' I dunno."

Jocko returned to the room as Charly was speaking. Even Duchess stepped inside the doorway. All eyes were on the ex-fighter. Every ear strained to hear every word, every intonation in his frightened, angry voice.

"You told him to bring me back," Melissa accused suddenly. "I remember. He told you he had beaten you once before. It made you angry. That's when you came out on the roof."

"I disremember that," Charly growled.

"You did. You did!"

Charly turned to the room at large. "They was gonna get theirselves killed. I was warnin' 'em, fer Christ's sake!"

"You climbed out onto the roof," she insisted.

Charly stood silent.

"George passed me by him." The tears began to trickle down her cheeks. "He told me to go on to the end and climb to the peak. We were going—" She tried to catch her breath to swallow a fit of hysterical sobs. "—To jump onto the other roof beyond. He smiled at me as if it were a great adventure. He said it'd be like Dickens. I already mentioned that, didn't I?"

Her eyes were wide with horror. Deep wells overflowing with tears, reflecting the light, reflecting the horror. She pointed an accusing finger at Charly. "He climbed out onto the roof."

Charly backed away, shaking his head. "I only took one step. Swear to Gawd."

"That's right."

Everyone looked at Bert. His words were barely discernible, but Charly nodded his head vigorously. "Tell 'em, Bert."

" 'E took one step, Charly did, an' 'is foot slipped. 'E

yelled. I looked out th' winda, an' 'e was down in the gutter."

"It was like glass out there," Charly supplied. "If m' foot 'adn't gone between them posts, I'd been gone over the side meself."

"So what did you do then?" the inspector asked.

"Wrapped me arms around the railin' an' prayed. Swear to Gawd."

"So you were down and out?"

Charly looked around as if he were ashamed of himself. "That's about the size of it."

"And what did you do?" Revill asked Bert.

"Stayed put." He shrugged his heavy shoulders, his eyes firmly fixed on the floor. "If Charly couldn't make it, it wasn't no use fer me to try."

Melissa looked from one to the other. She sniffed and mopped at her cheeks with her handkerchief. "If they were both back at the window we came out of, they couldn't have caused George to fall."

"Just tell us what happened."

Everyone in the room looked at her as Melissa went on. "I had climbed to the peak of the roof." She looked defiantly at Lady H through her tears. "I swore I would never, ever come back into that room again. I would have died rather than come back in."

"Was it very slippery?" Maria asked.

"Oh, sister, it was awful." She buried her face in her hands and struggled for control. "The ledge, the gutter, the tiles. They were so wet and slimy, my feet kept slipping. I was barefooted, and my toes and fingers—" She shook her head.

"Tell us about George," Cate suggested softly.

"I was on the peak of the roof, right ready to jump, but

I waited for him. He moved away from Charly and followed me. He was going so slow. It was dark, but we could see. Was there a moon? There must have been a moon."

She looked around for confirmation, but no one could remember whether there had been a moon or not.

"He came to the last window. He was almost past it. He was starting up the tiles. I swear he was. I held out my hand—"

"And pushed him," Lady H declared stonily.

"No!" Melissa held out her hand to the inspector. "I held out my hand to him. It was too far, but he was reaching for me and I was reaching for him. He smiled at me. And suddenly, he looked down." She thought a minute. "He had told me not to look down, but he looked down. He did look down. And then, he toppled backward over the rail."

She began to weep in earnest. Maria held out her arms and swept Melissa into them. "He fell. Oh, Maria. He fell. Our hands were only a few feet apart."

"She's lying," Lady H declared flatly. "The slut is lying to save herself. She was always trouble. Lying little whore."

"How many windows along that roof?" Revill asked.

"Four," Cate replied.

"Let's go to the fourth window and see what we see."

"There's nothing there."

"I'd like to see that for myself."

"I tell you there's nothing to see."

Surprisingly, Lady H joined in. "You'll be wasting your time, Inspector. You have the murderer right here before you. This slut led him on, teased him, lured him out onto the roof, and pushed him over when he tried to save her life."

Revill looked at the brothel keeper. "Madam, either you

have not been listening, or you are mad as a hatter. I myself and both of these young ladies first heard, then saw, the young lady you accuse screaming for help from the peak of the roof. Likewise, we saw your man with his leg stuck through the railing. Neither of them was within reach of the fourth window."

He nodded to Cate. "Lead us to it and be quick about it."

"We have to go back around the halls."

"Excellent. It will give me a chance to check each person's location. Mr. Stead, where were you and Lord Montague?"

The reporter thought a minute. "We stopped at the top of the stairs. The hall was empty. Lord Montague went into the second door on the left. We followed him. He looked around him. Looked under the bed, behind the screen. Er, I believe that's all. We watched him, but he paid no attention to us. Then we heard the screams again and we left that room. Several other people had thrust their heads out of doors, including several gentlemen."

"Was anyone actually in the hall?"

Stead thought a moment. "Several people actually. But I don't remember anyone in particular. They had either just stepped out or were poking their heads out of the doors." He looked a little embarrassed. "They didn't have many clothes on, Inspector."

"Of course."

"Then we heard more screaming. We hurried down the hall to this room."

"Was the door open or closed?"

"Closed. I'm positive. We went in and saw the two men, one in the room, one outside."

"Quite so." He turned to Cate. "Lead on."

"You won't see anything," she repeated stubbornly.

He took her by the arm.

"All right. All right. Take yer bloody 'ands off me, peeler."

He released her and she led them rapidly around the U-shaped hallway to its opposite end. No one noticed when Bert and Charly lagged behind and disappeared down the stairs. Cate stopped in front of two doors identical to the ones they had just left. She motioned to the one on the right, then waited.

"Let them in," Lady H sighed.

Pulling out her keys, Cate opened the door and entered. Again a match hit a striker. The darkness retreated before a red light caused by the ruby-tinted lamp chimney.

Revill stepped inside. "Good Lord." He closed his eyes.

Maria and Jocko followed him. Maria's face went absolutely white. The thief whistled softly.

Stead looked around him with a journalist's detachment. Then he began to write.

Melissa stopped in the doorway, then spun around and threw herself against Peter's chest with a pitiful cry.

"Take that child downstairs," Revill ordered.

Hermione Beauforty's face was ghastly beneath her paint. Revill swung round, his eyes riveted on her.

"There's no real harm goes on here," she tried to explain. "Some of the gentlemen like a little bit of a game now and then."

"I think you might very well kill one or more of them here," he said.

A penal stock for arms and head, a medieval torture rack, a pair of whipping posts were placed strategically around the room. One entire wall was pegged with chains and shackles, leather straps, and whips of every kind from long coach whips to pony quirts to a vicious looking cat-o'-nine-tails. Some of the things on the wall were so exotic as to be unfamiliar. On a table at the door, grinning like a human head, was an iron mask. A padlock lay on the table beside it.

The walls of the room were done in red velvet. The floor was painted black. All the lamps had red chimneys.

Revill walked to the window. A system of bars had been set across it. He reached between them and unlocked it. It slid up easily. "It's not nailed shut," he reported. "Obviously, because it doesn't need to be."

"No, sir." Maria's voice sounded thick.

"Are you crying, Miss Thorne?" he asked her softly.

"I never dreamed. I never knew anything could be this dreadful."

"Just so."

Jocko put his arm around her. "Want to leave, Ria?"

She shook her head. "Just keep your arm around me. I can finish this."

Revill was looking through the window. "Mrs. Beauforty. Mr. Stead. Lady Clarice, you may look only if you so desire."

Lady H came reluctantly to his side. William Stead came eagerly. Country-bred, her senses numb, Montague's young wife followed them, gamely determined to know the worst.

"Look." Revill pointed.

Stead shook his head and stepped back.

Lady H looked where Revill's finger indicated. "Oh, no," she wailed softly. "Oh, no. Oh, Georgie. Oh, no." She made her way blindly back across the room and out into the hall. None of them could doubt that her heart was broken.

"Poor George," Lady Clarice murmured. Head down, hiding herself from the horrors, she hurried from the room.

"Miss Thorne." Revill's voice was weary.

"Yes, Inspector."

"Please write this down as I dictate it. We are looking at a small area where the ledge has crumbled away. From the look of the stone, it has crumbled quite recently. The damage is very fresh. No darkening or weathering has occurred. Beneath that we see a broken lead gutter plate. At the point of the break, the metal is white and shiny."

"I'll note that, Inspector." Leaning against Jocko's strong chest, her hand shaking, she wrote Revill's exact words.

"As you came along here, Mr. Walton, you were deuced lucky that more of it didn't crumble under your foot," Revill noted.

Jocko leaned away from Maria to glance out the window. He nodded solemnly. "I was fair lying on the rooftop, Inspector. I never did look down. And I never put my foot on it. Just blind luck."

"No doubt. Mischance. Misadventure. Blind luck. Good for you. Bad for poor George Montague."

Jocko shook his head. "Got that, Ria?"

"Every word." Tears sparkled in her eyes. "You could have died, too." She hid her face against his chest.

"I have no doubt that if we go down to the kitchen basement, we'll find pieces of stone and perhaps a flake or two of this lead," Revill continued. "I'll send a constable around in the morning to have a look."

Gently, as if performing a benediction, he pulled the window down and locked it in place. Shaking his head one more time, he followed Jocko and Ria into the hall.

"Are you satisfied, Mrs. Beauforty?"

The lady's tears had become a storm of noisy, agonized weeping. She barely managed to nod.

"And are you satisfied with what you have seen, Mr. Stead?"

"I can see no other explanation, Inspector Revill."

"Then I will leave the report as it stands. George Montague met his death by accident and mischance."

Twenty-four

Between them, Revill and Stead supported Hermione Beauforty down the hall. As if her wrath had sustained her, she was in a state of collapse now that she had nothing left to stoke it. Her sobs were horrible to hear. Deep-throated, rasping, torn from her chest.

The others followed silently behind them. Jocko put his arms around both Melissa and Maria. They both leaned against him.

Silent tears trickled down Melissa's cheeks. "Is she really George's mother?"

Jocko squeezed her a little harder. " 'Fraid so."

"That's even more terrible for her."

The unspoken thought among the three of them was that the youth had died on the roof of the Lord's Dream trying to rescue Melissa from the life of prostitution that Lady H had callously planned for her.

"Saint" Peter moved ahead obsequiously. He assumed a formal stance at the head of the stairs and made a bow. "Shall we go into the salon?"

The three of them smiled. Jocko chuckled.

"A very good idea, Peter," Maria replied. "We mustn't keep Mrs. Shires waiting."

"My thought exactly, Miss Thorne."

The last two people in the hall faced each other. Cate's

pose was defiant. Suddenly, her black dress seemed ominous. She tossed her head and would have walked away.

Duchess caught her arm in a hard grip. "Where are my children?"

A corner of Cate's sullen mouth curled up. "Follow me." She opened a room midway down the back hall.

As Duchess crossed the threshold, she heard or felt movement behind her. Fortuitously, she ducked just when a footstool would have crashed down on her head. The miss was accompanied by a heartfelt curse uttered in a ten-year-old voice. She swung around to take the edge of a metal tray across her shins.

"It's me! Pansy! Betty! It's me, Duchess!" she yelled.

"Duchess!" With a cry of pure joy, Pansy launched herself from behind the door and into Duchess's arms. "Bet! It's Duchess."

"Duchess!" Bet began to weep. She leaped down from the chair and threw her arms around Duchess's waist. "Ye found us."

"Course she did," Pan said, planting a wet kiss on her idol's cheek. "I told 'er, but she was so scared."

Bet pulled away and placed her hands on her hips. "Liar. Y've been bawlin' all over me coat. Gawd! She 'bout drownded me."

Before Pan could answer, Duchess put her hand over the little mouth. "Let's go home. You can argue there to your heart's content."

Cate had watched the exchange curiously. "You really want those heathens?"

Duchess raised her eyebrows. "Of course."

"We love 'er." Pan hugged Duchess hard. "An' she loves us."

And that seemed to settle the matter.

* * *

In the main salon Clarice was attempting to rouse Lord
Montague from his drunken stupor. One eye drooping hor-
ridly, he stared at the young woman who hovered over him.
"Who're you?"

"I'm Clarice." She pulled him to his feet.

"Never heard of you." Saliva ran from the corner of his
mouth. His eyes rolled as he shook his head. The movement threw him off balance. He reeled sideways against
Clarice, looked at her again as if he had never seen her
and pulled himself away from her.

Revill and Stead had brought Hermione to the foot of
the stairs. The Russian held out his arms.

"Yaroslav," she whimpered.

Wordlessly, he gathered her against him. One big hand
cradled her head. Like a father with a child, he rocked her.

Revill and Stead moved away, thankful to turn the hysterical woman over to someone else's care.

Jocko led Maria and Melissa down.

"Saint" Peter marched behind them. He caught sight of
Mrs. Shires talking earnestly to Bert and grinned to himself. He could use a good sparring partner.

At first Montague's eyes were blank as he watched the
Russian comforting Hermione. Then there was a spark of
recognition. "You there! Get away from that woman!" He
staggered groggily. "Get your hands off her!"

He stumbled across the room. Clarice screamed. Revill
made a grab for him, but Jocko was quicker.

"Here now. None of that." The thief caught Montague
by the shoulder.

"You won't tell me what to do!" The baronet began

vindmilling with his fists. Jocko took them on his fore-
urms.

"Good job," Charly called.

Jocko was too busy to acknowledge the compliment. He
lucked under the drunken blows, caught Montague's right
urm, and spun him around. In the blink of an eye, the man
vas trapped in a painful hammerlock. "Somebody come
und get 'im. I don't want to 'urt 'im."

Montague howled in helpless rage. Words poured from
uis mouth—ugly accusations, vile epithets, insane ravings.
"My son!" he kept repeating between rantings. "My son!
My son!"

Hermione lifted her head in the Russian's arms. Almost
ull the thick *maquillage* had been washed from her cheeks.
Her skin was thin as parchment and a mass of tiny wrin-
kles. She looked infinitely old.

"Terry," she whispered.

He continued to scream and curse.

"Terry!"

He ceased. His rapid breathing sounded like a bellows.

"Terry, it's over now. He's dead. But I want you to
know—George was my son, but not yours. It doesn't make
uny difference now. George was not your son. Do you understand me? George was my son, but not yours." Her
words were clear and distinct, though her voice was very
hoarse.

His mouth sagged. His body began to tremble as he
sought to deny the dawning horror. "You're lying!"

"I was afraid you couldn't give me a boy, Terry. I
couldn't take that chance. You were too important to my
plans. If I hadn't given you a son, I'd have been cast off.
Just like poor Evelyn." She looked at Clarice. "And sure
enough, you couldn't give any of us boys."

Clarice's mouth pinched tight. She gave the faintest o
shrugs.

Jocko released Montague's wrist. The arm fell limply t
his side. The man looked dully round the room. "Evelyn,"
he whispered. "Evelyn."

"Who?" Stead asked.

"His first wife," Hermione supplied. "Poor thing. Sh
was glad to be dead and out of it."

Clarice wrapped her arms around her waist. "It's eas
to see why."

Duchess came downstairs, Bet and Pansy clinging t
each hand. Dressed in her elegant clothing, every hair i
place, she made quite a contrast to the ragged pair. Sh
was intent on leading them out without attracting attentior
but Montague saw her. He smiled.

"Evelyn." He held out his arms. "Where've you been?

Duchess tried to duck, but Hermione caught her an
pushed her forward. "Take her, Terry. Here she is. You ol
fool. This is not Evelyn. Evelyn's dead. This is Evelyn
daughter—you made her give her up and raise my so
instead. My son by another man. Oh, it's rich. Rich! An
now he's dead because of us. And this—this street whor
is your firstborn, your legitimate heir. If you can get any
one to recognize her."

Montague stiffened. He shook his head dazedly.

"I sent her to the schools the way you insisted, but
made her pay for keeping me from my son. I told he
every day who she was and why she was here. I love
telling her how her father and mother hated her, how they'
thrown her into a whorehouse because she wasn't a boy
She separated me from my George and I hated her. Whe
she ran away, I didn't try to bring her back. It pleased m
to see her walking the streets."

Revill looked with new interest at Duchess. Stead had used up one notebook completely and was writing on the back of an envelope.

"Loved you," Montague muttered. But no one knew whether he spoke to the image of Evelyn or to Hermione.

The brothel keeper shrugged contemptuously. "Not enough," she countered. "Never enough."

Montague's eyes rolled back in his head. He toppled backward and sprawled on the floor. For a moment the exhausted group could only stare as his body jerked and twitched in the grip of some kind of fit.

"Look what you do," the Russian chided softly.

"Good enough for him," Hermione Beauforty sneered. She turned her back on the spectacle and slipped her arm through the Russian's. "Will you take me home, Yaroslav?"

"Don't leave me until this is straightened out," Duchess pleaded.

"Never." Jocko put his arm around her shoulder.

"I want to go," she explained, "but I feel I should stay. I don't know why. After all, this really doesn't concern me."

"He's your father," Maria pointed out.

The younger girl snorted indelicately. "Not even in name. I suppose I feel a bit of morbid curiosity."

"We'll stay with you."

"In that case, Peter and I should take Melissa and the children home," Avory suggested. "Then you won't have to worry about them while you're getting this unfortunate business straightened out."

The old lady's face had an unpleasant gray tinge under the skin—a sure sign that she was wearing down physically. Otherwise, her eyes sparkled with her usual curiosity and concern. "Those poor babies need to be in bed."

Pan and Bet were sitting propped against each other on the red plush divan. Their eyes were closed.

"Oh, yes, please do." Maria took her employer's hands. "I can't ever repay you, dear lady."

"Nonsense." Avory leaned forward to kiss Maria on the cheek. "I haven't had such a fascinating time in years. I thought everything was over for me. I was sure I was condemned to a life of writing letters." She looked around appreciatively at the red velvet and gold tassels. "Now just look at the places I've been and the things I've seen. And all in the company of a handsome rogue." She laid a loving hand on Jocko's cheek, then stepped back smiling. "Come, Peter. Pick up the littlest girl. What's her name?"

"Pansy," Duchess said.

"Yes, pick up Pansy. And, Bert, you pick up—?"

"Betty."

"—Betty. Come, Melissa. We'll all have a good sleep."

The doctor came down the stairs. He looked around him, his mouth set in a moue of disapproval. Then he sighed. "Dear lady." He addressed himself exclusively to Lady Clarice, who rose to meet him. "In my opinion he's too ill to be moved."

"Oh, no."

"His condition is quite precarious. I fear some sort of disturbance in the brain. A dent slightly more than an inch in diameter and a quarter of an inch deep can be felt on his right temple."

"A dent?"

"Yes, ma'am. I believe that one of the plates of his skull

has shifted. Undoubtedly, he has had some sort of a stroke."

She sat down abruptly. "Dear God. Can he live like that?"

"In some instances. It remains to be seen whether he will recover entirely, partially, or not at all."

"He can stay here," Cate said.

"This is a brothel," Lady Clarice gasped.

"It's only right that he should. He owns the building. He owns part of the business." Cate had been sitting in a chair beside the fire, the chair Montague had vacated when he started the tirade that led to his collapse. She rose from it, a stern figure all in black, face whitened with cosmetics, lips blood-red with rouge. A curious sense of purpose seemed to energize her. "It's a good business. Plenty of money for his care."

The doctor looked around him disapprovingly, then bowed to the inevitable. "For the time being at least, here would be best."

"We'll give him every care," said Cate. "Charly can bathe him. The girls can take turns feeding him. I'll give him his medicine."

"But it's such an imposition," Lady Clarice objected.

"Not at all." Cate smiled her catlike smile. "In a sense this is his home, too. His name is on the deed."

Clarice looked uncertainly at Duchess. "You're my step-daughter."

"Forget it."

"But I can't. Terence has a sizable fortune. By rights part of it's yours." She swallowed. "Bethany and Juliet are your half-sisters."

"I wouldn't touch a penny," Duchess assured her. "Let them go on believing George was their brother. Let the scandal die."

Clarice smiled in relief, then frowned. "That's too easy. I'll instruct Terence's lawyers to pay you a quarterly portion."

"You really don't have to."

"Yes, I do. What is your name?"

Duchess looked away. "I don't have one."

"No name?" Clarice put her hand to her mouth.

"Duchess is what they call me on the street."

"But what was your name here? What did that woman call you?"

"Brat."

Lady Montague turned to Revill and Stead. "This is the most monstrous thing I have ever heard of. I'm sure you gentlemen agree. I'm calling on you as witnesses to this and you, Maria Thorne, and you—"

"Jocko Walton."

"Yes. You are all witnesses to this. You will stand in court if necessary when I have the legal papers drawn up."

They all nodded.

"You must have a name on the account I shall instruct the lawyers to open for you. You can touch it or leave it, but every quarter an allowance will be paid and deposited in the name of Evelyn Montague."

Outside in the street, the dawn was breaking.

Stead tipped his hat and caught a cab to the *Gazette*. He had the greatest story of his career, and more food for thought besides. The idea of little girls like Pansy and

Betty being kidnapped and taken into prostitution with no laws to protect them preyed heavily on his mind.

Something must be done. The power of the press must be brought to bear. As he rode through the waking streets, he began framing the campaign in his mind.

"I'll be taking that thief off your hands, Miss Thorne." Revill spoke to no one in particular as they watched the journalist drive away.

Jocko hunched his shoulders. "I only did what you told me to," he protested. "You got no call—"

"I have your signed confession," Revill reminded him.

"And you can use that confession for kindling." Maria thrust her chin into the inspector's face. "Or better yet, turn it over and write a reference on the back of it."

"A reference?"

"That's right. Mr. Jocko Walton, Esquire, will be taking an honest job very shortly. In fact, he has most experience in law enforcement. You've been using him without paying him. It's time to start paying him."

"Miss Thorne, you are right about one thing."

"What, Inspector?"

He shook his head helplessly. "I'll be glad to see the last of you."

She smiled. "I promise not to help him solve his cases after he goes to work for Scotland Yard."

"A thief to catch a thief." Revill did not seem opposed to the idea.

"Exactly. He'll come to work directly after we're married and take a short wedding journey."

"So that's the way the wind blows."

"Ria," Jocko cautioned. "No need to lay it on so thick."

"What do you mean *lay it on thick,* Jocko Walton?" She planted herself in front of them both and shook her finger in his face. "Do you mean you're not going to make an honest woman out of me? After you seduced me—"

"Ria!" He caught her by the shoulders, trying to silence her. "Listen, Inspector, she's—"

Revill might have chuckled. The noise was very suspicious, but his expression remained stern.

"He seduced me," she insisted loudly. "He had his way with me."

"Maria Thorne!"

"Well, I won't have it. You'll marry me and make an honest woman of me and an honest man of yourself in the process."

"Sounds as if you have your marching orders, Mr. Walton," Revill growled. "And I'll hold that confession as a surety that you do right by this girl."

"Oh, Lord," was all Jocko could say before she threw her arms around his neck and kissed him hard and long right there on the street in front of the Lord's Dream.

Epilogue

More than a dozen witnesses gathered in the narthex of St. Boniface's Church to watch Maria Thorne sign her maiden name for the last time in the register. Jocko signed his name after hers. Then while Mrs. Avory Shires and Detective Inspector Clive Revill signed as witnesses, he took her in his arms again. Their kiss was a promise of lifelong love.

"I must be dreaming," he whispered.

"I love you," she whispered back.

Bet and Pansy giggled.

Mrs. Shires beamed and nudged Revill. "Rogue no more. Right, Inspector?"

Her escort nodded, his chest swelling with pride. "A complete and thorough reformation."

Then the thief led his lady in her pink wool wedding dress and lace-trimmed bonnet out through the portal and into the sunshine.

Two little flower girls walked in front of them in pretty dusty-rose dresses with ecru lace collars. They carried tiny baskets from which they strewed rose petals. On their heads were rose bonnets tied with satin ribbons. Their smiles were like sunshine.

"Isn't this the loveliest sight? Jocko's so handsome." Pan burbled happily. "I want to get married."

"When ye grow up," Bet said with a great show of weary resignation, "ye 'ave to wait 'til ye grow up."

"I'm almost grown." Pan stood on tiptoe and thrust out her flat chest. "Seven is almost grown."

"Not grown atall."

"At least now I'm in school. I'm not a baby no more."

Duchess, dressed in an attractive wool suit with a modified bustle, put her hands on the shoulders of her two charges and whispered in their ears that they were to stop arguing. Today was to be a happy day.

Lady Clarice had been as good as her word. A check deposited each quarter to the account of Evelyn Montague paid for schooling for the little ones and had arranged for positions for Duchess's other charges. But Evelyn Montague remained a name on an account. While Duchess lived in a set of comfortable, though humble, rooms, she still dressed in her rags and prowled the streets, looking for girls in trouble.

"You look so beautiful." Melissa hugged her sister and then her new brother-in-law. "You look beautiful, too, Jocko. Do you know how lucky you are?"

His hair was brushed to guinea gold, his face flushed with happiness. He hugged Maria hard against his side. "I guess I do. Beautiful as an angel. And smart. I'm marryin' a type writer."

She beamed up at him. "Same to you, luv," she said in street accents. "Smart as a whip. Tough. 'Ey! I'm marryin' a bloody peeler."

Duchess put her hand on Maria's arm. "You take good care of him."

The look that passed between them spoke volumes. Maria lifted her chin. "I mean to."

Duchess's long lashes swept down, then back up again.

"I really think you will, Maria Walton. I think you'd let him steal if he wanted to."

Maria leaned toward her so their lips brushed each other's cheeks. Then Duchess stood on tiptoe to buss Jocko. He knelt to hug Pan and Bet, who kissed him enthusiastically.

Peter nodded happily from the box of Mrs. Shires's coach. Bert opened the carriage door with a low bow and a broad grin.

On the steps of the carriage, Maria handed her bouquet to her sister. She waved to everyone.

Jocko put one foot on the step, when Revill's left hand closed hard over his shoulder. The thief froze.

Grinning, the inspector held out his right. Jocko shook it. Paper crackled between them. "An extra wedding gift," Revill said in answer to Jocko's questioning look. "Something I won't be needing anymore."

As the carriage rolled away, Jocko unfolded it.

"What is it, sweetheart?"

Wordlessly, he held it out to her.

Revill had given him back his confession.

Maria ran her hands mindlessly over Jocko's hot, damp shoulders. With lips and tongue he caressed her breast. Her nipple throbbed and ached from his gentle torment.

He moved inside her with long, gentle strokes. Each one seemed to begin at the opening of her body and slide with an electric caress along the sheath of nerves that wept for more. Deep inside her she anticipated his power and gasped each time he touched the center of her body.

"Don't," she breathed. "Oh, please . . . don't . . ."

"Don't?" he whispered, taking her nipple between his teeth.

"Don't stop . . . oh, please, don't . . . stop."

He growled acquiescence and moved to her other breast. She threaded her fingers through his curls and held him tight against her. "Love . . . love . . ."

He rocked back on his calves and heels, lifting her with him, her ankles crossed to lock her tight around his hips. "Is that better? Do you like that?"

She opened her eyes, staring unseeing at the pleasant room, darkening as evening shadows grew behind lace curtains. All her senses concentrated on the exquisite pleasure with which he was tearing her apart and putting her back together.

"Ria?"

A minute's hesitation at the zenith of a terrible, beautiful desire. "Yes!" She arched her spine, pushing her body into his, making them one. "Yes! Jocko! Yes! Yes! Yes!"

Her sheath contracted with shudders that rippled through them both. With a cry of pleasure, he joined her, held her at the top. The crystal seconds flashed before their eyes before they slid together into a dark and honeyed bliss.

The room was full dark when she stirred. Sleepily, she found his face and began to kiss him—forehead, cheeks, lips, the strong column of his throat. He stirred, groaned, and began to kiss her back. His hand shaped itself to her waist, then slid over her hip.

For the moment they lay replete, luxuriating in the darkness and the caress of soft skin. "Jocko."

"Maria?" he replied sleepily.

"You don't have to be a peeler if you don't want to."

He nuzzled against her neck. His lips found and tugged at her earlobe. "Do you want me to be something else?"

"No. I don't want you to be something else. I want you to be what you want to be. Duchess told me that all your life, you've been what other people wanted you to be. But not with me." She kissed him harder on the mouth and tilted away to lie on her back. She stared into the darkness for a long time before letting out a deep breath. "You can even be a thief."

Silence followed her brave sentence.

Then he chuckled. "Ria, m'girl, a man's got to look to 'is future, and I've got nowhere to go as a thief. A peeler's the ticket, as I see it."

She reared up in bed. "Why?"

Almost lazily, he wrapped his arm around her neck and pulled her down for a long, satisfying kiss that rekindled their passion.

"Why?" she repeated dazedly as he rubbed his knee against the jointure of her thighs.

"Because I'm the best thief that ever was. I stole a life for myself and I'll never give it back. Never."

Epilogue the Second

Lord Terence Montague sat in the Bath chair that Cate had purchased for him. In point of fact, he was strapped into it. A leather belt passed over his chest and under his arms, buckling at the back. It kept him from falling over or slipping sideways.

Night and day, day and night he remained in the chair. It was tilted back when he wanted to sleep. A monstrous creature whom Cate addressed as Nessie cleaned him once a day and bathed his withering body once a week. Since he had to be diapered like a baby, the process was exceedingly humiliating.

He hated the chair, and his handlers, and all the world.

The stroke had left his legs and arms paralyzed, his speech destroyed, his bodily functions beyond his control. But he was fully aware of everything around him. Not that there was anything to be aware of. No one came into his room in the second story of the Lord's Dream except Cate and the amorphous Nessie.

At first he had listened for Hermione's voice, thinking surely she would relent and return. She had not done so. One day Cate, her dark eyes watching his face, had remarked that Lady H never came to the Lord's Dream anymore. She cared nothing about it. She spent her hours studying the stocks on the Exchange and entertaining the Russian, who came regularly to her house.

He had shifted his eyes away to look out the window. He had never forgotten how Cate had insulted him and kept him from going up the stairs. But for her, he would have saved his son.

Propped up in his chair and rolled to the window, he could look down onto the street all day. At regular intervals he was fed three meals. Because he had great difficulty swallowing, his weight was falling off. He supposed that eventually he would starve to death. That thought, like every other, infuriated him.

Once in awhile, Cate would remember how much he liked brandy and would include it with his evening meal. She never thought to hold a cigar for him.

At first he had tried to communicate. He had gone so far as to devise a simple system of sounds and make them over and over at the appropriate times. Any sound made to Nessie was ignored, and Cate appeared not to understand. One treated him as if he were a lump of coal. The other, as if he were an idiot.

Gradually, he grew discouraged and then ceased his efforts altogether. His unintelligible grunts and cries sounded like the wailings of an idiot. He had not made a sound for a week when Cate entered the room one evening.

She turned his chair in her direction and set down a bottle of whiskey at hand. Her color was high. When she called his name, he could smell the liquor on her breath.

He watched her pour an inch for herself and another for himself. Then she lifted hers and toasted him.

"From now on I think I'll call you Father."

His eyes locked on her, their vision piercing. The pupils widened as she moved closer, stepping out of the light, so he could see her face. When she was directly in front of him, she put both hands on the arms of his chair and brought her face down to within inches of his.

"I'm your daughter, you know. You don't even remember me. But I'm your firstborn. When your precious Evelyn's child died, Lady H's lived. You gave her this house. I'll bet you don't even remember. Lady H told me when I was little. I suppose she thought I was too young to understand or remember. Perhaps she even forgot that she told me. But I remembered—I always remembered. Even when she put me to work here at the Lord's Dream, I remembered I was Lord Montague's daughter."

He opened his mouth, struggling to speak, but only a braying sound came out. He sucked in air and tried again.

She laughed. "Oh, would Papa like a drink of whiskey?"

More dribbled out of the side of his mouth than went in, but she did not bother to wipe it away.

Smiling, she lifted her glass in a toast. "You can't move. You can't speak. You'll never be able to speak again. But you're not quite punished enough for what you did to me."

He rolled his eyes wildly. Spittle flecked his gaping mouth.

Cate laughed again. "When Duchess came to live with us, you paid for her care. She had a fine education, beautiful clothes, everything your conscience made you give to your second daughter. But for me—your first—nothing. Not even so much as a pat on the head."

He made a squealing sound like a hog dying.

"Too late now, Father dear. I can't understand your loving words. Too, too late. But you can understand mine. So listen to what I tell you. I killed him. I was at the window of the discipline room. I caught him by the ankle and tumbled him over the railing. Revill's constable Wilkie, the man you bribed, was supposed to come and look at the ledge. He didn't bother. He thought he wasn't supposed to find anything. Later, I went back up and took a hammer to it."

He brayed again.

She laughed. "They all had what they wanted at the end. Jocko, Maria and her pretty little sister, Melissa, even Duchess, my 'sister.' Every single one of them, except me. No one cared what I wanted. But I knew what I wanted when you fell to the floor. And now I have it. I have my dear father all to myself."

He tried desperately to move. Trapped in his dying body, he tried to throw himself out of the chair, tried to attack her, tried to tell somebody, but his misshapen mouth could only produce the pitiful braying.

She patted his limp hand where it lay on his withering thigh.

"Your dinner will be a little late, Father."

Author's Note

In the following year, 1885, William Stead arranged to purchase a thirteen-year-old girl named Eliza Armstrong from her parents. He transported her to a brothel in Paris without the slightest objections from any British customs officials along the way. In so doing he proved that the laws of Britain were so lax that they actually cleared the way for unspeakable vice. His efforts and the articles he wrote in the *Pall Mall Gazette* so inflamed the country that they led to the Criminal Law Amendment Act of 1885, familiarly called the Stead Law, which made procuration a criminal offense.

In many ways he set the example for the great investigative journalists of our own day. In 1912, on his way to America in pursuit of yet another story, he was lost at sea on the *Titanic*.

Deana James
Dallas, Texas

DEANA JAMES lives in Dallas, Texas, where she teaches creative writing at Brookhaven College and dances with the Dallas Metropolitan Ballet.

SURRENDER TO THE SPLENDOR OF THE ROMANCES OF F. ROSANNE BITTNER!

CARESS	(3791, $5.99/$6.99)
COMANCHE SUNSET	(3568, $4.99/$5.99)
HEARTS SURRENDER	(2945, $4.50/$5.50)
LAWLESS LOVE	(3877, $4.50/$5.50)
PRAIRIE EMBRACE	(3160, $4.50/$5.50)
RAPTURE'S GOLD	(3879, $4.50/$5.50)
SHAMELESS	(4056, $5.99/$6.99)

Available wherever paperbacks are sold, or order direct from the Publisher. Send cover price plus 50¢ per copy for mailing and handling to Penguin USA, P.O. Box 999, c/o Dept. 17109, Bergenfield, NJ 07621. Residents of New York and Tennessee must include sales tax. DO NOT SEND CASH.